SHADOW SISTERS BOOK TWO

QUINN NOLL

ISBN: 978-1-7353814-2-8 (Paperback)

ISBN: 978-1-7353814-3-5 (E-Book)

Warning: You are about to enter the mind of a serial killer. It is a playground for the demented—not exactly a tourist destination. Within this book, you'll find scenes of murder, mayhem, and abuse of every kind. Enter at your own risk and proceed with caution.

This is a work of fiction. The only thing factual within these pages is proof of an author's dangerous mind. Any resemblance to actual persons, living or dead, is entirely coincidental.

Cover photo: Zsolt Biczo/Shutterstock.com

Cover design by Brian Quinn

www.QuinnNoll.com

For Mom
The woman who has loved me unashamedly, unconditionally, my entire life.
If I had one-tenth of the strength, love, and faith you possess, I would be the richest woman in the world.
I love you, Momma

Sometimes, the most terrifying monsters are those that dwell within the soul...

PROLOGUE

Once upon a time, decades ago and in too many cities to remember, there lived an angelic child trapped beneath the thumb of an evil woman ...

The man with the knife in his chest lay sprawled on the floor, stinking of sweat and booze, his dingy T-shirt and boxer briefs covered in blood. Pink foam dribbled from his lips and over his day-old stubble, staining the corners of his mouth.

The boy standing at the dead man's feet inched closer, as if moving too quickly would rouse the dead. Circling the body, resisting the urge to poke the corpse's ashen skin, the child ignored the slosh of his shoes as he waded through the blood.

The ear-splitting shrill of a female on the edge of hysteria shifted his focus.

His mother.

Annoyed at the interruption, he pulled his gaze from the man on the floor and looked up at the screaming woman, the very one who'd plunged that knife into 'uncle' Bill's heart.

The first thing he noticed was the blood on her hands. It stained every surface, from her palms to all ten fingers, eventually settling into her nail beds and cuticles. Her pinched face, gasping breaths, and dark eyes were all too familiar to him.

A warning of her impending rage.

Over the years, his mother made it clear to her 'clients' that she would not suffer a leech, that payment was due upon services rendered.

But Bill reneged on their arrangement. And, although not the first man she'd sacrificed her son to, he was the only one who dared not pay what he promised.

Now, it seemed Uncle Bill had settled that debt with his life.

The boy returned his attention to the body on the floor, imagining it was he who pierced the heart of his abuser, he who'd plunged the knife to the hilt. An odd sense of satisfaction blanketed him from head to toe as he studied the man's terror-stricken eyes.

Eyes that, wide open in death, saw nothing.

Yet saw everything.

~

For as long as he remembered, the boy's mother never used his given name. She'd call him 'boy', or 'thing'. Sometimes, if she were feeling especially clever, she'd call him 'it' simply because she refused to think of the child as anything but her possession.

To address him by name was to give him power, comfort, even hope, that he was a human being who deserved kindness and respect.

They lived alone in a run-down apartment in a dangerous part of town. Night and day, the blast of gunfire and the shrill of sirens filled his ears. Few tenants lived in the building, and fewer still shared the second floor. The neighbors the boy did happen upon ignored his tattered clothes, blank stare, and the bruises on his arms.

Because shuttered eyes cannot see.

One day, the young boy awoke to the melodic tinkling of a bell coming from his mother's bedroom. Peeking into her room, he found her sitting on the side of the bed, a handsome silver bell between two fingers. His mother explained that she'd purchased it as a tool, one she would use to summon him, much like a hunter summons his hounds.

Soon, he was not merely ignored; he was invisible. He yearned to hear her call him 'boy' or 'thing' once again.

Even 'it' provided more dignity than the bell he would come to detest.

~

Living a childhood of neglect, with only himself for company, meant learning to take pleasure in the simple things. The boy's wooden toy box contained few possessions—an action figure with a missing hand, a deflated soccer ball, and his treasured book of fairy tales.

Night after night, the child would surrender to the darkness of his closet, only the dim light of a dollar-store flashlight and his precious books to keep him company. Crawling far inside his mind, he would become the Prince, the King, even the witch or warlock.

If the main character possessed the power to fight against an enemy, it mattered little to him whether they were good or evil.

As the years passed, the silver bell would ring more often as the child's chore list grew. Aside from his regular duties, it was the boy's job to see that the place his mother spent most of her time—on her back atop a well-worn mattress—was, at the very least, clean.

His mother had many friends that called on her, a seemingly endless supply of men to entertain. The boy was tasked with changing his mother's linens several times a day, ensuring that her next lover could not detect the scent of the man before him.

She believed it denoted class and good breeding.

Five days a week, from dusk until dawn, his mother would paste a smile on her face and greet countless 'gentlemen callers' at the door. Before they could even cross the threshold, the boy would escape to his room, eager to wrap himself within the darkness of his closet.

His Sanctuary.

He spent hours in this make-believe world, riding beside the dashing knight or dueling with a rogue swordsman. The adventures swept him away, transporting him to a magical world. They were the stories that sustained him, carried him through the roughest times and the bleakest days.

Within those pages, he found safety, humanity, peace.

Until the evening where immorality and the wickedness of society shredded the child-like wonder of an innocent soul; until a vile monster dared to enter his kingdom, constructing a reality he could never imagine.

And a nightmare unlike anything he'd read in his story books.

An unspoken line, a line of limits and morals and decency, would be not only crossed that evening but wholly shattered. And when it was over, the horror and shame of it all would cling to the child, draping him in darkness and threatening to swallow him whole.

On that fateful evening, immersed in his latest story and absorbing the words until they were a part of him, he never heard the turn of the doorknob or the hinges squeak in protest. It was a sliver of moonlight entering through the closet door that alerted him to another presence. He squinted in the darkness, his eyes trailing up a pair of shadowy silhouettes until they landed on his mother's icy stare.

Stomach cramping and heart racing, he pulled his gaze from hers and blinked in confusion at the stranger beside her.

He was an older man, with a paunch at the waist and hands the size of bear claws. The odor of cigars and whiskey and his mother's cheap perfume assaulted the boy's nostrils, and he gagged.

The stranger licked his lips, displaying a hunger unimaginable to an innocent.

Giving the boy a lopsided grin, the man stuck out his hand.

"Greetings, lad," the stranger said. "Whatcha got there? You like books, do ya? Your mother here told me you like books." He slid a look at the child's mother, and she nodded. "I have money, son. I can buy you as many books as you'd like. I can help you and your momma get out of this rat-infested building. All you have to do is be nice to me."

The stranger wiped a line of drool from the corner of his lips, reached into his pocket, and pulled out a coin. "If you are a good boy, there's much more where this comes from."

Terrified, though he didn't understand why, the boy bolted for the door.

But the old man was faster than he looked. Reaching out, he hooked an arm around the boy's waist and pulled him close. With breath ripe with the stench of rotting meat and booze, his words tickled the boy's ear.

"Don't worry, child," the stranger whispered. "It only hurts for a little while."

~

And so, it would become the night where the boy learned of a different kind of pain, a night where the wanton desires and despicable fantasies that crawled inside the mind of a pedophile came knocking on a lonely closet door.

It would become the first night of many, the clang of the bell announcing his mother had offered him to yet another visitor. In time, as hope was lost and thoughts of mercy forgotten, the boy learned to turn inward, disappearing inside himself.

Stoic, dry-eyed, free to enter the realm of his books.

But the same fables that prevented his mind from shattering into a million pieces were the very ones he despised for the childhood they symbolized—shocking, immoral, tarnished.

A double-edged sword that, as a young boy, he could neither wield against his enemies nor fall upon in defeat.

Now, as the small boy stared into the dead eyes of 'Uncle Bill,' he recognized the truth. His mother had not killed his molester out of maternal instinct or a desire to protect him. Nor was the man on the floor dead because of any love between mother and child.

He was dead because he failed to pay for his pleasure.

But with death, comes clarity.

The man with the knife in his chest could finally see clearly.

And now, so could the boy.

Once upon a time, decades ago and in too many cities to remember, there lived an angelic child trapped beneath the thumb of an evil woman ... He was only eight years old.

CHAPTER ONE

April 5th
Fredericksburg, VA
Callahan Residence

Callie Callahan crossed her arms and squinted at the black lab sitting in front of her. The dog peeked up through dark-brown eyes, occasionally diverting his gaze to the side as if he could not bear her judgment for long.

"So," Callie said sternly, "I see here that the bagel I toasted to perfection is no longer on the table where I left it. Curious, don't you think?" Shamed, the dog had the good sense to look away. "I mean, call me crazy, Blue, but I'm fairly certain I didn't eat it. So —any thoughts about how it just, like, disappeared?" Blue shook his head, chuffed in the air, and settled on the floor, head on his paws.

"Yeah, I thought so."

A chill swept up her back, settling comfortably at her nape, and she shuddered.

Behind her, a soft voice asked, "Did he fess up?"

Callie lifted her head from the alleged bagel thief and turned. The vision in front of her shimmered, a vibrating pulse of energy, a flickering of light that only Callie could see. The woman was beautiful, iridescent, calming.

And dead for over four months now.

Smiling, Callie winked at her sister. "Not a peep, Kates. I'm thinking he is so laden with carbs, he can barely speak."

"Go easy on him, Shadow. He's had a rough couple of months."

There was an awkward pause, an uncomfortable silence out of character for them. When Callie's twin, Katie, was alive, they filled whatever space they occupied with conversation and laughter.

Determined to get their rhythm back, Callie joked, "So, look at us. You've only been gone a few months, and we've already run out of things to say. I blame you—you never call, you never write. I mean, how busy could you be over there?" She smirked, happy for the opportunity to tease her sibling.

Katie chuckled, and her soul burned brighter. Katherine Callahan did not merely absorb light; she radiated it. She was the epitome of purity, of grace, and it both mesmerized and disturbed Callie.

Because, although her sister's presence was proof of life after death, it also served as a painful reminder that she was dead and never coming back.

"You'd be surprised, Cal. You mortals, thinking it's all harps and angelic music and spying on your former lovers in their bedrooms," she joked. "But our schedules leave us with little time for any of that. We have many fish to fry on this side, you know. We are incredibly important to the world." She grinned and gave a half-assed curtsy. "Anyway, I can't stay long. I just wanted to try one more time to talk you out of going after Jeremy."

Jeremy. Just the name of their half-brother sent shivers up Callie's spine.

Jeremy Sterling was a sociopath, a crazed serial killer obsessed with destroying Katie's life. It was because of him that

Katie and so many others were dead. Jeremy was why Callie had screws in her ankle and walked with a slight limp whenever she was tired.

He was the reason she broke out into a cold sweat, heart racing, in dark and cramped spaces.

And he was the reason she awoke screaming nearly every day since December, her nightshirt clinging to her damp body. Sometimes, her terrifying dreams left her vocal cords raw, and she barely recognized her voice the next day.

Jeremy. Except now, he went by several titles: Gabriel, the Apostle, Messenger of God.

Callie didn't care how many names he used—he would always be an asshole.

Four months ago, Gabriel began a killing spree based on an insane notion that Katherine Callahan had destroyed his life. In the process of going after everyone Katie loved, he killed several people, eventually completing his mission.

And right before he took Katie's life, he also admitted to killing their mother, Eileen Callahan, decades earlier.

At the time, Gabriel was just ten years old.

"So," Callie said, changing the subject, "tell me more about the afterlife. What do you do up there? Do you have a house?" She paused for a second, then snapped her fingers. "Hey! Have you seen Elvis?"

Katie huffed. "Oh, you're a riot, Cal. And I know what you're doing. It's the same thing you did when we were kids—deflect and redirect. But this is no childhood prank here, Sis. Seriously, what do you plan to do if you find Gabriel?"

Callie shook her head. "Me first, Kates. There's something I haven't asked you yet because I'm not sure I want the answer. I mean, once the words escape your lips, all hope is lost, isn't it?" She cleared her throat and pushed her shoulders back, hoping that a confident physical presence could sustain her emotionally. "Have you seen her? Mom? I know Gabriel confessed to killing her, but since we've never found ..." She stopped speaking, unable to say the words. There was no need to voice them out loud, anyway. Katie understood.

"She's here, Cal, with us all. Mom, Dad, Nana, and Stacy. We are all here, adjusting but doing well."

Callie swallowed the impossibly large lump in the back of her throat, the sting of tears threatening to fall. In her heart, she'd always known. But to hear the words, to see the truth laying bare on her sister's face, was like a punch to the gut. In an instant, Callie's crazy notions of her mom, alive and well somewhere, vanished.

She hadn't run away with a secret lover, hadn't been kidnapped by a religious cult or the Irish mafia, hadn't been whisked away into the Witness Protection Program.

Eileen Callahan was dead.

"I'm sorry, Shadow. I know you hoped for a different answer, and I wish I could give it to you. Just know that she is at peace and here with Dad and me. It is as it should be."

Callie chuffed and rolled her eyes. "Oh, brother. No offense, but you realize you sound like a dork, right? 'It is as it should be.' Who are you? The Dalai Lama?"

Katie laughed. "I do miss that sense of humor, Cal Pal. Now, how about we get back to the question I asked you? What do you plan to do if you find Gabriel?"

Callie picked up a sponge and wiped down the spotless counters in the kitchen. Her mom used to call it 'busy work,' and Callie was good at it. As she scrubbed, she searched for the right words to convey her mission. It wasn't just that she wanted Gabriel to pay for his actions. It was an intense, physical need to see justice prevail.

As if her entire future, and the only way she could move on, was to see him behind bars.

Or dead. She didn't much care either way.

Sighing, she wrung out the sponge and tossed it into the sink. It hit the faucet, ricocheted off the sprayer head, and came to rest inside the holder on the basin wall.

"Score!" she whispered. When Katie showed little reaction, Callie shrugged and took a seat at the table. "You want the truth, or you want me to pretty it up a bit?"

"What do you think, Shadow?" Katie said, folding her arms.

"Okay, but I can't promise that you'll like it. Look, Gabriel took everything from me, Kates. You, my best friend, Mom. He kidnapped me, beat me half to death, branded his fucking name on my thigh. Every time I change my clothes or take a shower, that damn tattoo stares at me, mocks me. And he got away with it all. How does that even happen?" Taking a shaky breath, she rubbed her brow, feeling a beastly headache coming on. "How does a ten-year-old kid kill Mom and get a pass? Keep his freedom so he can continue to kill, continue to destroy lives, and never have to pay?" She stood and paced the room. "There have been so many aftershocks to his actions, Kate. Bottom line? He went after you because of an accident you had as a child! What kind of maniac blames a little girl for the death of her father?"

It was a rhetorical question, one they both knew the answer to.

Callie and her sister were just six years old when Katie drowned in the family pool. Once resuscitated, Katie returned to life with the ability to see and feel the dead. After the accident, her father, guilt-ridden at nearly losing his daughter and ashamed of the kind of husband he'd been, turned over a new leaf. He chartered a plane, traveled to Laredo, and broke things off with his mistress, Meredith Sterling.

Gabriel's mother.

On his return trip to Virginia, Rowan Callahan's plane went down, killing everyone on board. In Gabriel's twisted mind, if Katie hadn't drowned, his father would never have been on that plane.

Katie's radiance dimmed. "I'm running out of time, Shadow. I understand you're hurting. I can still *feel* your pain, even from this side. But there is no future in revenge. You must know that."

In life, Katie could not only see the dead but could sense

their suffering. Months ago, as she lay dying on a musty basement floor, her psychic ability somehow transferred to Callie. Thankfully, her gift as an Empath did not.

Callie had no desire to go through the rest of her life bleeding for other people.

"I love you, Kates. I miss you so much that, some days, the pain takes my breath away. We all miss you. Jake misses you."

FBI Special Agent Jacob Devereaux was the man who captured Katie's heart. He was the man who held her hand as she lay covered in blood, struggling to breathe. And he was the man who beat himself up every damned day, and twice on Sundays, because he failed to protect her. Theirs was an all-too-brief love affair that, Callie believed, would have gone the distance if Katie had lived.

How different things would have been, Kates, if only you'd lived!

"And I miss you all," Katie whispered. "But it's different over here, Shadow. The line that divides the living, and the dead, is somehow blurred. The hands of the clock move like lightning here. Hours, days pass in the blink of an eye."

Dumbfounded, Callie stared, trying to absorb what her sister was saying.

"Don't you see? I can't miss your presence because time is relative. Eternity has no beginning and no end. So, while it may feel to you like decades until we are together again, in this dimension, it's minutes." Aware that the energy it took to manifest in spirit form was waning, she said, "I'm never far away, Cal. Even if you cannot see me, know that I am close. And that I love you forever."

Callie watched Katie vanish, hung her head, and, as always, cried.

⁓

Thirty minutes later, balanced precariously on the staircase, Callie wrestled an over-stuffed suitcase over the landing to the first step. Huffing and puffing, taking one step at a time, she yanked the bag forward, cringing as it bounced off the spindles on the handrail. The clatter on the steps masked the sound of the front door.

"Cal?" Darby Harrison, her current roommate and Katie's lifelong friend, stood at the bottom of the steps. She had plaited her hair into two long, blonde braids and wore a Bavarian jumper. "Christ, what the hell are you doing? Getting rid of the body?"

"Cute hairdo," Callie said with a grunt as she bounced down another step. "How's the yodeling going?"

Darby grinned. "Funny."

Callie grunted again. "Not to be pushy, but do you think you could give me a hand, Heidi? Unless, of course, you have goats to herd or something."

Darby chuckled. She was living in the main house now, ever since that dreadful day in December when she'd lost the best friend she'd ever had. Prior to that, she'd hung her hat in an apartment above the Callahan garage.

"Look at you, killin' it with the jokes!" She pirouetted, then curtsied. "I'll have you know, this outfit came into the shop the other day, and I couldn't resist!"

Darby was the sole proprietor of Time and Time Again, a small store specializing in clothing and toys from yesteryear. Everything in Darby's life, from her car to her clothes to her quirky mannerisms, was vintage. The quaint boutique matched her personality perfectly.

She met Callie halfway up the steps, then grabbed one end of the suitcase. "You sure you want to do this, Cal? Go to Montana, I mean. Katie's gone, and there isn't a dang thing you can do that will bring her back. If there were, I'd have done it months ago." Looking over her shoulder, she backed down the stairs. "And I'm fairly confident there is no chance on God's green earth she would agree to what you are planning. In fact, she would hate the idea. It's reckless and dangerous and, quite frankly, unnecessary.

Gabriel will get his comeuppance someday. You just gotta believe in karma, toots."

They reached the first floor and lowered the bag to the ground. "Woo-hoo," Callie said, "we did it! This monstrosity was the big bastard; the others aren't as heavy." Shaking her head, she added, "Honestly, I try to pack light. I just suck at it."

Darby grinned. "Samesies."

Adjusting the elastic band holding her hair, Callie said, "I have to find him, Darbs. Gabriel took too much from me, from all of us. My sister, my mom, my best friend. And sweet, lovable, Chance. Gabriel has so many notches in his belt. He has to pay."

"You know what blows my mind about this whole thing?" Darby asked. "I mean, aside from the obvious fact that he killed so many people? It's the number of victims. Thirteen. As in thirteen Apostles? Eerie."

"Technically, I think there were always twelve," Callie said. "Some consider Saint Matthias the thirteenth Apostle, since he took the place of Judas Iscariot after he killed himself. But when Judas died, it left eleven. Matthias just made it twelve again. It is weird, though. The whole thing is freakin' weird." She took a seat on the living-room sofa. Blue came towards her, his wagging tail nearly toppling a candle on the coffee table. "Hey, fella," she said, patting his head. "I'm gonna miss you."

Her original plan was to take Blue with her to Montana. Jake's brother, Jed, owned a private investigation company called Private Investigative and Personal Protection Services, or PIPPS. She'd tried to hire Jed to help find Gabriel.

Instead, he offered her a job.

Jed believed Callie, a psychologist by trade and ghost whisperer by chance, would prove invaluable to his investigative team. But his base of operations was in Montana, over fifteen hundred miles away, and Blue was a search and rescue dog. Taking him away from the rescue team, especially now that they were short a qualified dog with Chance's death, would be selfish. So, with a heavy heart, Callie decided to keep Blue in

Fredericksburg. Darby would continue his training and answer any calls to action.

It was the right thing to do.

Sensing her sadness, Darby said, "Don't worry, Cal. Blue and I will be okay."

"It just bites, you know? I hate to introduce yet another change in his life. He's missing Katie and Chance just as much as I am." Resigned, she added, "But it would be unfair to the families desperate to locate a loved one."

Darby nodded. "Very true," she said, absently playing with a button on her jumper. "So, in other news, have you figured out how to turn off your dead people radar?"

Callie shook her head. "Hardly. It's so damned freaky. Some nights, I wake with a start, just knowing someone is staring at me. When I finally get the guts to open my eyes? Bam, dead guy two inches from my nose!"

Darby grimaced. "Dang! You know, this may shock you, but I did a little digging."

Callie widened her eyes in mock exaggeration, fully aware of Darby's intense fascination with the supernatural. "Wow, you got me, Darbs! Totally blindsided over here."

"Anyhoo," Darby said, rolling her eyes, "the article I read talked about the need to give a signal to the spirit, like a stop sign or an off-duty tag. The lady who wrote the piece uses a wide-brimmed red hat to let ghosties know she is off the clock."

"What kind of friend are you to even suggest that?" Callie teased. "We both know I look hideous in hats. Katie could wear them, but I could never pull them off. I look like I'm dressing up in my momma's clothing."

Darby laughed. "Can't argue with you, there. But you do a great baseball cap!"

"I do, don't I? That's a stellar idea, my friend. And I know just the ..."

The doorbell rang, interrupting her.

"Expecting someone?" Darby asked.

"Jake. I'm going to follow him in my car on this ridiculously long road trip."

Callie strode to the door, Blue at her heels.

"Hey," Jake said. "You all set?"

"Yep. I just need to double-check I've got everything. Come in a sec."

"Um, before I do, I have something to tell you," Jake said, fumbling for words. "Well, show you. Well, show and tell you." He pulled nervously at his collar. "Not like that kind of show and tell."

"What's with you? Spill it, man."

Jake raked a hand through his dark hair. "Uh, there's someone here who's dying to meet you. I just hope you'll be as happy to meet her."

Callie tilted her head. "Are you gonna make me beg here, Devereaux?"

He grinned and pulled his hand from behind his back, tugging gently on the purple leash wrapped in his fist. In a blink, a gorgeous Golden Retriever puppy was jumping at Callie's feet.

"Ohhh!" she shrieked. "Who is this adorable baby?" She bent down and scooped up the fluffy ball of fur. Blue was going nuts.

Jake grinned and relaxed a bit. He hadn't been sure what Callie's reaction would be. "This," he said theatrically, "is a four-month-old orphan I bought from a friend. His momma didn't survive the birth of the litter, and this girl," he ruffled the dog's neck, "is the last of the bunch to find a home. I figured since you weren't taking Blue, you might need a friend."

Callie put the puppy down, and Blue, curious, walked a circle around Callie's legs, sniffing the new arrival. He quickly lost interest, as if saddened to discover this Golden Retriever was not his lifelong friend, Chance.

"I don't know what to say, Jake," Callie said, moved. "This is probably one of the sweetest things anyone has ever done for me."

Jake blushed, then rushed on to say, "She's a good girl, too, and smart as a whip. You won't believe her name, either. It's what sold me, the one thing that pushed me over and let me know I needed to take her."

When he just stood there, grinning like a fool, Callie said, "And?" She was beginning to understand why Katie once told her Jake could be frustratingly obtuse.

"Her name is Lucky and, according to the dictionary, the definition of lucky is to happen by chance."

Callie's heart squeezed. *Chance.*

Darby snuck around Callie, plopped on the ground, and reached out for the pup. "Come here, you beautiful girl!"

Smiling, watching Darby play with Lucky, Callie said, "I can't thank you enough, Jake. This dog is just what I need about now. And her resemblance to Chance is uncanny!" She slapped her forehead. "She needs a cushion to sleep on! Chance's bed is still upstairs in Kate's room. Be right back!"

Jake watched her jog up the stairs, a satisfied smile on his face, momentarily forgetting he wasn't alone. When Darby cleared her throat, he turned to find her squinting at him, sizing him up.

"What?" Jake asked innocently.

"Don't 'what' me, mister," Darby said, standing. "Good God, Jake! Does she know?"

"Know what? What the hell are you talking about, Darby?" Jake asked, jaw tense.

Darby backhanded his shoulder. "You know darn well what I'm talking about. And if you don't, you'll figure it out, eventually."

"I'm seriously lost here, Ms. Harrison," Jake said, frowning. "What do I have to figure out?"

She stared him down. "If I have to tell you, it's worse than I thought. Look, I like you, Jake. As sure as God made sunshine and little green apples, I do. But you were Katie's guy. And the thought of you and her sister ..." she trailed off. "Callie's been through enough without adding on heaps of guilt. And I will do anything to protect her. Even if that means busting kneecaps or breaking arms if someone hurts her."

"What the devil are you ..."

Just then, Callie came bounding down the stairs, a green canine bed under one arm, the other arm juggling three or four dog toys. She noticed a change in the atmosphere immediately.

"What? What'd I miss?"

"Nothing," Jake answered quickly. "You ready?"

As they passed through the door, Jake turned back, his eyes finding Darby's once more. Using two fingers, she gave him an 'I'm watching you' gesture, then quietly closed the front door.

He still hadn't a clue what the devil she was talking about.

CHAPTER TWO

"... when they began playing, one child said to the other, 'you be the little pig, and I'll be the butcher.' He then took a shiny knife and slit his little brother's throat." — *The Brothers Grimm*

Joey 'the Hammer' Fabrizio fancied himself a wiseguy, a hooked-up Mafioso whose last name would someday rival the notoriety of the Gambino family. He wore thousand-dollar suits and ate cannoli and kissed grown men on the mouth, just to prove how 'made' he was.

But the only things Joey would ever be infamous for were his Dolce and Gabbana shoes, his overactive imagination, and his delusions of grandeur.

The 'Fabrizio Five,' his so-called organized crime family, included himself, a brother, an uncle with dementia, and two distant cousins. Together, their combined IQs wouldn't fill a thimble. And while Joey readily admitted their shortcomings, he just as quickly excused them.

Most criminals were not rocket scientists, after all.

Joey and his quartet of mobster wannabes would meet one evening a week and regale each other with tales of sweet stings, successful money-laundering operations, and profitable stock market investments. Cousin Louie, a greasy, hairy man who reeked of garlic and body odor, embraced his role as the 'enforcer' of the crew, bragging that "sometimes you gotta break a few legs to get what the family needs, capeesh?"

'Fabrizio Fabrications,' Joey used to call them. Exaggerated tales, woven together to impress or intimidate, depending on the audience.

Still, they could be a formidable bunch, especially to vulnerable women and senior citizens. The Fabrizio Five specialized in scamming old-timers by duping them into giving away their nest eggs. It was despicable work—perpetuated on defenseless people—by the lowest of the low.

And The Hammer loved it.

Joey's office was on the ground floor of a four-story building; a brownstone he'd purchased in Brooklyn Heights. He believed appearing legitimate was the only way to find the perfect patsy. And so, by day, Joey masqueraded as a construction foreman, printing bogus business cards, placing ads, even creating phony work receipts. He filed a business tax return for Fabrizio Construction and dutifully paid his share of the yearly taxes, but it was all a front. The only thing Joey used his office for was to scout out another sucker.

He'd found one in Marjorie Whitman.

An elderly widow with no children and a sizable bank account, Marjorie was kind, giving, and a bit naïve, creating the perfect target. On a chilly November morning, Fabrizio Construction arrived to 'inspect' her home, free of charge. An hour later, they'd convinced her that her roof was falling apart, the home's foundation was crumbling, and her driveway was near collapse. She wrote them a check on the spot, one made out to a dummy corporation, for over forty thousand dollars. Joey cashed it that same day.

Marjorie Whitman never saw them again.

Things could have gone on for years like that for Fabrizio Construction; find a mark, investigate their assets, swoop in for the spoils. Unfortunately for him, Joey had one inescapable flaw: the inability to keep his mouth shut. A braggart and a cad, his boasting at a neighborhood bar describing the 'blue-haired lady with too much money and not enough tit,' reached the ears of the wrong man.

A man just looking for a reason to kill.

Three days after absconding with most of Marjorie Whitman's nest egg, Joey 'The Hammer' Fabrizio disappeared.

When Joey regained consciousness, he was in the basement of his brownstone, naked and trussed up like a Christmas goose. Hands and feet hog-tied behind him, he pulled against the nautical-type rope, grunting with effort, his arms slick with sweat.

He ordered himself to think, but terror prevented any rational thought. Thighs aching and eyes burning, he took a deep breath and gagged, the air ripe with the sharp stench of urine. Tears stained his cheeks while mucus left a thick film on the lower half of his face.

Joey Fabrizio was as far away from a tough guy as he would ever be.

The scrape of shuffling boots startled him, and he stifled a scream. Something, someone, stood just inches from his body, panting. Squeezing his eyes shut to avoid a reality he could not face, macho veneer all but gone, Joey prayed to a God he didn't believe existed.

Eventually, human curiosity won the battle, and he opened his eyes.

Instantly, he regretted the decision.

His captor, brawny and bald, paced the length of the room. Speaking in hushed tones, his words nonsensical, the bald man jabbed and sliced the air with his impossibly long hunting knife.

Slaying imaginary demons.

Joey gave up trying to make out the vaguely familiar words the man was chanting—something about children and a game of death. In the background, the pitiful cries of dozens of frightened pigs played softly on a loop.

"Here, piggy, piggy," the Hairless Man said, drawing closer to his victim. "I want to hear you oink."

Joey stopped whimpering, certain he'd heard the man wrong.

"Come on, you fucking swine! Squeal!"

Confused, struggling to break free, Joey almost made it to his knees before collapsing to the ground. "I don't understand!" he cried, not expecting an answer. "Why are you doing this?"

The Hairless Man bent over, his lips close to Joey's ear. In a whisper, he answered, "Marjorie Whitman."

The blade that slid across Joey Fabrizio's neck nearly decapitated him.

The Hairless man studied the corpse on the ground. The back of Joey's head rested somewhere between his shoulder blades, his sightless eyes directed toward the rear of the basement. Using a gloved finger, the man drew the word 'PIG' in blood on the cement floor, then placed a silver bell over the 'I.'

Simple clues for simple cops.

By the time The Hairless Man left Joey Fabrizio's brownstone and headed for home, he admitted this latest kill was not satisfying. It was a mission born out of another person's wound, an offense committed against Marjorie Whitman, and did not have the same 'feel' as the others. His philosophy on terminating vermin was simple—eliminate those not worthy of sharing the same air. He killed for himself, and himself only.

Putting his freedom on the line to settle a score for an old lady was unwise. He'd do well to remember that in the future.

Joey Fabrizio had been his third victim, and a risk he shouldn't have taken. Three suspicious deaths, three individuals killed in proximity to each other, all within the last two weeks.

Not smart.

If he hadn't noticed the stupid tattoo on his first kill, he might have let them all live. But he noticed. And he acted.

Still, it had been sloppy planning and entirely out of character. He needed to do better, be better. The murders would surely bring unwanted attention and scores of investigators to the area. They may even post a reward, pass out flyers, study red-light cams.

Were there any closed-circuit cameras operating in nearby businesses? Did Fabrizio have a security system?

Just the thought of being captured on video made him queasy. He would need to cut his vacation short, leave the state of New York for good. Moral decay thrived here, and if he stayed, the temptation to kill again would be too great. The dregs of society seemed to gather in the Big Apple. Besides, he had many precious memories to bring home with him, memories of his first victims and the joy they gave him.

Two prostitutes, he thought bitterly.

Two skanky whores working the streets of Manhattan. Not even people, really—more like objects, things that sold themselves for a quick buck.

Just like Mother.

It disgusted him. And, although he didn't intend to kill the first one, he'd been so turned on by her fear, he'd lost control.

She called herself Candy.

Candy was bony, hard-looking, and much too old for a hooker. But she had a glorious head of butter-blonde hair, too lovely to ignore, and a mouth that could suck the chrome off a trailer hitch.

She was miles away from what one would consider attractive, but Candy's rates were cheap, and she was a decent fuck.

As soon as the sex was over, she rolled out of bed and flicked on the nightstand lamp. Lighting a joint, she walked toward the bathroom, and he noticed it for the first time—the etching above her ass, the faded hearts framing the simplistic phrase.

The tattoo looked amateurish, as if done using the crude instruments found inside a prison's walls. He wondered briefly if she'd done time.

His hands began to shake, and his vision tunneled into narrow cones of light.

The tattoo read 'Happily Ever After.'

A flash of anger hit him, intense and unexpected, and he vaulted out of bed. Reaching her in three strides, he yanked her by the hair and hooked his forearm around her neck.

Then he squeezed; the flesh of her throat pillowed and warm in the crook of his elbow. Her carotid pulse beat frantically against his forearm, and he felt his groin stir. He didn't understand what drove his reaction. Or overreaction.

It felt instinctual, like scratching an itch or taking your next breath.

Candy, meanwhile, had instincts of her own. She bucked and kicked and gnashed her teeth at the arm around her throat, desperate to break free. But the Hairless Man just giggled, drunk with the power he possessed, and pressed harder. Within minutes, a startling yet satisfying crack echoed in the room.

Or maybe it only reverberated in his ears. No matter.

Candy went limp, her head thrown unnaturally to one side. Transfixed, he gazed at the paleness of her neck and the crimson dots that speckled the whites of her eyes.

And came for the second time that night.

Later that evening, after tucking a lock of her hair into a pocket, he went home, confident that he would kill again. He had never felt so free, so alive. He was like an addict, craving just one more fix.

He got it with girl number two in a seedy motel in the heart of Manhattan.

~

"Are ya smooth all over, baby?" Leaning into the car, Amber cracked on a piece of gum and winked at the man behind the wheel.

The Hairless man nodded. "Mostly. It's called Alopecia. It's genetic."

A lie, born out of desperation to keep everything about him

anonymous. In the end, though, he knew how the evening would conclude.

Making confidentiality ... lunacy.

The actual cause of his baldness, trichotillomania, was a condition that manifested as an irresistible urge to pull one's hair out. Classified as a mental health disorder, sufferers claim the act can successfully relieve stress and frustration.

The Hairless man had been yanking on his hair for years, leaving bald patches in his scalp and blood trails covering his skull. Still, his anxiety remained.

So, to deal with the stigma and embarrassment of the disorder, he shaved his head.

Amber smirked, showing a row of rotting yellow teeth. She stood straighter, smoothing back her greasy, dark hair. A crude tattoo of Betty Boop humping a stripper pole peeked out from beneath her black miniskirt.

"Genetic, huh? Well, I'll tell you, sugar, it's making me cream my panties." She smiled again and lit a cigarette. "So, how much you willin' to spend for a good time? Miss Amber would love to wrap her lips around some smooth right about now." She took a drag from her cigarette and pushed out her chest, the sheer fabric of her blouse outlining small breasts beneath impossibly large nipples.

The Hairless man forced a smile, trying to hide his contempt. "How about fifty for an hour of your time?"

Amber nodded. After she extinguished her cigarette, he ushered her to the passenger side of his vehicle. Fifteen minutes later, they found a roach-friendly motel in a dicey section of Central Park West.

Once inside their room, he stripped her and dug into his knapsack for a roll of duct tape.

Amber was well-versed in the unconventional fantasies of her clients and went along at first, finding his tastes kinky but harmless. And, although she stiffened when he lashed her to the bed frame with the tape, she said nothing.

But when he asked to gag her mouth, Amber felt the first niggling of fear seep through her bones.

"Aww, you don't wanna do that, baby," she purred. "How will you hear my groans of pleasure when you make me feel soooo good?"

The Hairless Man shrugged, giving her a boyish grin. "Please?" he pleaded. "It really turns me on."

Weighing the promise of fifty dollars against the very slim chance that this particular John was a nutcase, Amber's greed triumphed.

She could do a lot with fifty bucks.

"Okay, big guy," she said, batting her non-existent lashes. "But not too tight, okay?" Despite her resolve to see this through, she was feeling the tug of panic once again. "Um, if I can't speak, how will you know when I don't wanna play anymore?"

The man frowned, his pretense at concern convincing. "Yes, I can see that could be a problem." After a moment, he smiled and snapped his fingers. "I know! How about if you blink? When I ask if it feels good, you blink once for yes, twice for no."

She bit her lip. Everything about this was making her uncomfortable.

She agreed anyway.

He wrapped the silk scarf he'd brought gently over her mouth. Once she was secure, he returned to his knapsack, withdrawing an enormous pair of scissors.

Amber's eyes widened in confusion, then fear, and she screamed, the sounds beneath the gag muffled and distant.

"Hush," the Hairless Man whispered, leaning into her face. "Do you have any idea how incredibly repulsive you are, Amber? Is that even your name? Pathetic piece of shit! Did you seriously think I took you here to have sex? With you?" He sneered, then spat in her face. "Lady, I wouldn't fuck you with someone else's dick."

Amber's eyes widened in panic. Sobbing uncontrollably, snot gathering in the crease above her lips, she followed his movements as he waved the shears over her body. Her heart thumped faster than she thought possible, drowning out the screams echoing in her mind.

The Hairless Man dipped in closer. "Do you want to play a game, Amber? I do!" He clapped his hands and jumped in place. "Let's play a game!"

He reached back into his bag and pulled out a black cord. It was a power cable, about three feet long, with a USB-type connector on one end and a plug on the other. Climbing on the bed, he straddled her hips and smirked.

Amber twisted and bucked, bile clogging her throat, until he slapped her, hard, across the face.

"Knock it the fuck off!" he growled.

Amber, in a mad panic, began to hyperventilate beneath the gag.

Ignoring her terror, he smoothed a hand down her now-reddened cheek and whispered, "I like to call this game 'Options' because there are so many varieties, so many ways to play. We will start slowly, enjoying the game as you learn the rules. I'll even let you choose how we start today. Cords, fists, or scissors?" He snickered. "It's like the game we all played as children—the rock, paper, scissors game! We already have the scissors, and we can use this cord for the paper part, and my fists in place of the rock! Oh, this will be lovely!"

He bounced up and down on her lap, unable to contain his glee. Amber grunted with each jolt, the breath leaving her body. Her mind raced, trying to recall if she'd told any of the other girls who worked the same street corner where she was going.

She hadn't.

The Hairless Man grabbed the scissors and ran them up and down her bare torso, occasionally stopping to explore a valley or hill while crooning an unfamiliar tune. He pressed the tip of the scissors into the flesh of her lower abdomen, and she jumped, the puncture igniting nerves and lighting a fire near her midriff.

A steady stream of blood flowed past her hip, and she screamed through the gag over her mouth.

He stabbed me! Oh, God, please! Help me!

He chuckled, then painted a small daisy on her tummy with her blood, using her belly button as the flower's center.

"What's next, bitch? Shall we try fists?"

Snickering, he pulled back a fisted hand and began pummeling her face and body. Her head whipped back and forth with each blow, shooting blood and saliva across the room.

Finally, exhausted but not yet satisfied, he stopped punching long enough to wrap the electrical cord around her neck.

"Are you ready for the next part of the game, Amber? I could honestly play all day, but since I only have the room for an hour ..."

His eyes were glazed, the lids heavy. They were the eyes of lust, of passion; a lover's eyes caught in the throes of ecstasy.

Amber understood the look and, recognizing him for the dangerous animal he was, resumed her muffled screams. Whipping her head back and forth, she successfully dislodged a corner of the cloth that bound her mouth. A weak scream escaped her lips, more like a kitten's mew than the cries of a dying woman, but she continued to fight, to hope.

The Hairless Man repositioned the gag, then punched her already swollen face.

Amber heard the unmistakable crack of her jaw breaking.

"Don't try that again!" he snarled, inches from her face. "If you do, I assure you the game will take a very dark turn!" He squeezed the cord around her neck until her face turned smokey gray and her eyes bulged. Seconds later, she lost consciousness.

When she came to, she took in her surroundings, and her heart jumped to her throat. The Hairless Man was straddling her, teeth bared and drool dripping from the corner of his mouth. He squeezed the cord once more.

Amber blinked frantically, ridiculously, hoping to convey that the game was over, that he needed to stop, needed to obey her 'safe' signal.

He laughed and pulled harder on the cord, spittle spraying from his mouth, sprinkling her face and ears. The blood vessels in her eyes burst, and her tongue poked through swollen lips. The sight excited him further, and he ejaculated beneath his jeans.

Time marched on, and he continued to play—long after Amber had left the game.

~

Sheridan, Wyoming
Mid-April

His world had turned to shit. Just a few short months ago, he had life by the balls. He'd been the master of his destiny, captain of his ship, second to none. Now, he played a cruel game of hide and seek. A game where he'd gone from predator to prey, forced to conceal himself from his enemies, forced to continue this charade while pretending to be something he was not.

Father Gabriel.

He despised the title. He wasn't a Kool-Aid drinking, slave to social norms type of man. He never feigned piety. He didn't have to ... he was the Apostle. He had plans, countless ideas to rid the world of the diseased in both mind and morals. But his agenda, his aspirations, became thwarted, courtesy of his two sisters and that FBI agent.

Oh, sure, he'd gotten his revenge. Before it all came crashing down, he'd been able to see not only his sister, Katherine, dead, but he effectively removed several other vermin he'd encountered along the way. People who'd contributed nothing to the planet, leeches that sucked on the teats of society.

Like his lying bitch of a mother, begging for forgiveness and crying crocodile tears. Pathetic. And that mouthy fucking cheerleader, Stacy.

And Katherine's ex-boyfriend, ol' Kyle what's-his-name, sticking his dick where it didn't belong.

He'd taught them all.

Still, it was not without sacrifice on his part. In the process of his work, his sister Callie blinded him in one eye with a nail and that FBI prick shot him in the thigh. He hadn't fully recovered from that leg wound and so, had a considerable limp. On the unbearably long days when he visited the sick, the injury forced him to use a cane.

He'd hated those hospital visits. Giving blessings on the infirm and the weak went against everything he believed in. But it was part of the job description, part of the facade, so he went along with it.

Go along, get along!

He checked his watch and sighed. It was nearly time to enter the confessional. Congregants from St. Michael, the Archangel Church, would come in droves to confess their paltry sins behind a wooden screen that provided privacy and anonymity.

Their confessions were tedious, monotonous, as compelling as watching paint dry.

The sinners in Sheridan, Wyoming, were a lame bunch, to be sure. How he longed to hear someone reveal to him their deepest, darkest secrets—secrets that told of wicked thoughts or hungry desires that led them to commit unspeakable offenses.

Instead, womanizing, drinking, and gambling seemed the only transgressions the weak townsfolk could muster. Gabriel longed for something with a bit more bite, something tawdry and juicy and vulgar that would raise the eyebrows of even the most decadent of people.

As fate would have it, today would be his lucky day.

~

The third man in the confessional line stepped behind the privacy screen, kneeled, and began the act of contrition. The

Apostle yawned, thinking about nothing but the leftover lo-mein and pork fried rice that waited for him in his refrigerator.

"Bless me, Father, for I have sinned. It's been," the man hesitated, "it's been too long since my last confession."

"We don't use a calendar here, son," Gabriel said wearily. "Just free your soul from the burdens of sin, and God will forgive all."

The man nodded and folded his hands in his lap. Clearing his throat, he began his confession.

"I have sinned, Father. I've committed horrible, unforgivable sins. Mortal sins."

Gabriel stifled a yawn and picked at a cuticle. "Go on, my son."

"I, um, I have taken a life, Father. More than one, actually."

Gabriel's ears perked up. *A life? Could that be true?*

"I see," Gabriel said, keeping his voice even. "And how, exactly, did this happen? When did this happen?"

The man rubbed a hand over his face. "There were three of them, three people I ... targeted. Two women and a man, all from New York, all sinners. The women were prostitutes, and the male was a charlatan who fleeced an old lady of her life savings." He clucked his tongue. "They all deserved to be punished for their misdeeds. What they did was immoral. Disgusting."

Gabriel had trouble containing his glee. His brain worked furiously, creating ideas, devising strategies. In his mind's eye, he envisioned the possibilities.

I could continue my work! Through this man, I could banish the blight, the unholy stains that have taken hold on this earth!

Gabriel chose his next words carefully. "I understand, my son. There are many sick individuals in this world whose souls deserve to be freed. But you must be smart, cautious with whom you reunite with God." He made a show of blessing himself, mumbling a few words he believed would sound genuinely holy, and continued.

"Let us contemplate how best to go about this new task—a task that shall bring you glory in the eyes of our Lord. Come back to see me next week. Until then, reflect on any past transgressions, say three Hail Marys and two Our Fathers, and understand that you have transitioned into a higher purpose."

The man stood, and, hiding a smirk, left the confessional. Gabriel remained seated for fear his trembling knees would not hold his weight. Once again, the Creator had opened a window when all doors appeared closed to him. It cemented his belief that he was doing God's work.

He could exploit this man. Mold him and twist him and subjugate him into service. Finally, after all these months of living in darkness, Gabriel's face would, at last, feel the sun.

The Apostle was back.

CHAPTER THREE

C allie clicked the leash on the Golden Retriever's collar and glanced at Jake. "I thought you said you knew where you were going."

"I do know where I'm going," Jake snapped. "Just give me a minute to get my bearings."

Callie rolled her eyes and coaxed Lucky to the dog-walking area of the Iowa rest stop. It was day two of their cross-country trek, and they'd taken a wrong turn on a lonely road somewhere near Bloomfield. "Well, did you think to check the GPS? She ought to get us back to the interstate, no?"

"Yeah, she's a peach; keeps putting us back on the roads she originally kicked us off of because of detours." He raked a hand through his dark hair and grunted. "This is what I get for trying to avoid rush hour on the Chicago Skyway."

Callie squatted in front of her dog. "You need to pee, baby girl. Hopefully ..." she frowned at Jake, "... we can stop for the night soon. Who knows? With any luck, we'll have a repeat of last night's lodgings." Whispering to Lucky, knowing Jake could hear, she added, "You know, girlfriend, any ol' motel can boast a threadbare comforter, broken coffeemaker, and stale donuts. But it takes a particular brand of magic to offer guests an entertaining game of 'count the cockroaches' and 'identify that bed stain.'" She turned to Jake and raised a brow. "Good times."

Jake grunted, opened the rear door of his Ford Explorer, and grabbed an apple from the cooler. Resting his muscular arms on the door frame, he asked, "How the hell was I supposed to know the place sucked? Looked okay from the outside. But, yeah, sure, we can stop soon if that's what you want." Lifting a shoulder, he took a bite of his Granny Smith and added, "Princess."

"What I want," Callie said through gritted teeth, "is to be on the highway that will get us to Billings, Montana, while I'm still in my twenties. Oh, and a meal that's not stuffed into a cardboard box and picked up at a drive-thru window." She pursed her lips. "A smooth Chardonnay and a clean bed for the night might be nice, too." Gently tugging Lucky further onto the pet path, she tossed over her shoulder, "But stop me if I'm asking too much."

Jake hid a smirk, violet eyes sparkling with mischief. "I think I can do that. I checked, and it seems there is a decent hotel about twenty miles from here. Think you can wait that long?"

"I don't know, Agent. Think you can find it?"

Jake chuckled and closed the back door.

~

Thirty minutes later, they pulled into the parking lot of a pet-friendly hotel that boasted both a restaurant and a bar. Callie groaned and stepped out of her Jeep Wrangler, silently berating herself for not taking Katie's Denali.

I'm going to have to rethink this Wrangler thing. Cool car, but not exactly a practical choice for a woman with dogs.

Exhausted but famished, they paid for two rooms, settled Lucky in her bed for the night, and headed downstairs to the restaurant.

"So, how long are you planning on wearing that baseball cap,

Blaze?" Jake asked her, as the hostess seated them and took their drink orders.

"Blaze? Oh, this should be good."

"You know, red hair? Like Kate's?" Jake said. "You both have the same auburn-colored hair. I called her 'Red,' but I'm thinking, with your fiery temper and all, 'Blaze' suits you better."

My fiery temper? I'll show you a temper, asshole!

"That's a bold statement coming from a man who hardly knows me," she clipped. "You know, just because I don't agree with every damn thing you say or curtsy when you walk in the room doesn't mean I have a temper." Her clenched fists and reddened face told a different story. "Frankly, Agent, you seem to be the only person I know who can aggravate me with just a look."

"That so?" he said, bemused.

Forcing herself to calm down, confused as to even why she was so pissed off, she continued. "Yes, that's so. Here's a novel idea, bud. How about we call each other by our given names? Otherwise, I might have to get creative and come up with something nifty for you. How about I call you Raven? You know, for *your* hair color?" She turned her mouth down in an exaggerated frown. "Or is that too girly? Wait, I've got it! Barney! You know, like that bumbling old-time TV cop from Mayberry?" She lifted a brow. "What do you think?"

Jake shook his head dramatically. "Geesh, you're cranky today. Maybe it's a blood sugar thing. We better order before you start chewing glass."

Callie's retort died on her tongue as soon as their drinks arrived. After the server took their dinner order, Callie took a swallow of her white wine and closed her eyes.

"That good, huh?" Jake teased.

"You have no idea. I've been thinking about rolling this deliciousness around my mouth for the last eighty miles." Moaning in pleasure, she added, "This is, quite possibly, better than sex."

Jake grinned and tipped his beer bottle in acknowledgment. "Not sure I'd go that far, but it definitely hits the spot."

When their order came, Callie, though ravenous, pushed her food around the plate.

"No good?" Jake asked. "I can grab the server and order something else if you don't like your steak."

Callie shook her head. "No, it's not that. The food looks delicious. It's just that I … I was thinking of something you asked me about before."

Jake stared, trying to read her body language. When she hesitated, he urged, "And? Do I have to guess or something?"

Eyebrows drawn, she shot back, "Hold your horses, Barney, I'm getting to it." She bit her lower lip, and Jake felt a sudden and severe sadness wash over him; Katie had done the same thing when troubled.

"It's about the baseball cap, about why I wear it. You know how, when Katie died, her ability to see the dead somehow transferred over to me?"

Jake nodded.

"Well, apparently, there's a trick to turning that psychic crap off, but for the life of me, I can't figure it out. People have been coming to me, night and day. Dead people. All kinds of spirits— young and old, sweet, or sour. They come when I'm awake, they come when I'm trying to sleep. Hell, some perverted bastard dropped in while I was in the shower last week. All seeking, I don't know … something. Some 'thing' from me I don't know how to give. It's exhausting, depressing, and terrifying at the same time." She took a gulp of her wine. Then another.

Jake finished his beer, waved the waitress over, and ordered them both another round.

"Anyway, I was explaining things to Darby, and, Darby being Darby, she set off to find a solution to my problem."

Jake cocked his head. "And that solution involved headwear?"

"It did. She unearthed a story about a psychic across the pond, a woman who shared the same issues controlling her gift.

The article explained that no matter how much she tried to turn them off, the dead hounded her twenty-four-seven. Frustrated, she eventually confronted the spirits and declared that, on that particular day, she would be off the grid. Then she plopped on a hat and, to her astonishment, as soon as it landed on her head the activity stopped."

After being served another round of drinks, Callie lifted her glass. "So, from that day on, the red hat became a kind of symbol for the ghosts, a message to the dead telling them she was unavailable or off-duty. According to the author who wrote the piece, it worked like a charm. I figured, why not? So, I stood in the center of my house and spoke to thin air—like a crazy person —then grabbed a baseball cap. Voila! So far," she knocked on the wooden table, "it's working. At least it has for the last twenty-four hours."

"Huh," Jake said skeptically. "So that's your answer, then? You're just going to wear it all the time? For like, everything?" He waggled his brows. "Call me loco, but I think that'll get really old, really fast."

"No shit, Sherlock," she grumbled, once again annoyed at his flippant attitude. "I'm working on a solution. If I could understand what they wanted, I could help them move on. But, until that happens and as long as it's working for me, the hat stays. You don't understand how overwhelming it can be. I thank God that I don't have Katie's Empath abilities as well. I cannot fathom how she did this without going bonkers." Eyes downcast, she added sadly, "Jesus, I miss her."

Jake nodded, but said nothing. There was nothing to say anyway, no words that would make Katie's passing any easier. They finished the rest of their meal in silence and headed to their rooms, pensive and lost in their memories.

⌇

The next morning, they headed out early, determined to make it as far as Rapid City, South Dakota. It would be a grueling ten-hour day behind the wheel, but it meant their last day of travel would only be a five-hour drive. They were eager to get to Jed's home in Billings and get started on the hunt to find Gabriel.

Jake's leave of absence from his job as an FBI agent based in Quantico, Virginia, had an expiration date. He had just six weeks to find Jeremy Sterling, a.k.a Gabriel Devine. After that, he would need to decide whether to continue with his current assignment in Quantico, transfer to the field office in Billings, or join his brother's company as a private investigator.

It was a tough decision. He loved his job with the Bureau, but he missed his family in Montana. And, after Katie's death, a change of routine may be just what the doctor ordered. He'd become disillusioned with certain aspects of the job and wasn't sure he would ever get back the spark and drive he enjoyed years ago.

Callie had to make some career decisions herself. Months ago, she received her Ph.D. in Psychology and was looking forward to working in the field. In the last year, she'd tossed around several career paths that interested her; assisting battered women to leave their abusers, serving the mental health needs of the homeless, protecting traumatized children.

But it was the idea of a career in forensic psychology that got her blood pumping. Dissecting the inner workings of an evil mind, such as Gabriel's, could lead to improved methods of predicting future serial killers and preventing another family from experiencing the horrors that visited her family.

It was more than appealing to her.

Those career dreams would have to wait, though. For now, she would soak up every drop of knowledge Jed could offer her about finding someone. Gabriel could be anywhere. Grudgingly, she admitted her half-brother was not a stupid man. The chances he'd stayed on the East Coast were slim to none. Knowing that, it mattered little where she and Jake were in the country as they pursued the investigation. Wherever the clues led her, she would follow, no matter the cost.

Even if those clues led her straight to Hell.

∼

At seven that evening, Jake and Callie arrived at the last stop before their ultimate destination, Jed's home in Billings, Montana.

Earlier in the day, afraid to leave the choice to Jake, Callie did her own search for a motel. She was delighted to find a quaint little bed-and-breakfast in the Bad Lands area of South Dakota. Not only did the stunning Victorian home offer gorgeous views, but their rates also included a hearty morning meal. The owners were a lovely middle-aged couple named Tammi and Victoria Andrews. Callie had phoned Tammi from the road, booking two of the six cabins that surrounded the main house.

The rooms were spacious, comfortable, and tastefully decorated. Callie's was done in various shades of cream and colonial blue, while Jake's room was sleek in black and white. Each suite had a small kitchen, a dorm-type fridge, and a fireplace.

After taking care of Lucky, Callie and Jake returned to the main house and their hostesses. The four of them sat in a comfortable living room, drinking English tea and nibbling sugar cookies beautifully arranged on a blue China platter.

"Are you sure your pup will be okay without you?" Tammi asked. "It's our shoulder-season right now and business is slow if you want to bring her in."

"Thank you, but she's fine," Callie said. "Last I checked, she was snoring softly by the fireplace."

"It is a comfortable room." Victoria said proudly. "Say, I'm not sure if she mentioned it when you phoned, but both Tammi and I are realtors. Tammi believes that this part of South Dakota is the most gorgeous part of the state. I agree, although the Black Hills will always be my favorite. So majestic!"

Tammi bobbed her head in agreement, addressing Callie. "Oh, yes. Why, there's Mt. Rushmore, a'course." She brought the teacup to her mouth, then set it down without drinking from it. "Then there is the City of Presidents, Custer State Park, all kinds of museums and parks." She was gasping for breath, as if she'd run a marathon. Apparently, the woman had found her passion. She raised the cup again, only to set it down once more without tasting a drop. Her lack of focus was driving Callie nuts.

Oh, for the love of God, woman, drink your tea!

For the next several moments, Callie and Jake listened politely as Tammi rambled on about the local hot spots. More than once, Callie battled to stifle a yawn and suppress a stretch. Jake seemed to be fighting that particular battle as well.

Finally, after what seemed like hours, Victoria smiled knowingly and grabbed Tammi's hand. "I'm sure you are both exhausted from your travels. We serve breakfast in the main house between seven and nine a.m. Tomorrow, if you're interested, you can pick up some of our free brochures detailing the area's popular attractions." She glanced at Callie and winked. "I believe there may even be some coupons tucked inside the pamphlets, Mrs. Devereaux."

Callie froze, Jake choked on the cookie he was eating, and Tammi cringed.

"Um," Tammi said to Victoria, "they booked separate rooms, love. I don't believe they are married."

Victoria blinked, and her face reddened. "Oh, I am so sorry. I just assumed ..."

Jake, doing his best to hide a grin, failed miserably. He glanced at Callie, still frozen in place, and cleared his throat. "Oh, don't give it another thought, Victoria. It happens to us all the time."

Now it was Callie's turn to choke. She discreetly kicked his shin, then stood. Her head was pounding, her eyes mere slits. She could sleep for days.

"Well, thank you for your hospitality, ladies," she said, adjusting her cap. "I think I'll call it a night. See you both in the morning."

They said their goodbyes and Jake, after nabbing a few more cookies, followed her out of the house, still smirking.

"What the hell is wrong with you?" Callie said when she was sure they were out of earshot. She watched his smile widen as the twinkle in his eyes became annoyingly bright. He enjoyed taunting her, and it showed.

She bit back a response. He was poking the bear, looking for some teasing banter, but she was too tired to give it to him. Instead, she brushed past him. "I plan to be on the road right after breakfast, with or without you."

Disappointed that she didn't take the bait, Jake plodded back to his cabin.

~

"What a frustrating man!"

Callie slammed her overnight bag onto the bed and picked through the contents until she found a nightgown. Lucky lay just where Callie had left her, on a small rug in front of the fireplace. She wagged her little puppy tail but refused to rise, instead rolling to her back, waiting for a tummy rub.

"What kind of watch pup are you? You don't even get your butt off the floor, let alone bark, when someone enters the room. We need to work on that, Luck!" She bent down and gave her dog a vigorous rub from chest to gut. Yawning, she changed into her nightgown, washed her face, and climbed under the covers.

And didn't stir until morning.

. . .

After a quick breakfast of coffee and blueberry muffins, Callie and a sleepy Lucky headed out, Jake right behind them, determined to make Montana by afternoon. The early morning sun was brilliant, the temperature a comfortable sixty-five degrees. Traffic was light, but the cracks and potholes of the right lane caused her concern. She flipped her blinker and switched to the middle lane, checking to make sure Jake was still behind her.

Just as she did, a shadow darted from right to left in the backseat. Lucky growled softly, as if she'd seen it too. Adjusting the mirror, Callie scanned the rear seat but saw nothing.

As she drove, her thoughts turned from Jake to Katie. Unashamed, she began speaking to her sister as if they shared the same space.

At the moment, they did not.

"So, Kates, I gotta be honest here," she said, as she took in the breathtaking mountain views, "I don't know what the attraction was to Jake. I mean, sure, he's easy on the eyes. And that body? Good God, it's what sweet dreams are made of. But none of that means anything if it's wrapped in a package of arrogance and ego, am I right?" As she spoke, barely stopping to breathe, she emphasized her points by flapping her hands inside the car.

Callie had always spoken with her hands.

"So, anyway, while I can appreciate the beauty in the man, his character flaws would make me give him a hard pass. No offense, of course." She said the last in an apologetic tone, as if offending her sister about her choice in men was taboo.

From somewhere in the backseat, a soft voice chimed in. "Yeah, but you haven't seen him naked."

Callie glanced into the rearview mirror and laughed. "Well, hello there, my sister. And no, I haven't seen him naked. I'm surprised that even matters to you, though. I thought you were all about a man's mind." She raised and lowered her brows.

Katie grinned. "A mind is a wonderful thing, but it won't keep you warm at night."

Engrossed in the small talk with her dead sister—and in how bizarre that felt—Callie failed to notice the erratic driving of a tractor-trailer traveling in the eastbound lane. A low-pitched rumbling, followed by the wail of an air horn, caused her grip on the steering wheel to tighten. Anxiously scanning the highway, she spotted the massive truck as it flew over the center divider, horn blaring and out of control. The back of the rig fishtailed; the creak of metal thunderous as it swerved into the middle lane on the westbound side of Route 90.

Callie was directly in its path.

"Go left, go left!" Katie screeched from the back. "There's a pickup broken down in the right lane! Veer left—now!"

Callie cranked the wheel to the left, her tires barreling over the rumble strip on the shoulder's edge. She slammed the brake pedal, her head and body flying forward, until the car came to rest on the grassy median. Jake, because of instinct or concern, followed her off the road to the left shoulder, kicking up gravel and careening in behind her.

The trailer whizzed by them both.

Thankfully, the vehicle traveling behind Jake was far enough away to avoid a collision, and the semi-truck eventually came to a screeching halt in the center lane.

Callie took a few breaths and, still holding the steering wheel in a vice-like grip, glanced at the rearview mirror to check on Jake. Reaching behind her, she stroked Lucky's chest. "You okay, girl? Holy shit, that was intense." She turned in her seat to check on Jake again, as if not trusting the mirror. Bringing her eyes to Katie, she said, "Thanks, Kates, I'm pretty sure you just saved our bacon. Check that—there's no 'pretty sure' about it. You definitely saved us." After a moment, she added, "But, are you in trouble now? Isn't interference of any kind in the life or death of a mortal being a no-no?"

"It is, Shadow. And under normal circumstances, I could not have interceded on your behalf. But something big is coming. There's a wrong to be righted, a situation that must be resolved. And it's something destiny has decided only you and Jake can remedy."

Riddles again, Callie thought. *I need to buy a decoder ring.*

Katie's image flickered, fading into nothingness. Although no longer visible, her voice reverberated within the walls of the vehicle. "Know this, Shadow. Whatever is coming is big. It may already be here. And it's something so threatening, fate has ignored the rules of the universe."

CHAPTER FOUR

"If I die, then bury me beneath the juniper tree." —*The Brothers Grimm*

Sunday Services
St. Michael's the Archangel Church

Gabriel stood behind the altar, searching the sea of faces in front of him. Desperate, he scanned the pews, calculating the probable, tossing out the improbable.

Too old, too fat, too young, too thin.

He estimated the unknown man, whom he had dubbed the 'Disciple,' to be in his mid-thirties to early forties, judging by his voice. When seated, his silhouette measured under Gabriel's height, leaving him in the five-ten or five-eleven range.

Of course, he could have short legs, Gabriel thought. *Oddly short, like a fucking midget from the Wizard of Oz. Was that even possible? A killer who could get a job as a circus freak?*

Frustrated, Gabriel struggled to concentrate on his sermon. The Disciple would come to him, must come to him, but also must believe it was his idea to share his work. Otherwise, the plan would falter while the two men engaged in a fight for control, a pissing contest for top dog.

Gabriel could ill afford to waste time pandering to the bruised ego of a thin-skinned novice. No, it had to appear as though the Disciple was calling the shots. Then, when the time was right, Gabriel would swoop in and take the reins.

Before 'Sideshow Bob' could cave and throw in the towel.

Before he could fuck it all up.

~

The Hairless Man coughed into his fist to hide a smirk, doing his best to appear captivated by Father Gabriel's uninspired sermon. Only an imbecile would savor the emptiness of Gabriel's words.

Apparently, the pews were awash with imbeciles.

No matter. He understood what the priest was doing—seeking him out, searching the rows and rows of congregants, trying to figure out the game.

He would not make it that easy.

Ever since his confession, he'd felt lighter, freer, as if his path had become crystal clear, the road unobstructed. But he would tread cautiously when moving forward with this new alliance. The last thing he needed was a butt-hurt holy roller with an inflated sense of self-importance. He would use the priest, let him think he was in control.

Until it was time to prove otherwise.

Ten Sleep, Wyoming
8:45 a.m.

For the third time that morning, Richie Biggs found himself closer to his brother's ass than he ever wanted to be.

"Jesus Christ, Bobby Joe," Richie said, nearly stepping on Bobby's heels. "You gonna keep walkin', or should we sit a spell while you catch your damned breath? Ain't like we got all day to finish this hike, man. How 'bout you quick draggin' your balls and move it?"

Bobby muttered an oath, dropped his bags, and turned to face his brother. "How 'bout you shut the fuck up, Richie? In case you ain't noticed, I'm carrying both my crap and Casey's gear over here. These trails are tough. Instead of bitching about it, you might offer to spell me a mile or so."

Bobby Joe's girlfriend smiled and stood between both men. "I done told you, Bobby," Casey said, her accent telegraphing her southern roots, "I can carry my own stuff. And Richie," she said, pointing a finger at his chest, "you hush now. It's early yet, and besides, there ain't no clock when you're hiking God's country."

Richie repositioned his backpack and moved past the couple. "Whatever. But if it's all the same to you, I'll go on ahead. I'd just as soon hit the clearing while I'm young enough to enjoy the bitch."

Casey laughed and rubbed Bobby's back. "Don't pay him no never mind, baby. We got this. I'm so dang proud of you!"

Moments later, with his brother no longer in sight, Bobby Joe and Casey huffed their way forward, determined to catch up to Richie before his lead over them became insurmountable. Just as they crested a slight rise in the wooded basin of Ten Sleep Canyon, they heard a terrified, primal scream. It echoed off the distant mountains, froze their blood, sent goosebumps scurrying down their spines.

Richie.

～

Special Agent Curtis Valdez of the Wyoming Division of Criminal Investigation zipped his jacket against the chilly morning, his unruly black curls waving in the wind. Spotting a few uniformed officers standing near the yellow crime-scene tape, he made his way to the group.

Expression grave, Curtis addressed the man with the highest rank. "What do you have, Mason?"

Sergeant Mason George tipped his hat back to meet Curtis's gaze. He was a short and round man, with an enormous belly that strained against the bottom button of his uniform shirt. "Howdy, Curtis, been awhile. Didn't know HQ was sending in a man from DCI." He pulled his hat back down. "Not that we don't appreciate the help, you understand. So, how are things? How's your momma doing?"

Valdez did his best to hide his impatience. He knew Mason George as a local cop who tried too hard at being a 'good ol' boy.' Curtis found the man's affinity for small talk irritating, especially when he knew the sergeant couldn't give a fat rat's ass about his mother.

Pasting on a smile, Valdez answered. "She's right as rain, Mason. Thanks for asking. Enjoying her retirement and developing quite the green thumb. So, what can you tell me about our guy here?" He cocked his head toward the naked, lifeless male propped against a large Juniper tree. The victim's head tilted at a peculiar angle; a bloodied bandana wound tightly around his neck.

The man's eyes were wide and frozen in fear, as if privy to secrets known only to the dead. Next to the corpse, creating a macabre sense of normalcy, sat a basket of red apples, a can of black bean soup, and a silver bell.

Mason hitched up his trousers. "Whelp, this here is a fella by the name of Arthur Sinclair. He teaches math—algebra, I'm thinkin'—and coaches the JV track team over at the Trinity high school. I recognized him from an assault complaint a few years back. 'Course, he looked a might better back then. Not much, but better than this here." He paused, recollecting the scene of that past brutal crime. "Nasty business, it was. Mr. Sinclair here was the victim of a mighty ugly beating by an unknown subject or subjects. The offense took place behind the high school, right after track practice. Anyway, one evening, these unknown suspects cornered the poor bastard and bludgeoned his head like a baby seal. Used Sinclair's own baseball bat to do it, too." He licked his lips. "Guess what they did when that didn't kill 'em?"

Curtis shrugged rather than roll his eyes. *Guessing games at the feet of a dead man—what a charmer.*

Mason grinned widely; a crooked front tooth coated in silver glinting in the morning sun. He enjoyed the power that came with knowledge. "They damn near cut his head off, is what. Hacked at his neck with a butcher knife until the man passed out from blood loss. Luckily for him, a few fellas passing through chased 'em away before they could finish the job. Medics got there and found him underneath the bleachers. Just dyin', I expect."

Curtis tucked that information in the back of his mind. Squatting down, he studied the front of Arthur Sinclair's body, noting the crimson blotches of livor mortis that colored his abdomen and buttocks.

Lividity, the pooling of blood to dependent areas, begins about thirty minutes after the heart beats its last and peaks between eight and twelve hours later. To Curtis's trained eye, the pattern of blood settling meant they were at least eight hours beyond the time of death. He turned, his eyes doing a quick sweep of the immediate area.

"What about the witnesses, Mason? Where are they?"

A foot shorter than Curtis, the sergeant tipped his head back again, squinted, and took a pair of sunglasses out of his chest pocket. Despite the cool temperature, the sun was quickly going from brilliant to blinding. "They gave their statements an hour ago. They were pretty shook up, I'd say, and paler than shit. I figured for sure the kid who found the body was gonna hurl." He chuckled and winked at Valdez. "So I sent them home, warning them not to leave town and all that. Cause, you know, we might gonna wanna interview them again."

Valdez cringed at Mason's uncanny ability to butcher the English language.

"Right," Valdez said sourly. "We just might gonna wanna do that."

Sergeant George seemed not to notice the mockery.

After carefully examining and documenting their findings on the victim's anterior side, investigators circled the body, preparing to slide Arthur away from the tree to inspect his back. Mason George volunteered officer Clyde Jessup, a young cop barely two months into his law enforcement career, for the unenviable task of moving the corpse.

As a rookie, Clyde was still navigating through an unspoken rite of passage—the inescapable truth that the lowest in rank were usually tasked with the worst assignments.

Resigned, he gathered the courage needed to touch the cadaver's waxy legs, grabbed Arthur Sinclair by the ankles, and yanked. The dead man's head bounced cruelly down the tree trunk before jerking wildly to the side, rolling off his shoulders, and landing with a thud near his left hand. Then, as if starring in a second-rate horror movie, the head began a slow roll, coasting like a child's ball before stopping at the feet of the young officer, a Juniper needle impaled into one milky eyeball.

The rookie cop screamed, stumbled backward, and vomited all over the crime scene.

~

Curtis Valdez was puzzled. His career in law enforcement spanned over a decade. He had miles of experience, yet this case was unlike any he'd seen. He'd been on the scene for hours now, watching the crime scene technicians work, reviewing the possibilities. The background info of what he knew about the victim was thin; an unmarried, all-around good guy, well respected by his peers. A virtual pillar of the community and a saint among men.

Unless, of course, you factored in the complaints filed months ago by the parents of two of his prized track stars alleging abuse and improper contact.

Both female students, in sworn depositions, accused Arthur Sinclair of 'inappropriate contact and lecherous advances toward a minor child'. Specifically, they alleged their track coach 'did knowingly and willingly engage in unlawful and unwanted fondling while using sexually explicit language' during late-night practices and individual strategy sessions.

The charges were relatively recent and remained under investigation.

Thirty minutes after the initial investigators discovered that Arthur Sinclair was decapitated, Deputy Daniel Cummings of the Sheridan County Sheriff's Office arrived on the scene. Daniel and Curtis had known each other for twenty years.

"What do you think, Curt?" the Deputy asked, his vibrant voice seemingly out of step with his gaunt appearance. He rubbed his hands together, the late April breeze cold and damp. "Seems like a lot of trouble to go through, doesn't it? Not only the act of decapitation, but the extra step of securing his head to his torso. It's almost as if the killer is taunting us, playing with us."

Valdez nodded. "I agree. And while my gut tells me the guy is having a laugh at our expense, it's also telling me there is something else we're not seeing. It's right there in the back of my mind, like something we're missing, something I recognize."

"You think you've seen a similar crime scene? Maybe heard of it?"

"Nah, I'm not sure yet. I just know something about it is familiar. I have a few contacts I can reach out to, both at the local and federal level. If I can't find anything in NCIC or ViCap, I will give them a shout." Lost in thought, he glanced back at the remains of Arthur Sinclair. "Call it gut instinct, Danny, but something tells me this is only the beginning."

~

Gabriel waited patiently in the confessional. It was Monday evening, normally a light one for the sinning folk of Sheridan, Wyoming. But he wasn't here for them; he was here for *him,* the one who would lead Gabriel to victory. All he had to do was mold him. If he could nurture their union, his work could continue.

Head pounding, ass numb from sitting on a wooden bench, Gabriel's patience was waning. It had been fifty minutes and four confessions later, yet the fool he was waiting for had yet to make an appearance.

Who did this guy think he was? He is going to make me wait? Fuck that! I ought to drop a dime on him, set up a sting, then watch as they toss his ass in jail!

But, of course, he could never do that. Number one, it would be too risky. He would have to be an imbecile to draw attention to himself, even if the focus of that attention was directed toward another. And, of course, he was not an imbecile.

Far from it.

And secondly? As much as he hated to admit it, he needed the stranger. Needed him like a person needed food and water and sunlight.

The man was the key, Gabriel's personal messiah.

Just when he was about to give up, the confessional door opened, and the silhouette of a man came into view. He wore a wide cowboy hat that, once removed, revealed long hair pulled into a ponytail. Once seated, the man tugged off his light jacket, folded it neatly on his lap, and cleared his throat.

Discreetly, he dug at his scalp beneath the wig he wore. Since he began his cleanse, he no longer felt the urge to rip his hair out by its roots. Still, regrowth was slow, the itch intense.

Gabriel held his breath, waiting for him to speak. *Come on, man, can you be any slower? Spit it out!*

The man in the confessional was enjoying taunting the priest, toying with him. And why not? Father Gabriel wore anticipation and impatience like a cloak around his shoulders. The priest was nearly giddy, drooling at the prospect of hearing the sordid details of his parishioner's darkest sins.

In a few minutes, the man began. "Bless me, Father, for I have sinned. It's been a few days since my last confession."

Gabriel closed his eyes in relief. It was *him*, the messiah. "Go ahead, my child. Tell me of these sins you speak of and be absolved."

The man picked at a fingernail. "Well, Father, as I said in my first confession, I have killed several times. The first two were nothing but whores, hardly worth a mention. The third was that man who fleeced a poor old lady out of her life savings." He chuckled. "Although, since God understands my mind and my heart, I suppose I should be clear; it was more about my annoyance at him than any offense committed toward the old lady. He reminded me of ... something. Someone from my childhood. Honestly? I couldn't give two shits about Marjorie Whitman."

A killer without a conscience? Gabriel thought, invigorated at the possibilities. *This could work out even better than I'd expected!*

"I see, my son," Gabriel said, fighting to keep his voice neutral. "And is there anything else you'd like to confess?"

The man clucked his tongue. "Well, as a matter of fact, I do, but ..." He held the words back, floating them like cheese in front of a rat and enraging Gabriel.

C'mon, fucker! I'm about ready to punch through this confessional screen and rip your heart out with my teeth!

"Well, you'll probably read about it in the papers, anyway, so I might as well tell you." Sitting up straighter in his seat, he puffed out his chest. "Yesterday, I killed a man from Worland, a man who escaped death years ago. His end was, shall I say, poetic justice?"

Enthralled, Gabriel needed details. "How, um, how did you kill him?"

The man snickered like a child. "It was quite satisfying, actually. After hitting him behind the ear with a tire iron—several times, if memory serves—I relieved his head from the rest of his body and left him in the woods in Ten Sleep."

Gabriel gulped, momentarily startled. "You decapitated him? How?"

"Does it really matter, Padre? He was a pervert who liked to diddle little girls. So, I cut his fucking head off."

Gabriel noted the sudden flash of anger in the man's tone and decided to tread lightly. "I see. And are you planning any more of these, em, vengeance killings?"

"Why, of course, Father. As many as I can. I've constructed a plan, a kind of cleansing of the morally skewed, if you will. But, in the interest of fair play, I've left tiny clues for the brainless cops working the case." Tilting his head, he asked, "Does any of this upset you, Padre? Does any of this make you uncomfortable?"

Gabriel shook his head. "Quite the opposite, my child. I applaud your efforts to rid this world of the belly crawlers, the lowest of the low. But you must be smart. There are many who will try to stop your work and many more who will seek to destroy you." He steepled his hands, deep in thought. "We shall call you the 'Disciple,' for you are spreading the doctrine of the Lord. I will help you, but we must forge a pact to succeed. We must agree on the targets chosen and put great thought into the planning of the, what did you call it? Oh, yes. The cleansing."

The Disciple rolled his eyes. He needed no help, especially if it was coming from a preacher. Still, there was no risk in listening to what the man had to say. The sacred vows Gabriel took as a priest would ensure his silence.

A man of the cloth could not break the seal of confession, not if he wanted to continue to wear the collar.

"Alright then, the Disciple it is. And what shall I call you? Gabriel? Father?"

Gabriel stood, exited his end of the confessional box, and opened the door to the Disciple's side. He stood there a moment, taking in his progeny, sizing him up.

Then he smiled, as if greeting an old friend.

"Me? You can call me the Apostle."

CHAPTER FIVE

Callie pulled in behind Jake's Explorer and gasped at the size of the home at the end of the driveway. Most of the front of the raised timber and log ranch was glass, allowing for spectacular views of the landscaping and open land below. Gray slate covered the shrub-lined front walkway, leading to a decorative wall of stone. To the left of the main house sat a quaint log cabin surrounded by white and red flowers that served as the guest quarters. On the right, a three-car garage with an apartment above where Callie would stay. A quick calculation left her with no doubt that this was a seven-figure property.

Jake walked to her car and opened the driver's side door. "So, this is it. Casa de Jedidiah. What do you think? Miles away from mediocre, right?"

Callie smiled and stepped out of her Jeep. Moving to the passenger side, she opened the door for Lucky and hooked the leash to her collar. "Mediocre? My God, Jake, this is gorgeous! Look at those windows!"

Jake smirked. "Yeah, no kidding. Apparently, there's a killing to be made in investigative services. C'mon, let's go check out the inside. If you think this is good, just wait until you see the layout of the interior."

They turned toward the house just in time to see a little boy of about five or six peeling out the front door, the shouts of a woman chasing after him.

"Git back here, ye wee eejit, before ah skelp yer arse!"

Wide-eyed, arms pumping, the boy sped past Jake and Callie without so much as a nod.

Jake raised a brow. "Well, you don't see that every day."

Lucky pulled against her restraint, trying to chase after the little boy. "Who is that?" Callie asked.

"Not sure," Jake said with a shrug. "Let's go find out."

A harried-looking woman stood at the door, brows furrowed, wearing an apron that proclaimed 'Slainte' in bold colors. She was a natural beauty, a tiny woman with caramel-colored hair fashioned into a long bob and animated green eyes. Pushing a strand of hair back from her face, the stranger eyed Jake and Callie suspiciously as they reached the alcove by the front door.

"Kin ah help ye?" she said with an unmistakable Scottish lilt.

"Hello, there," Jake said warmly, "I'm Jake Devereaux, Jed's brother? And this is my friend Callie Callahan. Jed is expecting us."

The woman's hand went to her throat. "Oh, ah am an eejit. How could ah nae see the resemblance? Why, ye must ken yer Jedidiah's twin!" She wiped her palms on her apron and awkwardly stuck out a hand. "I'm Faith, Faith McTavish. It's lovely tae meet ye."

After they shook hands, Faith turned to Callie. "And ye, lassie. Callie, was it? Why, yer a bonnie thing, are ye not?" Bending forward, she reached out a hand to Lucky. "And who is this wee pup scramblin' aboot?"

Callie stroked the animal's neck. "This would be my new partner in crime, Lucky. I hope it isn't too much of an imposition that I brought her with me. It's a long story, but her companionship has been ..." she hesitated, "has been just what I've needed."

Faith patted the dog's head. "Dinnae give it a thought, lassie; yer pup is most welcome."

Callie extended her arm, shaking Faith's hand in greeting. Looking over her shoulder, she asked, "Was that your son who just flew past us? Handsome kid."

"Aye, that's mah Caleb. Full o' piss 'n vinegar today, mind ya. You'll hae tae forgive ma language, but ah dinnae ken what gets into that lad."

Jake winked at her, "I would say that youth has gotten into him. Hard to believe looking at my angelic face, but I seem to recall I was a handful to my mom at that age."

Callie turned to see if the child was in sight. "Well, he's a cute kid. Fast runner, too."

Faith smiled. "Aye, 'n' he dinnae get that from me. If ye see me runnin', it means ah'm bein' chased." She gave them both a lopsided grin. "He's the only bairn ah ken who riles me so, ah cannae help but return tae mah Scottish tongue." She opened the front door wide. "But here ah am, dithering aboot. Come in! Come in!"

She led them through the front entryway into a rustic but luxurious living room. Exposed logs framed the vaulted ceiling, while several old-fashioned gas lanterns hung strategically around the room. The lights cast a warm glow, surpassed only by the brilliance of the flames burning in the stone fireplace. The room smelled like wood and leather, exactly the aroma Callie had expected. The house was a cross between the stylish décor of a country cabin and the grand architecture of an American Craftsman's home.

Faith invited them to sit on one of the rich leather sofas surrounding the fireplace, then left to get Jed.

"Holy crap!" Callie said in awe. "I could get used to this. This is one of the most beautiful homes I've ever seen." She walked, with Lucky on her heels, to the wide French doors that led to the backyard. "I keep expecting to see a horse running through the grass."

"We had a horse when I was a kid. Beautiful little filly named Summer's Eve."

Callie held in a laugh, choking into her fist. "Summer's Eve? You named your horse Summer's Eve?"

Jake frowned. "I know, I know. *Summer's Eve* is a feminine hygiene product, right? Sure, I know that now. Not so much when I was twelve. At twelve, Summer's Eve sounded exotic. Mysterious."

"Refreshing?" she teased, then mimed locking her lips, "Don't worry, your secret is safe with me." Continuing her assessment of the yard, she said, "Did you see this patio? The pavers are stunning. And talk about your outside kitchens! Even from here, I can see that his outside kitchen has nicer appliances than my inside kitchen." She walked back and forth in front of the doors, peeking here and there. "Oh my God, is that a wooden swing? I think I may never leave this place!"

From behind, Callie heard a chuckle and an unfamiliar voice. "And you are welcome to stay as long as you like."

She whirled and locked eyes with a man who was clearly Jake's brother. Jed Devereaux leaned against the doorway to the living room, arms folded, a sly smile on his face.

Callie flushed, and her eyes flicked to Jake. He was reclining in an easy chair, a smirk on his handsome face as well, enjoying her discomfort.

She raised her brows at him, a silent plea for help.

He only smiled wider.

"Uh, sorry about that," she stammered, "it's just that your home is so beautiful, so inviting, it's hard not to want to live here forever."

"Nothing to apologize for," Jed said, walking toward her. He was taller than Jake, with the same raven-colored hair and chiseled features. Aside from the obvious height difference and a noticeable scar Jed had on top of his right eye, they could have been twins.

"Don't give it another thought," he continued. "I still wake up some mornings astounded that this is my home. The view never gets old. Anyway, welcome to Montana. I believe that once you're here for a visit, it's damn near impossible not to stay for a lifetime. At least, that's what all the brochures say." They shook hands, his grip firm and warm. He bent down and gave the dog a vigorous rub on the nose.

She responded by sniffing his groin.

Callie grabbed the pup's collar and pulled her away from Jed's crotch. Squatting down, she took Lucky's snout in her hand. "No, no, Lucky! Bad doggie!" Embarrassed, she glanced up to find Jed grinning. "I'm so sorry. She is still learning her —boundaries."

Jed's grin turned into a chuckle. "No worries. That's probably the most action I've had in some time."

Callie giggled, and, looking between both brothers, said, "No getting around the fact that you two are related."

"Yeah, I'd appreciate it if you kept that to yourself," Jed said. "The fewer people who know about that, the better."

Jake grunted. "How 'bout you kiss my ass, little brother?"

Callie was doing her best not to laugh. They were like two toddlers, having a tug-of-war with a favorite toy. It was hysterical to watch.

Ignoring Jake, Jed addressed Callie. "Let's get you settled in your apartment so you can unpack and unwind. Afterward, I'll show you around. Dinner is at six, and we can talk shop then. Sound good?"

Callie nodded. "Better than good. Lead the way."

At six o'clock, Callie met Jake in the foyer. Fresh out of the shower, his dark hair still damp, the man looked and smelled amazing. He wore a pair of faded jeans with a flannel shirt that oozed masculinity.

When Callie caught sight of him, her heart sped up, and her

breath caught. Annoyed at herself, she trained her eyes on the floor, the ceiling, everywhere but the man next to her.

Just don't look, idiot! Don't inhale his scent, don't gaze into his eyes!

She smoothed a hand down her long skirt, adjusted her off-the-shoulder blouse, and concentrated on not tripping in her cowboy boots. Lucky, already fed and walked, was currently in her crate, listening to Blake Shelton and taking a snooze.

Jake and Callie strode side-by-side to the dining room, matching steps in an easy gait. To anyone watching, anyone not privy to their inner thoughts, they appeared comfortable and familiar in each other's company.

They looked like the perfect couple.

Sensing that, suddenly a million miles away from comfortable, Callie hurried to her seat.

"Where's your cap, Blaze?" Jake asked. He was uncomfortable as well, his mind knocking on forbidden doors when he caught sight of her shapely calves peeking from beneath her skirt.

"Oh, that," Callie said. "Well, it turns out it's not all it's cracked up to be. Last night, I went to bed with the cap on and at least three dead people decided it was the perfect night for a slumber party. And this morning, despite keeping that blasted hat on through my morning routine, two more spirits dropped by. Just dropped in, waved, and went on their merry way. I wish I knew what ..." She stopped when she felt Jake's gaze on her bare shoulders. Adjusting her blouse, she said, "So I guess the cap trick doesn't work for me. It's just as well. Hat hair makes me sad."

Jake's laughter filled the room. It surprised Callie how much she enjoyed the sound.

What the hell is wrong with me?

She turned away from him, away from the treacherous thoughts that seemed to spring from nowhere, and focused on the room. A table made of mahogany and dotted with square nail heads gleamed beneath the wagon wheel light fixture above. Deer and moose heads stood silent sentry on the walls, mounted over the rifles that had undoubtedly claimed their lives. A worn safe, circa the early 1900s, took up one corner of the room. Another corner held an old trunk draped with a Native American-style blanket. A woven throw rug in the center of the pine floor added to the sense of warmth and welcome.

Jake, seated next to her, noted the wonder in her eyes as she took in her surroundings. "Nice room, huh?"

"Nice?" she whispered, turning to him. "That's not exactly the adjective I would use. Breathtaking? Stunning? Amazing? Those are more in line with what I see."

Jake snickered, then turned his attention to the young boy seated across from them. Head bent, hands in his lap, the child had yet to say a word. "What do you think, Caleb? You like this room?"

The boy, startled to hear his name mentioned, jerked his head up, but remained silent.

Jake tried another approach. "So, how old are you, son? You look like a kid, but you run like a cheetah. I bet I clocked you at thirty miles per hour."

The child dropped his head again, trying to hide a grin.

Callie studied him, wondering why he did not speak. Judging by his ability to sprint, he seemed healthy enough, at least physically. He also appeared to understand the spoken word. She was debating whether to follow-up Jake's question with one of her own when Faith and Jed entered the dining room, arms full of platters and plates.

Callie jumped out of her seat. "I'm so sorry. Instead of sitting here daydreaming, I should pitch in. Let me help you." She grabbed a platter from Faith's outstretched hand, then peeked shyly at Jed. "Your gorgeous home has my head in the clouds. I swear I'm not usually such an idiot."

Jake coughed into his hand, then winked at Faith. "Right. She may be stubborn, have the temper of a honey badger, and is always itching for a fight, but she isn't an idiot."

Glaring, Callie muttered, "Jackass."

Faith clapped her hands sharply. "Jesus, Mary, and Joseph! Cut that oot, mister! Yer bum's oot the windae with such blather!"

Callie nodded in agreement. "Yeah, what she said!" Then, perplexed, she whispered, "What exactly did you say, Faith?"

Faith chuckled. "Ah am sorry, lass. Been in America fer a long time, but sometimes ma heid forgets tae remind mah mouth. Ah said his ass is oot the windae with such nonsense, meaning he has nae idea what he's talkin' aboot."

Callie chuckled. "Well, you're not wrong. And please don't apologize for your accent. I find it lovely."

They began the meal, falling into an easy camaraderie. Jake and Jed shared stories about their childhood and the fierce sibling rivalry that existed to this day. Callie listened, a bittersweet nostalgia settling over her as she recollected her childhood with Katie. Since she felt it was too soon to speak of the relationship they shared, she instead soaked up as much information about the brothers that she could.

"Okay, so answer me this," Callie teased, looking pointedly at Jake. "Which one of you gave your parents the worst headache?"

Jed tossed his head toward Jake. "I think you know the answer to that, Callie," he joked. "My mom always says that it was a miracle she agreed to have a second child."

Jake squinted at his brother. "That right, little brother? Because, as I recall, Mom always told me if you were her first, you'd be her only."

Faith laughed. "Hah! Pure, dead brilliant, that was Jacob! Ah kin see how you kept Jedidiah on his toes through yer wee years!"

They continued the conversation, and the good-natured banter, for several hours. Finally, Faith stood to clear the table. When Jed, Jake, and Callie rose to help, Faith shooed them back.

"Ye cannae help and have yer meetin' as well. Caleb and ah will take care of this. Ye go on an' git yer work completed."

Jed shook his head. "Nonsense. You're off the clock now,

Faith. Jake will get himself and Callie a nightcap while I help you in the kitchen."

When Faith protested, Jed held his ground. "Save it, McTavish," he said jokingly. "This is how it's going to be."

Faith shrugged. "Suit yerself, but no dawdlin', ye hear?"

She walked out of the room, back stiff, and headed to the kitchen. Jed turned, winked at his brother and Callie, and said, "Ain't she the best?"

"So, are they a couple?" Callie asked Jake, as they sipped on blackberry brandy.

Jake looked over his glass. "You mean Faith and Jed? Not that I know of. According to Jed, Faith is like his right arm around here. She does everything from office work and bookkeeping to housework and stakeouts. In return for cooking and cleaning, she gets to live rent-free in the carriage house, while her PIPPS job gives her a generous salary."

Callie chewed that over in her mind. "Hmm. Well, if you ask me, there is something else going on here." She tipped her head toward the kitchen door as if replaying their exit. "There are very few men I know who would fight to do dishes." Smiling, she added, "I think he likes her."

"Wow," Jed said, entering the living room a moment later. "Beautiful and perceptive, just as my brother described you."

Flustered, Jake cleared his throat while Callie, just as rattled, blushed.

Jed smirked. "Relax, guys. Anyway, in answer to your question, Callie, yes, I do like Faith. A lot. But she is very protective of both her son and her past. Something happened to them, something highly unpleasant, and it's left lasting scars. So, until I get her to let me in, I'm afraid any romantic relationship remains on the back burner. Now, let's get down to it, shall we? Tell me what you know about Gabriel's whereabouts."

"Unfortunately, not much," Jake said. "After he shot Kate and fled the basement of Callie's childhood home, he was in the wind. We had every resource available trying to track him, from search dogs to local and state cops to private investigators. Hell, Kate's best friend, Darby, even brought in a psychic. No luck with any of them."

Callie rested her hands under her chin. "We also made flyers and posted them all over town. A coffee shop owned by a family friend held a fundraiser, collecting thousands of dollars in reward money. Nothing worked. It's hard to believe no one saw this creep. He had a gaping hole in his thigh, courtesy of Jake's service weapon, and I blinded the bastard with a nail. He must have looked like something out of a nightmare. So, how does he get away?"

"Maybe he had help," Jed said. "A getaway driver? Someone he could stay with until he healed?"

Callie shrugged.

"Okay, so tell me what you do know about him."

"Not much, I'm afraid. Jeremy Sterling is my stepbrother, one I never knew existed until the killings started. What I know about him wouldn't fill a teacup. He targeted my sister because, in his mind, she was responsible for my father's death."

Jed nodded. "I remember Jake telling me about that. Something about Katie's drowning having forced your father's hand?"

Jake snorted. "Yeah, twisted, right? So, in this asshole's deluded mind, it was Katie's fault that Rowan Callahan died." He looked at Callie, brow raised, seeking permission to tell Jed the entire story. As if reading his mind, she nodded.

"Okay, here it is in a nutshell. Rowan was having an affair with a woman in Texas named Meredith Sterling. The affair produced a child, Jeremy, who displayed characteristics of a sociopath from an early age."

Callie joined in. "Yes, and as an adult, Jeremy changed his name to Gabriel Devine, his deluded way of announcing to the world that he was a messenger of God. He coined the title of

'*Apostle*' and has committed at least a dozen homicides that we know about. Chances are, there are even more."

Jed gave a low whistle.

"Yep, that kind of crazy," Jake added. "Anyway, after Katie's accident, her father flew to Texas to end the affair with Gabriel's mother. On the way back to Virginia following the breakup, Rowan's plane went down. Gabriel, in his fucked-up brain, believes the death of a six-year-old ignited all the negative events in his life."

Jed sat speechless for a moment. Once he gathered his thoughts, he said, "I'm sorry, Callie. Talk about being served a shit sandwich. And while I can't change the past, I can promise that we ..." he looked at Jake, who nodded in agreement, "... we will do everything in our power to find this dirtbag and get justice for Kate. Count on it."

Jake turned to Callie, held her gaze for a moment, then winked. "Count on it, Blaze."

CHAPTER SIX

I t was late, close to three a.m., when Callie finally rolled out of bed. She'd been wide awake for hours, solving world hunger, searching her memory for the name of her first crush in elementary school, planning her next career move.

And daring to hope they would soon get a lead on the man who took so much.

Knowing sleep was futile until she calmed her mind, she threw on her robe and made her way to the tiny kitchen. Aside from Lucky snoring softly in the corner, the room was silent. She filled the teakettle and lit the burner, then wandered to the big bay window to wait for the water to boil. Pulling back the dainty lace curtain, she peeked outside.

The night was clear, the full moon a golden globe in the sky. The teak porch swing she'd admired earlier swayed gently in the Montana breeze. It looked just as somber and lonely as she, and strangely, seemed to call to her. Changing her mind about the tea, she turned off the stove and slipped out into the night.

The main house was dark, with only a dim light glowing from Jed's office on the second floor. Creeping on bare feet, pulling the robe tighter against her body, she went straight to the swing and sat. Rebel strands of auburn hair escaped her satin hairband

and curled around her face. Her toes, barely scraping the paver stones beneath her feet, pushed off, and she began to swing.

The gentle motion soothed her, and she immediately thought of Katie. She would have loved it here, loved the quiet cool breezes and the cloudless sky bursting with the light of a million stars.

As if flicking a switch or unlocking a door, Callie's throat tightened, and her heart squeezed. The pain of loss was a different kind of pain. It wasn't a sliced finger or ruptured appendix that would, with time, heal, scab over, scar. It was an intangible, evasive 'thing,' a wound that was difficult to describe and impossible to pinpoint. But it was always with her, hiding in the light, lurking in the dark.

It was nowhere. And everywhere.

She bent her legs, pulling them up to rest on the swing, and wrapped her forearms around her knees. Emotion overtook her, and she sobbed quietly, fearful of waking the household. The creak of the patio door opening startled her.

"I don't mean to intrude, but I'm an incurable insomniac," Jed explained. "I couldn't help but hear ..." he hesitated, a knowing look in his eyes, "your pain. Is there anything I can do to help? Anything you need?"

Embarrassed once again in front of Jake's brother, Callie cleared her throat, a lingering sadness in her eyes. "I'm so sorry, Jed. Here I am, a stranger, sitting on your porch in the dead of night, bawling like a newborn. I suppose I'm feeling nostalgic and, I don't know, lost?" She clenched her fists and dug her nails into her palms, desperate for a physical pain to carry her away from the wave of sorrow. Mumbling, she said, "Feeling damn sorry for myself, truth be told."

"Beg your pardon?"

Callie shook her head. "It's just that ... oh, never mind. You don't need to hear my sad-ass story."

Jed stepped closer and took a seat on the other end of the swing. He pulled a tissue out of his bathrobe pocket and handed it to her. They sat like that for a few moments—Callie softly crying while Jed propelled the swing to a simple rhythm. Finally, when her sobbing subsided, he spoke.

"Better?"

"I am, thanks. Guess I needed that." She wiped her eyes and tipped her head back, studying the stars. "For nearly five months now, I've ignored the gaping, oozing crater festering in my core. My heart is, for lack of a better word, shredded, I guess. Some days it's a challenge just to get out of bed in the morning." She put her feet on the ground and helped him to push. "Katie was more than my sister; she was my best friend. She knew what I was thinking or feeling long before I did, and that had nothing to do with her empath abilities. As corny as it sounds, it was a twin thing."

A rustling, like leaves dancing across a field, came from the corner of the house. Peering into the darkness, Callie searched for the source, but saw nothing. "Anyway, most of the details from the night my sister died are a blur. Blur might be an understatement. In truth, I have a huge chunk of time missing from that night, time I cannot seem to account for. But there are things, memories that do stand out, that will stay with me forever."

"Like what?"

"Sights and sounds, mainly. Like the wail of the ambulance siren and the flashing lights of the patrol cars as they arrived at the house where we grew up, the house where Gabriel made his last stand. If I quiet my mind, I can still hear the paramedics' heavy boots pounding down the basement stairs, their medical bags thumping into the wooden stair rail." She smiled weakly. "But you want to know what plays over and over in my mind?"

"I do," Jed said truthfully.

"It was the look in the first medic's eyes, a look that told me they were out of options. He was an older man, calm, competent, obviously experienced in the field. But his eyes gave away everything. They pitied me and sympathized with me and looked everywhere but directly at me. Because he knew Katie was beyond help, knew, somehow, that if he made eye contact with me, the knowing would be too much. My chest would explode, my heart would burst, and I would wallow in a storm of grief I could never recover from."

Jed nodded. "I see."

"I have so many questions," she continued. "Why her? Why not me? I would give all that I have, all that I am, to switch places with her. I mean that sincerely." She dropped her head. "I've lived in her shadow my entire life. Kates was the 'good' daughter, the child other parents wished they had. She was the sister with the most poise, the most beauty, the bigger brain. She was voted 'most likely to succeed' by my parents and, later, by my grandparents. They all expected great things from her." She stopped speaking for a moment, lost in the memory.

"That had to be tough for you," Jed said.

Callie cocked her head a bit. "I can see how you would think that, but, truthfully, it wasn't hard at all. It just … was. I was the frailer of the twins, saddled with two serious conditions—severe asthma and an attitude problem. I proudly wore a badge of 'I don't give a flip' about almost everything. But Kate? Man, she shone brighter than any star in the sky. I knew it, accepted it, almost reveled in it as I watched her enjoy the spotlight. The only thing I feared was becoming an afterthought in her eyes. So as long as I remained a part of her world, I never blinked at being second best." Callie rubbed her shoulders, chilled. "I know, I know. I sound pathetic, don't I? But honest to God, I was content to hide behind her, watch her move forward while I stood still, because I truly believed."

"Believed what?" Jed asked softly.

"Believed that she was the important one, the sister fate decreed would do great things for this world." Callie swallowed the lump in her throat. "Katie was the one who needed to live that day. I still believe that. I still believe that God took the wrong sister."

Jed's eyes narrowed, disturbed by both her honesty and her point of view. Unsure how to respond, he changed the subject.

Sort of.

"I don't suppose that Jake ever told you why he became a cop? Or why I created an investigative agency?"

Dabbing the corner of her eyes, Callie shook her head.

"It's because of our sister, Lacy."

"Sister?" Callie asked. "I didn't know that you had a sister. I thought it was just the two of you."

"We don't bring it up much. In the Devereaux family, if you drop the ball or can't fix the situation, it's best not to speak of it again."

Callie blinked, digesting the bitterness in his voice.

"Anyway, we had a sister. Her name was Lacy Jane, and she was just the cutest, sweetest five-year-old in the world. Jake was twelve, and I was nine, when we lost her."

Callie gasped. "Oh my gosh, Jed. I didn't know. How did she die?"

Jed shook his head. "That's the hell of it. It wasn't death that took her. It was a kidnapper, a son of a bitch who grabbed her right under our noses. You know, back then, kids played without fences or barriers, free of fear. The day she went missing, we'd all been in the front yard playing with our dog, Mr. Pipps. Mom called us in for lunch, and Jake and I tore into the house." He shrugged, smiling. "You'll never find a Devereaux boy passing up a meal. Lacy, however, stayed outside with the puppy. Ten minutes later, when Mom went to call her in, Mr. Pipps was still there, but Lacy was nowhere to be found." He rubbed his chin, recalling one of the most horrific days of his life. "My God, we were terrified. Mom called the cops, then jumped in her car and started searching. Jake and I called my dad at work and then took to our bikes, turning that neighborhood upside down. The only thing we found was a tiny cowboy boot at the end of the driveway. My parents had gotten her those boots for her fifth birthday."

Callie's eyes filled once again. They'd lost a sibling as well. "I'm so sorry, Jed. It's all so cruel. Lacy deserved to live a full life and your family deserved to watch her grow and flourish. How tragic and heartbreakingly random."

Jed nodded. "It is. The feelings of helplessness remained with us for years. Leads came and went, sightings anywhere from the next town over to Lima, Peru. But we followed them all, even the heartless cranks. Did you know there are nut cases in this world who get off on deepening a person's pain just because they can? Bottom line, though? We never found her. Not her body, her clothing, nothing. It's still listed as an unsolved case, but investigators soon changed the classification from an endangered person to a murder investigation."

Jed stopped talking and stood, smiling down at Callie. "You're freezing."

"No, I'm okay. Finish the story."

"That's pretty much it," he said, leaning against the chain of the swing. "Lacy would be about your age right now. Most of the leads we had dried up a decade ago, but we will never give up. Jake and I both check ViCap frequently for new major case crimes that involve the kidnapping, rape, or murder of a child. We seem to have hit a brick wall, but I don't care. As long as there is breath left in my body, I will search for her. Jake and I have an unspoken pact; we will continue to look until we find her and bring her home."

Callie stood and gave Jed a warm hug. "I sincerely hope you do find her someday. I know what it's like living with that kind of nightmare. When my mom went missing ..." She stared down at her bare feet, embarrassed. She should be providing Jed support, not entering a 'me too,' contest with him. She blew out a breath. "Anyway, I'm here if you need an ear. It's the not knowing that can keep you up at night."

He winked. "No kidding. Why do you think I'm out here, hanging with you at the devil's hour instead of walking through dreamland?" His eyes danced playfully. "Not that your company isn't delightful, you understand."

Callie chuckled and rolled her eyes. "The Devereaux men are smooth talkers. I can't wait to meet your dad."

Eyes twinkling, he said, "And you two will get on splendidly, I'm sure. But right now, I think we both need some shuteye. Tomorrow is going to be a busy day. I have some colleagues joining us here for a strategy session, and you and I still need to discuss your job here at PIPPS. I need to show you the basics of what we do, how we operate, but the job itself will be more of a 'learn as you go' kind of thing."

Callie nodded. "Yeah, we did kind of skirt the details before I jumped at the job offer, didn't we? Well, as a hands-on type of learner, on-the-job training is perfect for me." Her head whipped around at the crunch of dried leaves at the back of the house. Scanning the shadows, she asked, "Did you hear that?"

Jed squinted into the darkness. "Probably a rabbit. We have tons of them around here."

They said their goodnights, and Callie, senses heightened, hurried back toward the garage. Jed watched from inside until she reached the apartment, then locked the slider and turned off the lights.

Tucked into a dimly lit corner on the edge of the garage, Jake watched Callie enter the apartment. He hadn't meant to eavesdrop, but after hearing her sobs, he'd come out to comfort her.

Before he could get to her, Jed was there.

Once she started talking, once she began sharing her thoughts with his brother, he froze. It was as if her pain burrowed into his core. It curled inside his chest, got comfortable in his space, demanded he stay where he was, hidden in the shadows.

A voyeur peeking into her soul.

Which, he admitted, was a scumbag thing to do. Still, he stayed where he was, waiting until Callie was safely inside the apartment.

Contrite, he stuffed his hands into his pockets and retraced his steps to the main house and his bedroom upstairs. Thoughts jumbled, he fell into bed and closed his eyes.

He did not sleep.

~

"Good morning, sunshine!" Jake said to Callie, as she made her way to the main house early the next morning, Lucky at her heels.

Dressed in jeans and a faded Ohio State sweatshirt, her hair pulled back into a ponytail, Callie could have passed for a college student during finals—minimal make-up, purple smudges under her eyes, sallow tint to her skin. Yawning, she gave Jake a sideways glance.

"Don't tell me, let me guess—you're a morning person, right?" Muttering more to herself than to him, she added, "Of course you are. Why wouldn't you be?"

Jake chuckled. "And if memory serves, you are not. At least, not until we pour some coffee into your yap."

Callie yawned again. "Well, unless I'm dreaming, I think I smell it brewing now. Lead the way."

Following the tantalizing smells of fresh-brewed coffee and bacon, they made their way to the kitchen. Faith stood at the stove, apron in place, flipping pancakes. Ignoring the humans for the moment, she smiled down at Lucky. "An' how are ye, Miss? Kin ah offer ye a lovely egg?"

Callie chuckled. "If you offer it, believe me, she will take it."

"And how aboot the two o' you? I'm cookin' up a feast fit for a king."

Jake smiled. "Appreciate that, Faith, but we are fairly self-sufficient. I make a mean egg and cheese sandwich, and Callie here, well, she eats what I make."

Callie rolled her eyes for the billionth time since meeting Jake Devereaux. "Have you noticed, Faith, that all I seem to do is roll my eyes to the back of my skull whenever I'm around this cheese ball? If I'm not careful, they'll stay that way. At least, according to my grandmother."

Faith slapped at Jake's arm. "Yer a buster, ain't ya? Rather than dig yerself a deeper hole, how 'bout mindin' yer tongue and grabbing us some plates?"

"Yes, ma'am."

As Jake set the table in the dining room, Callie poured herself a cup of coffee and took a seat next to Caleb at the kitchen counter. He was working on a picture, scribbling furiously with a red crayon, his mouth turned to the side in concentration.

"Good morning, Caleb. Whatcha drawing?"

Caleb, hunched over his masterpiece, stopped working and squirmed in his chair.

"Looks like a pretty cool rainbow," Callie continued, pointing to the center of the picture. "I especially love how you've blended the colors here."

Caleb shrugged, but sat up taller. Laying down his crayon, he held the drawing closer to her face so she could get a better look. Jake walked behind them and squinted down at the paper.

"Caleb, did you draw that?" When the child nodded, Jake whistled. "Dang, that's some outstanding work."

Grinning, Caleb looked down shyly, suddenly interested in his shoelaces. Jake glanced at Callie and winked. "You ever think about coloring for a living, son? I've seen pieces that don't hold a candle to that rainbow."

Caleb lifted his head. He was beaming.

Faith jumped in, spoiling the moment. "I'd be thinkin' he first needs tae master his ABC's." Ruffling the boy's head, she said, "Off ye go. Go on and get yer breakfast."

After Caleb scurried off to the dining room, Callie said, "I think Jake has made a friend. I haven't seen him smile like that since we got here."

Faith nodded. "Aye, he's taken a right shine to ye, eh? Tae ken what that means is tae ken how much Caleb keeps tucked inside. He's not had it easy, that lad. Suffered a trauma early on, and now, he doesnae speak. Not a word." She wiped her hands on her apron. "It's a long, sad story and one yer no needin' tae hear right now. But I didnae want tae forget tae tell ye I appreciate yer buildin' up ma boy. He surely needs it."

Jake tipped his head in acknowledgment. "Don't mention it, Faith. He's a good kid."

Callie cleared her throat. "If you don't mind my asking, is he capable of speech?"

"Aye, physically, he kin speak. He just doesnae hae a mind tae anymore. Oh, I've tried everything, but the lad willnae say a word."

Callie chewed on that for a moment. "You know, I'm not sure if Jed told you, but I'm a psychologist. I could talk with Caleb, see if I can get him to open up if you'd like."

Faith's eyes flashed, and her demeanor changed from open and honest to guarded, suspicious.

"'Tis none o' yer concern, Callie. A'll no be needin' yer kind of help." Pushing a stray hair back behind her ear, she said, "Now, breakfast is gettin' cauld. We'd do well tae get in there afore Caleb eats it all." Back stiff, she headed out of the kitchen to the dining room, Jake's eyes following her the whole way.

Stunned, Callie looked at Jake. "What did I do?" she whispered.

Jake, still watching Faith's retreat, shook his head. "Damned if I know, Blaze. Damned if I know."

∿

As she hurried to the dining room, Faith did her best to stop shaking, her racing thoughts asking questions she could not answer.

Why didnae Jedidiah mention what Callie did for a livin'? How kin ah keep hidden the secrets surrounding ma son's silence?

Most importantly, knowing that Callie was almost living under the same roof, Faith's mind screamed a question she had no answer to …

And how, in God's name, dae ah keep her away from ma Caleb?

CHAPTER SEVEN

"I looked through the window and saw not you, but, as I verily believe,
the devil himself with a head of fire." —The Brothers Grimm

Nora Grant stared at the computer screen, her finger hovering above the "send" button. Was she really going to do this? Was she truly going to share her worst fears and heaviest regrets with a group of strangers? Chewing on a thumbnail, she backed out of the page and clicked on another tab. In bold, flashing letters, the name "LiveFeed" shouted at her.

LiveFeed was a site she'd discovered merely by accident. Trolling around the internet, earphones on, trying to drown out the sound of her two screaming children, Nora's mind was frazzled, her soul tired.

She was looking for an escape, hunting for an exit from what had become dull and routine. Nothing in this life had turned out as she'd planned. Gone were the fantasies of the idyllic marriage, the angelic children. In their place were the responsibilities of a single parent dealing with chicken pox and stomach flus and temper tantrums, trying to make ends meet.

All thanks to her ex-husband Matthew and the selfish decisions he'd made three years ago.

"Babe, do you know what time you'll be home tomorrow night?" Nora asked. "I have that parent-teacher conference for Bailey at seven. Pain in the ass, but I promised I'd be there."

Her husband, thirty-three-year-old Matthew Grant, looked up from his plate of macaroni and cheese, a greasy strand of long hair clinging to his right eye. Sneering, he said, "Nora, I have no fucking clue what time I'll be back. Why do you always gotta be like that? I told you I have an important meeting tomorrow with the boss. What, you don't believe me?"

Nora rocked her head. "No, no, of course, I believe you. It's just that," she paused, choosing her words carefully, "it's just you've been out late nearly every night this week. I could sure use a break from these kids." She smiled and rolled her eyes, hoping that he would get on 'team Nora' and sympathize with her. Instead, he rose angrily to his feet.

"You know what? I'm done here." He threw down his napkin and tossed his head to the side, the oily strand of hair flying upward, sticking awkwardly to the opposite side of his head. "Every night, I have to listen to your whiny bullshit. 'Matthew, I need this, Matthew, I need that,'" he mimicked in a sing-song voice. "I'm so sick of it! Sick of you!"

Nora rushed over to him. "Oh, I'm sorry, babe. I don't mean to. Honestly. You go on and do what you need to do. I will figure something else out."

Matthew gulped down the rest of his iced tea and stepped away from the table. "It's too late for that now. I wasn't planning on telling you tonight, but since you've forced my hand ..." Standing up straighter, he looked her in the eye. "I'm leaving you, Nora. Tonight, if possible. The truth is, I don't love you anymore." Shaking his head, feigning a sadness he didn't feel, he said, "You're not the girl I married. I mean, have you looked in the mirror lately? Have you no pride? You've let yourself go, woman. You've become nothing more than an overweight, nagging shrew. Frankly, I can't stand the sight of you." He dabbed his mouth with a *napkin and headed for the stairs, a spring in his step, as if he hadn't a care in the world.*

As if he hadn't just shattered her universe.

"I'll send you my new address when I know it. As far as the kids go, I guess we'll figure out a custody thing. I don't know; it's not like they give two shits whether I'm here, right?"

And that was that. In an instant, Nora Grant found herself a single mother, struggling to stay afloat and care for her children.

Alone.

Nora snapped back to the present and the website in front of her. LiveFeed was a site that encouraged its users to share their struggles, fears, and regrets with other users, whether off-camera or on. The site had several private rooms, each with its own theme to explore. There was a room called 'Funny Pages' where users would share jokes and humorous true-life situations. 'Larger than Life' was a room whose participants acted as cheerleaders, supporting overweight members struggling to get fit. And one of her favorites, 'Twenty minutes til Chow,' a room where users shared their timesaving, easy recipes geared toward working moms.

But it was the room called 'Confession' that intrigued her the most. The people who entered here were people looking for absolution, forgiveness, even salvation. Every week, the site administrators would post a new topic for consideration. Users could comment or share personal feelings on that topic using their actual names or an alias. A side chat was always open with a direct message feature for those who wanted to get to know each other better.

This month's topic was fears, phobias, and how they developed in your life. Some people took it a step further, delving into whether karma was at hand, dishing out retribution for sins of the past.

Going back to the response page, Nora reread what she'd

written. While she would never choose the 'live' option, could not choose it, a part of her felt liberated relating her story. It was cathartic, releasing some of her secrets.

She poured over the passage a third time, then hit send.

When I was a child, my home life was sad, lonely, chaotic. While all my friends were playing kickball and going to parties or sleepovers, I was a prisoner at home, forced to babysit my little brother every day. Our family was extremely poor, and both of my parents worked extra shifts just to make ends meet. Consequently, my brother and I were left home alone most days, expected to fend for ourselves.

Because of this, I resented my parents for years.

One day, feeling exceptionally petulant, I found myself in the living room, playing with wooden matches I'd discovered in a cupboard. At twelve years old, my parents had forbidden me from touching them, making my defiance much more attractive.

It was as if I was giving my parents the middle finger, only from a safe distance.

Anyway, there I was, striking match after match, my six-year-old brother upstairs in his room with his hand-me-down train set. I had just struck what was probably my twentieth match when the phone rang, startling me. The next thing I knew, that match was on the sofa, licking at the upholstery. That slow burn quickly morphed into a miniature inferno, and I watched, horrified, as the couch burst into flames. Panicked, not thinking of anything except the wrath I faced if my parents found out, I ran to the kitchen to get—something. I'm not even sure what. Water? Towels? It doesn't much matter now, though, does it? The bottom line is when I returned to the living room, fire had engulfed every stick of furniture we owned; the chairs, the mantel, the television. Flames licked up the sides of the wall to the ceiling, the dining room, and finally, the staircase.

The staircase that led to my little brother Jeffrey.

I'm ashamed to admit there was a split second of hesitancy before I called to him. No, that's not true. It was more like two or three minutes of standing by, doing nothing but watching my home burn. All I could think was, what if I didn't warn him? I mean, if he died, my imprisonment would be over, the chains broken. Does that make me a horrible person? Possibly.

Probably.

Eventually, guilt won out, and I shouted to him, screamed at the top of my lungs, even as the black smoke and heat made me choke. But Jeff didn't respond, didn't even come to the top of the steps. In fact, there was no movement on the second floor at all.

The smoke got thicker until I could barely breathe, the scorching heat melting my plastic watchband to my wrist. I had to get out, get help. I left through the back door in the kitchen, still calling for my brother.

He never answered. He would never answer again.

So, surprise, surprise, my greatest fear is being burned alive. And my greatest regret? Knowing that if I hadn't played with fire, if I had acted quicker, Jeff would still be alive.

And living with the truth that, when it came down to it, I killed Jeffrey.

∿

The Disciple sat at his desk and logged onto his new favorite site, LiveFeed. He entered his usual room and, eyes glued to the pages, scanned the dozen or so new posts added since last he logged on. Most of them were boring, generic, safe 'confessions.' Pathetic stories hardly worth his time.

"Ever since I was young, I've been afraid of spiders," he read aloud, his tone dripping with contempt.

Who the fuck cares?

"My worst fear is that of rejection from my peers," he said in a sing-song voice.

Which means you're a tool and everyone knows it.

"My biggest regret is not having loved more!"

Jesus, I think I just puked in my mouth!

On and on they went, one story more laughable than the

next. Just when he was about to toss in the towel, the word 'fire' caught his attention.

Hmm. This one might be interesting.

For days, he'd scoured the LiveFeed site in search of his next project. He was seeking people whose sins were unknown to the world and, therefore, went unpunished. People who flaunted their offenses to the masses without fear of repercussion.

People who thought themselves invincible.

People like 'Nora G.' Licking his lips, he clicked on her bio and studied the profile picture she'd provided. Judging by the angled hairstyle, it was most likely a dated photo, going back seven or eight years ago.

Probably taken before the kids she mentions in her 'About me' section. Typical female.

Gathering his thoughts, he composed a private message that conveyed an understanding and sensual man; a man who believed that behind every good man stood a better woman.

Playing on her vanity and inner ego, he showered her with compliments on her strength of character and unparalleled beauty.

Then he waited until she took the bait.

Their correspondence occurred almost immediately. Nora, flattered that out there, somewhere, was a man who thought she was beautiful, jumped at the chance to engage with him. She'd hidden in the shadows for three years now; it was time to bask in a little light. So, she answered his response to her story immediately. Soon, all she could think about was her next conversation with 'Samuel J.'

A week after their initial introduction, Nora agreed to meet Samuel at a coffee shop just outside of her home in Dayton, Wyoming. Her friend Evelyn agreed to babysit the kids.

"Are you sure you want to do this, Nor?" Evelyn asked, as she fixed the clasp on Nora's necklace. "I mean, you don't even know the guy. What if he's like a weirdo or something?" She grabbed her throat, a frightening thought popping into her head. "Oh my gosh, what if he's, like, a crazed killer?"

Nora giggled. "Then it will be the most excitement I've had in, like, forever. Seriously, Ev, it's fine. We'll be in a public place, and it's just coffee. Not like we are going out on the town, right? It's broad daylight and I'll be less than ten minutes from home. Relax, girlfriend, I got this."

Nora grabbed her purse, patted her two children on the head, and headed for the door.

"Wait!" Evelyn yelled. "Tell me his name at least! I'm gonna need it for the suspect list when the cops find your body."

Nora smiled. "Funny. It's Samuel. Samuel Jackson."

When Evelyn raised her brows, Nora joked, "Yeah, I know. Sam says he gets that all the time. Be back in a bit!" With a wave, jingling her keys, and humming a tune, she walked out of her door.

~

"You look nice."

Nora and Samuel sat at a corner booth in a little-known coffee and donut shop on Highway 14 in Ranchester. She twirled her coffee cup, uncomfortable with what to do with her hands. She was so far away from where she was fifteen years ago when she played the dating game. Now, everything seemed forced, artificial.

What the hell is the matter with me, anyway? She thought nervously. *Say something!*

"Th-thank you, Samuel. You do, too."

And he did. He wore tan pants, an olive-green shirt, and a light jacket. He was a clean-shaven, average-looking man with short, curly hair and deep-set eyes. If she had passed him on the street, she wouldn't have given him a second look. But here, chatting with him, she could see the possibilities.

Samuel reached out and squeezed her hand. "Thank you for agreeing to have coffee with me today. It's strange, but after having read your story and spoken with you online, I feel a strong connection to you." He dropped his head and smiled softly. "I know, I know. I sound like a dork."

Nora felt her cheeks flush. His focused attention was unfamiliar, leaving her feeling self-conscious and vulnerable.

How do I respond to that? she wondered.

"I-I'm happy to meet you too, Sam. It was lovely of you to reach out. I don't have many opportunities to sit and chat with a big person, having two young children." She smiled, beaming, congratulating herself for her straightforward response.

They continued like that, laughing at life, discussing, in depth, the LiveFeed website and how it seemed cathartic, almost empowering. It was as if their conversation could go on forever, an infinite inspection of thoughts and feelings, free from any awkwardness or judgement. When they finally, reluctantly, stood to leave, Samuel made a suggestion.

"Ok, Nora, this is going to sound totally random," he wiggled his eyebrows playfully, "and it may start the neighborhood talking, but do you like to hike? I have a gorgeous spot I found that I'd love to share with you. It has flowers and trees and the most beautiful waterfall I've ever seen. It's close to Dayton, just about fifteen or twenty minutes away. If you're game, we can meet here tomorrow, and you can follow me in your car. But wear hiking boots or sneakers—the terrain is kind of rough in some parts. Believe me, though, it's worth it. You won't be sorry."

Nora pursed her lips, conflicted. Picking up on her apprehension, Samuel jumped in.

"I mean, if you are uncomfortable or it's too soon, I get it." He let those words dangle a moment before grinning. "After all, what if I'm a psycho bent on sacrificing you to woodland nymphs? Or a werewolf, waiting to devour you and use your bones as wind chimes? Or, heaven forbid, a serial killer luring you to your death?"

Nora chuckled, "Oh, I don't know, Sam. What are the odds that two serial killers will occupy the same location at the same time? Must be astronomical."

Samuel laughed; a genuine belly-type laugh. He was enjoying her company.

What a pity she would be dead soon.

"Is this it, Samuel? It's lovely." Nora gaped at the beauty before her, astounded that such a place existed. Secluded, the scenic spot was on a bluff twenty-five feet above Tongue River Canyon, giving an unobstructed view of the Tongue River and the surrounding Bighorn Mountains.

Rangers deemed the trail they hiked as 'moderately difficult' and, with its icy patches and sudden dips, it proved challenging. Nora lost her footing once or twice and Samuel, ever the gentleman, kept her upright.

When they reached the top of the bluff, he stood behind her and they absorbed the stunning view.

"It is lovely, isn't it?" he said. "I used to come here with my best friend, Eliot. We came here often, pretending we were cowboys, our silly Nerf guns at our sides, protecting our cattle from rustlers." He clucked his tongue. "Of course, that was before Eliot died."

Nora gasped and turned back to look at him. "Oh, how horrible! I am so sorry, Samuel. That must have devastated you!"

Samuel nodded. "It did. Especially how he died."

Nora turned back around and waited. When nothing was forthcoming, she croaked, "How did he die, Sam? What happened?"

Samuel looked beyond her to the rocks and river below. "Eliot had an older sister named Miriam. Seems Miriam was always in charge of him, making his meals and bathing him and such. Eliot's parents worked obsessively and were seldom home, leaving the parenting of eight-year-old Eliot to their thirteen-year-old daughter."

Nora, back still toward him, felt her gut tighten.

"Anyway, Miriam hated the boy. Took him up here one sunny afternoon and let him play wherever he wanted, unsupervised, ignoring the seduction a high cliff has to a child. In fact, rumor had it that she encouraged him to go higher up the ridge, and soon the inevitable happened. Eliot climbed a bit too high, lost his footing, and plunged twenty-five feet to the rocks below. He was killed instantly."

Of course, the Disciple thought, *this entire tale is bullshit and nowhere close to how Eliot actually died, but it is fun telling it.*

Nora gasped. "Oh, that's terrible. What was Miriam thinking? It's almost as if she wanted him to die!"

The minute she said the words aloud, she felt sick to her stomach. Miriam's story was too close to her own.

"Yes, it is like that, isn't it? As if she wished death on her little brother." His face flushed and his fists clenched. "In fact, it's almost as bad as, say, lighting a match and burning your house down with your brother trapped inside!"

Nora blinked rapidly, the man standing behind her becoming a looming threat; a threat that had her trapped on top of a cliff. Scared to death, she turned fully around to face him.

"I want to go home now, Samuel," she said tersely. "I don't know what kind of game you're playing, but whatever it is, I'm not interested."

Samuel spat on the ground, just missing her boots, and grinned.

"I mean it! I want to leave, now!" She attempted to walk around him, but he blocked her path. Frustrated, becoming angry, she shouted, "What the fuck, Samuel? What do you want from me?"

He placed his hands on her shoulders. "What do I want, Nora? Well, isn't it obvious?" He kissed each cheek softly, then shoved her backward, watching her flail as she plummeted, her screams echoing in the canyon.

"I want you to die."

When he reached the bottom of the cliff's face, Nora's body lay crumpled on a rock grouping, her legs at an impossible angle and nearly touching her ear. A massive amount of blood pooled around her head, while her soft moans and gurgles were lost in the sounds of rushing water.

The Disciple bent down, placed a hand on her shoulder, and studied her face.

Nora's mouth was open, as if frozen mid-scream. Her eyes darted frantically as her damaged brain attempted to assess her situation. She tried moving her legs, a foot, her arms, but she could feel nothing.

The connection between her sensory and motor neurons was severed. Her nervous system could no longer control anything below her neck.

But her thought processes remained intact, allowing her to understand her back and neck were broken, her limbs paralyzed. Fresh fear washed over her as she realized just how vulnerable she was.

Her wide eyes finally found those of her attacker, and she tried to speak. But her words were garbled and unintelligible.

"Don't say anything, Nora. It wouldn't help you, anyway." He patted her cheek. "I want you to know that, after spending time with you, I really have grown fond of you. Of course, it goes without saying that I still plan on killing you, but I thought you should know I do it with a heavier heart than usual."

Nora's heart pounded and fresh tears streamed down her face.

Oh, God! Please help me!

The Disciple grabbed her ankles and pulled, dragging her into a wooded area several yards away from the edge of the falls.

Once there, he gathered branches, leaves and moss, and tossed them into a pile.

When the pile reached close to three feet, he stepped back, walked to a nearby aspen tree, and retrieved a metal container that was hidden behind it. He glided back to where Nora lay and moved her to the pile of kindling.

Terrified, comprehension slammed into her brain and she fought to scream, to move, but found she was unable.

Once he settled her atop the branches, the Disciple opened the canister and shook the lighter fluid, bathing Nora and the kindling she lay on.

When he pulled an old wooden match from his pocket, the same kind used to set her home ablaze, all she could muster was a silent scream. She prayed that her death would be quick, that paralysis would dull or mask the pain.

When the orange flicker of flame spread across her torso, she was stunned that she didn't feel a thing. But then, as the white-hot fire licked at her neck, skipping across the slope of her throat to her face, she felt every nerve catch fire.

And in the brilliant glow of the morning sun on Tongue River Canyon, Nora Grant burned alive.

Just as her little brother Jeffrey did all those years ago.

CHAPTER EIGHT

J ake yawned, leaning back in his chair. "So, who all is coming to this shindig, anyway?"

Jed, Callie, and Jake sat in the dining room, waiting for the other participants of their meeting to arrive. A fresh pot of coffee and a plate of sugar cookies sat in the center of the table, compliments of Faith. Jed snagged a cookie, then passed around notepads and pencils.

"A couple of cops who help me out occasionally, pro bono. In return, I do some covert investigating for them on certain cases. It's a symbiotic relationship that benefits us all."

"No pay?" Callie asked.

"It can be construed as a conflict for a cop still on the job to make side money working for a company like Jed's," Jake explained. "Most agencies forbid it. But, if no money changes hands, consultations between PI's and law enforcement can be a win-win."

"It's worked out great so far," Jed said. "One guy on the team is Curtis Valdez, an agent from the Wyoming Division of Criminal Investigation. Curt has been a close friend of mine for, geesh, must be ten years now. He's an excellent investigator, nose like a hound dog. I figured we could pick his brain about this case."

Jake sat up and reached for his own cookie. "And the other guys? Anyone I know?"

Jed smirked. "Does the name Jim Ford mean anything to you?"

Jake let out a whoop and clapped his hands together. "No shit? You got Jimmy to work for free? How is the old coot, anyway?"

"Ornery as hell and can still kick the crap out of either of us."

"Yeah well, the big bastard would have to catch us first."

Raising her hand, Callie asked, "Pardon me for interrupting this stroll down memory lane, but who is Jimmy?"

Ignoring her question, Jake continued as if she hadn't spoken. "So, Jed, what is Jimbo doing for you, anyway? Wait! Don't tell me—he's undercover in a nudie bar?"

What am I, a potted plant? Callie fumed. *What's wrong with him?*

Jed looked ready to knock Jake out of the chair as well. "You ever tire of being an asshole, Jake?" Turning to Callie, he said, "I apologize for this ignoramus. James Ford is an FBI legend who went from being front-page news to relative obscurity by his own choosing. After a career that most only dream of, he transferred here, to the Billings Residential Office, to finish his time with the Bureau. On the weekends, when he isn't chasing skirts, he's tracking down leads for me."

Jake stood and stretched. "Yeah, he's a real charmer. Jim Ford never met a female he didn't like. Or want to bed." Chuckling, he added, "Bastard is in his early fifties and still has them lined up. I wish I knew his secret."

Callie sipped her coffee, her eyes piercing Jake's over the cup. "I'll take a stab at it and say that he meets the requirements of 'not an arrogant putz' on a woman's checklist."

Jake's eyes twinkled, and his lips quivered as he struggled to suppress a laugh.

Callie addressed Jed. "Who else is on that list besides Curtis and Jim?"

"Abby Moore, a gal that used to work for the Feds in cybersecurity but now works in the private sector. She's a genius at computer technology, electronic surveillance, coding—you name it, she's done it."

"Hallelujah!" Callie shouted. "Finally, some more estrogen to level out all the testosterone in this group!"

Jed smirked. "True, but not the reason I hired her for this case. Abby is just that good. I figured we would need the best for scouring and deciphering just where this scum Gabriel might be."

The mere mention of his name elevated Callie's heartbeat and caused her to scrub self-consciously at the tattoo carved into her thigh.

As if that will wipe away the horror of the last four months, Callie thought angrily. *As if it will erase the fact that my sister is dead!*

She'd made a promise to herself to get that abomination on her leg removed, knowing that surgeries and skin grafts would never obliterate the truth. Gabriel's name, boldly tattooed on her inner thigh, would stay with her forever. She would always feel it when she touched her leg, see it when she closed her eyes.

Whether visible or not.

For now, she'd vowed to leave it in place, obnoxiously undisturbed, until they caught the bastard. It served as a brutal reminder, an impetus to keep going.

Climbing out of those dark memories, she said, "Well, it sounds like we're lucky to have such an elite group of investigators." Winking at Jed, she added, "It's nice to know my new boss has so many connections."

For the first time, Jake recognized Callie intended to stay in Montana to work for his brother, even after Gabriel was caught and punished. He felt a twinge, a stab of something unfamiliar, and pushed it aside.

The three of them sat in comfortable silence, each in their

own thoughts, until the chime of the doorbell broke the spell. Jed left the dining room to answer it, leaving Jake and Callie alone.

Leaning toward him, Callie whispered to Jake, "I can't stop thinking about Faith. Do you think she's angry with me? What did I do?"

Jake shrugged and shook his head. "It's not on you, Callie. Something is going on with her, something tucked beneath the surface that we can't see. I plan on asking Jed about it later tonight. Don't want to step on any toes here, but I have a strange feeling about the whole thing."

"What kind of feeling?"

He hesitated. "Like there is something Faith's hiding. From us, from Jed. And me and dishonesty? We aren't exactly friends —especially if it messes with my family."

A few moments later, Jed entered the room, followed by a huge, dark-skinned man with a shiny bald head and a beautiful smile.

"Son of a bitch, if it isn't Jimbo the giant, the paparazzi's favorite investigator!" Jake said, jumping up and grabbing the man in a bear hug. They slapped each other's back, each grunting with effort, trying to be the one who squeezed harder.

Callie peeked around the two men and looked at Jed. "I can't wait to hear the story about these guys!"

The men separated, allowing Jim Ford to notice Callie for the first time. He covered the length of the large dining room in three long strides, took her hand, and bowed slightly.

"And who do we have here?" he said with a grin. "Whoever you are, I curse my ophthalmologist. If he wasn't so good at his job, I'd still be cross-eyed and could see you twice."

Callie burst out laughing. "Oh, wow, does that line ever really work?"

"Not sure, but I'm leaving here in an hour." Jim waggled his brows, then winked. "If you're with me, it worked."

Jake stepped between the two. "Don't listen to him, Blaze. He's a legend in his own mind. Callie, meet James Ford, better known as Jimbo. Or just, Ford."

Callie curtsied, a cheeky move mimicking his bow, and said, "Pleased to meet you, 'Just Ford.' Callie Callahan here." Grinning, she stuck out her hand, and he took it.

Ford held her hand a bit too long, then turned to Jake. "Oh, beauty, brains, and a wise guy. I'm impressed."

Jake grumbled something unintelligible, and the four took a seat. Jed checked his watch, then began his meeting.

"Okay, I guess we will get started. Hopefully, Abby and Curt will be here momentarily. So, I suppose we should start at the beginning, get everyone up to speed." He looked at Ford. "How much do you know about this case?"

Ford shrugged and poured himself a cup of coffee. "Just what I could gather from Jake. As you know, we've been friends a long time, worked many a case together when I was with him in Quantico. Hell, I practically raised him from a pup." He winked at Jake. "Anyway, we've kept in touch through the years, emails and phone calls, and I have the gist of what went down." He gave Callie a sympathetic look. "I'm truly sorry for what this bastard has taken from you, Callie. Jake has spoken highly of both you and Kate, and he isn't one for giving false praise."

Callie felt odd at the thought of being the subject of Jake's conversations with Ford. Squirming in her seat, she pulled at the collar of her blouse, wondering if the others could sense her disquiet.

Thankfully, Jed stepped in. "Alright, so let's start with what we know about Jeremy Sterling, aka Gabriel Devine." He pulled over a manila folder that sat to his side, opened it, and began reading aloud.

"Jeremy Sterling was born on December 18, 1987, to Meredith Sterling and Rowan Callahan. He was the product of an affair ..." he looked apologetically at Callie, "and lived alone with his mother in Texas for a time. At ten years old, Jeremy killed

Callie's mother, Eileen Callahan, in a fit of rage. According to reports, soon after the murder, Meredith became a reclusive alcoholic. Eventually, she could no longer care for him and relinquished her parental rights."

Jim stretched toward the plate of cookies. "This Jeremy guy sounds like a real charmer."

Jake nodded. "You don't know the half of it."

The doorbell rang again, and Jed rose. "That must be Curt and Abby. Be right back."

While he was gone, Ford played with his pencil, occasionally sneaking glances at Callie.

Uncomfortable, Callie stared back. "What? Do I have spinach in my teeth or something?"

Jake blinked, the simple sentence pulling him back to a day with Katie. She had uttered the exact phrase to him when she'd found him staring at her. In that case, it was her frilly, barely there pajamas that had him gawking and drooling like a lovestruck teen. Her teeth had been the last thing on his mind.

Ford laughed. "Good God, but it's nice to meet a woman unafraid to speak her mind!" He clucked his tongue. "The truth?"

Callie nodded.

"Well, Miss, the truth is, you're stunning. I keep looking for a flaw, a hideous and hidden imperfection to spoil the vista of your gorgeous face or your silky-smooth skin. But there's nothing. You are, simply, that beautiful."

Callie felt her cheeks flush. She hated being the center of attention.

Jake cleared his throat, uncomfortable himself. "Okay, Casanova, settle down. This is supposed to be a professional meeting, not a pickup joint."

Ford shook with laughter, his bellow echoing off the walls of the room. "A pickup joint? You really were born in the wrong era, weren't you? But I get it, JD, and I'm sorry about that—I didn't realize you two were ..." His words trailed off when Jed and the others entered the room.

"Look what the cat dragged in!" Jed teased, pointing to Curtis. "I swear, they'll let anyone out on a day pass!"

Smirking, Curtis replied, "Kiss my ass, Devereaux." He walked to the table and the three individuals surrounding it. "Mornin', folks."

Jake, Ford, and Callie stood as one.

"Hey, Curt, it's good to see you. Been a long time," Jake said, shaking the man's hand. "You know the big guy here," he nodded toward Ford, "but I don't think you've had the pleasure of meeting my associate."

Associate? What am I? A banker?

Callie stepped forward. "Callie Callahan. And I like the term 'partner' better. It's a pleasure to meet you."

Curtis shook her hand and smiled. "Pleasure is all mine."

Abby, as if waiting for the green light to speak, stood awkwardly to the side. She was a young, plain-looking woman, muscular, with cropped hair, a nose ring, and about a dozen tattoos.

"Hello," Callie said, extending a hand. "You must be Abby Moore. I'm Callie Callahan."

After the introductions, Callie continued. "Jed has been filling us in, extolling your virtues. Your talent with technology is quite impressive. I have trouble logging onto my laptop to get my email, so I am looking forward to learning from you."

Abby smiled. "Oh, it's not so hard once you learn a few tricks. I would be glad to teach you sometime." Stuttering, she added, "If-if that's something you would like to do. No pressure or anything. I mean, I don't want to imply that you're incompetent or need teaching. Gosh, no, quite the opposite. Jed told me you are super intelligent." She gnawed on a fingernail. "Nevermind, forget I said anything. I meant no offense."

Callie furrowed her brows. "None taken. And, of course, I'd love some help!" Then, grabbing her hand, she pulled Abby toward the table. "Now, what do you say we take a seat and get this party started, huh?"

. . .

Two hours later, the group broke for lunch. Sitting on a stool in the kitchen, watching Faith assemble some roast beef sandwiches, Callie spoke up.

"Can I help you with anything, Faith? I feel like an idiot just sitting here, watching you work."

"Well, we dinnae want ye tae feel like a dunce now, dae we? Ye kin give mah soup a stir."

Callie walked to the stove and grabbed a slotted spoon. The mouth-watering scent of spices and the sea made her stomach growl. "This smells amazing. Chowder?"

Faith nodded. "Aye, New England clam. 'Tis Jed's favorite."

"Well, I'd love the recipe. Grams absolutely adores clam chowder."

Faith merely grunted a response.

The conversation continued that way, with Callie asking questions and Faith doing her best to keep her answers cordial, but short.

This is ridiculous!

Finally, having had enough, Callie said, "You know, Faith, in my family, if there's an elephant standing on the balcony, you give it a front-row seat. I don't know if you've noticed, but we've got a big-ass mammoth pounding at the door right now." She swept her hair to the side. "I honestly don't know what I did to make you angry, but whatever it was, I apologize. Sincerely, I do. I would never deliberately hurt you or Caleb. Is there any way we can fix this?"

Faith closed her eyes and took a breath. She needed Callie as an ally, not an enemy. Choosing her words, not wanting to tip her hand and spill buried secrets, she said, "Nae, lass, the apology is mine tae make. Caleb cannae speak for himself, so ah speak for him. Ah be needin' tae learn tae trust again. Ah am sorry, lass."

Callie smiled softly. "Apology accepted. Now, how about we

97

get this grub out to the others? If Jed is anything like Jake, an empty stomach creates a temperamental monster."

At three o'clock, meeting winding down, Jed assigned everyone a task to follow up on.

"Jim, you have a ton of out-of-state contacts in the Bureau. Many more than Jake here." Jed nodded his head toward his brother.

"That's because he's been around longer." Jake growled. "Tell me, Jimbo ... what was it like to serve under J Edgar?"

Ford chuckled. "I'd say it was a damn sight better than serving with you, Junior. At least I didn't hafta pat him on his little head and wipe his ass for him."

Callie rolled her eyes. "Focus, boys, focus."

Jed stood and stretched. "Yeah, what she said. I only meant that Ford, having served in several areas, knows more agents. We need to go back over everything and anything remotely resembling this guy's MO. Wants, warrants, data entries in ViCap, the works. And since Jake is on leave, it will be much easier for someone on the inside to look around. Discreetly, mind you. We don't need to draw attention to the fact that we're looking. Maybe we check with the Department of Defense, get a copy of his DD214."

"DD214? What is that?" Callie asked.

"It's a military record," Jed answered. "Sort of like a personnel file."

"They house all inactive Federal field records of both civilian employees and military personnel in the National Personal Records Center," Jake explained. "These files, called Reports of Separation, contain information about an individual's standing upon discharge. Things like the person's character of service, whether it was an honorable or dishonorable discharge, or any red flags that appeared during their active status. DD214s are usually only available to the service member or next of kin, but we FBI guys have our ways." He gave her a brilliant smile, and she felt the gentle brush of butterflies fluttering in her stomach.

Jeepers, creepers, what the hell is with me?

Trying to stay on track, ignoring that her belly flipped every time Jake smiled at her, she said to Jed, "Okay, I can see where you are going with this—the more information we find out about his character, or lack thereof, the more ammunition in our stockpile."

Jed smiled at her, a beautiful smile but one that failed to cause her body to react as it did with his brother. "Exactly." Turning to Ford, he said, "Think you can get through that kind of red tape?"

Ford rolled his eyes. "Is a frog's ass watertight? I'd like to bring my old partner, Sawyer, into the mix if he is available, too. I worked with him when he first came west and started in Billings. Now, he works out of the Casper office. Real, on-the-ground shit, too, not like me—an old fart sitting behind a desk following paper trails and making phone calls. This kid is sharp, edgy. He can smell a lead faster than a fly smells a lawn full of dog shit."

"I remember him," Jake added. "Met him at the academy when I was doing a class there on Defensive Tactics. Good instincts."

Jed nodded. "Well, if he is available, I have no problem with it."

Abby stuck her hand up shyly. "What do you want me to do, Jed?"

"Abby, I'd like you and Curt to look for spikes in internet searches, maybe specific keywords or phrases involving Katie Callahan's death, her background, that kind of thing. If you find anything even the least bit promising, Curt can run with it. I'd also look closely at social media sites. Sometimes, a group of people get together, play amateur sleuth, and try to solve a mystery or crime on their own." He flipped a page in his notepad, scribbled down some thoughts, and continued. "Check for hits having to do with Katie, her death, or any of Gabriel's other victims. We all know these assholes like to relive their crimes. Since the good guys forced him to pause his agenda, he might be getting his jollies from past articles or pictures. There may have been an attempt to hack into the case files and access the crime scene photos. It's been four months. Interest has waned, so someone revisiting the investigation could be golden." He cringed and shot a look at Callie. "Sorry."

"No, you're right. Unfortunately, my sister's case has grown cold, and there aren't as many eyes looking at it right now. But just because I know that doesn't mean I have to accept it."

Curtis's phone rang, and he excused himself, walking out of the room.

"Okay, so what about Callie and me?" Jake asked.

"Glad you asked," Jed said, eyes bright. "I think there may be a treasure trove of information to discover about Gabriel's previous life. Did he have any relatives on his mother's side? Friends he stayed in contact with? Maybe a former employer or church official? We know about his obsession with religion and that he believes himself to be a liaison between God and man. So, it would stand to reason that he would have frequented a church at some point."

"All valid ideas," Jake said. "So I guess we're heading to Texas, then?"

"I think it's a start. Maybe your contact in the Laredo PD can lend a hand."

"Laredo contact?" Callie asked. "Is that the guy you and Sully interviewed? Katie told me about it."

Jake nodded. "Investigator Adam Dempsey of the Office of Criminal Investigation. Good cop with superior instincts. He already knows what a douchebag Gabriel is, so he'll jump at the chance to help take him down."

Curtis came back to the room, hands in his pockets, brows furrowed. "Well, folks, that's a wrap for me. I just got a request from the Sheriff's Department to respond to a nasty crime scene in Tongue River Canyon. An officer from the Forest Service found a burned body out there in the woods and, although a Sheriff's deputy is on the way, they're requesting an assist from DCI." He grabbed his windbreaker from the back of his chair. "Jed, I'll call you later, and you can fill me in on what I missed."

"Will do," Jed said, standing. "I think we've covered everything anyway, unless anyone has questions?"

Abby stood, awkwardly wriggling into her jacket. Jim stepped over to her, helping her find her sleeves. "Uh, thanks," she said, face flushed.

"No problemo, little lady," Jim smiled. He turned to Jake and stuck his hand out. "Good seeing you, partner. Catch you on the flip."

After Jim and Abby had gone, Callie spoke up. "You think it is okay if I leave Lucky with you? Obviously, we can't take her with us to Texas, so I'll need a dog sitter."

Jed smiled. "Of course. She and Caleb have become inseparable in such a short time. I think having that dog here is doing him a world of good."

Jake raised his hand. "Speaking of Caleb ... what's the deal there if you don't mind my asking? Callie and Faith had a bit of a run-in earlier, after Callie offered to speak with the boy as a therapist. Faith essentially freaked out at the offer. Struck me as very odd, Jed."

"It's fine, Jake," Callie jumped in. "We ironed it out earlier today."

"Still strikes me as off, Blaze, regardless of whether you two patched things up."

Jed cleared his throat. "I'm sorry if things got a little weird, Cal. There is a history there, one that I know exists between Faith, Caleb, and her ex-husband. Unfortunately, she's a very private person and has said little about that period in her life. All I know is that Caleb witnessed a horrendous event, one that led to his catatonia, and he's been that way ever since." He gathered up his notes and placed them in his folder. "Anyhow, I'd appreciate it if you didn't push. I hope that one day Faith will believe in me enough to let me in."

"Understood," Callie said. "We'll back off, right, Jake?"

Jake nodded but remained unconvinced. In his opinion, it wasn't space that Faith and Caleb needed right now.

It was a couple of trusted friends.

CHAPTER NINE

Tongue River Canyon
4:30 p.m.

"I t's just over this ridge here, Agent Valdez. I apologize for
the bumpy terrain," LEO JP Burke of the USDA Forest
Service called over his shoulder. The wind was fierce through
this part of the canyon, causing him to compete against both it
and the whir of the ATV motor.

Curtis shouted back. "No problem, JP. I appreciate the lift."

Leaving his truck on the trail about a mile back, Curtis sat
behind JP on the ATV, his gear over his shoulder. There were
sections of Tongue River where the forest was so dense, it was
impossible to get a standard-sized vehicle through it. Where
passage proved impossible by truck, the Forest Service used
ATVs and motorcycles to cut through the thickly treed areas.

And when those failed, they took to their feet.

Spotting a few people standing together outside the yellow
tape perimeter, JP pulled the Polaris Sportsman XP a few feet
behind them. Hopping down, Curtis took in his surroundings.
The roar of the Tongue River echoing off the giant stone walls of
the canyon was almost deafening. An acrid scent assaulted his

nostrils, a mixture of burning hair, sulfur gas, and cooked meat. He subconsciously rubbed his nose, as if the simple action could wipe away the offensive odor, and nodded to the other investigators.

"Afternoon," Curt said, swallowing hard and trying his best not to gag. "Curtis Valdez, Wyoming DCI. Sheriff's Office requested an assist on this one."

The tallest man in the group stepped forward, his red hair blowing in the chilly breeze. "Pleased to meet you," he said. "I see you've met LEO Burke. I'm Sawyer Mills, FBI agent out of Casper. Thanks for coming out to give us a hand. I take it you know Deputy Dan Cummings?"

"I do." Curtis shook Sawyer's hand, then nodded at Cummings. "Good to see you again, Danny. We gotta stop meeting like this." He placed his bag on the ground at his feet. "So, Mills, huh? I've just come from a meeting with a friend, Jed Devereaux, and your name came up. Feels like I should know you." Curtis said.

"Devereaux?" Sawyer asked. "I knew a Jake Devereaux from my academy days."

"Jed's his brother. He owns his own PI company and has been working on an old serial killer case. We've formed a kind of squad or task force to find this son of a bitch who has, so far, given law enforcement the slip. One of the elite members of this team is Jim Ford. He thought maybe you'd climb aboard our investigative train."

Sawyer chuckled. "I shoulda known. Only Ford would offer my services before he's even asked. But, sure, I'll do what I can to help."

"Appreciate it," Curtis said, taking in the cordoned-off scene ten or twelve feet away from him. Within the 'Police Line; Do Not Cross' tape and surrounded by a circle of rocks sat the remnants of a campfire, its ashes still smoldering. At the core of the ring, nestled inside burned edges of leaves and twigs, lay a blackened form.

Curtis sighed. He knew this was going to be a bad one. "Christ, what happened to this poor bastard?"

Sawyer nodded at the body. "Impossible to tell right now. We are waiting on the M.E. to arrive, but according to the purse we found, the deceased may be a woman named Nora Grant. A friend reported her missing late last night after she failed to return from a date. JP here found the body while on routine patrol."

Burke's head bobbed quickly. His wide-eyed look and reverent tone telegraphed his youth. "That's right. I thought it was the remnants of an illegal campfire at first. We sometimes get out-of-town folks who think nothing of starting their own little cooking fire out here, regardless of the time of year or wildfire risk. It was only as I got closer that I realized there was, uh ..." he hesitated, "... there was a hand coming up from the ashes."

Curtis frowned. "Seems an elaborate way to dispose of a body, doesn't it?" He looked over at JP. "Did you touch anything, Burke?"

Burke shook his head. "No, sir. As soon as I realized what it was, I backed off and radioed my commander. He notified the Sheriff's Office, who reached out to ya'll." Uneasy, he unzipped the bottom of his jacket, allowing for easier access to his service weapon. They were in an isolated part of Tongue River and a killer was on the loose. Cell service was spotty, and back-up could be miles away.

"Anyway, there's no telling how long she's been here." Burke shifted his stance and frowned. "We have a lot of acreage to cover," he said defensively, "so it was just dumb luck that I stumbled upon her."

"You did great, kid," Deputy Cummings said. "If it wasn't for your due diligence, she may not have been found for weeks."

The crunch of leaves from behind drew their attention. A thin man, with slicked-back hair and dressed in coveralls, stopped before them. "Hey, whatsup Curt? Now, I bet you are thinking, 'Well, what did I do to deserve this!'" The man stuffed his hands inside his pockets. "Glad you asked! It seems HQ put the call out for an evidence tech in case you needed it, and, lucky you, here I am! So, tell me—what are your next two wishes?"

Valdez frowned, squinting at the newcomer. He'd seen him around the DCI lab the last few months and wasn't a fan. Something about the guy seemed off. Curtis couldn't recall his name at the moment. "Hey, yeah, we may need something from you. Stick around if you can. We'll take care of the pictures and sketching the scene layout. Stay behind the tape until we need you, but be ready."

The technician nodded, giving Curtis a thumbs up. "Okey dokey, big guy."

Valdez cringed.

Taking a camera out of his bag, Curtis turned to Mills and Cummings. "I'll grab a few pics of the area before we get closer. There are some extra gloves and shoe covers in my bag if you don't have them."

The trio donned protective gear, and Curtis began taking the preliminary photographs. Initial investigation into a homicide included taking hundreds of images of the scene, the body, and the surroundings. While Curtis snapped pictures, Mills and Cummings did a scene walkthrough, establishing a path of entry and exit to reduce scene contamination.

"What do you need from me, Deputy Cummings?" JP asked.

Dan looked past him, beyond the crime scene tape and toward the main trail. "I'd appreciate it if you could go back to where you picked up Agent Valdez and chase down the M.E. He should be here any minute now."

Curtis bent down and studied the remains. What was left of the body remained hot, with small plumes of smoke blowing in the westward wind. The woman's face was unrecognizable, but portions of her body were visible among the soot and ashes: a foot, both hands, part of a thigh.

Should be enough for a positive ID, Curtis thought grimly. *At least, that's something.*

Agent Mills crouched down alongside Curtis. "You know, it doesn't matter how many years I do this job. I don't think I'll ever get used to the shit people do to each other."

"That's a fact," Curtis said somberly. "Anything else around the scene worth noting? Tire impressions? Footprints? A big-ass sign identifying who did this to her?"

Sawyer shook his head. "Don't I wish. Except for the purse, not much left behind. I'd bet dollars to donuts the perp used an accelerant, but there's no container or can around. We can have the tech bag the ashes, check for fibers. I don't know, maybe we can pull a print off the rocks." He tipped his head back in thought. "We are gonna have a hell of a time determining time of death though. It's not like we can get a liver temp or check for rigor, right? And it's anyone's guess if this is where she was killed or if it's just where the bad guy dumped her."

Determining where the crime took place, as well as time of death, was often the key to solving a crime. Curtis tossed a glance at Deputy Cummings. "What do you think, Danny? Anything jump out at you? Maybe something in her purse?"

Dan shrugged. "Nothing in her purse, but I did find something weird. Not sure if it ties in at all, though. Follow me."

Curtis trailed behind the deputy to a spot a few yards away from the body and behind a large fir tree. There, on a flat rock, sat a perfectly square, unblemished block of wood. It reminded Curtis of a smooth piece of corner trim one would find in a home improvement store. On top of it was a silver bell, along with a necklace of beads coiled into what looked like the number three. When Curtis peered closer, he realized it was not a necklace.

It was a set of rosary beads.

. . .

Thomas Palmer slid off the ATV, medical bag in hand. He inhaled and turned his head on a swivel, his mind registering the sights and sounds of death. He knew he should be somber; he knew it was wrong of him to love these types of call-outs. But the truth was, he loved his job.

So sue me.

He snapped on gloves, lifted each foot to slide on a yellow shoe covering, and ducked beneath the crime scene tape. Whistling, he walked over to Dan and stopped.

"What do you have, Danny boy? It looks like a crispy critter but smells like French fries and pork roll."

Dan frowned. "Jesus, Thomas, could you be any cruder? A woman is dead here."

The coroner shrugged. "Can't bleed for 'em all, Danny me boy. Can't bleed for 'em all."

Dan's eyes flashed with anger. "Not asking you to bleed for anyone, Palmer; just asking for a little respect for the dead. Anyway, nice of you to join us—we've been standing here, holding our johnsons, for over an hour."

Annoyed, Thomas growled, "You aren't the only ones dealing with a death, Cummings. Our office handles several counties. I got here when I got here."

Overhearing the heated exchange, Curtis approached the men. "Doctor Palmer? I'm Agent Curtis Valdez, DCI. Appreciate you coming out."

Thomas gave Curt a weak handshake. "Not a doctor, son, just a man familiar with death. Nice to meet you," he said half-heartedly. "What can you tell me about the deceased?"

Curtis turned and walked toward the body, looking behind to ensure the coroner was following. "The remains appear to be female, burned beyond recognition facially, but with some appendages intact. We've taken photos and measurements, scouted around for tire or footprint impressions, and searched for bullet casings or anything else that appeared off. No luck there, but we found a few cigarette butts and a soda can, which we've bagged. There was also a block of wood, a silver bell, and a set of rosary beads nearby, though we don't know yet if they come into play here. We can't see any obvious blood or bodily tissue on any of them."

"I see," Palmer said, opening his bag and pulling out a notebook. "Has your tech found anything?"

"Not so far. He's taken several samples from what's left of the body and bagged a good portion of the ashes. Impossible to tell right now if she was clothed. If she was, maybe we can get some hair or fibers within the ashes to help with a positive ID. It looks like both hands and a foot survived the flames, so maybe we get lucky with prints." Walking a few feet away, he called out, "Hey, JP? Any suggestions on how we get her out of here?"

Burke's face flushed. "Um, sorry fellas, but I think we have to hoof it. I can bring you a basket stretcher, and we can carry her back to the trail. Since I'm used to it, I can do most of the heavy lifting. Unfortunately, out here, it's our only option."

Super, Curtis thought grimly. *Guess I can skip the gym today.*

Callie shoved a make-up kit into her small suitcase and attempted to zip it. She'd miraculously crammed everything she would need for her trip to Laredo in the suitcase, but now it wouldn't close. She'd tried pulling and pushing, leaning her body weight on top of the luggage. Frustrated, she blew the hair out of her eyes, climbed onto the bed, and plopped down on the case.

"You know, you could ask someone for help," Katie said from somewhere in the room.

Not looking up, grunting with effort, Callie replied, "Not on your life, sister."

Amused, Katie said, "Yeah, well, I'm dead, so ..."

"Always the wise ass, aren't ya? Honestly, have you been paying attention to these jokers, Kates? I swear, if assholes could fly, this place would be an airport. The last thing I need in this house full of testosterone is to play the damsel in distress card. I'd rather walk around the streets of Laredo, naked and blindfolded, then ask anyone in this joint for help."

Katie clucked her tongue. "Cutting off your nose to spite your face, huh? How perfectly Callahan of you. And they used to say I was the stubborn one!"

"You *were* the stubborn one, Kates. I was the more, shall we say, cautious of the two."

Katie grinned. "Cautious my ass, Shadow. Pig-headed? Maybe. Saucy? Definitely!" She sat on the edge of the bed. "Tell me, what's going on in Laredo?"

Callie wriggled off the suitcase and faced her sister. "Wait, you don't know? Jake and I are headed there to look for someone, anyone, who may have been close to that pinhead, Gabriel." She pursed her lips. "I'm confused. You're a ghost, so aren't you supposed to, like, know stuff?"

Katie laughed. "Just because I'm dead, Shadow, doesn't mean I'm omnipotent. I know about as much as you do, usually. But every now and again, the powers that be allow me to see a little more; feel a little more."

"Like when you warned me about the tractor-trailer fixing to turn me into its new hood ornament?"

"Exactly like that."

Callie nodded. "And have those finicky beings on the other side handed you any other insights?"

Katie shook her head. "Unfortunately, no. I don't know where Gabriel is hiding, can't even sense him anymore. Something, or someone, else has taken his place. And, although I cannot see them, I can feel them, feel their dark and wicked soul."

"Someone worse than him? Jesus, Kate, I hope you're wrong."

"I wish I was, Shadow." As she faded away, she added, "Be careful, Callie. I love you."

⌐

"You about ready? Our flight leaves in a few hours."

Jake stood at the open doorway to Callie's apartment, bending down to greet Lucky. Callie had set her suitcase outside the door and was doing a last-minute walkthrough. Although they only planned on being in Texas for a few days, she couldn't help but feel like she forgot something.

She called to him from her tiny kitchen. "Just give me a few minutes. I feel as though I'm missing something. Do you think Jed is okay with dog-sitting Lucky? I don't want to overstep here."

Jake lifted her suitcase. "It'll be fine. Lucky is a good girl, and I'm sure Caleb will have a blast with her. You worry too much, you know that, Blaze?"

Callie huffed. "For your information, Barney, it's called having good manners. You should try it sometime." Pushing her hair away from her face, she snipped, "Honestly, Jake, you could start an argument in an empty house."

Jake's chest heaved as he struggled to hold in a laugh. She was cute when she was pissed off. Instead, he blinked with feigned innocence. "Me? Why, I'm probably the most well-mannered guy you'll ever meet. I'd put Emily Post to shame."

Callie shot him a chilly look. "Right," she said dryly. "Well, how about you take the dog over to the main house while I get his bowls and food together, Emily."

Jake smirked and adjusted the suitcase in his hand. He whistled for Lucky, and the pup followed him down the stairs to the driveway. Callie took one more glance around, picked up her wallet, and turned for the door. Out of the corner of her eye, she saw a flash, a shadow dart from one end of the kitchen to the other. It was about four feet tall, black, and unidentifiable as either animal or human.

What the hell was that?

Spooked, she crept away from the front door, through the living room, to the entrance of the kitchen. Peeking around the doorframe, she scanned all four corners of the room, heart pounding, then chastised herself for being afraid.

Jesus, Callie, get a grip. There's nothing there!

Still, she couldn't shake the irrational fear that something actually was there, watching. She looked around one last time, then headed outside, making a mental note to call Darby as soon as possible.

If anyone could provide clarity on what she may or may not have seen, it was Darby Harrison.

"So, when do you think you'll be back?" Jed asked Jake as they stood inside the foyer.

"A few days tops. I think the whole thing may be a bust, but we may as well give it a shot."

Jed nodded. "And you and Callie? Is everything okay there?"

Jake looked at him blankly, so Jed tried again.

"You two seem," he pressed his lips and arched a brow, "there seems to be a tension between you two. Just an observation from an outsider, mind you."

"What the hell are you talking about?" Jake asked, suddenly annoyed.

"You know, things seemed a bit ... strained at the meeting." Jed held up his hands. "Don't kill the messenger, but do you want to know what I think?"

"Not particularly."

Ignoring him, Jed continued. "The whole thing reminds me of Harper DeLuca. Remember her?"

Jake felt his face flush. "My ex? What does my ex, one from fifteen years ago, have to do with Callie and me?"

"Well, see, I remember how torn up you were when she dumped you for that other guy. You know, the law school dude? What was his name again?" Jed asked, already knowing the answer.

"Can't recall," Jake lied.

Blake Cobb! Jake's mind screamed. *The guy's name is Blake Cobb. It's tattooed on my brain!*

Jed hid a smirk. "Anyway, so old what's-his-name came into the picture and stole her heart. You left for the academy, and they went out for what? A New York minute? Afterward, I'd occasionally see her around town, and she would stop to ask about you." He shrugged. "I tried to ignore her, tried to hate her even, but you know what? She was a good person, Jake. Pretty, funny, smart. And even though I associated her with the pain you went through, I looked forward to running into her. I was, I don't know, drawn to her."

Jake growled low. "So, what then? Are you saying you wanted to be pals? Do each other's hair and nails? Or, maybe, you just wanted to fu—"

Jed stopped him. "No, not like that, Jake. I mean, not that the thought hadn't crossed my mind, but, no, that isn't what I am saying at all."

Jake strode to the front door and reached for the handle. Without turning around, he asked, "Then what are you saying, junior? 'Cause I gotta be honest, you're really starting to piss me off."

Jed scrubbed his face. "What I'm saying is that maybe you need to let it go. You're holding on to the past so fiercely, it's blinded you to what's right in front of you. I think when you look at Callie, you're reminded of her sister." He stepped behind Jake and placed a hand on his shoulder. "All I'm saying, Jacob, is that Callie isn't Kate. She is a living, breathing, gorgeous woman who, I think, could be good for you. So don't let the dreams of something that will never be mess with the possibility of something that could damn well be your future. That's all I'm saying."

Shrugging out of Jed's grip, Jake opened the door and stepped outside. As he stormed away, he tossed back, "Callie is the only one on this crew with a psychology degree, little brother. You'd do well to remember that."

The slam of the door brought Faith into the foyer. Drying her hands on a towel, she asked, "Dae ah even wanna ken what that was aboot, then?"

Jed smiled. "I'm not sure. Could be that I hit a nerve Jake didn't even know he had." He threw an arm over her shoulder. "C'mon, I'm starved. Let's go eat."

~

Mood foul, the Disciple glared at his computer screen and flipped through the entries in the Confessions Room on Live Feed. He was looking for something special, something that would prove more challenging than Nora Grant had been.

Scrolling through the dozens of posts, eyes glazed, he found it difficult to concentrate. After watching Nora burn for a while, he left the canyon and went straight to St. Michaels, to Father Gabriel, eager to share with him the glory of the kill.

"And you did what I said?" Gabriel asked, eyes searching. "You left the rosary?"

Annoyed, the Disciple squirmed in the confessional booth, sitting on his hands to avoid reaching through the screen and throttling the priest. "You know, Padre, you suck at listening. I already told you I did. Now, do you want to hear about how she died or not?"

"Of course, I do," Gabriel placated. "I just wanted to make sure you were sticking to the plan. Everything we do from here on out hinges on discipline and caution. If you slip up, our mission is over. Now," he said, hands folded on his lap, "tell me all about it."

And so he did. The Disciple left nothing out, feeling his groin stir as he described Nora's last moments alive. Reliving it left him euphoric.

"Did you see anything when she died? A light or a glow?" Gabriel asked. "How about the scene? Did you take anything from her, like clothing or jewelry? Trophies can only lead to discovery, my son. Don't give anyone a reason to suspect you."

"No, Padre. Sorry to disappoint, but I saw no bright lights, colored stars, or white angels. And I took nothing except the joy of watching her die."

And a lock of her hair, but you don't need to know that, asshole.

After he left the church, the Disciple hurried home, giddy with the possibility of finding another victim. Although, truthfully, he thought of them more like sacrificial lambs than victims. Their deaths would prove to the world that consequences had actions, that you couldn't just shit all over people and expect them to shake it off, beg for more.

Now, as he scrolled through all the posts on the Confessions site, he worried he would not find as suitable a victim as Nora Grant. And then, just when he was about to give up for the night, he'd found her.

Naomi Vaughn.

CHAPTER TEN

"... and if at the end of that time you cannot tell my name, you must give up the child to me." —The Brothers Grimm

Naomi Vaughn sat on the toilet lid, whispered a prayer to the heavens, then sliced the razor across her skin for the sixth time that day. She watched, unashamed, as blood dripped from the freshly opened wound, slid around the crescent shape of her upper thigh, and landed with a plop on the bathroom floor. The cuts from her earlier sessions, crusted with dried blood, nestled snugly among the older scars that marched up and down her thigh.

Yet, despite the many attempts to release her pain, nothing changed. She still felt numb, disconnected, unworthy.

The sound of a baby's cry brought her to her feet. Cassidy needed to eat. Cassidy would need to be changed. Cassidy would need to be swaddled and rocked and shushed.

She was beginning to detest Cassidy.

Naomi tried to be a good mother. She set up play dates, posted the appropriate number of pictures to her social media accounts, made sure all of Cassidy's foods were organic. Her friends told her what an amazing mom she was, and her coworkers lavished her with praise for juggling the single-mom routine.

But none of them had a clue of the battle she fought every damned day when she was alone. No one was aware of the frightening thoughts that banged on the doorway of her mind, begging to be released, forcing her to acknowledge the truth.

She hated being a mother.

To twenty-five-year-old Naomi, babies were needy and gross and time-consuming. She believed that once fate gave someone the gift of bringing a new life into the world, it demanded you give something in return. And so, every day for the last two-hundred and twelve days, she felt another piece of herself break off and dissolve into nothingness. Chunks of what she once was crumbled to the ground as the universe sucked at her soul, chipping away at her very core.

Until all that remained was a shell of the woman she once remembered.

It was like suffocating in a bag no one else could see.

Needing an escape, Naomi revisited a coping mechanism she'd developed as a teen—the art of cutting. Years ago, she'd picked up a razor more than once, attempting to escape the dysfunction of her family. It was about reminding herself that she was a real person, one with fears and hopes and feelings—a person who mattered.

A person who bled.

Some days it worked, some days it didn't. But one thing it always seemed to do was give her a sense of control.

Until Cassidy.

Cassidy, her second child, was the product of a one-night stand involving a gorgeous stranger, a van, and a shameful amount of tequila. Cassidy's father, a confirmed bachelor and self-proclaimed 'player', sent Naomi child support checks every month, but had yet to meet his daughter. Naomi didn't really blame him for that. After all, he thought he was just getting a quick lay with an easy girl. He never expected the hook-up would produce a child.

Her first-born, a boy, was delivered on the evening of her sixteenth birthday party at a local bowling alley. Naomi, unaware that she was even pregnant, gave birth on lane three, while a dozen or so teenage friends looked on in horror.

Shortly after his birth, she gave baby boy Vaughn up for adoption. Ignoring the scarlet letter she wore on her chest after his birth, Naomi continued her education despite the hostile glances and schoolgirl gossip. In public, she held her head high, refusing to let the others see how hurt she truly was.

But privately, the pain of rejection by her peers was crushing.

Naomi fared no better with her family. Ostracized by her siblings, constantly criticized for her past, she turned to self-harm to gain some semblance of control. Now, after caring for her unwanted child for the last seven months with no support system, she found the razor in her hands once again. It was the only thing that made her feel connected to humanity.

Except for LiveFeed.

LiveFeed was her guilty pleasure; the Confessions room, her salvation. Within that community, she could be herself, share and bitch and say out loud what she'd felt in her heart since Cassidy was born.

She did not want her child.

After giving birth, the motherly instincts—the nurturing, loving, selfless traits said to visit every mother—never arrived. That fierce need to protect your child, knowing you would sooner rip off your legs than hurt your offspring, failed to materialize. Instead, she was left feeling hopeless and hollow, a void filled only by sharing her secret with others.

Mothers who, like her, resented their children.

She wiped the blood from her thigh and stiffly, robotically, left the bathroom to care for her child. Naomi knew she would never hurt Cassidy, could never hurt her. After all, she was just a baby.

It wasn't Cassidy's fault her mother was a fucked-up nightmare.

After feeding and changing the baby, Naomi put Cassidy down for a nap and went to the kitchen. Opening her laptop, she scrolled down through the latest posts in *Confessions*, occasionally stopping to read an entry. Today, the participants seemed especially shy about sharing their stories.

To Naomi, the lack of transparency was like waving a red flag at a bull. She felt an overwhelming need to tell her story, to start the conversation.

So she did.

Hey everyone! So, today was an exceptionally shitty day. I admit, I almost bailed on more than one occasion. It's so frustrating! I want nothing more than to adore my child, to be the mommy that she deserves. But the truth is, every day, I feel more and more like a rat in a maze, frantically seeking that reward of a block of cheese.

And desperately searching for a way out.

I'm ashamed to tell you, but recently, I resorted to some old, self-destructive habits. The feel of the blade as it glides through my skin, the sudden burn as the flesh splits apart, seems to center me.

Cutting is my crutch when I need release, distraction, and the freedom to be me again. It's the only way I've found to fight my biggest fear—losing control.

But, surprise, surprise, this time, cutting didn't work.

How can I be like this? What kind of mother doesn't love her child, doesn't want to be with her? It isn't fair to Cassidy, and it isn't fair to me. I need help, serious help. I should give her up, right? She would have a much better life if she were with a family who loves her, dotes on her. Don't you guys think?

Please, just please, give me some advice. Because right now, heaven help me, I would sell my kid to the highest bidder just to save myself from the prospect of raising her.

And that, my friends, is the definition of fucked up.

She punched the 'enter' button on the keyboard. And waited.

"It's nice to talk to someone who doesn't look down on me or judge me for my past." Naomi typed into the chat. "For the longest time, like forever, I've beaten myself up for giving up that baby at sixteen. I think that's why I kept Cassidy. I did it out of guilt, not love." She toyed with a string on her hooded sweatshirt. "Does that make me a horrible person?"

The Disciple smiled. He had this bitch right where he wanted her. "Of course not, Naomi. On the contrary, I think recognizing that your motives for keeping the child were less than altruistic makes you an honest, as well as beautiful, woman. And we can surely use more beauty in the world, can't we?"

Naomi blushed. "Elijah Price! If I didn't know any better, I'd say you were flirting with me!"

The Disciple tapped a finger on the table, deciding what to write next. He didn't want to rush her, but neither did he want to listen to her whiny, pathetic drivel longer than necessary. They'd been chatting for two days already, and as far as he was concerned, it was two days too long.

"Say, I know just what you need! Do you hike?"

Naomi laughed. "Hike? Like, in the woods?"

"In the spectacular Bighorn Mountains! The sweet mountain air and gorgeous scenery will do you a world of good! Can you meet me there?"

Naomi chewed a thumbnail. It would be reckless of her to agree to a trek into the mountains with a stranger. Reckless and dangerous and foolhardy.

But irresponsibility was what she craved. She was sick of the chains of motherhood. Sick of being tied down, missing out on everything she should be enjoying at her age.

It was her time now.

"Okay, I'll do it!" she typed quickly before she lost her nerve. "Where should I meet you?"

"There is a picnic area in Little Goose Canyon, west of Red Grade Road on Bighorn Mountain. You ever hear of it?"

"Oh, sure," Naomi said, "I've been up there with a friend who is a photographer. She wanted company as she photographed some pictures of the view. It was stunning."

The Disciple smiled. "Yes, it surely is. If you meet me at the picnic area, we can head out from there. I know a trail that will lead us straight to a magnificent waterfall. I tell you, you get a gander of that, and you'll feel like a new woman."

She shouldn't. She knew she shouldn't. She didn't care.

"Yes, Elijah, I will meet you. When? What time?"

He closed his eyes, basking in his victory. He would never tire of this part of the ritual; setting the bait, casting the net, reeling it all in.

"Tomorrow," he said, finally. "Meet me at the picnic area tomorrow at noon. Oh, and Naomi? You won't be sorry."

Naomi ended the call, hands shaking and knees weak.

What the hell did I just do? she asked herself. *Meeting a man in the mountains? A man I don't know? In the middle of bum-fuck Wyoming? I must be nuts!*

She peeked in on Cassidy, who was still fast asleep, and then went to her bedroom. Rummaging through her dresser drawer, she pulled out a pair of blue tactical pants and a long-sleeved T-shirt with a target in the center and the words 'I Aim to Please' lettered inside. Placing the clothes on her bed, she walked to the closet to find her hiking boots. Then, taking a deep breath, she phoned her best friend, Suzanne, to ask her to watch Cassidy tomorrow.

She was seriously going to do this.

Naomi looked around the deserted picnic area of Little Goose Canyon, its rusted hibachi grills and battered tables a testament to a long-forgotten destination, and bit her lip. There was no sign of anyone. No cars, no motorcycles. Just her, the piece of shit Honda she called Tonka, and her nearly new hiking boots.

I'm such an idiot!

Taking one last glance around, angry with herself for falling for such a cruel trick, she opened the car door, threw her knapsack into the back, and tucked herself into the driver's seat once again. She'd no sooner fastened her seat belt and started the car when a knock on the drivers-side window caused her to jump.

A man stood outside, tapping the glass with a gloved fist. He wore a black hooded sweatshirt, jeans, and an apologetic smile.

Naomi tensed, wary.

"Naomi? It's me, Elijah Price. Sorry I'm late!" He smiled again, warm and genuine, and she felt her guard lower.

Rolling down her window, she said, "Oh, hi. I thought maybe you weren't coming."

He shook his head. "No, no, nothing like that. I just figured I would get an extra few miles in today, so I parked about a mile and a half from here." Shrugging, gleam in his eye, he joked, "I suppose my body never got the memo from my brain that said, 'You're not in half as good a shape as you think you are.'"

Naomi giggled. It was going to be alright. It was going to be just fine.

They hiked for thirty minutes before stopping to sit on a rock at the edge of a rolling stream. Grabbing a water bottle from her backpack, Naomi said, "It truly is stunning, isn't it? It's as though God created this tranquil corner of the world specifically for the downtrodden. Like, with the wisdom only He possesses, he conjured up a retreat or a haven, one meant to rejuvenate the soul and release your worries. I should get up this way more often." She looked at Elijah and smiled sadly. "Unfortunately, with a seven-month-old and a full-time job, getting away is damned near impossible."

The Disciple narrowed his eyes. "Yes, I'm sure," he said coolly. "About that. I must say I was quite taken with your honesty. Writing what you did, baring your soul, couldn't have been easy. After all, few people would admit to hating their child."

Naomi's head snapped up, her eyes meeting his. "I—I don't hate Cassidy. I just don't feel like I love her with a mother's love is all."

"I see." He stood, pacing in small circles as he spoke. "So all the talk about giving your child up, selling her to the highest bidder, resenting having to care for her? All of that was just what? Venting? I'm not sure Cassidy would see it that way."

Naomi was becoming uncomfortable. And angry. Who was he to judge her?

"Well, since she is an infant, the way she sees things isn't a concern. And, since you have no children of your own, you really have no business offering me advice or making judgments." She stood as well. "I thought you understood what I was going through, Elijah, understood the torment I feel. It's obvious to me now that I was mistaken." She picked up her backpack and slung it over her shoulder. "I'd like to leave now. I think I've had enough for the day. I need to get back to my daughter."

The Disciple was in front of her in a blink, taking two angry steps, getting within inches of her face. He clenched his jaw, his breath stale and hot upon her cheeks. "*You've* had enough? You *need* to get back to your daughter? That's rich, coming from a woman who's made it her mission to shit on her children." He grabbed her throat and moved forward, pushing her toward the tree line. "We are going to take a little walk now, Naomi. Play nice with me, and maybe I won't kill you. Nod if you understand."

Naomi's eyes were wide, her fingers pulling at the hand that was crushing her windpipe. When she didn't nod, the Disciple squeezed harder.

Oh God, oh God, oh God! Her mind screamed. *I'm so stupid! Why did I come here!*

Tears streaming down her face, her heart galloping and lungs gasping for air, she nodded. He nudged her, and they began to walk, he forward and her backward. Naomi's eyes never left his face, her brain aware he had yet to let up on the compression to her throat. Her thin fingers continued to tug at the hand gripping her neck.

But the Disciple was too strong, his hand massive against her slender throat.

In a few moments, minutes that seemed an eternity to Naomi, the Disciple stopped inside a thick grouping of aspen trees. He shoved her to her knees, letting up ever-so-slightly on the pressure to her neck.

"Say my name," he said, his eyes cold, his voice dead, emotionless.

Naomi blinked her pleading, terrified eyes. "Elijah," she croaked roughly. "E-Elijah Price."

The Disciple shook his head. "Nope, try again. I will give you three guesses. If you don't come up with my name, I will kill you and steal your child."

Naomi blinked in confusion, fighting the storm of panic raging in her mind.

What the fuck is he talking about? Oh, please! Someone, help me!

"You have two more guesses, Naomi," he said calmly. "Choose wisely. Death by strangulation is not ..." he hesitated, "... not a pleasant death. Minutes can feel like an eternity when your brain is starving for oxygen. Now, my name."

Naomi scrambled for ideas, clues as to his real identity. But there was nothing. She'd only known him as Elijah Price, which, obviously, was an alias. He'd given nothing away in their conversations.

"Please," she whispered hoarsely. He still had a tight grip on her neck. "How can I know that? Please, let me go! I won't tell!"

"Tick Tock, Nay Nay."

Jesus Christ, help me!

"Levi," she blurted, voice strained. She wasn't sure why she'd called out the name. It was the first name that popped into her head.

Cassidy's father's name was Levi.

The Disciple made a buzzer sound, as if her incorrect response was part of a game show. "Wrong answer, Nay Nay. One more try."

Her stomach cramped, and she thought she would vomit. Urine ran down her legs, a consequence of both her fear and the reduced oxygen to her brain. If only he let up. If only she had a minute to think, maybe she could come up with the answer.

But her time was up. She could see it in the glint of his eyes.

"Satan!" she rasped. "Your fucking name is Satan! And your father was a cunt, your mother, a whore!"

The Disciple laughed. "You have no idea how spot-on you are about that, my dear. But, sadly, my name is not Satan. Although, how cool would that be?" Not waiting for a reaction, he dug into a front pocket with his free hand and produced a length of golden string, thick as a cord. Naomi kicked at his groin and punched his back and head with her hands. He grunted, but successfully pushed her against a tree and wrapped the cord around her neck.

Screaming without uttering a sound, vision fading, Naomi kicked feebly, her punches becoming pathetic and weak. Her legs were heavy, her hands incapable of making a fist. He grinned, squeezing hard, saliva bubbling in the corners of his mouth.

This was the best part.

. . .

Whistling a cheerful tune, he stripped Naomi's still form of her clothing and positioned her, legs splayed suggestively, beneath a nearby pine tree.

You spread your legs in life, it's only fitting you spread 'em in death.

He opened his satchel and dug deep, rummaging around the bottom of the leather bag. His fingers wrapped around the container he was searching for, and he pulled it free. Releasing the lid, he removed the items from inside and looked around. He needed the perfect spot to display them. His eyes landed on a fallen tree about ten feet away from the glassy-eyed corpse that was once Naomi Vaughn. The log lay perpendicular to the body, with a broad base and a flat, smooth surface, like a tabletop. Or an altar.

Perfect.

CHAPTER ELEVEN

"Are you sure you want to park the Explorer here for days?" Callie asked. "The airport is not always the safest place to leave a car."

Jake shrugged. "Most convenient thing for us to do, since we have no clue how long we will be in Laredo. Long-term parking is well-lit, and there are usually people milling about. It will be fine."

"You say so. It's your ass, Cochise. Well, it's your car, anyway."

Feisty little thing, Jake thought, smirking.

They walked through the terminal and to their departing gate with an hour to spare before boarding for Laredo.

"How about I go get us a couple of coffees?" he asked. "I need to check in with Jed, anyway. And I want to call Sully, get an update on Gus."

Sully was Ian Sullivan, Jake's partner in DC. He was caring for Jake's Bernese Mountain dog, Gus, while he was in Montana on leave.

"Sure. I think I'll call Darby and check on Blue as well. Maybe we should suggest a play date for the dogs. You know, get them together with their caretakers." She wiggled her brows, and Jake laughed.

"Don't think I don't know what you're doing, Blaze. Matchmaking? Cute thought, but asking Darby and Sully to arrange a playdate might be a little obvious, don't you think?"

Callie shrugged. "Stranger things have happened. Besides, the dogs love each other." She looked away, dispirited. "And with Chance gone, Blue could sure use a friend."

Ever since Gabriel killed Blue's best friend, Chance, he had been a different dog. Solemn, endlessly roaming the house, occasionally issuing a mournful whine. Losing both Katie and Chance had devastated him, and Callie wasn't sure how to help.

Jake unzipped his carry-on bag and took out his cell phone. "Don't beat yourself up, Callahan. Blue will adjust." Beneath his breath, he added, "Just like we've all had to do."

Callie heard him, but didn't respond. There was no need. Gabriel's vicious actions left them all hurting.

"Be right back. Stay where I can see you. And don't talk to any strangers, you hear?" Jake told her, only half-joking.

As he walked to the small coffee kiosk, Callie called after him. "You bet, Mister Boss Man, sir. Thank God you're here to protect me from the perils of society."

Jake stopped a few feet away from her and turned. "Why do you always have to be like that?"

She shrugged. "Same reason you always have to treat me like a child and an imbecile, I guess. Entertainment."

"Imbec ...?" he stuttered, shaking his head. "You're a lot of things, Callahan, but an imbecile isn't one of them."

She watched him leave, surprised at her knee-jerk reaction to his words and feeling a tug of remorse for mocking him.

But he can be so condescending!

Sighing, she pulled out her phone and dialed a number she now knew by heart. Darby picked up on the first ring.

"Cal? Jesus, how are you? You had me worried! Why haven't

you called? Is Jake okay? What the dickens is going on in Montana?"

Darby had a habit of chattering non-stop when nervous. Usually, Callie found it endearing, but today, with so much on her mind, it was distracting.

"We're fine, Darbs. Don't worry so much, you're gonna give yourself a stroke. The minute things go sideways, you'll be my first call, alright? Anyway, I was calling for a few reasons. First, though, how is my boy?"

"Holding his own, I suppose. I swear, Cal, sometimes when he looks at me, I can almost hear his thoughts. Weird, right? Maybe it's his expressive Labrador eyes, but good golly, Miss Molly, I can get right inside his head."

Callie sighed loudly. "That bad, huh? Maybe I should come and get him. He may do better here, with Lucky and Caleb to focus on."

"Caleb?"

"Oh, yeah, I haven't spoken to you in a while. Caleb is the adorable son of Faith McTavish, a woman who works for Jed. The boy has taken quite a liking to Lucky. They're pretty much inseparable lately."

"Aww, that's sweet. Well, it's up to you, but that is such a long-ass ..." she stopped, then snapped her fingers. "Hold the phone, Gertrude! What if I came out there with him? To you, I mean? I'm due a vacation anyway, and I'd love to see you guys. I can drive out, have Trish manage the shop. She's out of work right now and would love that!"

Callie's cousin, Trish, was the daughter of Eileen Callahan's brother, Tim. Tim Kelly helped Callie's grandmother raise the four Callahan children—Finn, Katie, Callie, and Ryan—following the loss of their parents.

Callie smiled. "You know I would absolutely love it, Darbs, but that's asking too much. It's a long trip from Virginia. Plus, you love your store. How will you be able to stay away?"

Darby huffed. "You listen up, missy. First, you aren't asking too much because, if you remember correctly, you didn't ask, I offered. And second, 'Time and Time Again' will do just dandy without me. Honestly, I could use the distraction, Cal. Katie's absence is fudging up my Feng Shui. I need to get centered again, balanced. And my self-help books can only do so much. You guys would be helping me out, not the other way around."

Callie smiled. "Okay, it's a deal! We're heading to Texas to follow up on a potential lead, but I'll call you when we get back. Now, speaking of your self-help books, I had something strange happen to me before we left, and I wanted to get your take on it." Callie paced in her small corner of the seating area, keeping her voice low and an eye out for Jake. She wasn't ready to include him, or anyone else in the airport, in this part of the conversation.

"I'm all ears."

Callie studied a poster on the wall, an advertisement for a brand of Irish whiskey that depicted four dogs playing canasta and drinking from highball glasses.

Well, that's silly—everyone knows dogs prefer poker.

"Strap in, buttercup, 'cause this is gonna sound strange." Her eyes roamed around the immediate area, stopping on a woman who stood near a collection of garbage cans. She wore an airport employee uniform and was trying to gather up trash bags near the escalator.

Which was proving impossible, given that she was dead.

Seeing spirits in the airport now, Callahan? Super! What's next? A ghost trying to serve your order of fries at Mickey D's?

She closed her eyes and focused on her conversation with Darby. "Sorry I'm so scattered today, Darbs. My brain is jumping around like hot grease on a skillet."

"Welcome to my world."

"Yeah, no kidding. Anyway, a little while ago, at the apartment at Jed's house, I saw a dark mass, a shadow that stood about four feet tall and was quick as lightning. Honestly, I couldn't say if it was human, spirit or ... something else. It was in and out of my field of vision that fast. I think I may have seen the same shadow in the back seat of my car recently as well."

As she spoke, she heard Darby scribbling on a notepad. "Hmm, weird. I'll have to do some research on this one. Not sure what it could be."

Callie looked up just as Jake approached with two steaming coffee cups. "I have to go now, Darby. Talk soon. Let me know when you are planning on coming, okay?"

They hung up, and Jake handed Callie her cup. "Coming? Is Darby planning on visiting out here?"

Callie blew on the steaming beverage and took a tiny sip, the flaming liquid stinging her tongue and burning her throat.

"Egad, but that's a hot cup of Joe," she said.

Jake laughed.

"Yes, Darby wants to come out here and bring Blue. I told her we would love to have her." She peeked at him under thick, lush lashes. "I hope that's okay?"

Jake studied her for a moment. "Why wouldn't it be? You worry too much, you know that Blaze? Someday, it's gonna give you ulcers."

"I think that ship has already sailed. On another topic, though, I wanted to tell you I did one of those ancestral DNA kits the other day. I put a rush on it, so I am hoping I get the results while we are still in Laredo."

Jake looked at her blankly. "DNA? What for?"

The airport loudspeaker interrupted her, announcing it was time to board. They both slung their bags over a shoulder and began the short walk to the gate, tossing their unfinished coffees into a nearby trash can.

"Well," she explained as they walked, "we don't know if Gabriel has any other family. I mean, I loved my dad with all my heart, but he was an adulterer. What if he fathered more than one illegitimate child?"

Jake squinted his eyes. "Okay. What if?"

"If I'm his half-sister, any relatives who've done an ancestry-type test should come up as kin for me. A long-lost brother or sister out there will be swimming in the same gene pool. So maybe the psycho bastard found out about them and reached out, tried to connect? Worth a shot, anyhow."

Jake looked at her, impressed. "Yeah, Blaze. Definitely worth a shot."

～

Agent Curtis Valdez and Deputy Daniel Cummings pulled in front of the modest brick ranch that was once Nora Grant's home. The place was in rough shape, its peeling paint and broken shutters a startling contrast to the perfectly manicured lawn and beautiful gardens. Evidently, Nora preferred the serenity of the landscape over the aesthetics of the building.

Curtis stepped out of the Sheriff's vehicle. "Did you phone the house ahead of time, Danny?"

"I did," Dan said, as they walked to the front door. "Evelyn Leonard, Ms. Grant's friend, is staying here, looking after the children until the family makes other arrangements. Seems those kids got a raw deal in life and will need a steady hand rowing the boat over the next few months, not a rudderless ship."

"What do you mean?"

"Let's just say those kids are strangers to stability. Their father, Matthew Grant, is out of the picture which, after reading his old arrest records, may not be a bad thing. Nothing too crazy, certainly nothing that immediately screams 'suspect' in this killing, but worth a look."

"True that. Remind me to look at Matthew Grant's rap sheet when we finish up here." Curtis rang the bell, then glanced down at his notes. "The local police report states that Evelyn was the last person to see Nora alive. According to her statement, she became concerned when Nora didn't come home right away, but not shocked. Apparently, it wasn't the first time Ms. Grant stayed out later than planned. I'm just hoping ..." He stopped speaking when the front door creaked open.

A middle-aged woman with graying hair and sad eyes stood behind the glass storm-door. Unhooking the latch, she swung the door wide, holding it open for them.

"You must be the investigators. I'm Evelyn Leonard. Come in, come in."

They thanked her and stepped into the foyer. "We don't mean to take too much of your time today, Ms. Leonard," Daniel said. "We just need to ask you a few questions, maybe look around a bit. Would that be alright with you?"

"Of course, of course. Please, come sit down." She led them into a country-style living room with a floral couch and two easy chairs. Easing herself down into a winged-back chair, she offered the sofa to Curtis and Daniel. "The kids, Bailey and little Matty, are in the playroom watching a movie. I'd rather not disturb them if we don't have to. They're so young and," she hesitated, her eyes teary. "Well, they've had a rough go is all. I've finally found something to distract them, at least for a while."

Curtis nodded. "Understood. We may need to speak to them in the future, but for today, we will give them their peace."

"Appreciate that," Evelyn said. "Can I get you anything? Coffee? Water?"

"No, we're good, thank you," Curtis said. He flipped open his notebook and began. "Miss Leonard, can you tell me what you remember about the last time you saw Nora?"

Evelyn reached over the stenciled trunk that served as a coffee table and pulled out a tissue from a box of Kleenex.

"Nora was excited and anxious all at once that day. She'd met someone online, someone new, and was going to see him. She'd already gone out with him once, the day before, for coffee at a local place." Evelyn dabbed her eyes and continued. "Her mood when she came back from that first date was ... giddy, I guess you'd say. Like a teenager swooning over her first kiss, Nora couldn't stop talking about the guy, said he'd invited her to go on a hike the next day. She was happier than I'd seen her in a long time."

Daniel cleared his throat. "Tell me, Evelyn. Is it okay with you if I call you Evelyn?" At her shy nod, he continued. "Evelyn, did Nora tell you anything about this guy? His name? Where he lived? How about the coffee shop they were going to?"

"Nothing about where he lived, although I assumed he was a local. I mean, he knew about that small coffee shop in Ranchester. You would think someone who knew about that had to be from the area, right?"

Curtis and Daniel nodded in agreement.

"And she told me his name. Such an odd one, too. It was Samuel. Samuel Jackson."

Curtis glanced at Daniel. "Not the most original alias I've ever heard."

Daniel shrugged. "If it is an alias. Could be his real name."

"Evelyn, is Nora's computer still here?" Curtis asked.

"Her laptop, yes. It's in her bedroom. Do you want me to get it?"

He shook his head. "If it's all the same to you, we'd like to look around first. We can get the laptop after we search her room."

Evelyn paled. "Search? Whatever for?"

Curtis stood and moved to the easy chair where she sat, then squatted down. "Clues, mostly. Sometimes, people jot things down, even subconsciously. Doodles and such. We need to check around, see if anything can point us to this guy." Smiling sadly, he added, "You know, sometimes it's the strangest things that pop up that can solve a case. Your cooperation in this whole thing will help us catch the person who did this to your friend."

Deputy Cummings listened, impressed. Interviewing a witness was an innate talent, an art. One that Curtis Valdez seemed to have in spades.

"Of course, whatever I can do to help." Evelyn stood. "Follow me. Her bedroom is right down the hall."

Investigator Adam Dempsey of the Laredo Office of Criminal Investigation stood at his open office door, grinning like a fool.

"Hot damn, son!" he said to Jake, shaking his hand enthusiastically. "So good to see you again!"

Jake grinned back. "You too, cowboy. How goes it? Sully sends his regrets that he couldn't make it out this trip, but, as I said on the phone, I'm operating kind of off the radar right now." He gently scooted Callie up next to him and said, "This is my assoc—" he caught himself, earning a wink from Callie. "This is my partner, Callie Callahan. Kate's sister."

Adam stuck out his hand, and they shook. "Pleasure, ma'am. I'm truly sorry to hear about the loss of your sister."

Callie nodded. "Thank you. I appreciate all you did to help the investigation. Both Jake and Sully have told me a lot about you." Raising a brow, she added quickly, "But don't worry, it was all good things. Mostly."

Adam laughed. He was a big man with kind eyes who could have been a poster child for a Texas rodeo: blue jeans, boots with spurs, Stetson hat. Everything about him screamed cowboy.

"I'm glad. I, on the other hand, have done nothing but trash talk them both to anyone who'd listen." He grinned again and stepped back, opening his office door wider. "But enough about this bozo. Come on in, take a load off. Can I get you anything? Food? Drink?" He hooked a thumb at Jake. "A one-way ticket away from this pompous jackass?"

Callie chuckled. "Don't tempt me. We appreciate you seeing us on such short notice."

"Happy to help. Have a seat."

They sat on the opposite side of Adam's desk. Jake loosened the tie around his neck and smirked. "You still love hearing yourself talk, don't ya, Dempsey? Glad nothing has changed since last I saw you."

"You know, Devereaux," Adam said, eyes playful, "you

Yankee's are like hemorrhoids. A pain in the ass when you come down, and always a relief when you go back up."

Grinning, Jake deadpanned, "Funny."

Callie shook her head and sighed. "Why do I always feel like a school monitor around you and your friends?" she asked. "Can we get to it, boys? Please?"

Adam's eyes found Jake's, and he smirked. Turning back to Callie, he said, "My apologies, Miss. I'm happy to help. So this brother of yours, this Gabriel/Jeremy guy? Well, it seems he's slicker'n owl shit. Ever since Jake called me, I've been runnin' all over hell's half-acre, trying to dig up some dirt on this guy, trying to find anyone he was close to. But, nada, zilch, nothing. Seems most folk recognize a snake when they see 'em."

Callie's shoulders slumped. "So, there's nothing then? I felt sure we would find someone he connected with."

"And didn't kill," Jake said sourly.

"Yeah, that too," Callie said. "So, what's next? Any ideas?"

Adam stood, walking over to a file cabinet. "Give me a little more time. I have some feelers out, contacted a few informants that'd sell their momma for a song. I figured it was reasonable to question whether he was into burglary, theft, or drugs. He has no work record that I can find, yet he had to live on something aside from hate and crazy, right? So, it could be the rat bastard made a living stealing. And if that's the case, the underbelly of Laredo just may have run into him."

"Sounds good. I'll reach out tomorrow," Jake said. Extending his hand, he added, "Can't thank you enough, brother. You've no idea how badly we want this son of a bitch."

"No thanks necessary. I'd like to take a piece of his hide myself."

~

"What now?" Callie asked, as they stepped into the bright afternoon sun.

"Let's hit the library. We can dig through old newspaper articles, focus on military news. Who knows? Maybe there is an article about our boy. Afterward, how about we grab a pizza and a six-pack and head to the hotel to eat? Not sure about you, but I'm getting mighty peckish over here."

Callie laughed lightly. They were following a course of action, had a strategy they were employing.

And just knowing that they had a game plan lifted her spirits considerably.

Hours later, they left the library with little information. There were two articles about Jeremy Sterling in a weekly column entitled "Call to Service," a section dedicated to spotlighting area servicemen and women and their families. One article simply stated that Jeremy was a local kid, Army bound, with no mention of his family.

The other article, only one sentence long, announced his reenlistment.

Jeremy's foster parents, Billy Ray and Jolene Porter, were strict disciplinarians with a history of physically abusing their charges. They housed Jeremy for a few years until he turned eighteen and aged out of the system.

Once the state checks stopped coming in, Billy Ray and Jolene kicked him out, and Jeremy joined the military. A few weeks later, the Porters were found dead in their basement.

Beaten, strangled, each with a set of rosary beads by their bodies.

Disappointed they didn't find more, Jake said, "You know, according to Adam Dempsey, Jeremy was a person of interest in the rape and murder of a neighbor, Samantha Norman. He was never charged, though. Apparently, his mother, Meredith, gave him an alibi for the time of the killing. Maybe we take a look at that murder and see if anything pops."

Callie agreed and, fifteen minutes later, they read a disturbing account of the torment Samantha Norman endured at the hands of her killer.

Callie left the library feeling grimy and weak-kneed.

"Well, that was a lovely way to end the day. Nothing like peering into the mind of a twisted psycho to make you feel all warm and fuzzy," Callie said, as they made their way to the car.

Jake nodded, somber. "Yeah, that was rough." Flicking his gaze toward her, he teased, "Hey, aren't you psychologist-type folk supposed to avoid using the term 'psycho'"?

Callie frowned. He was right ... she really shouldn't use that term. It was condescending, outdated, and cruel.

She didn't give a shit.

Thirty minutes later, they arrived at the hotel. Callie found it fancier than most of the hotels she frequented. Faith had made the arrangements, all on PIPPS dime.

Jed explained it was a business expense, a deductible he could use during tax time. Reluctantly, Jake and Callie agreed.

"I'll check us in, then we can commiserate over this miserable day with food and booze," Jake said. "I spoke to my brother earlier, and he tells me they secured us a suite on the top floor. Two bedrooms, two baths, and a tiny kitchen. Are you okay with us sharing a suite? If it makes you uncomfortable, I can get you another room."

"Don't be silly, it's fine. I am looking forward to a hot shower and some grub, though. I haven't eaten anything since that stale granola bar you offered me on the plane."

"Beggars can't be choosers, Blaze."

"Yeah, well, next time, bring jelly donuts."

He laughed and checked them into their suite. They took the elevator to the fourteenth floor, then followed the signs to Suite 1424. When they entered, Callie gasped.

The suite was newly renovated, with freshly painted walls and lush carpeting. She inhaled deeply, the fragrant mixture of pine cleaner, lavender, and sunshine tickling her nose.

"Good God, look at this place! Your brother sure knows how to live. This suite had to cost a fortune! I don't know about this, Jake. It's too much."

"Nah," Jake said, waving a hand. "You'd be surprised at the contacts Jed has. I'm sure he got this for a song." Rubbing his hands together, he said, "Now, let's find the delivery menu and order something. I'm starved."

They ordered a large pepperoni pizza from a local pizzeria, then plopped on the couch with the beer Jake picked up on the way to the hotel.

Clinking glasses, Jake said, "Cheers. Here's to a more informative day tomorrow."

"Right," Callie said, "although at least we know we are covering all our bases." She stood, walked to her overnight bag, and pulled out her laptop. "I'm going to check my email. I put that rush on the DNA test and want to see if anything came in."

Jake nodded. "Okay. While you do that, I'm going to jump in the shower. I should be out by the time the pizza gets here." He hopped over the top of the couch just to see if he could do it, picked up his beer from the end table, and headed to his side of the suite. Callie rolled her eyes.

Who does he think he is? Chuck Norris?

Signing into her email account, Callie began scanning her in-box. Most of the mail was junk: credit card offers, coupons for stores she never shopped in, life insurance pitches. But one email caught her eye, the subject line intriguing.

"Evidence/For Your Eyes Only," she read aloud.

What the hell?

The email came from an unknown sender and included an attached file. She knew better than to open something like that. It could be a virus, a hacker trying to get her passwords, child porn from a twisted spammer. But that one word called to her, got into her mind, planted a seed of hope.

Evidence.

She clicked on the email, hovered over the attachment icon for a second, then opened the file. It was a video, grainy and lacking in quality, the audio muffled and distant.

But she immediately recognized the location and players on the screen.

Fighting her rising panic, heart hammering, she tried to reconcile what she was seeing, her mind searching for a benign explanation. When comprehension dawned, adrenaline crashed through her, and she did the only thing her paralyzed body would allow.

She started howling; her anguished cries echoing off the pristine walls.

CHAPTER TWELVE

J ake was toweling off from his shower when he heard the first scream. Admittedly, it was more an angry roar, a bellow that erupted deep from the gut, than a scream. Throwing the towel over his hips, hair still dripping wet, he grabbed his gun from the dresser and silently made his way to the living room.

Callie was bent forward on the sofa, rocking at a nearly imperceptible pace, her eyes fixed on the computer screen. Jake swept his gun in front of him, raking the room in search of an intruder. He scrambled past Callie to her bedroom and bath, confident that he would find a trespasser hidden in the shadows.

He found nothing.

Adjusting the towel around his waist, satisfied they were alone, he walked back to the living room and studied Callie with a trained eye. Her skin was pale, her hands shook. She frantically bounced her right knee, her attention on the screen before her.

"Blaze?" he said, laying a hand on her shoulder.

She jumped at his touch, whipping her head around to face him. Her eyes were wide, the muscles beneath her shoulder taut.

"Callie, what is it? What's happened?"

Without saying a word, she rewound the video, then angled

the laptop to give him a full view of the screen. She pushed play and averted her gaze.

She didn't think she could bear to watch it a second time.

Jake placed his weapon on the end table and slid onto the couch beside her. His mouth was dry, his palms sweaty, as he studied the picture in front of him. Although the video resolution was poor and the image distorted, he had no trouble identifying the location.

Kate and Callie's cellar? Shit!

The Callahan family home, the place where, once upon a time, there were only sweet memories of childhood. Nearly five months ago, it became a house of horrors for the Callahan sisters.

The place where Callie sustained severe physical injuries and lasting psychological scars.

The site where Katherine Callahan, Callie's sister and the most important person in her life, bled to death in Jake's arms on an unforgiving cement floor.

And it was where a maniacal killer, hellbent on revenge, carried out his final 'lesson.'

The Callahan basement.

Jake felt his stomach cramp as recognition slammed into his brain; a woman, nude and bound by chains, sat slumped on the floor, covered in dark splotches of ... what? Dirt? Blood? Her auburn hair, clumped with grime, hung limply around her face as she hunched over, motionless.

Callie.

Callie had been Gabriel's prisoner for hours in that basement ... drugged, tormented, abused physically and mentally. But this video began near the end of her captivity, after she'd gouged his left eye with a nail and he responded by beating her nearly to death.

Jake turned and caught her studying a random spot on the wall. Anyone else would define her demeanor as detached, emotionless. Jake knew better.

"Where did you get this?" he whispered hoarsely.

"Email," she croaked.

He turned back to the video, hands fisted, and jaw clenched. Forcing himself to watch the recording, knowing what was coming—knowing the ending—was one of the most challenging things he'd ever had to do.

Fortunately, the audio quality was poor. Jake heard snippets of conversation as the recording ran, catching only every third or fourth word, and he counted that as a blessing.

He was so angry that hearing Gabriel's voice would push him over the edge.

He stopped the video just as Katie came into the frame. Turning slightly, eyes still on the laptop, he said, "Hey Blaze, why don't you try out the jacuzzi tub in my bathroom? I swear, there must be a dozen jets guaranteed to pulverize this shitty day into oblivion. I'll call you when the pizza gets here."

He didn't want her to have to relive the worse day of her life.

Callie, blindsided and horror-stricken by the video she just watched, was willing to overlook Jake's protective instincts for the moment. She nodded dully, eyes dry and face calm, knowing the walls she'd erected months ago were crumbling.

Bits of plaster and mortar, falling into a dark void as her mind silently screamed.

Lost in the shadow of her own fury, she wanted nothing more than to rip her eyes out of her skull and unsee what she'd just seen. Instead, she walked on trembling legs, hiding her inner breakdown, until she made it to the safety of the bathroom.

Once she left the room, Jake resumed the video. He watched as Kate ran to her sister's crumpled body and cupped Callie's face; watched as Gabriel came from behind and ordered her to her knees.

Oh, Red ...

Jake swallowed the bile in his throat. He fought the urge to scream, tear his hair out, rip Gabriel Devine to shreds. Instead, he squeezed his shaking hands between his thighs to prevent them from punching a hole in the screen.

Katie and Gabriel were facing each other now, trading barbs, each in a boxer's stance. Jake found himself talking aloud to Kate, instructing her.

"No, left! That's it, move to the left, Red. Watch his eyes! Your gun, pull it now!"

As if his words could change the inevitable and alter the outcome. Of course, they could not. Within a few moments, in the shadows of that dank, dark basement, Katie Callahan would be dead.

A knock startled him, and he paused the video, listening. He'd been so engrossed in his fantasy of changing the past, he had trouble processing the sounds created in the present. Another knock followed the first, and he realized it was the door to the suite.

Dinner, he remembered.

"Be right there!" he called out.

Jogging to his bedroom, Jake tugged on his jeans and a T-shirt. Returning to the kitchen, he grabbed his wallet and paid the delivery girl. After setting the pizza box on the counter, he took a seat on the sofa and hit 'play' once more.

Eyes glued to the screen, he watched a few minutes of what appeared to be some sort of stalemate. Then, Katie finally made her move, pulling her gun but not firing.

Why did you wait, Red? I told you, never wait! You take your shot when you can! If only you'd listened ...

But Jake knew that was an unfair assessment of her situation. Katie was the one living that moment, the one reading the room. He had to trust that she drew her weapon when she deemed it safe enough to do so.

Riveted to the screen, he watched Katie force Gabriel to his knees (*good girl*), watched as she aimed the gun at his head. He heard her say 'keys' and stretch out her palm, presumably for the key to Callie's shackles.

And then, in the blink of an eye, chaos and speed filled the camera lens. Gabriel was lunging, flying at Katie, hate blackening his eyes. They rolled on the ground, him trying to take her gun, her fighting to control it.

And Callie, helpless, her mouth in a perpetual scream. She was kicking, barefoot, at Gabriel, frantically trying to land a blow as best she could. At that moment, Jake had an epiphany of sorts. He'd never met two women as courageous and determined as the Callahan twins. He paused the video again and studied Callie's face, frozen mid-scream.

Beaten and broken, yet still trying to save your sister. Bravo, Blaze.

Jake's jaw was set, his fists clenching and unclenching. He took a steadying breath and resumed the video, recalling the layout of the basement.

Where the fuck was that camera? How did we miss that?

Kate and Gabriel had temporarily rolled out of the camera view. Callie lunged, stretching as far forward as her chains allowed, leaving only her bruised legs in the camera frame.

At that moment, Jake had never hated anyone as much as he hated the son-of-a-bitch who called himself Gabriel Devine.

You fucking coward! When I get my hands on you, I'm gonna rip your head off and shit down your throat!

He was so enraged when he saw the flash of light as the gun fired, so heartbroken when Katie came into view, grabbed her chest, and crumpled to the ground, that he was deaf to the soft footfalls padding up behind the couch.

On the screen, Katie Callahan's blood was everywhere. Deep crimson liquid pumped a steady rhythm from her chest, leaving jagged lines that snaked in a sinister pattern around her body. It covered her shirt and her face, the sheer volume pooling above the minuscule crevices in the concrete floor. The bullet that had pierced her chest did a colossal amount of damage, the fatal round nicking the aorta where it rose from her heart.

The coroner later explained that, even if Gabriel had shot her in a hospital operating room, surrounded by surgeons, she would still have succumbed to her injuries. It was that kind of rolling disaster—fast, grievous, lethal.

There was nothing anyone could have done to save her.

The quick intake of breath from behind startled him, and Jake turned. Callie was behind him, unmoving, her eyes glued to the screen. Jake stood, closed the laptop, and walked around the sofa. His shoulder brushed hers, and he caught a brief nuance of her scent. She smelled of fresh air and roses, mixed with just the right amount of honey.

She smelled of life.

"Blaze, why are you doing this to yourself?" he asked quietly, his hand hovering at the small of her back but not touching her. "This isn't healthy. I thought you were in the tub."

"I was, but then I heard the door and got nervous." Voice shaking, she added, "We don't know where he is, Jake, and you were out here alone. I didn't much care for that thought."

Jake knew that the 'he' she referred to was Gabriel. He pressed his lips to her temple, a gesture intended to calm her mind, not to ignite a flame. Yet, feeling Callie stiffen made him immediately regret the innocent kiss.

Smooth, Devereaux, smooth.

Ignoring her reaction, he said, "It was just the pizza delivery. You hungry?"

She shook her head.

"C'mon, Blaze, you gotta eat. We've had one helluva day. In fact, it was so crappy you gotta drink, too," he joked, handing her a beer.

She took the bottle and gulped greedily as if, at that moment, she wanted nothing more than to be blind, stupid drunk.

In a damned hurry.

They sat at a short table in the kitchenette and ate in silence. Jake was the first to speak.

"I've been wondering. Why do you think that asshole sent you the video? Why now?"

Callie shrugged and took a sip of beer. "Not sure. He's

psychopathic, so it could be a power play. Do you think he knows we're looking for him?"

Jake shook his head. "Nah, I think it's more likely that he's bored and has had time to stew. We've boxed him in, shut him down. At least, for now. Hell, you blinded him with that nail; I shot him in the leg. Physically, he is probably still healing from those wounds." Jake gathered their paper plates and tossed them in the trash. "He's pissed off that he can't hunt, so he is doing the next best thing ... tormenting you."

Callie nodded. "I guess that makes sense. But why now? Maybe it's a 'revenge is a dish best served cold' thing?"

Jake grinned. "Katie told me you were a Star Trek fan. I admit, it is curious that he didn't send the recording earlier. And, since we never found a camera on scene, either it's still there, or he went back and got it."

Callie shuddered. "Well, that's a scary thought. Do you want to know what's even scarier, though? The thought that there are more recordings out there."

"Yeah," Jake agreed, leaning against the sink, "that is a scary thought. When we get back to Jed's tomorrow, we'll have Abby look at your laptop to see if she can determine where the email came from. In the meantime, don't open any others you may get until she can get a handle on this. Okay?"

Callie's hands curled into fists, and she pounded on the table. "Fuckity, fuckity, fuck, fuck! Son of a bitch, this pisses me off!"

Jake did his best to hold back a smile. The animated cursing uttered in her light, pleasant voice was unsettling but adorable. "Easy there, Champ. I get it, and believe me, I'm just as pissed off as you. But Gabriel is smart. We need to keep cooler heads. Out-thinking the bastard may be the only way to nail his ass."

"Yeah, I guess. I can't fathom watching another video from him, anyway. I don't think I could bear to climb inside his demented mind for one more second." She rested her chin on her hands and sighed. "If that makes me a coward, then so be it."

Jake narrowed his gaze, frowning. "No, Callie, that doesn't make you a coward. It makes you human."

~

The Apostle stood in the vestibule, humming as he polished a forgotten chalice that sat on a shelf in the dimly lit alcove. He was pleased with himself, pleased with how well things were going. Manipulating the Disciple had been easier than he'd planned. Right now, the dumb fuck was huddled over his computer, scrolling over dozens of heart-felt confessions, practically foaming at the mouth.

Putz.

Gabriel would never stoop to such nonsense. It was beyond pathetic and below his dignity. Instead, he would orchestrate the kills, choreograph the Disciple's moves like Geppetto choreographed Pinocchio, and slake his thirst for purifying the world.

Remaining a ghost to the police was an extraordinary advantage. There was no one dogging him, no one scrutinizing him. He was free to just ... be. And, in that freedom, he was able to trace Callie's email address, courtesy of her published dissertation entitled, "Prefrontal cortex alterations during episodes of manic behavior."

Oh, please ...

Although he felt the topic lame, it got him the author's contact information he needed. He followed the trail from a dissertation database, one of the country's largest repositories, back to an online survey platform Callie used in her research. The questionnaire asked for opinions and relevant experiences by individuals diagnosed with bipolar disorder.

The survey's conclusion included her email account for participants to send additional thoughts, medical test results, or further survey suggestions.

Dumb fuckin' move, Sis.

The dissertation, the survey, none of that mattered to Gabriel. His focus now lay solely on making Callie squirm. He intended to toy with her, much like a cat with a mouse, until he tired of the game and went in for the kill.

Initially, in his quest for revenge against Katie, her twin sister hadn't even been a blip on his radar. In fact, for the first time in his life, he thought he'd felt a niggling of remorse when he captured and contained her in that basement; a tinge of regret when she feigned bravery in her chains. But then, like all the women in his life, she turned on him, destroying the sight in his left eye with a simple ten-penny nail.

Afterward, he beat her nearly to death. And felt nothing but redemption.

Looking back on it now, his only regret was not choking the living shit out of her when he'd had the chance. He dreamed of the day when they would face each other once again. In the meantime, he would play.

Setting up the camera to record Katie's end was an afterthought. His original plan was to take pictures of the final events of that day, but logistically, he'd found that to be an impossibility. He would be far too busy exacting his revenge to remember to memorialize it in a few photos. Instead, he purchased a wireless security camera, hid it high atop a metal shelf in the basement, and paired it to his cell phone, enabling him to monitor and record any activity. It was an ingenious plan ... until it wasn't.

Who the fuck knew that dickhead FBI agent would get there when he did?

Gabriel fumed. Dealing with the injury to his eye was bad enough, but being shot in the thigh by Jake Devereaux was damned near catastrophic. It took all his energy to fight his way up the steps to the Bilco doors and freedom without collapsing. There was no way he would have had time to hop over to that musty corner, balance on his good leg, and grab the monitor.

So, he left it, convinced it would be in the hands of the police in a matter of hours.

But the assholes missed it! Those crackerjack Eliot Ness wannabes fucking missed what should have been their most valuable piece of evidence!

He was astounded. Day after day, he'd follow them on his phone screen, watching them scurry like cockroaches caught in a sudden burst of light, moving here to there in the cellar and never noticing the damned camera.

Never even looking up.

Thinking about it now made him euphoric. Adrenalin coursed through his body as he recalled the day, weeks later, when he returned to the house where his sisters grew up and retrieved the camera.

Gabriel watched the video several times, reliving that day. It hadn't gone as planned, he didn't count on Callie interfering, stealing the show. Still, it was a win, one that would have been sweeter if he'd been able to witness the *Splendor,* that glorious moment of a soul's transition. But the fool camera suffered a glitch, a disturbance that scrambled the signal as she was dying, fading to black before she succumbed.

No matter. Someday, somehow, he believed the *Splendor* would reveal itself to him.

And although Katie was dead, rotting in the ground and no longer an itch to be scratched, Callie could not go unpunished. She became his new rash, his fresh irritation demanding to be soothed, healed, eliminated.

He sent Callie the video.

The following day, Callie awoke early. She'd slept restlessly, finally getting out of bed at five in the morning. Moving quickly, she tiptoed to the living room to retrieve her laptop, her Crimson Tide sleep jersey barely covering her bottom. Since she didn't know that she and Jake would be sharing a suite, she hadn't thought to bring a robe.

Sweeping the laptop from the coffee table, she was working her way back to her room when Jake spoke.

"Couldn't sleep either?" he asked. Standing at the entrance of his bedroom, Jake leaned against the door frame. He was shirtless and barefoot, his pajama bottoms hanging loosely around his hips.

Callie froze, mortified. *Shit!*

"Um, yeah, not really. I thought maybe I would check for those DNA test results. Sorry if my walking around disturbed you."

He moved toward her, his toned torso contracting with each step. She jerked her head to the side, suddenly fascinated by the olive-drab draperies.

"Not at all. I've been up for hours, studying the messed-up corners on the molding. You know, for a room that appeared as put-together as this, they could sure use a good carpenter."

Callie laughed. "Didn't notice. Sorry. Anyway, I'm going to look at this in my room. What time are we supposed to meet with Mr. Yates?"

Owen Yates was an eighty-four-year-old man who was, at one time, a neighbor of Billy Ray and Jolene Porter. Owen, one of the last originals in the neighborhood, agreed to speak to Jake and Callie about what he remembered of Jeremy's years at the Porters'. Since it was quite a long time ago, they weren't sure how much help he could be.

"I told him we would swing by about ten o'clock. Afterward, I thought we could stop by the police department and see if Adam found out anything from his sources. Then we can grab lunch and see where we are. If nothing else screams at us, I say we head back to Montana. No sense hanging around if it does us no good, right? What do you think?"

Callie bit back a smile. Months ago, Jake would never ask what she thought. He was used to giving orders, making unilateral decisions as the man supervising so many agents. The thought that he was trying to change his mind-set and include her in the decision-making process warmed her heart.

Maybe there was hope for him yet.

"Sure, that sounds like a plan." She swallowed against the lump in her throat, a lump growing exponentially the longer she stared at his half-naked body.

She needed to move. Now.

"Alright, I guess I'll see you in a bit. Maybe you should go back to bed." The minute she said it, a flush rose to her chest and landed squarely on her face.

Blast that Irish heritage!

Jake pressed his lips together to hide his smile. He knew exactly why she was blushing and found it sweet.

Maybe even sexy.

"Uh, nah, that train already left the station. I'm going to make a pot of coffee. Whenever you're ready, come on out and get yourself a cup." Winking, he added, "I've been told I make a mean cup of coffee."

Callie slipped back into her room, trying to ignore the pounding of her heart. This was all wrong.

Jake was all wrong.

And she needed to get him out of her head. Fast.

CHAPTER THIRTEEN

"Appreciate you seeing us, Mr. Yates," Jake said to the hunched figure in front of him. The man was balding and frail, an ornate cane clutched in his left hand.

"What's that?" Owen Yates said, cupping a hand to his ear.

"I said thank you for seeing us," Jake yelled, probably louder than necessary.

"Okay, okay," Owen said, "no need to scream it, man. I may be a tad deaf, but I'm not daft."

Callie chuckled, immediately liking this man. She tossed her head toward Jake. "Don't mind him, Mr. Yates," she said conspiratorially, "I think he's interviewed one too many bad guys. He expects everyone will play at being deaf and dumb."

Owen laughed, a hearty laugh that morphed into a coughing spasm. When he regained control of his lungs, he said to Jake, "I like her. She's got spunk!"

He guided them to an old sofa bathed in dog hair, crumbs, and a multitude of stains. Taking a seat in a sage-green recliner, he asked, "What can I do you for?"

Jake flipped open a notepad. "We'd like to talk to you about your former neighbors, the Porters. Specifically, we'd like to ask about one of their foster children, Jeremy Sterling. Jeremy has become a suspect in several crimes. Do you remember? It would be quite a few years ago now, sometime in the early 2000s."

Yates scratched his chin. "Oh, sure, I remember him. Don't expect I'll ever forget that kid, even if I live to be a hundred." His hooded eyes slid from Jake to Callie. "Pardon my French, Miss, but the kid was a peckerhead. Trouble with a capital 'T' if you want to know the truth."

Owen stretched across his body and dug inside the chair cushion, pulling out a backscratcher. Moving his arm above his shoulder, he angled the device, shaped like a screaming monkey, downward until it reached the small of his back.

It appeared that, at least momentarily, he'd forgotten he had guests.

Jake lifted an eyebrow at Callie, who shrugged. "Um, so, Mr. Yates," she said. "You were telling us about Jeremy?"

The old man looked up, then smiled sheepishly. "Oh, sure. Sorry. I got me a raging case of sumac yesterday and can't seem to quell the itch."

"Calamine," Callie said softly. "I have an intense allergy to sumac, too. Calamine is the only thing that helps."

Refocusing, Owen nodded, more to himself than anyone. "Thank ya, kindly. I'll have to get me some. Where was I? Oh yeah, Jeremy. God as my witness, that child gave me the willies. I always made sure to lock this place up tighter than a clam's ass at high tide if I had to go out." Reddening, he said, "Again, my apologies, Miss."

Callie tossed a hand in the air. "Please, Mr. Yates, I have two brothers. I've heard worse." She smiled at him slyly. "I've said worse."

Owen grinned. "Somehow, I doubt that, Miss."

Jake raised a brow. "Don't let her innocent act fool you, Owen. She can swear like a sailor when the occasion calls for it."

Callie discreetly kicked Jake's shin.

Amused, he continued. "Do you recall if he had any friends

that hung around? Any visitors that stopped by or maybe a job he held?"

Owen shook his head. "Sorry, can't say I remember any of that. Those Porters were a strange couple, God rest. Kept to themselves mostly. Occasionally, I'd hear hollering and such over there, but most of the time, it was just a confounded silence. Rarely saw the kid after the first year. My understanding was they homeschooled him right after he got hisself in a bunch of trouble." He sat forward, then glanced left and right as if he was about to drop classified information into their laps.

"But the real reason I was nervous about the kid? I caught him, many a time, hanging with the cats in the neighborhood. He'd chase them, grab them by the tail, hoist them over his shoulder. Whenever he seen me lookin', he'd just smirk and keep walking." Owen shivered. "Some of those cats and kittens were pets; some were strays. But you want to know the part that gets your hackles churning?" He stopped and rubbed his arms.

"What?" Callie asked gently. "What does?"

Owen shivered. "Those critters he was with? No one ever saw them again."

⁓

"Hey, Faith! Have you seen Caleb?"

Jed was in the foyer, calling to Faith as she folded laundry in an upstairs bedroom. Lucky was pacing, her signal for potty time, and Jed thought he'd ask Caleb to accompany them. He tried to include the boy in as many tasks as possible, hoping something would break through his self-imposed verbal prison.

"Aye, he's up here, scampin' aboot," Faith called back. "Ah'll send him down."

A minute later, blond hair slicked back from a bath, Caleb's tiny hand gripped the banister, and he pranced down the stairs. He stopped at Jed's feet and looked up at him.

"Hey, Tiger," Jed said, ruffling his hair. "I have to take the

Luckster out for a walk and, well, it seems she'd rather go with you." Smiling down at the boy, he shrugged. "Go figure, right? I mean, what kind of crazy dog wouldn't want me all to themselves?"

The boy's eyes danced mischievously, as if he had the perfect comeback, but couldn't reveal it. He skipped to the hall closet, pulled Lucky's leash from a brass hook, and clicked it on her collar. In a moment, they were sailing through the door to the front yard.

"Are ye off, then?" Faith said from the top of the staircase.

"I suppose we are," Jed said. "Be back soon." He cleared his throat. "Um, Faith? Maybe when we return, you and I can sit on the porch, watch Caleb and Lucky play, and have a chat? I think it's time we talked, don't you? There are folks here who care about you and Caleb. We're worried."

Faith inwardly cringed. She knew this day was coming, but hoped to put it off.

"Aye, ah ken you are concerned, Jedidiah. We'll hae a good talk when ye return."

Faith watched him leave, her heart heavy. It seemed like forever ago that she and Caleb arrived in Montana. She'd tracked down Jed for a reason and, instead of going with her original plan to watch him from a distance, ended up taking the job he'd advertised. So far, her time as his live-in assistant had been wonderful, and accepting the job was one of the best decisions she'd ever made. She took it as a sign that she was on the right path.

Now, everything would change. No matter how she handled it, things would change.

She wandered back down the hall to her laundry, her mind concocting a background that would both satisfy Jed's curiosity and fulfill her obligation to explain her past. It would be an account jam-packed with innuendo and euphemisms.

A story stitched with half-truths, woven together by lies.

"It's difficult to draw pure water from a dirty well." — Scottish Proverb

Jed and Faith sat on rockers on the front porch, sipping on fresh lemonade and watching Caleb throwing tennis balls to Lucky.

"He really loves that pup, doesn't he?" Jed asked.

"Aye, that he does. Caleb never had a pet. Ah always feared he was too young for the responsibility, but eyeing him now, ah am not so sure."

She paused, shielding her eyes from the morning sun as she turned toward Jed. "Ah suppose we should start from the beginning, hadn't we? His name was Graeme Duncan, an American laddie born in a wee town in Ohio, and, before ah git tae far ahead o' the story, you need tae ken it wasn't always bad. Nae all the time, anyway." She turned back to watch Caleb, now spread out on the grass, trying to teach Lucky to roll over. "In the beginning, the time Graeme 'n' ah spent th'gither was near perfect. Aye, his temper frightened me a bit, but ah've gone off half-cocked myself, ye ken, so, glass houses 'n' all that. For years, we enjoyed a kinship maist would envy. Ah cannae recall so much as a cross word between us in the beginning."

"So, what changed?" Jed prompted.

"Ah suppose real life stuck her nose intae our fantasy. Graeme's obligations were like anchors, weighin' him down. Drownin' him." She shook her head sadly. "We both had a rough go as wee ones, and ah believe it gave Graeme an inflated sense o' responsibility. His struggles started fur him as a bairn, when his parents forced him tae shift from the only home he'd ever kent back tae his faither's hometown o' Glasgow. Graeme left behind his school, his friends. He hated Scotland, nae fur any reason except it wasn't Ohio." She brushed some imaginary crumbs from her skirt. "Several years later, missing the States and in search o' fortune, Graeme left Scotland 'n' headed back tae America. By the grace o' God—an' a lonely widow in charge o' new admissions—he got intae Harvard law school."

Jed whistled. "Harvard, huh? Impressive."

"Aye, but as ah said, he got help by takin' a desperate woman tae his bed. In time, he passed the Bar Exam and took a job in a law firm in Philadelphia. He was twenty-eight years old."

"And you? Were you in Philly at the time?"

"Nae yet. Ah was in Edinburgh—a twenty-one-year-old waitress 'n' dreamer, filled with grand ideas 'n' fancy aspirations, but na money tae make those dreams a reality. We first crossed paths when he came back to Scotland to help an auld friend who'd gotten himself into a wee bit o' legal trouble."

Jed nodded occasionally as she told her story, but said nothing. She was like a skittish foal, biding her time, waiting for the opportunity to break free. He didn't dare startle her by speaking.

"The day he walked intae the café, he caught mah eye immediately. Ah felt mah heart skip as he strode tae the breakfast counter, a man o' confidence 'n' stature, a man on a mission. I dinnae mind sayin' he was easy on the eyes." She blushed and tucked her hands into her lap. "And, though nae as handsome as you, his hazel eyes 'n' full lips demanded an audience. Aye, he swaggered in like he owned the place, with his fancy pin-striped suit 'n' well-manicured hands. Hands that belonged tae an accountant or a surgeon, nae a laborer. We chatted, hit it off right away. Before I knew it, ah was fallin' hard." She sighed heavily. "The man swept me off mah feet 'n' ah'd ne'er seen the broom."

Jed smiled. "I imagine there were plenty of men around you who carried a broom."

"Nae hardly. But he was smitten with me, that ah know. Ah couldn't wrap mah head around the idea that this big-shot lawyer wanted me. Faith McTavish, a lassie with nae education and only forty-five pounds in the bank; a lassie who belonged tae a family of drug-addled degenerates. My faither was an angry, selfish man who moved the family from Scotland tae the U.S. when ah was wee. And nae because he was searchin' for more job opportunities or better pay, mind ye. The man was lookin' for a bigger high, was all. My mum was sick, fighting the cancer in her bones, and could nae travel. We took our leave anyway, left her there tae die."

Faith's hands curled into fists, her face flushed, and her brow dropped. Her quick transformation from indifference to anger took Jed back.

Aware that Jed was watching her, she relaxed her hands and continued. "Da took mah brother and me to California, set us up in a lovely apartment," she said, her voice dripping with sarcasm. "Right next tae a crack house, complete with its own cockroaches 'n' rats. Three months after we arrived, we got word that mum was dead. Six months after that, mah faither overdosed on heroin."

"Jesus, Faith," Jed whispered.

"Oh, it gits better. Mah wee brother, being in that environment, got hooked on the stuff as well. He's currently doing time in Pelican Bay State Prison for aggravated assault and armed robbery. Crimes he committed tae get money for his next fix. Lovely family, eh?"

Jed just shook his head.

"After that, ah lived with my paternal grandparents—beastly people, by the by—until ah graduated high school and could move back to Edinburgh. Ah had to work two jobs, one at the cafe and one as a tutor, just tae pay mah monthly bills. But ah didnae mind. When Graeme came into mah life, it all changed. Before ye could say 'Bob's your uncle,' ah was plannin' a fairy-tale wedding and scouring the real estate listings in Pennsylvania. Ah pure thought my dreams had come true."

Jed sighed. "Can I get you anything before you continue? Another lemonade, maybe? With a shot of bourbon or tequila?"

She agreed to just the lemonade, straight, and watched Jed enter the house. Caleb and Lucky were now running in a line, racing each other, Caleb's head thrown back in glee. How she loved that boy. He was hers, and she would do anything to protect that.

She stood and leaned against the porch column, rehearsing her story in her head. This was where the fork in the road lay, the place where lies and the truth intersected. The place where she would follow only one path.

Deception.

A few moments later, Jed returned and set another glass of lemonade beside her. The morning was warm, the sun bright, and she watched, mesmerized, as trickles of condensation ran down the sides of the glass, forming a wet ring on the wooden cocktail table.

"He's dead, you know," she said flatly. "Graeme, ah mean."

Jed scratched his jaw in thought, his face expressionless. "How did he die?"

Faith looked him in the eye. "Graeme Duncan got everything that was coming tae him. It matters nae how he met his end. All ye be needin' tae ken is he was an evil man who got his kicks from the suffering of others. He was a bully and a monster, and his death will nae be mourned by many."

Jed frowned. He'd been an investigator for much of his adult life and could tell when someone was dodging the truth. Faith was being evasive, maybe even deceptive. It was clear he'd hit a wall trying to figure out her past. Maybe it was time to bring in some reinforcements.

"What do you say we take a break, huh?" Jed asked. "Let's grab Caleb and Lucky and go to the park for a bit. We can pick this up later tonight."

Faith shook her head. "Truth be told, Jedidiah, ah am workin' on a wicked headache. Would ye mind if ah stayed here while you 'n' the boy went?"

"Not a problem. Get some rest. We'll be back before you can miss us."

Faith watched as he and Caleb walked to the truck, Lucky

dancing happily beside them. A migraine, no doubt brought on by stress, really was brewing inside her skull, and she massaged her temples. All she could think about was getting to her room, to her journal. She needed to make today's entry, to write about what she related to Jed.

Her journal was full of letters addressed to him, notes that he would never see. It was her way of keeping her story straight while absolving herself of the sin of lying.

Because everything she had told Jed was to the right of the truth. Way right.

Yes, Graeme Duncan had been a dangerous man. Certainly, he was abusive physically, mentally, emotionally. But he never raised a hand to Faith. His target was closer to home.

His target was his wife.

~

Dear Jedidiah:

I am so sick of playing this game, pretending to be happy, pretending to be carefree. Pretending to speak with the thick Scottish accent I fucking lost years ago.

I'm sick of being forced to write in this damned journal. And terrified that someday you will discover this book and everything I've worked for will unravel.

I'm not a bad person. But I refuse to be shit on, treated like I don't exist. I lived that way for years, a mouse in the corner, afraid of my own shadow—afraid to stand up for myself, to stand up to her.

Emily Duncan.

I never claimed to be Emily's friend. After all, why would I be? She had everything I wanted—wealth, beauty, brains.

Most of all, she had Graeme.

Truth was, Jed, I hated her. Hated her perfect hair and perfect teeth and the way she said, "Hello, lovely," with a slight wave of her hand, as if she were the fucking Queen of England.

Most of all, I hated she had it all, but was too stupid to realize it.

Sure, Graeme knocked her around some, but she had no one to blame but herself. If she'd just learned to keep her big mouth shut, she wouldn't need to spend a fortune on concealers or ice packs.

Blackened eyes, a dozen fat lips, and countless broken cheekbones aren't exactly a good look for a girl. You'd think she would have learned self-discipline.

Do you want to know why I made the move to Philadelphia when Graeme asked me? It was because I needed a role, however small, in his life.

My God, I loved that man! Completely, selflessly, with an intensity that sometimes scared me to death.

But he was married, betrothed to Emily Duncan, a highly respected photographer with beauty and poise and class. And no matter how many times Graeme promised to leave her, I knew, deep down, he would never divorce her. Graeme's lifestyle required a polished and educated wife on his arm while attending fundraisers, banquets, and fancy dinners.

He had no room in his circle for me, an uneducated spitfire from Scotland.

He did, however, have room in his bed.

I remember how we laughed at Emily's stupidity when he told her the story of the young homeless girl who needed a job and a place to stay. The pretentious bitch clucked her tongue and shook her head and lamented how tragic a story it was. I've no doubt she told all of her friends about the poor dear living in the upstairs suite of their gazillion dollar home.

And I admit I grew more and more resentful. It was hard not to be angry at how things were turning out. I went into this whole fucking thing believing Graeme and I had a future together.

Fat chance. A divorce would cost him a fortune. He would never leave her.

We continued our affair for years, right under the bitch's nose. In fact, it became a game, this forbidden love of ours. And each day, excited at tempting fate, we grew braver. We'd brush hands in the kitchen or steal kisses in the hallway, just daring her to catch us. We were walking a razor-thin line, playing with fire.

It made me nervous. It made Graeme horny.

Still, I bided my time, planning. I grew weary of being second best, was sick to death of being an afterthought. I promised myself that someday I would have all that Emily had, no matter the cost. I promised myself that I would win.

And, in a way, I did.

CHAPTER FOURTEEN

"In the fifteenth year of her age, the princess shall prick herself with a spindle and shall fall down dead." —The Brothers Grimm

Shell, Wyoming
May 1st

Madison Gibbs stood at the end of her driveway, arms crossed, furiously tapping her foot. She was not just annoyed, not merely frustrated, but knock-down, drag-out, scare-your-grandma and hide the children, pissed off.

Her boyfriend was late. Again. It was the third time that week.

After dating Stanley Brighton for almost a year, Maddie was aware of his many shortcomings.

Painfully aware.

His future was questionable, his grades abysmal. He possessed an aversion to bathing and, if cleanliness was, in fact, next to godliness, divinity was well beyond his reach. In Stanley's eyes, hygiene was more a kindness than a necessity.

Most days, he wasn't very kind.

To Stanley, none of it mattered, and everything was a joke. He was a prankster, a clown who specialized in one-liners and toilet humor.

"Hey, Maddie," he would say, *"poop jokes aren't my favorite, but they're a solid number two,"* or *"Why don't little girls fart? Because they don't have assholes until they're married!"*

Hilarious, if you are a ten-year-old boy. Maddie wasn't.

On top of all that, he was a mouth-breather, called her 'baby,' and had an uncanny ability to micro-manage every little situation. As if taking apart a problem piece by fucking piece could magically change the outcome.

She hated that kind of happy-happy, joy-joy bullshit. Life didn't work like that.

But the thing that grated most, the one thing she could not abide, was his incessant tardiness. Stanley was late for everything; school, track practice, dinner with her family. But Maddie had hoped today, of all days, would be different.

Today was the day she'd prepared for all her life.

At four p.m., she would meet with the Big Horn County Fair judges at the community center. Maddie studied sample questions for weeks, practiced her answers before a mirror, and tore through her closet, looking for the perfect outfit.

The perfect outfit that she'd changed five times in the past hour.

Because Maddie was desperate to make an impression. She wanted the judges to remember her, Madison Eleanor Gibbs, local girl and high school track star. They needed to believe, to trust that she would fulfill all her obligations if given the title of County Fair Queen.

She needed that freaking title.

Instead, she feared they would remember her as the girl who showed up late for her evaluation.

Stanley was the one with a license; Stanley was the one with a car. The only wheels Maddie owned were a pair of rusted roller skates and a bicycle with no brakes. Neither of which would get her across the county, anyway.

She had one month left before her sixteenth birthday, one month before obtaining her driving permit. Until then, she relied on family and friends to take her where she needed to be.

She relied on Stanley.

Reaching into her oversized purse, Maddie dug until her fingers wrapped around her phone. Scrolling angrily through her contact list, she tapped on Stanley's number. After six rings, his voicemail picked up.

"Hello? Hello? I'm sorry, I can't hear you—can you speak up? Haha, fooled ya! You've reached the amazing Stanley Brighton. If you are getting this message, it means I have better things to do than jaw with you. Leave your digits at the tone, and if you're lucky, I'll hit you back!"

Maddie rolled her eyes. Stan could be such a tool sometimes. She folded an arm around her waist while she waited for the beep. "Well, hello, Stanley. This is your girlfriend, Madison. Remember me? I'm the one who's not finding you so fucking 'amazing' right now! Where the hell are you, Stan? You know I wanted to be early to this thing. Now I will be lucky to make it on time! Call me!"

She ended the call, stuffed her phone back into her bag, and paced in a circle, her mind racing. Her parents were away on a retreat, as usual. They thought nothing of leaving Maddie and her thirteen-year-old brother alone for days at a time while they sought serenity or meditation or some such bullshit at Zen-like compounds all over the world. Her aunt and uncle, who checked in on them daily, were both at work and nearly two hours away. The next-door neighbor, Mrs. Crouse, was spending the day in Jackson Hole with her granddaughter.

There was no one else to help her.

Near tears, she stuffed a hand back in her bag and rummaged around for her phone once more. Tires crunching on gravel drew her attention, and, looking up, she spotted a dark-blue Toyota heading her way. The vehicle was unfamiliar, the driver impossible to see through the tinted windows. Maddie lived in an isolated area, and, except for Mrs. Crouse, there were no neighbors for miles. Cars seldom traveled down her unpaved road, so she found the appearance of this one curious, if not unsettling.

Within a minute, the Toyota rolled to a stop at the end of her driveway, kicking up pieces of gravel and leaving plumes of dust in its wake. Reflexively, Maddie took a step back, both from the dust choking the air and the man behind the wheel. She bent to peer into the car, squinting as the passenger-side window rolled down. Benny Mardones' 'Into the Night,' boomed from the radio, and the driver turned down the music to speak.

"Madison, is that you? Why, hello! I was just passing through, hoping to leave you this brief note of encouragement." The man waved a small white envelope in her direction. "I'm surprised to see you're still home. I thought you'd be halfway to the interview about now!"

He shrugged coyly, a dimpled smile creasing his cheeks. Madison thought he looked familiar, but couldn't place him.

"Do I know you?" she asked warily, studying his features.

He was a harmless-looking man with a plain face and winning smile. Her first thought was that he was old, but, to be fair, she realized that any person over thirty was ancient in the eyes of a teenager.

The stranger chuckled. "Well, we haven't met in person, but we've talked for ages on LiveFeed. It's me, Abel."

Maddie smiled her first genuine smile all afternoon. "Abel! Holy hell, am I glad to see you! I'm in a bit of a jam, and I'm hoping that you could help me? Pretty please, with sugar on top?" She batted her lashes and dipped her head into her shoulder playfully.

Thank you, Jesus, she thought happily. *At least something is going right today!*

Maddie knew a lot about Abel Turner. She'd spoken to him for hours in an online chat room and felt comfortable doing so.

Comfortable enough to spill some of her deepest, darkest secrets.

Secrets like ...

"You know, I really hate my parents, Abel. Sometimes, I picture myself at their funeral—they die together in this fantasy, so their coffins are side-by-side—and you know what? I'm not the least bit sad. Like, not at all."

And ...

"I get that I can be a not-nice person, Abel. Hell, I cheat on Stanley constantly. I've fucked so many guys behind his back that I lost count. And it's not because I don't love him. I do. It's just that, well, I like sex. A lot. And he seems to be not as into it as me. Plus, sex with him is like doing business with a bank—he makes his deposits, but I'm the one who gets penalized for early withdrawal if you get my drift. Besides, I'm not about to beg to get laid, you know? Yeah, I love sex. And I'm not ashamed to say I've used it as a weapon before. Hell, this one time, I traded the fry boy downtown a blow job for a Big Mac. Does that make me a slut or a whore, you think?"

And the biggest confession of them all. One she'd admitted to no one for fear it made her look weak ...

"Remember when you asked me about fears and shit? Like what I'm most scared of in the whole entire world? Needles, dude! Fucking syringes full of shit jabbed into my arms or my ass. One time, I went to the mall to get my ears pierced, but I couldn't go through with it. Just imagining that dagger shooting through my earlobe damned near made me shit my pants. Yeah, needles scare the ever-loving fuck outta me!"

Yes, she'd trusted this man with some hefty secrets. The least she could do was trust him to take her to Big Horn. She sent a quick text to Stan, telling him not to 'bother' himself about taking her to the interview. Her tone was short and snippy, and Stanley would, no doubt, have a lot of groveling to do later.

Abel leaned across the seat and opened the passenger door. "Hop in!"

As she climbed inside, Maddie got a better look at the man behind the wheel. She smiled, trying to ignore the sudden ache between her legs that surfaced when she wondered about the size of his package, curious about what kind of lover the old fart would make.

Curious about the lock of hair that was dangling from the rearview mirror.

And curious about just where in the hell Stanley could be.

Abel got off Highway 14 and instead took Black Mountain Road, a steep and winding climb up the face of Bighorn Mountain. He drove at a snail's pace, navigating the hairpin turns and blind corners of the narrow, two-lane road.

Annoyed, Maddie fidgeted in her seat.

"Hey, Abel? Not to be an asshole, but can you pick it up? I'm in a time crunch here. Maybe get back on Route 14, huh?"

Abel pursed his lips, slowed, and pulled the car to the shoulder of the road. He turned and faced Maddie.

"Why is this so important to you, Maddie? This interview, I mean."

Madison frowned. "Well, because it's a coveted spot. It can open doors for me." She played with the strap of her purse. "Look, I live in a little backwater ghost town, okay? Shell has maybe, what, a hundred people? Most of those are old farts, too, no offense. This County Fair can put me on the map. I've heard stories where modeling agencies and talent scouts got their latest stars from little contests like this. So, yeah, I'm gonna take a chance that this will lead to bigger things, to my being discovered."

Abel laughed. "Discovered? Is that what you truly believe? Oh, Madison, the only thing people will know you for is being a slut and a selfish little bitch. Don't these contests have rules or codes of conduct?"

Maddie's mouth dropped, and her face reddened.

"We both know you spread your legs for anything with a

dick. Do you really believe those judges won't see you for what you are?"

Furious, Madison did what Madison always did—snap back. "Yeah, well, fuck you, you piece of shit! Who are you to judge me? No one! You're an old, ugly loser. I can't believe I trusted you! I'm out of here!"

She gathered her purse in her lap and grabbed for the door handle. The ominous plink of the automatic locks clicking into place sent a chill down her spine. Screaming in frustration, she ran her fingers across the armrest of the door, searching for the unlock button. Instead, she found a gaping hole, covered by duct tape, where the button should have been.

Oh, God! Help me!

Panicked, howling in fear, Maddie gripped the door handle and rattled it wildly, slamming her shoulder against the door. Her feet stomped in place, her heels producing a frenzied rhythm that echoed inside the car.

As if she were running for her life, but going nowhere.

"Let me out of this fucking thing!"

In her periphery, she saw Abel's hand fly toward her face, and she jumped. A sharp jab to her neck, the pierce of the needle through her skin, and instantly her legs became putty. She found herself descending into darkness, even as her mind clawed and scratched to remain conscious.

But it was no use. In the end, Maddie fell head-first into a blackness she could neither describe nor escape.

When Madison Gibbs regained consciousness, she found she was still in the passenger seat of Abel's car, idling on a secluded access road near Shell Canyon. Shivering from fear and the effects of whatever drug he'd given her, she reached out to turn off the radio, but her leaden arm fell back onto her lap. Groggy, she looked around, searching for her captor. Her gaze found him at the side of the dirt road, satchel in hand, heading toward a steep embankment.

Moaning, her body operating at a snail's pace, Maddie reached for the passenger door handle but quickly discovered her fingers refused to take direction. Repeatedly, she swiped at the side of the door, looking for the handle, but grasped only air. Sapped of strength and spatial awareness, groaning louder, she tried to move her feet, but they too betrayed her brain's commands.

Come on, dammit!

Maddie's heart thundered, and her breath quickened. Shaking the cobwebs from her mind, forcing herself to calm down, she concentrated on one thing—moving her right hand. Her fingers swept over the inside of the passenger door, reading the landscape like a sightless person read braille, until her palm landed on the metal handle. Triumphant, she squealed and pulled up on the handle.

On the third attempt, the door swung open. Jubilant, Madison lifted her legs with her hands and turned in the bench-type passenger seat, willing her body to cooperate.

"Hello, Maddie. I trust you slept well?"

Wailing, raising her arms defensively and crying for her mother, Madison leaned forward and vomited all over Abel's shoes.

I am going to die here.

Madison fought the thought, tried to imagine how she would tell the story of her kidnapping to the cops, to the world. She pictured the newspaper headlines, the photo of her emerging from the mountain, a first responder blanket wrapped around her shoulders.

"Local girl saves herself!" or *"Meet the luckiest girl alive!"*

But, as she lay on the cold ground, surrounded by dirt and leaves and bear shit, she understood that would never happen.

They were miles off the main road and Abel had her tied up 'tighter than a camel's ass in a sandstorm,' as Stanley would say.

How she wished he were here, stupid jokes and smelly feet and all.

But he wasn't. And the cold hard truth was, she could scream for days, but there was no one to hear her. The thought reminded her of a famous question posed during an obnoxiously boring philosophy class.

Sort of.

If a girl screams in the forest and there's no one there to hear it, does she make a sound?

Shaking the useless thought from her head, she attempted to refocus on her options, limited though they were. The only way she could see to get out of this was to out-think him, trick him into untying her.

She could outrun him. She was the fastest girl on the track team. But first, she needed to get him talking. Currently, he was hunched over his leather bag, rummaging around in the contents.

Maddie's panic rose as she contemplated what was in that bag. She needed to make a move.

Now.

"You know, my parents have money, Abel. Lots of money. I could get you some. We could go to the ATM in town right this very minute. What do you say?"

Abel snickered. "You think this is about money? You're an even dumber bitch than I gave you credit for."

Grunting, Madison tugged on her restraints and tried to roll away. Abel kicked her.

"Unless you want another kick in your ass, you better hold still, child."

His words echoed in her mind, giving Maddie another idea. One that she'd buried deep inside her mind, revolted by the thought.

Still, desperate times and all that.

"How about I give you something else then, Abel?" she rasped, trying to sound seductive but in reality, sounding like a three-pack-a-day smoker. "You like head, Abel? You've never gotten a proper blow job until Madison Gibbs sucks you off." He seemed neither angry nor interested, so she pushed on. "Or would you rather just fuck me? Whatever you want, we can do. Nothing is off-limits for me, Abel."

Her strategy was to use his name several times, even though the sound of it rolling off her tongue made her gag. She'd watched a documentary once where the cops said it was important to humanize yourself, to connect with your captor.

I'd like to connect an axe to your motherfuckin' skull and watch your brains slide down your neck, you inhuman piece of shit!

Maddie held her breath, waiting for Abel's response. He was still crouched low, bent over that stupid bag.

What the hell is he doing?

After what felt like an eternity later to Maddie, Abel stood and faced her. In his hands, taunting her, were dozens of pre-filled syringes, each with needles of varying lengths. He smiled and walked toward her.

"What a coincidence, Madison. Nothing much is off-limits for me, either. Shall we begin?"

Maddie opened her mouth to cry out, but found that fear had paralyzed her vocal cords. The only noise she could create was a pitiful squeak, no louder than the chitter of a church mouse.

But deep inside, within the walls of her mind, her screams rumbled off the forest floor, bounced over the dense woods, and echoed off the canyon walls.

And no one heard.

CHAPTER FIFTEEN

Billings, Mt
12:30 p.m.

Callie pulled her suitcase across the parking lot at Billings Logan International Airport, stopping every few feet to adjust her grip. A cool breeze danced across her bare legs, and she cursed herself for the billionth time for wearing a skirt and heels.

What the hell was I thinking?

Ignoring the inner voice that was currently scolding her, she pivoted around a pothole, the wheels of her luggage squealing in protest. "Did you get in touch with your brother?" she asked Jake.

"Not yet. Cell service was not the greatest in the terminal, so I figured we'd call him on the ride back." He watched as she struggled with her luggage and lifted a brow. "You sure you don't want me to take that?"

"No, thank you," she said stiffly. "I'm perfectly capable of handling my own bag."

Her statement would've had more impact if she didn't punctuate it with a wheezing breath and a wipe to her brow.

Jake grinned. "Suit yourself." Then, taking pity on her, he added, "We're almost there, Blaze. A few more yards, and we're home free."

"Yippee," Callie said dryly. "Next time we get called away, if there is a next time, remind me to leave the big boy home and just bring a backpack."

He laughed, the sound rich and genuine. Eyes twinkling, he said, "What, and miss all the fun of watching you sweat? Not on your life, Callahan."

Once they loaded Jake's car, Callie used the time to text Darby and let her know they were back, while Jake called Jed.

At his desk and poring over the Department of Defense files provided by Ford, Jed answered on the first ring. "Jesus, Jake, I'm glad you called. I've been trying to reach you."

Jake hit the speaker on his cellphone. "You're on speaker, Jed, so keep it clean. What's going on?"

"We might have a promising lead." Jed paused and added, "Hi, Callie. Are you guys back in Montana?"

"Hi, and yes, we just got in. We tried phoning you several times earlier, but the signal out here is terrible. I wanted to let you know we're bringing my laptop to you, hoping that Abby can look at it."

"Why, what's happened?" Jed asked.

Jake discreetly glanced at Callie as she rubbed her inner thigh, still trying to erase the crude tattoo that lived there. It was the same ritual, performed again and again, an impossible attempt to deny Gabriel's existence.

It made Jake's blood boil.

Starting the car's engine, he snapped, "Gabriel's happened. Again. That scumbag sent Callie a video, a play-by-play of her kidnapping and imprisonment. The recording is about fifteen or twenty minutes long and includes when Kate ..." He ground his teeth. "Fucker must've had a camera somewhere, though, for the life of me, I can't believe we missed it. I'm going to go over the police reports, find out who oversaw the search of that basement. Someone's ass is gonna burn for this."

"That's some sloppy police work, I'll give you that."

"No kidding. A few of my guys went looking for the camera yesterday, practically tore the place apart. Wherever the prick had it stashed, it's gone now."

"Christ. What exactly was on the video?"

Jake glanced at Callie once again. "All of it, brother. Everything from that last day. Callie being beaten nearly to death, Kate dying, all of it."

"My God. Just when I think he can't get any lower, the fucker proves me wrong." He cleared his throat. "Sorry for the language, Callie."

"No need to apologize, Jed. He is a fucker."

"We're hoping Abby can come up with the IP address of the sender," Jake said. "So, that's our story. Your turn."

"Okay, so an interesting homicide case has fallen into our laps. Just after you left for Laredo, an officer for the Forest Service, a guy named JP Burke, found a body up by Tongue River." Jed shuffled some papers, grabbing the one with his notes. "The victim's name was Nora Grant. Even without being present at the scene, I can tell you someone did a number on her. Not sure of the cause of death yet, but she was burned beyond recognition." As an afterthought, he added, "Hopefully, it was after she was dead."

Puzzled, Jake asked, "Tragic, but how does she fit in to our case?"

"I'm not sure yet that she does. It was the rosary beads left near the body that caught our attention."

Callie mumbled, "Holy shit."

"That's not all, though. Sawyer is on his way to another homicide, this one in Little Goose Canyon. No police on scene yet, but the calling party reported finding the body of a woman near a stream up there."

"And you think it's connected?" Callie asked.

"I do. Especially since the caller mentioned a set of rosary beads near the body."

Jake gave Callie a questioning look. "That's two scenes, two sets of rosary beads. Coincidence?"

"Someone once told me there is no such thing as coincidence, only design. That leaves one explanation ... Gabriel."

"Or a copycat."

Callie shuddered. "Are you thinking what I'm thinking?"

Jake nodded. "Jed, Little Goose is only about two hours from here. We want to get a first-hand look at that crime scene. Do me a solid and call Sawyer or Ford, get a precise location of that homicide, and tell them to expect us."

"You got it. And Jake? There will be people from several agencies up there. Try to get along, okay?"

Jake hung up without responding, then noticed Callie's wide grin. "What? I get along just fine with people."

Callie shook her head and smiled. "Whatever you say, Barney. Whatever you say."

"Are you familiar with Little Goose Canyon?" Callie asked Jake as they drove. The afternoon sun beat mercilessly through the windshield, bringing a flush to her face. She cracked the window, then laid her temple against the cool glass.

"Are you too warm? I could turn on the air," Jake said.

"No, I'm fine. I'm excited about maybe finding some evidence on that tape, and when I get worked up, I get hot."

Jake slid her a look, then quirked a brow and grinned mischievously.

"Oh, come on! You know what I meant!" She felt her face flush even hotter.

He laughed, and Callie felt herself smiling as well.

"So, about Little Goose," Jake explained. "Yes, I know it well. It's a magnificent spot if you know how to get there. It's about five miles from Big Horn, off a two-track road, so it's difficult to find unless you know the area." He turned and found her watching him, obviously rapt in his words. He felt a twinge of something—warmth? intimacy?—and, rattled, ignored it. "Legend has it that Jesse James, at one time, had a cabin up in Little Goose. He needed a place to rest in between rustling cattle and horses."

"Well, sure. Exhausting work." Callie said dryly.

"You know it," Jake winked, not missing a beat. "Rustling's a backbreaker. When I was growing up, I heard fascinating stories about Jesse's adventures in Wyoming. According to the tales, he fell in love with the seclusion and beauty of the mountains and built himself a cabin in the woods. One day, a fire broke out and the entire structure burned to the ground. Supposedly, the only thing left standing was the fireplace. People swear it's still up there, standing tall, Jesse's initials carved into the mantle."

Callie whistled low. "Wow, that's a story to tell the grandkids, huh? How much of it is true?"

Jake shrugged. "There aren't many people alive who can relate the stories their great-grandparents told, so it may be more legend than fact. Still, it's a cool story."

Callie opened her mouth to speak, then stopped when her phone pinged, indicating she had mail. Anxious, she swiped through her apps until she got to her mailbox, Gabriel's last message on her mind.

"Trouble?" Jake asked with a frown.

"Not sure. I just got an email notification which, under normal circumstances, would be no big deal. But now, after the video ..."

"You know, you don't have to open anything now, Blaze. It can wait."

She shrugged and looked at the sender. It was from the ancestry site where she'd sent her DNA. She thought it possible that Gabriel, looking for shelter and anonymity, had reached out to a long-lost and, yet unknown to her, sibling.

How strange it was to hope that her father had sired not one, but two illegitimate children.

She quickly scanned the results, glossing over the percentages of ethnicity. She didn't particularly care that she was 78% Irish or 20% English or had a touch of German blood running through her veins. What she cared about was the link at the bottom of the email that directed her to 'View all DNA matches.' She clicked the link, and a list of names popped up— people with similar genetics who took the test. The tally of names was short, four or five people, probably just second cousins she'd never known about. But it was the first name listed that stopped her in her tracks. It was a name she did not recognize, a twenty-two-year-old female who lived in Denver, Colorado. Callie gasped as she read the statistic, a probability match of 92%.

The young woman's name was Amara Grace Davies.

"You're sure?" Jake asked, as they pulled into the Little Goose Canyon picnic area. "How do you know she's not a long-lost cousin rather than a sibling?"

"Because the results come up as 'Close Family,' sharing twenty-five percent of my DNA," Callie answered. "The only other option at 25% shared DNA is a grandmother or aunt, which, clearly, doesn't fit. If she were a cousin, it would be half that amount. A full sibling? Fifty percent shared DNA. The only thing I don't know for sure is if she is my dad's child. Logically, I cannot fathom that my mom had an affair that produced a child, but since they are both gone, getting DNA for comparison is a moot point."

Jake thought for a second. "You said she is twenty-two, though, right?"

Callie nodded.

"Okay, well, I've always sucked in math, but if your mom died when you were seven, and you are twenty-nine now, that's twenty-two years ago. Your mom died in October, so unless she was pregnant in the last year of her life, it doesn't add up. The child would have to have been born the same year that your mom died." He shrugged. "I would think you'd remember your mom being pregnant when she disappeared. Even if she conceived right around the time your dad died, that would put the birth of the baby four or five months before she went missing."

Callie tried to wrap her head around the time frame. She was sure her mother hadn't been pregnant the last year of her life. But her father could have impregnated someone before he died. It was dizzying trying to digest the time frame.

Jake turned off the engine and faced her. "Look, we can deal with all this later, okay? It's not like Amara is going anywhere, right? Let's make our way to the scene and find out what the fuck Gabriel has been up to."

Callie nodded and stepped out of the car, pushing her thoughts and questions to the back of her mind. She squared her shoulders, determined not to let what she'd just learned overpower her.

Amara Grace Davies. It seemed they shared not only a father, but the same middle name. She whispered that name now, feeling it roll off her tongue, imagining the possibilities. It was a beautiful name.

Amara Grace Davies ... my sister.

CHAPTER SIXTEEN

Little Goose Canyon
Sheridan, Wyoming
3:15 p.m.

"Jake, Callie!" Agent Sawyer Mills called out. "We're over here, about fifty feet to your right."

Callie searched the woods, her eyes landing on the yellow crime-scene tape amid a thick cluster of trees. The trail had become progressively more treacherous—so much so that it was in danger of disappearing altogether—and she kept a close eye on the ground, treading lightly. Thanks to Gabriel's crushing, MMA style foot stomp months ago, her right ankle was weak and unreliable. Pins, screws, and the occasional prayer secured together the splintered bones both above and below the joint.

Just one more reason to hate you, Gabriel.

Jake held back a low-lying branch dangling from a spruce tree, an oddity among the groupings of aspen and pine, and allowed Callie to pass. "After you," he said with a slight bow.

"Gee, thanks," she said, acknowledging his kindness was a double-edged sword. Did she really want to cross this line, enter this hallowed ground? It would be her first murder scene, her baptism by fire into the true-life workings of a homicide investigation, and she wasn't sure how she would react. Sure, she'd lived a nightmare, held her dying sister in her arms. But somehow, this was different.

A terrible thought dangled in front of her, refusing to be ignored.

What if the victim is still here, her ghostly form beckoning to me? And worse ... what if I can't decipher her message?

They made their way to Sawyer, who nodded in greeting, a clipboard in one hand and a handful of gloves in the other. Around his neck, a camera dangled from a multi-colored strap.

"Hey, Jake. Long time, no see. Hello, Miss. Agent Sawyer Mills, FBI out of Casper." He held out a hand.

"Hi. I'm Callie Callahan, Jake's partner," she grasped his hand. "Pleased to meet you."

"Likewise," Sawyer said, holding out the gloves. "I figured since you came directly from the airport, you might need these."

"Thanks," Jake and Callie said in unison. They both donned a pair while Jake surveyed the area. "We're pretty deep in the forest, Sawyer. Who found the body?"

"College kid, majoring in Wildlife Biology, came up here hoping to find a species of bird rare to the area. Eventually, he spotted and followed his assignment—a Snowy Egret, whatever the hell that is, as it made its way over the treetops. Almost tripped right in ..."

The crunch of footsteps interrupted Sawyer as Deputy Cummings approached them from the left.

"Hey," Dan said, nodding to Jake and Callie. "I suppose Sawyer has filled you in. This one is a real heart-breaker."

Jake shook his head. "We were just getting to that."

"Yeah, it's a damned shame," Dan continued, oblivious to taking over the conversation. "Woman was twenty-five years old. Pretty. We found a backpack with her wallet and a few pictures of a baby girl. The photo on the license in her bag matches her face. Her name is Naomi Vaughn, lived in Big Horn County."

"Cell phone?" Jake asked.

"Yes, but unfortunately, it's locked. And it's a smartphone."

"Shit," Jake grumbled.

"What?" Callie asked, looking first at Dan, then Jake. "Why 'shit?'"

"Certain model phones are notorious for their security," Jake explained. "Unless we find someone who knows her password, we're out of luck discovering any text or call history."

"Oh. Well, that sucks."

"Anyway," Dan said, "at least the bastard left her ID. It gives us a starting point."

As they approached the scene, Callie scanned the area, feeling like a voyeur as they trounced through the woods. She believed that people, especially those who left this earth by another's hand, deserved, at the very least, a modicum of privacy. Knowing that Katie had been prodded and swabbed and photographed in death only strengthened that belief.

Unfortunately, discretion and anonymity flew out the window the instant you became a homicide victim.

As a group, the four moved closer to the body. Callie could see Naomi now, naked and bruised, her legs spread in a suggestive, vulnerable pose. It was degrading, vile, and perverted, suggesting the culprit had a warped sense of morality and power.

And hinting at a killer with an untold amount of rage toward women.

Her mind turned to Gabriel as she analyzed the scene. Callie understood a lot about her half-brother, about how his mind worked. He was a sociopathic narcissist, a delusional but organized killer who drew pleasure through the pain of others.

He was also a meticulous planner. This scene appeared rushed, impulsive. Even so, rosary beads were the Apostle's 'thing', his signature that no one outside of law enforcement was privy to.

However, it was still too early to tell if this was Gabriel's work.

Too early to rule the sick fuck out, either.

She shivered, the woods strangely silent, the absence of chirping birds or buzzing insects eerie. It was as though nature took a pause, a breath, a moment of silence to respect the magnitude of the loss. The deep tone of Sawyer's voice nearly made her yelp.

"Not sure if she was sexually assaulted," Sawyer growled, "but whoever did this wanted us to think she was. You can see that, besides the objects left behind, the killer left a message on her abdomen."

They all stared down at Naomi's midsection, the hastily scrawled words ugly and glaring and red.

"Reaper?" Jake asked Sawyer. "Have you ever seen this before?"

"Nope. You?"

"Negative. Wonder what the hell he means by it. Is he saying he's like Joe Black? Like death personified?"

"No clue," Sawyer said, "but the coroner and a tech from DCI are on the way. Dan and I established the reference points for baseline measurements, and I expect the coroner will repeat and validate those once he gets here. We left the diagram sketching to you, though," he shrugged in self-depreciation. "I suck at drawing."

Jake nodded. "Not a problem. How about Curt?"

Sawyer shook his head. "Unfortunately, he's getting some pushback about getting too involved in these cases since both the Sheriff's department and FBI are working them now. I hear DCI has several agents on assignment investigating a child sex ring, meaning they're shorthanded working other cases."

"Damn," Jake muttered.

"But the good news? Since we asked for his help on the Nora Grant case, he has permission to continue that investigation. Maybe if we can connect Nora's murder with this one, they will allow him to join us on this case."

Jake nodded and stepped carefully around the body, stopping

near Naomi's head. Callie cautiously traced his path, shadowing his footsteps to reduce scene contamination. When he pulled out a notebook to diagram the scene, she squatted low, attempting to gain a different perspective of Naomi's body.

Dan stepped beside her, squatting down to meet her eyes. "Nasty stuff, right? Although you gotta give it to him—the guy has a flair for staging. Aside from the cuts and bruises, she looks gorgeous."

Irritated, Callie said, "I don't think she looks gorgeous, Deputy. I think she looks dead."

Dan blushed. "Of course. I-I didn't mean it like it sounded." Embarrassed, he walked away, pretending to check his cellphone messages.

Callie studied the body on the ground, feigning nonchalance while secretly trying to slow her racing heart. Naomi Vaughn was a classic beauty with dark, gleaming hair, a noble nose, and a skin tone that hinted at Middle Eastern heritage. A gold-colored crown, cheap, cheesy, and reminiscent of a prop found in a Halloween costume shop, sat crookedly on top of her head. A fallen log to her left held a loop of gold thread, a silver bell, and a set of rosary beads. A butter-colored cord, striking against her olive skin, twisted tightly around her neck.

And in bold letters, the eerie message recorded on her torso.

Tilting her head, Callie studied the sky. It was nearing late afternoon; the temperature dropping as rapidly as the sun. She wrapped her arms around her middle, unsure if it was the circumstances or the cold that made her shiver. Turning back to the scene, she noted Naomi's clothes, a pair of tactical pants and a brightly colored T-shirt, scattered haphazardly around an ancient pine tree. A pair of brown hiking boots sat near her backpack.

Callie's eyes darted between the clothing and the body on the ground. Something about the colors of the T-shirt, or the angle of Naomi's thin wrist as her hand pointed skyward, was familiar.

Shaking, mind whirling, she peeled back layer upon layer of memories until she found the truth.

It's the hand.

Naomi's delicate hand bent slightly at the wrist, her long fingers outstretched as if reaching for hope, an anchor, salvation. The realization, the familiarity of it all, took Callie's breath away.

Oh, God! Kates.

The memory exploded behind her eyes, slamming into her like a freight train. Katie's thin wrist, pale and motionless, resting against her temple, while the gaping hole that bubbled in the center of her chest mocked her as she gasped for air that would not come.

Oh, please! Callie's mind screamed. *I don't want to see this again!*

Her vocal cords spasmed, creating an inhuman, animalistic whimper that was foreign to her ears. She stood on shaky legs and, backing away, staggered deeper into the woods, not knowing where she was going but urgently trying to get there.

She stopped alongside an eight-foot-tall boulder that seemed out of place, as if someone dropped it from the heavens just so she could rest against it. Gulping in air greedily, convinced that the next breath would be her last, she failed to hear Jake come from behind.

"Blaze? What is it?"

Keeping her back to him, hiding the tears that rolled down her cheeks, she croaked, "I ... I just need a minute, Jake. Please?"

He stepped closer and gently placed his hand on her back, rubbing her shoulder. That humane gesture, that simple act of kindness, acted as a key, opening the gates to an agony Callie had never allowed herself to experience. She bent forward and caught her knees, her throat burning as she retched up nothing but bitter, hot bile, and waited for her heart to burst.

She had never known such pain in her life.

. . .

Jake stood quietly, his eyes glimmering with unshed tears, and forced his mind to focus on anything but the hurt he felt inside. His emotions were all over the place, running the gamut from sorrow to regret to an 'I need to punch something' kind of madness.

It was more than just a protective instinct, more than a kind of chivalry toward a female friend. It was... something else. A nameless, faceless urge to shield Callie from harm.

Puzzled, choosing to ignore whatever was stirring inside him, he waited until the relentless wave of spasms that assailed her gut had subsided.

Callie stayed like that, hunched forward, hands propped on her knees, long after the retching had ended, and her tears dried. Jake wasn't sure if it was because she'd forgotten to rise or because she lacked the strength to stand.

But eventually, she straightened and, tossing her shoulders back, swept an errant strand of hair from her cheek and faced him.

~

"Feel better?" Jake asked thickly. "I wondered when you were going to get it all out. You've never grieved her properly, have you?"

"Have you?" Callie snipped, unsure of where her anger was coming from.

Jake shook his head. "You can't compare us, Blaze. I grieve for what could have, should have been. But I only knew Kate for a month. We were just starting out, had only dipped our toes in the waters of our relationship. Of course, I miss her. She was a beautiful, amazing woman that I thought just might be 'the one.'" He stuffed his hands into his pockets, suddenly uncomfortable speaking about his relationship with Katie. "Jesus, Callahan, she was your twin sister. My grief can't hold a candle to yours." He narrowed his eyes. "So, I'll ask you again... have you mourned your sister?"

Callie scrubbed her hands over her face, then folded her arms protectively around her waist. "I've been too busy trying to hold it together, chasing shadows and looking for Gabriel." Embarrassed, she added, "I'm so sorry, Jake. I can't believe I just heaved all over your crime scene."

He snorted. "You didn't." Hooking a thumb, he pointed over his shoulder. "The crime scene is over there, remember? You just upchucked on Mother Nature is all."

"Maybe. Still, it wasn't very professional of me, was it?" A look of horror crossed her face. "Oh, man. Sawyer and Dan must think I'm a head case."

"Fuck 'em if they do," he grinned.

Despite herself, she laughed for a second, then became somber. "I guess I should have expected this. Christ, I'm a psychologist. How do I not know that skipping steps in the grieving process would catch up with me? I skipped right over denial and pain and headed straight to anger and bargaining. Do not pass go, do not collect two-hundred dollars."

She peeled off her gloves, stuffed them into a pocket, and climbed up the craggy face of the rock. Taking a seat at the top, she rubbed her hands together, mesmerized by the cloud of dust that fell to her lap. "I swear, it was like being hit by a bus. I saw Naomi's hand, the position of her wrist, and all I could see was Katie in that filthy basement, dying." She gulped, the sting of tears once again threatening to fall. "I flew back to that moment, dredged up the horror of staring at her ashen hand, begging you to help us while holding her head in my lap."

Jake frowned. "You know, not to sound like an asshole, but maybe you should talk to someone. PTSD isn't just for soldiers and cops. Don't feel you have to wade through this shit by yourself." He placed his foot on the rock, leg bent, and rested his forearm on his knee. His stand was casual, his tone friendly, and Callie couldn't help but recognize the lunacy of the situation.

Just two people, fifteen feet from a dead woman, having an informal chat.

"I've seen it more times than I can count," Jake continued. "I've seen it with me. In me. And I realize now that the person who stands alone with his burdens soon collapses from them."

Callie snickered. "Where the hell did you hear that? A fortune cookie?"

Jake winked. "I am chock-full of valuable pearls of wisdom, kid."

Raising a brow, she teased, "You're chock full of something, that's for sure. Anyway, you may be right about the PTSD thing." She waited a moment, afraid to voice her feelings out loud. Her heart was raw and tattered; the shrapnel left behind after Katie's death, jagged and sharp.

"It tears me up inside," she said finally. "I mean, I know I still get to see her occasionally, and that's a rare gift that I'm grateful for. Truly, I am. But, at the same time, I *see* her, you know? I see the truth—see the 'she's dead and never coming back,' Kate. Some days, her visits only serve as a reminder of what I've lost, what the world has lost. And that, that just sucks."

Jake stared at her for a moment, then held out his hand. Callie grabbed it, stood, and scrambled down from the rock. "Yeah, it does. But you know what doesn't suck, Blaze? Knowing that we are gonna catch the bastard that blew up your world. So, come on, let's do this."

～

Thirty minutes later, Jed phoned Jake with an update.

"Tell me something good, brother," Jake said, waving Callie over from Naomi's body. When she was near, he put the phone on speaker.

"Nothing you want to hear, unfortunately. I just spoke with Valdez. He and Abby got nada from the security camera footage at that Ranchester coffee house where Nora and Samuel Jackson, or whatever his real name is, met. For about an hour that morning, the tape was nothing but fuzz. Then, miraculously, the feed came back up. Abby figures he had some sort of radio frequency jammer in use while he was there. A device like that sends out a stronger signal on the same frequency as the one the camera is using, so it overrides it. You can get a device like that anywhere. Frightening, right? They sell ones that are portable, no bigger than a deck of cards. Then, once you turn it off, the signal is no longer blocked, and the system becomes fully functional again."

"Well, shit," Jake muttered.

"Yeah, what he said," Callie added. "Obviously, this dude knows his way around technology.

"Right. In other news, Valdez is checking in with the State Crime Lab. They're analyzing the fire debris found at the Grant homicide, looking for fibers, accelerants, etc. Oh, and Adam Dempsey called."

"He called you? Wonder why he didn't call me or Callie."

"He did, actually. Said it went straight to voicemail."

"Yeah, some spots up here are dead zones. What'd he say?"

"He says, in his words, he has 'bupkis.' Jeremy Sterling was an altar boy during his time in Laredo, literally and figuratively. He either did his crimes using an alias or was an exceptionally gifted felon. In any event, not one of Laredo's informants are talking."

"Geesh. Got any good news, Junior?"

Jed smiled. "I do. Your pal Ford is on the way to you."

"Really?" Jake said, surprised. Ford seldom left the office anymore. "What's so urgent it's dragging him out of his comfy office chair?"

"Matthew Grant, Nora's ex-husband. Ford was running down a lead on him nearby that turned out to be a dead end. He said he might as well turn lemons into lemonade, so he was coming out to give you a hand."

Jake chuffed. "Lemons into lemonade? He really said that?"

"Well, um, no. What he said was that today was, and I quote, 'as useless as a cock in a convent.' So, sue me. I improvised for Callie's sake."

Callie smiled. "You're a good man, Jed Devereaux."

"Yeah," Jake muttered, "you are—when you aren't being an asshole."

Twenty minutes later, Ford announced his arrival in his usual manner, charging in, balls to the wall, like a bull in a China shop. His quiet cursing and thundering steps announced a man who could dominate whatever space he entered.

Making eye contact with Jake, who stood twenty feet away, Ford nodded and, huffing and puffing, headed his way.

Jim Ford had long ago traded his healthy diet and gym membership for greasy burgers and craft beer.

In his haste to reach the others, Ford plowed, face-first, into a tree branch. The sudden spurt of blood that gushed from his nose was immediate, and he swore, dragging the back of his hand under his nostrils and across his face. The blood smear left a heavy trail along his cheek that thinned slightly as it neared his ear.

"Oh, boy, that's gotta sting," Callie said sympathetically. She dug into a pocket and held out a white bandana lined with green shamrocks. "Do you think you broke it?"

Ford accepted the neckerchief, pressing it firmly against his nose. "Thanks, doll. No, I didn't break it, just pissed it off some. I'm used to this. It will stop in a minute."

"Ever hear the word 'klutz', Jimbo?" Jake asked.

Ford narrowed his eyes. "Ever hear the word 'schmuck,' Jakey?"

"Okay, then," Callie interrupted, "now that we've examined the whole 'schmuck vs. klutz' thing, would you care to see the actual crime scene?"

They walked a few feet away to where Naomi lay, the snap of twigs crunching underfoot, breaking the silence of the forest.

Sawyer and Dan flanked the body, cell phones glued to their ears. Sawyer finished his call first, glanced at Ford, and chuckled. "Jesus, Jim, you're bleeding all over my crime scene. You get into it with Smokey the Bear?"

Ford grunted, squeezing the fleshy part of his nose, the white cloth above his lip saturated in blood. "Tree branch, shithead. And I ain't bleedin' on your scene, so shut yer pie hole."

Dan cleared his throat. "Good to see you again, Jim. I, um, I have a first-aid box in my truck if you need an icepack or something. I just got called to an accident scene, but I can grab the kit before I leave."

"Nah, I'm good. Bleeding has slowed down a bunch, but thanks."

"Alrighty," Dan said to no one in particular. "I'm off. Keep me in the loop, will ya?"

"You bet. Thanks, Danny," Sawyer said.

Ford turned to Jake. "So," he said, voice nasally as his fingers clamped around his nostrils, "coroner get here yet?"

As Jim spoke, two unfamiliar male voices reached their ears. The newcomers, chatting amicably about pitching stats for the Colorado Rockies, came into view, dipped below the yellow tape, and stopped beside the body.

The minute Jake recognized one of them, he growled. "What the actual fuck is...?" He turned to Sawyer. "This is a joke, right? Has to be."

Confused, Callie studied Jake's profile, then looked back at the strangers.

The younger of the two spoke first. "Well, well, well, if it isn't the notorious Jake Devereaux, protector of women and agent extraordinaire!"

Jake clenched his jaw with such force, he expected to hear the crack of a molar. "What the fuck are you doing here, Simon?"

Simon? Callie thought. *The creepy bastard from the FBI lab Kates told me about?*

The larger man standing next to the crime scene tech spoke

up. "Well, now, this is awkward. I take it you and Mr. Simon have a history together?"

Eyes never leaving Tucker Simon's face, Jake asked, "And you are?"

"The names Palmer, TJ Palmer, Sheridan County coroner. My day begins when yours ends." It was an old homicide investigator joke, and he waited, expectantly, for his joke to make an impression.

No one laughed.

While Jake had no acquaintance with TJ Palmer, he knew all about Tucker Simon, a former intern in Quantico's Forensic Anthropology Program. Jake assigned Tucker to assist Kate Callahan with her examination of human remains found on Sugarloaf Mountain. Instead of helping, Tucker Simon did his best to terrorize and humiliate her.

Eventually, Jake witnessed the weaselly-eyed bastard threaten Katie after she'd rejected his sexual advances and he fired him on the spot.

"Excuse me," Callie clipped, addressing Tucker, "but I understood you were out of the business, so to speak. Well deserved, considering how you treated my sister." Clenching her fists, she added, "Consider yourself fortunate that I knew nothing of your interactions with her when she was alive. If I had, you'd be walking with a limp and questioning your ability to father children in the future."

Tucker smirked, showing a row of yellowed, rotting teeth. The repulsive image reminded Callie of the clown from the movie 'It.'

All you need is a red balloon, dickhead.

"Not only do you look like your sister, but you have her temper as well, I see. I guess the apple doesn't fall far and all that. As for your question, I didn't change careers. I was asked to," he hesitated, "to relocate. It was for the best, really. Wyoming DCI lab is a much better facility than Quantico." He pinned his gaze on Jake. "And it has a much higher quality of people who work there. Especially," he drew out the word, "the women. Women who are, frankly, as attractive as my former co-worker, without the added 'bitch' factor."

Callie swore, and Jake lurched forward. A beefy hand encircled his bicep and stopped him cold.

"Easy, partner," Ford said quietly. "This prick ain't worth it."

"Gentlemen, are we going to have a problem?" Sawyer asked, stepping between them. Squinting his eyes at Tucker, he added, "Because, while we need Jake's expertise here, I can easily replace a crime scene tech with just one phone call."

Tucker raised his hands. "No problemo, Chief. I'm just here to do my job."

"Wonderful," Sawyer said sharply. "Then do it."

Seething, Jake shrugged away from Ford's grip and looked back at Callie. "You okay, Blaze?"

She nodded, but the flush on her face, the curl of her lip, betrayed her. She was far from okay.

She was livid.

"Okay, let's get this scene processed," Jake said. "Suddenly, I feel the urge to puke."

Palmer opened his bag, donned a second pair of gloves over the first, and squatted down. Simon mimicked the move, and they went to work, speaking in hushed tones, jotting things down, taking measurements.

Ford glanced at Jake, wary. "You good?"

"Peachy."

Stepping around the victim's feet, heading toward her head, Ford picked up Naomi's wallet and said, "You're gonna need to fill me in on this Tucker asshole."

Less than a minute later, as Jake and Callie were comparing theories about how Naomi Vaughn ended up in Little Goose Canyon, Jim Ford barreled past them, arms pumping, sprinting away from the scene.

"Wait! Where the hell are you going?" Jake called after him.

"Hey, Jimbo! That irritable bowel acting up again?" Sawyer joked.

Ford never turned, never acknowledged Jake's question or Sawyer's teasing.

"Uh, what was that?" Callie asked.

Jake raised a brow. "Damned if I know. The Jim Ford I know doesn't run. Ever."

CHAPTER SEVENTEEN

A few hours later, with daylight waning, the body of Naomi Vaughn was transported to the coroner's office and the scene secured.

Callie hugged her torso. She was chilled to the bone and, although the air was damp, it was the horrific event that brought them here that caused her to shudder.

"You're shivering," Jake said, taking off his jacket and wrapping it around her shoulders.

"No, no, you keep it. You're only wearing a light shirt, and I refuse to be held responsible if you freeze your ass off."

He smirked. "I had no idea you were so interested in my ass."

"Oh, I'm not," Callie said coolly. "Just interested in saving mine." For the hundredth time in the last few months, she cursed her fair skin.

Her blush gave away everything.

"Seriously," he lied, "I'm not cold." He tucked his hands inside his pockets and pulled his elbows closer to his torso, seeking warmth.

He wasn't worried about freezing his ass off—that ship had sailed thirty minutes ago.

"But," he continued, tensing his jaw so his teeth wouldn't

chatter, "it is getting late, and Billings is at least two hours from here. You look exhausted. My family's cabin up in Pitikin Falls is only about twenty minutes away. We can scrounge up some grub for dinner, get a little rest, then head back to Billings in the morning. What do you say?"

Callie hesitated. A warm cabin and some comfort food sounded magnificent. But being with Jake, alone, in a cozy house high in the mountains? Why did she feel like a lamb being led to slaughter?

"Are you sure your parents wouldn't mind? Because, honestly, I am tired, physically and emotionally. Plus, I'd like to sit and digest all we've learned today."

He grinned. "Are you kidding? It would thrill my mom to know the place is being used. She keeps it well-stocked, hoping Jed or I will use it more often."

Jake's cell rang as they walked back to the car. "Hey, Jed, what's up?"

"Plenty, brother. What time are you coming home?"

Jake stole a glance at Callie as she plodded through the woods, shoulders slumped. He swore he could *hear* the fatigue in her steps. Purple smudges occupied the spaces beneath her eyes, accentuating her current ashy-gray skin tone.

There was no way in hell he was going to force this woman to travel another two hours.

"Tomorrow morning. We're wiped and are going to head over to the cabin for the evening. Why? What's happened?"

"Abby's happened. The girl is a freakin' genius. She's following up on a few promising leads, and, honest to God Jake, I think we may finally catch a break here."

"Hallelujah to that," Jake said. Then, hesitating, added, "Have you heard from Jim Ford today?"

"Uh, no, why? Was I supposed to?"

Jake rubbed the back of his neck, frustrated. "To be honest, I'm not sure. He hauled ass out of this crime scene with no explanation. It was as if he'd seen a ghost." He glanced at Callie and raised a brow. "And we all know only one of us in this crew can do that."

Callie rolled her eyes.

"Huh," Jed said, puzzled. "I don't believe I've ever seen Ford haul his ass anywhere."

"Yeah, that's what I said. If you hear from him, let me know. I'm going to reach out later, see what the hell is going on. Meanwhile, you have me curious. Anything concrete you can tell me about what Abby found?"

Callie tugged on his sleeve and mouthed, 'Speaker, please.'

Jake hit the speaker button and said, "You're on speaker. Callie is here with me."

"Hi Cal," Jed said. "We have a few developments, not confirmed but promising. The biggest one is a potential connection between the Nora Grant homicide and one that was committed 120 miles south, in Ten Sleep. In that case, the victim, Arthur Sinclair, was discovered in a wooded area damned near decapitated. Curtis and Dan are both working that case and confirm that the killer left behind a few items, including a silver bell. No rosary beads, though, like the Nora Grant case."

"But a bell like Nora," Callie said.

"Right. Investigators at the Sinclair homicide also found a basket of apples and a can of soup. Bizarre."

Jake frowned. "Bizarre is right. At the scene we just left, there was a silver bell, some yellow string, and a rosary near the body. The victim was nude, posed in a vulgar position, and had a dime-store crown on her head. But in this case, the killer left a message on the body—the word 'Reaper' written in blood."

Jed clucked his tongue. "Damn."

"It seems to me the killer is adding information with each murder," Callie said. "As if he's dangling clues like carrots."

"How do you mean?" Jed asked.

"The first homicide had only the bell, right? But in the Grant murder, he left behind both a bell and a rosary. And now, we have a bell, rosary, and a message." She bit her lip in thought. "Nora was burned so the killer couldn't leave a message on her body. But what about Arthur Sinclair? Maybe we missed the rosary or a message. Both scenes sound gruesome, so it wouldn't surprise me if investigators wanted to be in and out of there quickly."

Jake agreed. "Yeah, neither of those scenes sound like they were a picnic. I'd want to be out of there PDQ myself. Maybe we'll have Curt revisit the Sinclair homicide location, just to be sure. Gabriel used to string his rosary beads up high, where people seldom look. Hell, I nearly missed a set wrapped around a tree branch at the Dixon/ Wurster dumpsite. Thankfully, Katie spotted them."

Laura Dixon and her father, Henry Wurster, were among the Apostle's first victims after he arrived in Virginia from Laredo, Texas. Investigators surmised that Dixon and Wurster encountered Gabriel in Dulles International Airport and were killed simply because he needed their car. There was no ritual, no high moral standing in his warped mind for these murders.

Rather, Laura and her father died as a matter of convenience.

Months later, their decomposed remains were discovered on Sugarloaf Mountain, just north of Washington, DC. It was on that mountain, at that crime scene, that Jake and Katie first met. He smiled, reliving that first awkward meeting.

"What?" Callie asked. "Are you remembering something?"

"You could say that. Nothing relevant to the case, though."

"Hello?" Jed asked. "Are you two still with me?"

"Yeah, sorry, brother. What were you saying?"

"Just that I will give Curt a call when I get off here with you. I need to ask him to the meeting tomorrow, anyway. Either of you have any guess about what all these objects left behind could mean?"

Callie scoured her brain for a connection, a thread that could weave all the clues together. "Jed, did they find anything else at the Nora Grant homicide besides the rosary and bell?"

He flipped through his notes. "Looks like just a block of wood, about the size of a brick."

Callie bit her lip in thought, searching for a parallel. "A block of wood, a basket of apples, a can of soup. And at this scene, we found a crown and some golden thread. Let me think about it a bit."

"While you're thinking, here's another thing to chew on—Abby found a link between Sinclair and Grant. It's a website called LiveFeed."

"Never heard of it," Jake said.

"I wouldn't expect that you would," Jed replied. "It's a place people go to swap recipes or decorating ideas or find a no-strings hook-up. It's also where some go to bare their souls in a chat room called 'Confessions.' I did a cursory glance, and a few of the more popular topics centered on either voicing your biggest fears or relating your lowest moments. Still trying to wrap my head around why anyone would choose to show their warts to a room full of strangers."

"You'd be surprised, Jedidiah. Some folks grow a pair when hiding behind a computer screen."

"I guess so. Anyway, Abby is working on gathering a chat history from the Grant and Sinclair laptops. I'd bet you dollars to doughnuts that we can trace your latest victim to LiveFeed as well. By chance, did you find the victim's cell phone at this last scene?"

"Yeah, but it's gonna be a tough nut to crack. It's locked tight, with no way to get in unless we find someone who knows the code."

Callie frowned. "How about a court order?"

"Nope," Jake said. "Although many have tried that route, I don't know of any agency that has succeeded. Like I said earlier, security and anonymity have become the rallying cry these days."

"And," Jed chimed in, "companies that build that kind of reputation don't give a rat's patootie why you need to gain access to that info. It's a no-win situation."

"The Kobayashi Maru," Callie whispered.

Jake cocked his head. "The Koby what?"

"The Kobayashi Maru. It was a training exercise in StarFleet Academy, a no-win situation whose only point was to gauge how a cadet would do under pressure. The simulation involved a stranded ship in a dangerous zone that was off-limits to any starship. The cadet had to choose between saving that marooned ship or entering a perilous area that jeopardized his or her own ship and crew. Whatever path they chose would end badly. No one in the history of StarFleet had beaten it. Until James T. Kirk."

Jake smirked. "Star Trek? Okay, Ms. Trekkie, how did Kirk beat it?"

Callie winked. "He reprogrammed the test so that it was a winnable scenario."

"So, he cheated," Jed said.

"He did. Still beat it."

"Boy, Kate wasn't kidding when she said you were a Star Trek fan," Jake teased. "But how does that help us?"

Callie tipped her head. "What if we change the conditions of our situation, work around it? Live Feed must have an administrator, right? Someone who monitors the chat rooms? Maybe, instead of going through the cellphone records, we go directly to the source to get what we need."

"Worth a shot," Jed said. "In the meantime, I'll check with Ford, ask him to see if Naomi had a laptop or tablet that Abby can tap in to."

"Keep Ford out of it for now," Jake said. "Not sure what, but something spooked him at that crime scene. Until we know what's crawled up his ass, I would check with Dan Cummings or Sawyer Mills."

Callie jumped in. "Try Sawyer first."

Jake quirked a brow. "Why?"

"I just think Sawyer is more on the ball."

Jake didn't question her further. If she was feeling squirrely about Dan Cummings, she must have a good reason.

"Got it," Jed replied. "What time do you want to meet tomorrow?"

"We should be back by mid-morning. Why don't you get in touch with the rest of the Scooby Gang and see if we can meet around noon?"

"Will do. And Jake? I got a bad feeling about this case. Watch your back."

～

Thirty minutes after leaving the Naomi Vaughn crime scene, Jake and Callie pulled into the driveway of the Devereaux family cabin. Located in the tiny town of Pitikin Falls, the home had a rustic exterior, with two stone chimneys rising from the roof and several small windows dressed with lacy curtains. A quaint front porch held two rocking chairs, a small table made from a pallet crate, and a weathered wooden swing. On the side of the house, a small footbridge, illuminated by solar lighting, perched above a rocky stream that ran the length of the property.

"Don't let the outside scare you," Jake said as they approached the front door, "it looks rough, but the inside is up-to-date and bigger than it appears."

"I love it! Talk about a great place to escape to!"

"For sure. Come on, I'll show you around."

Jake climbed the front steps and reached overhead, scooting his fingers along the interior eave of the porch roof.

"Bingo!" he said proudly, waving the key like a child who'd just found the last Easter Egg.

Callie grinned. "I'm surprised. Never figured you for a 'hide the key' kinda guy. Too risky."

"It used to be even easier to find when we taped it to the underside of the rocker," he said, walking through the door. "Progress, right?"

Callie found the interior of the cabin just as inviting as the exterior. Warm pine floors complemented the bright floral patterns of the sofa and loveseat. A built-in corner cabinet housed the TV while the far wall held a rifle rack above a stone fireplace. The country-type kitchen boasted a cast-iron stove, walnut cabinets stenciled with light pink roses, and a square oak table.

He gave her a quick tour, pointing out the bedroom she would stay in.

"My gosh, this is all so lovely. Your parents have done a wonderful job here."

Jake's face reddened at the compliment. "Yeah, not too shabby, huh? There's a good stream for fishing, and my dad set up a shooting range on the south corner of the property. We have about five acres to play in, so the neighbors don't mind much. Why don't you have a seat on the porch while I rustle us up some dinner? You want a beer or something?"

"A beer sounds great. But first, can I use your bathroom? I want to freshen up after that puke fest at the crime scene."

He laughed. "Be my guest. Bathroom is the last door on the right and extra toothbrushes are in the medicine cabinet if you need one."

A few minutes later, Callie met him in the kitchen. "Can I help with anything?"

"Nah, I got it. Go on out and enjoy the view. I'll bring your beer in a sec."

Callie stepped out onto the porch, inhaling deeply, the air saturated with the scents of lilac and earth and spring. She chose a chair and rocked back and forth, admiring the early blooms of a Meadowlark forsythia bush.

Lost in thought, she jumped when the screen door opened. "Here you go. It's a pale ale from a local brewery." Winking, he added, "Good stuff, but be careful. The alcohol content may be higher than you're used to."

Callie rolled her eyes. "What makes you think I can't handle a beer or two? In case it's gotten past you, I'm Irish. I could probably drink you under the table."

Laughing, he sat next to her in the other rocker. "Okay, but don't say I didn't warn you. I put some water on for pasta, and we have some dinner rolls in the freezer. That work?"

"Sounds divine."

They sat in silence for a while, just enjoying the peace and, if they were honest, the company. Finally, Jake spoke.

"So Jed was talking about this website, the one the victims frequented called Confessions, and it got me thinking. Fear is a subjective thing, right? I mean, what scares the crap out of one person could be a walk in the park for another." He took a swig of his beer. "So, what's your greatest fear, Blaze?"

Callie said nothing.

"I'll go first.," Jake prompted. "Snakes. I freaking hate 'em. Always have, ever since I was a kid. How about you?"

Callie's eyes clouded, and she shrugged. "I've already lived my biggest fear, Jake. I lost my sister."

"Ah, I'm sorry. I can be such an insensitive ass sometimes. I shouldn't have brought it up. Of course, losing Kate was your biggest fear."

"Don't worry about it. The last thing I want is for you to feel the need to walk on eggshells around me. As for the question, I can tell you what my next greatest fear is if you're interested."

"Shoot."

"Anything to do with not being able to get that next breath. So many possibilities there, right? A hand over my mouth, running out of air in a confined space. Anything that hinders me from getting that next breath. But especially drowning. Did you know I don't swim anymore? As a kid, I was a fish. My parents couldn't get me out of the water. But after Kate's accident, after I understood she died because she couldn't get air into her lungs, I guess I turned her experience into a phobia. Shit," she laughed, "I don't even like to wear a scarf or a mask. Guess that means I'll never be a runway model. Or a burglar."

Jake chuckled. "You would suck at it, anyway. That red hair would be like a flare to the cops."

He excused himself to check on dinner. A few seconds after he entered the house, Callie heard his cell phone ringing.

~

Twenty minutes later, Jake walked outside and, head down, sat heavily on the porch steps. His eyes were puffy, his nose red. Callie could see he'd been crying.

She joined him on the stairs and took his hand. "Jake? What is it? What's happened?"

He coughed and, voice cracking, muttered, "Death in the family."

"Oh my God! I'm so sorry! Who?"

Jake ignored a tear that slid over his cheek, across his face, and onto his lip. "Good ol' Gus. Sully said he was fine this morning. He went for a walk, had his breakfast, snuggled with Sully for a few minutes. Hell, he even made it down the townhouse stairs without help. It's damn stupid I'm sitting here blubbering like an idiot." He sniffed and looked at Callie. "The dog was fucking ancient. Do you know the life expectancy of a Bernese Mountain dog?"

Callie shook her head.

"Six to eight years. Gus was nearly double that, just turned twelve in February. Like I said, damned stupid to be sitting here crying about it."

Callie leaned in and nuzzled her shoulder into his arm. "Come on, Jake, you know better than that. Gus was family, and you gave him a beautiful life. It was because of your love and care that he beat those longevity odds. Mourning him is anything but stupid."

Jake rubbed his eyes, her words giving him permission to grieve. Sobbing quietly, Callie tried to comfort him, whispering soothing platitudes and patting his back. Nothing was working, and she was becoming desperate. She hated seeing him so wounded.

It was an odd feeling. His pain was making her feel helpless, uncomfortable. She needed to do something. Impulsively, she took his head between her hands and, using her thumbs, softly brushed away his tears.

Then she kissed him. Seriously kissed him.

Jake groaned like a man who'd spent a lifetime waiting to taste her lips. He cupped the back of her head, kissing her just as thoroughly, just as passionately.

Callie felt herself falling, dropping into another dimension in time where nothing else existed except for the two of them. She melted into him, greedily accepting his kisses, aware that she could stay in this moment forever.

Until, as suddenly as she'd fallen, one word dragged her back to the surface, the name popping into her mind, intrusive and uninvited. She struggled to surface from beneath a wave of passion, kicking and screaming, horrified by what she'd done.

Katie.

Pulling back, gasping, she jumped up and vanished into the house.

Jake groaned again, but this time, it wasn't in desire. It was in regret.

Callie paced the small bedroom, her hands clutching the top of her head, pulling at her hair in frustration. "Jesus Christ, what have I done?"

Eyes filling, ashamed, she continued to walk in circles, reciting mindless words in a bizarre act of contrition.

"I'm sorry, I am so damn—I can't believe it; I can't fucking believe..." She stopped and cringed at the knock on the door.

"Go away, Jake," she whispered. "Please, just go away."

She waited, holding her breath, until she heard his footsteps fade down the hallway. Resuming her self-degradation, she muttered, "What the hell is the matter with me, anyway? Who does this? Who betrays their sister like that?"

Feet dragging, she sat on the bed, bent her head, and buried her face in her hands. A slight tap on her shoulder startled her.

"Shadow? What is it?"

Katie stood before her, all light and beauty and love, and Callie moaned. "Oh, God, Kates," she cried, "I'm such a shit! I let my emotions and hormones overtake common sense! I'm a terrible sister."

Katie frowned. "What the devil are you talking about, Cal? You're the bee's knees in the sister world!"

Callie vehemently shook her head. "But I'm not. I dishonored you, let you down. I zeroed in on the one thing I can never have. I—I kissed Jake," she blurted. "Practically threw myself at him."

"Shadow, it's not like that. I already..."

Callie cut her off. "Please don't be mad at Jake. He's been nothing but a gentleman. I'm the one who messed up. I'm the shameless hussy here."

Katie smiled at first, then roared with laughter. "Shameless hussy? Really? Who are you? Grams?"

"It's not funny!"

"But it is," Katie replied. "Look, I had a wonderful time getting to know Jake. And who knows what would have happened if I had lived. But Jake is not...."

Katie turned toward the bedroom door at the sound of approaching footsteps.

"Listen up, kiddo. We don't have much time. Do you remember I told you about a darkness I saw coming?"

Callie nodded. "Yes. You said it could be even worse than Gabriel. As if."

"Not worse, just... different."

Callie thought for a moment. "I've seen some things, Kates. Shadows, dark masses that look neither human nor animal. Just forms without light."

Katie nodded. "Yes, that's what I've seen, too. I think it's a manifestation of malevolent intent, like a visible form of evil."

Callie quirked a brow. "So, I see a trait or emotion or intention in a physical shape? A force or energy so powerful, it takes on a corporeal form? Sorry, but I call bullshit."

"You are a stubborn woman, Callista Callahan. Mark my words—one way or another, you are going to see the truth. And when you do, you'd best learn how to deal with it. Or else."

"Or else what?" Callie said, defiant.

Katie shook her head sadly. "Or else it will consume you."

Callie watched, heartbroken, as her sister faded into nothingness. Every time Katie appeared to her, Callie felt joy. And each time she watched her leave, she felt broken. It was a devastating merry-go-round of emotions, all packed into a sliver or two of time.

The day that Katie died, Callie understood the futility of believing in the future. There was no such thing as tomorrow. Instead, life built itself around a yesterday people yearned to relive, and a today that people took for granted. Tomorrow was an illusion, a lie we told ourselves to trick our minds into thinking we had all the time in the world.

And I adopted that lie. I took it in, inhaled it, made it a part of me. In a world full of inexperienced idiots and vain morons who foolishly believed that time was limitless, I was king. And now, I have nothing left but stolen moments. All because I lost sight of the big picture, failed to nurture and hold precious the time we spent together.

Sobbing, Callie laid back on the bed and reached for a lemon and cream-colored throw at the foot of the mattress. Settling in, the irony of the cheery colors on the blanket mocking her, she eventually cried herself to sleep...

. . .

Shackled to a Lally column in the dank basement, curled on her side, Callie peered into the blackness, searching for any source of light. The icy cold of the damp cement sent chills up and down her nude body. Her ankle throbbed, a fiery heat that traveled along the path of a nerve, terminating at the knee.

She took a deep breath, trying to steady the pulsing ache, and instantly regretted it. White-hot pain slammed into her side, flaring with each breath. She didn't need a chest X-ray to know that Gabriel had fractured several ribs. With each inhalation, the jagged edges of broken bone swept over one another, grinding and clicking along her ribcage. It was a synchronized chorus of pain, a melody that sang in tune with the agony of her crushed tibia.

Gabriel was responsible for all of this. He beat her nearly to death as she lay defenseless, cuffed and bound by iron chains to a metal pole.

She struggled to sit, nausea building as she fought the rising panic in her chest. Biting her lip, throat raw from screaming, she tested her restraints. Taking shallow breaths, she moved gingerly, yanking at the chains that held her. The iron clanged and rattled, the obnoxious clamor reverberating in her ears until she thought she would go mad with it.

Terror and pain heightened her senses. She could hear the rasp of her breath, feel each bead of sweat as it trickled down her spine, eventually coming to rest in the curve of her lower back. A hazy fog lingered in the air, creating a wavelike distortion to the walls and ceiling. To her left, an enormous grandfather clock stood sentry, its thunderous ticking with the passage of time unnerving.

A clock? But that wasn't right. There was no clock in that basement, no haze in the atmosphere, no twisting of the walls of her prison.

Just a dream, she decided. A nightmare, one she begged would release her.

Still, she slept.

Her vantage point in the dream quickly shifted. She found herself not only a victim, but a spectator, forced to watch the nightmare unfold, aware of what was to come but helpless to stop it.

In the distance, on the cellar steps, a shadow emerged, floating down the warped staircase. The smoke-like gloom seemed to part in front of the figure, and she stepped toward Callie.

"Kates!" Callie called out, "no, no! Get out of here! Go!"

But the clicking of the clock remained deafening, swallowing up her words.

Katie moved closer.

Callie's screams echoed in her ears, panic rising as the seconds ticked by. Ignoring her pain, she sat up taller and waved her arms, praying the movement would get Katie's attention.

Katie seemed not to notice, continuing forward. Behind her, Gabriel materialized, a gun in his left hand and a rosary in his right.

"Oh, God, please! No!" Callie's mind begged. "Kate, turn around!"

Unaware of the sinister form at her back, Katie smiled and reached out a hand. "I found you, Shadow! Come on, let's blow this popsicle stand."

Nearing hysterics, screeching, Callie rocked her head. "No, no, no! Behind you, Kates! Please!"

A brilliant flash, followed by a thunderous crack, shook the room. Katie's smile fell, and her brows drew together quizzically. She raised a shaking hand to her chest, then pulled it away, staring in wonder at the blood that covered her palm. Looking down at Callie, she mouthed, "It's not your fault, Shadow. I'm sorry," then dropped to her knees.

Callie screamed again and again, convinced she would never stop, could never stop. Her heart squeezed, and she felt it splinter—a shattering of glass, an avalanche of crushed pieces falling to the earth.

Until all that remained was a void in her chest that could never be filled.

∾

"Blaze!" Jake shouted, shaking her shoulders. "Wake up!"

Callie groaned, fighting to emerge from that dark place in her mind, tears staining her face.

"Come on, sweetheart," Jake soothed. "It was just a dream. Wake up, now."

Jake's words finally cut through the cloud, and Callie shot up in bed. Heart hammering, she grabbed his arm, gulping in air, starved for oxygen. The dream was still there, vibrant, terrifying, and threatening in its intensity.

Sitting next to her on the bed, he pushed a strand of hair behind her ear. "Tough one, huh?"

She sniffed, nodding.

"I'm sorry. But you'll be happy to know that your screams reached my ears, and I'm a heavy sleeper. Truth be told, that hollering probably reached the neighbor's ears." He smirked, adding, "And they're miles away."

She didn't laugh, didn't even crack a smile.

Concerned, Jake rubbed her back. "You wanna talk about it?"

Callie sighed. "No. I just want to lie here for a bit. Will you stay with me until I fall asleep?"

Jake swallowed hard, her vulnerability reaching a part of him he thought he'd lost forever. Wordlessly, he laid down on his side and tucked her snuggly against his chest. Resting his chin on her head, he patiently waited until her breathing was even, and he was sure she was asleep. Then, pulling her closer, he touched her ear with his lips and whispered, "I'm here. And I'm not going anywhere."

CHAPTER EIGHTEEN

Big Horn Sheriff's Department
Basin, Wyoming

Stanley Brighton fidgeted in an antique chair in a corner office of the Bighorn County Sheriff's Department, the heated gaze of a uniformed officer prickling his skin.

Bouncing a leg and studying the popcorn ceiling, Stanley wondered if it was possible to sink through the scarred oak seat into oblivion. He didn't much care for the line of questioning and the accusatory tone of the on-duty deputy.

After all, Stanley came here in good faith; Stanley came here to report Maddie missing.

Stanley didn't need a fuck-ton of bullshit.

"Tell me, again, son. What makes you think your girlfriend is missing? It's only been a few hours, right?" the deputy asked.

"Well, yeah," Stanley said glumly, "but you don't understand. Maddie fuckin' lived for this interview." He sneered, then rolled his eyes. "Big Horn County Fair Queen. Shit, it's all she talked about for like, months. I went to meet her where she was interviewing, apologize for fucking up and not driving her there. But the guy in charge said she never showed."

"I can do without the profanity, son," the deputy said dryly. "Now, tell me again, what time was the interview? And why, exactly, didn't you pick her up?"

"I told you already. I come out of the video store to find two flat tires. Had to call the garage and get a tow. You got any idea how much two new tires cost? Garage guy said they both had, like, holes the size of fuckin' craters in them." He shrugged and added, "Sorry about the cuss word, but sometimes you just gotta swear."

The deputy frowned. "Right. So, just to be clear, you never made it to her house then?"

Stanley sighed. *What was with this dude? The clock's ticking! How many times I gotta tell the same fucking story?*

What Stanley didn't realize, what nobody realized, was that it didn't matter whether he told his story once again or a thousand times over.

The clock had run out for Maddie hours ago.

~

Shell Canyon
Five miles from Shell Falls
Bighorn National Mountains

Otis Hunter stood in a clearing deep in the woods of Shell Canyon, lifted the brown paper bag to his lips, and sucked out the last drops of Jim Beam bourbon nestled inside. He tossed the bag aside, the harsh shattering of glass echoing through the canyon.

"Oops," he giggled.

Staggering, blind drunk, he bobbed and weaved toward his 'home', a crude hut made of lumber scraps, tree branches, and plastic bags. In twenty-four months, Otis Hunter had gone from champagne and caviar to cheap wine and dumpster diving.

It was a long, long way to fall.

In his former life, before the booze and the astronomical gambling debts to his bookie, Otis held a lucrative position in an investment firm. Two years and several bouts of pancreatitis later, he'd lost not only his job but his family, his friends, his home. Nowadays, he took to begging in the town square for spare change or, occasionally, a cot at the homeless shelter on a frigid night. The 'regulars' there would give up their bed for the night if the price was right.

Sometimes, if he were lucky, a passer-by would bring him a sandwich or a Happy Meal.

Shuffling along, humming the *"Wellerman"* sea shanty, his foot caught an exposed tree root, and he tumbled forward, landing face-first on the forest floor. Cursing, he pushed himself onto his hands and knees and looked around, checking for an audience. Satisfied that no one had witnessed his clumsiness, he shook his head, spitting out the dirt and crawling insects that existed only in his mind.

"Sumbitch and fuck yer grannie," he called to no one. "You tryin' to kill a man?"

Looking over his shoulder, his eyes scanned the ground for the guilty tree root, but found nothing.

There were no trees here.

Confused, wondering if he'd hallucinated the whole thing, he crawled nearer to the place he'd stumbled and saw a shoe—dainty and out of place—emerging straight up from the earth and decomposing leaves.

Wha' the fuck's tha'?

He inched closer, squinting, hoping against hope that by bringing his upper and lower lids together, he could sharpen his alcohol-induced double vision. His gaze traveled slowly from the shoe upward, but all he saw was a mound of twigs surrounded by what looked like Barrel or Prickly Pear cactus. The heap appeared arranged, the branches deliberately placed one atop the other, as if their creator was gathering kindling for a fire.

And the cacti, acting as a barricade, a briar hedge, protecting what lay beneath.

Otis knew little about nature, but he did know one thing; the closest grouping of trees was at least fifty yards away. Which meant someone had to bring these limbs, and their thorny guardians, to this spot.

Someone who was hiding something. Something valuable.

He stood slowly, rocking back on his heels, the alcohol in his veins causing the ground beneath him to shift. Mumbling, he took a shaky step, arms extended to the sides like an acrobat tiptoeing across a high wire. Bending forward, his eyes roamed over the pile before him. At first glance, he saw nothing.

Then he noticed the hand.

Ascending from beneath the leaves, the feminine hand reached skyward, four slender fingers hooked into a talon-like claw. It was like a morbid caricature of a gothic Poe tale, an ashen appendage lunging and straining, struggling to break free of the damp earth.

A phoenix rising from the ashes.

Otis brought a fist to his mouth, smothering a scream, his lungs desperate for air. Heart pounding, hyperventilating, he moved closer to the top of the mound, kicking at the web of branches, freeing them from their tangled prison. Inebriated and unsteady, it took him a long time to uncover what lay beneath the tree limbs.

And when he discovered the truth—a truth he knew he would find—he clutched his stomach, dropped to his knees, and howled.

$\sim$

Hours later, two officers from the Bighorn National Forest/Medicine Wheel district discovered Otis on the ground, crumpled and hoarse, a trembling hand pointing to the mound beside him. His eyes were wide, and his body shook. He did not speak.

Hours of screaming left his vocal cords raw and incapable of generating anything beyond a croaking whisper.

Both officers stepped cautiously to the pile, hands grasping their service weapons. There were many dangerous species living out here in the canyon, from rattlesnakes to venomous spiders to mountain lions. They saw none of those creatures.

Instead, amid the Ponderosa leaves, sagebrush, and grime that littered the forest floor, they spied the body of Madison Gibbs, dirty, naked except for her stilettos, legs spread wide. On her head was a paper crown that read 'Princess,' and across her breasts, the word 'Reaper,' written in blood.

And, in her clenched fist, a blood-soaked piece of cloth.

But it was what covered her body that truly shocked. Dozens of half-filled syringes, rising like pillars and impaled into her skin. They littered her arms, her legs, her torso. Sharp, hypodermic needles, standing shoulder to shoulder, crowding her navel, her hips, the labial folds of her vagina.

A platoon of miniature soldiers, a legion of infantry, marching in combat formation.

But for Otis, it was three syringes, driven deep into her sightless right eye, that he could never unsee. It was a memory that would continue to stir and claw and rake at his soul.

Until all that remained were the tattered pieces of a previously sound mind.

And the shell of a man who would never recover.

The Disciple sat on a cracked-leather barstool, sucking on pistachios and nursing a gin and tonic. Benny's Bar and Grill, one of the seedier taverns in the area, was an establishment that served up drug deals and fistfights at a greater frequency than any drinks or burgers.

The owner was a gruff ex-biker known for his tough talk and even quicker fists. Bar brawls never drew the attention of police, simply because they were over almost before they began. Customers soon learned that, unless they wanted to get an ass-whipping, any hostility or bloodshed needed to be carried outside and away from the premises.

It was that kind of security and anonymity that made Benny's Bar and Grill the perfect place to conduct business. As he waited for his associate, the Disciple dug deep into his jacket pocket and pulled out three photographs. Laying them across his lap and away from prying eyes, he studied them, feeling his pulse quicken and his respirations increase. Remembering, excitement building, he repositioned himself on the stool, his pants growing tighter.

He was hard.

Rock hard. Sporting a boner, a chubster, a stiffy. He giggled, scouring his memories of grade school and the countless names his classmates coined for an erection. Sensing a presence, the Disciple looked up to find a hulking shadow, a bartender named Bobby, standing directly in front of him behind the counter.

Bobby was Benny's brother and had the same gruff, no-bullshit philosophy about running a bar. Furiously drying a whiskey glass, he drew his brows together and gave the Disciple a sour look.

"What the hell is so funny, pal? You got somethin' to say to me?"

The Disciple's smile fell, and he rocked his head. "Oh, no sir, no sir, I don't. I'm just sitting here thinking about my old lady." He snickered, then winked, as if they were comparing notes in an all-boys club. "She's so fucking stupid. She thinks I'm at church."

Which, since he was unmarried and had no girlfriend, was a lie.

Bobby squinted, judging whether the explanation was the truth or a line of crap. Returning the whiskey glass to its shelf, he grabbed another towel and wiped down the bar.

"Whatever, dude," Bobby grunted. "Just keep that shit to yourself."

The Disciple nodded, picked up his drink, and waited for his associate to arrive.

~

The minute he walked into the dimly lit bar, Gabriel frowned. He hated this place—hated the atmosphere and the clientele and the stench that assaulted your nostrils the minute you stepped through the door. But for whatever reason, the neanderthal he'd hooked up with loved the joint.

Uncouth dickhead.

Peering into the darkened room, he skimmed past dozens of flannel-wearing, unshaven men, huddled in groups with beer bottles in hand, until he spotted his target. Smoothing his jacket—*because I'm not a fucking barbarian*—he pushed his way through the crowd and walked to the far end of the bar.

"Glad you could make it," the Disciple said into his gin and tonic. "I was starting to think you bailed on me."

Gabriel took a calming breath. His immediate reaction was to kick the shit out of this whining, lowbred asshole. "Some of us have work to do, sir; some of us have a higher calling."

He took the barstool next to the man, ordered a bourbon, neat, and continued. "Meeting like this is extraordinarily dangerous. I hope you have good reason."

The Disciple smiled, then slid the three photographs face down across the bar. "I thought you might be interested in these." Smirking, he added, "I consider them a blessing, Father Gabriel."

Gabriel stiffened. Without acknowledging the pictures, he quietly dropped his hand into the Disciple's lap.

Scooting to the edge of the stool, the Disciple whispered, "What the hell, Padre?"

Ignoring his question, Gabriel found the man's testicles and grabbed them in the palm of his hand.

Then he wrenched. Hard.

"Ow, ow, ow!" the Disciple grunted, his voice a whisper. "What the fuck? That's my package, dude!"

After one last twist, Gabriel released him. Under his breath, teeth clenched, he spat, "If you ever use my name in public again, I will end you. Painfully. Are we clear?"

"Jesus Christ, yes, yes! I'm sorry, okay? I just got excited and forgot." Hands shaking, he took a gulp of his gin and looked around nervously.

No one seemed to notice that his balls were just in a vise. Or, if they did, they didn't care.

After one last withering look, Gabriel gathered the photographs in his hands, one behind another. The first picture was one of a smoldering pile of ... something. If not for the hand rising from the blackened cinders, it would be impossible to identify the cadaver as human. In the second photo, Gabriel saw the body of an attractive woman, crown on her head, just another corpse in the woods. He was about to move on to the third picture when two figures in the background caught his eye.

"What?" the Disciple asked excitedly. "It's the message, right?" Chuckling and practically patting himself on the back, he said, "Clever, huh? I came up with it at the last minute. Get it? Reaper?" Wiping his eyes, he added, "Sometimes, my wit takes even me by surprise."

Gabriel couldn't hear him above the pounding of his heart against his ribcage. "These people," he tapped the photo over their image, "they look familiar. Who are they?"

"Just a cop, another clueless investigator. Oh, and some broad he dragged to the scene. Not sure what her story is."

"Names?" Gabriel asked, certain of the answer, even though the couple stood far away from the camera lens.

The Disciple took a leisurely sip of his drink. "Why do you want to know?"

"It's none of your fucking business why I want to know. Now, who are they?"

"Jesus, you're a jumpy one, aren't you? Guy's name is Devereaux. He's an FBI agent out of Virginia. The sexy lady is Callie Callahan. Like I said, aside from making me hard just looking at her, I'm not sure what purpose she serves."

Gabriel said nothing, his mind a whirlwind of questions without answers. *Why are they here? Are they looking for me? If so, how did they find me?*

"You okay, partner?" the Disciple asked.

Composing himself, slowing his ragged breaths, Gabriel said, "I've been waiting for the right opportunity to meet these two again. Callie Callahan is ..." He stopped for a moment, staring at a group of decorative beer steins lining the wall while deciding how much to divulge. Lightly stroking the eye patch over his left eye, he said, "Our last encounter did not end well." He turned to the man next to him. "I need to know everything about them— where they're staying, how long they're here, anything that will help me prepare for another meeting."

Gabriel hid a smile as he imagined the possibilities, more convinced than ever that he was God's messenger. Why else would He bring them here? Serve them up on a silver platter?

"Yeah, sure, whatever you say," the Disciple replied. "But first, take a gander at the third picture. It's the best one yet."

Gabriel tucked the second Polaroid in his jacket, ignoring the ugly looks from his companion as he took possession of the image, and picked up the third photo. As he stared at the body on the ground, his hands fisted, and his jaw clenched.

"Is that a kid?" he growled, spittle forming in the corner of his mouth. "A fucking child?"

There was little doubt that Jeremy Sterling was a sociopath, a twisted and narcissistic murderer who killed who he wanted, when he wanted. He changed his name to Gabriel to align himself with an Archangel and coined the phrase *The Apostle* because he believed he was a messenger of God.

All behaviors that exposed his demented thinking.

But even the most hardened heart, even the evilest among men, had an imaginary line they would not cross. For Gabriel, that line was crimes against children.

"What?" the Disciple asked, his armpits growing damp. He was getting good at reading people and right now, it was not admiration or pride the man to his right was emanating.

Gabriel held the picture below the level of the bar and stared. After what seemed an eternity to the man who had taken the photograph, he finally turned to face him.

"A kid? You killed a fucking kid? Is that what I'm seeing?"

The Disciple squirmed in his seat, bile rising in his throat. Later, when he reflected on this conversation, he would think of a dozen comebacks, a host of responses meant to put Gabriel in his place.

At the moment, though, the man was just thankful he hadn't pissed his pants.

"Um, uh ... no, not a kid. I mean, yeah, she was young but definitely not a child." He took in Gabriel's features—the thin line that had once been a full lip, the deep vee of his brow—and stuttered on. "It's, it's not like she was a good girl, either. She was a slut, a whore, a tease with no respect for her family. Don't you see? I had to do it!" He wiped the beads of sweat dotting his brow. "Maddie Gibbs got what she deserved."

Gabriel pushed the pictures back across the bar and stood. Leaning down, hand on the Disciple's shoulder, he whispered, "If you want to play this game with me, you must stick to the rules. Kill another person under the age of eighteen, and I will cut off your dick and shove it up your ass. Children are not participants in this cleanse. Do you understand me?"

The Disciple swallowed, choosing his words carefully. He knew Gabriel would do what he threatened. "Right, right. No problem. I meant no offense." Then, standing, desperate to get away from this man, this bar, he said, "Well, I'm off to work. No rest for the wicked, right? See you Sunday at Mass?"

Mass, the Disciple thought, disgusted. *What a joke! How does an alleged 'man of God' threaten to cut off someone's dick?*

Standing shoulder to shoulder, Gabriel, although only a few inches taller than his companion, seemed larger than life. "Sunday. And remember what I said. I've no tolerance for attacks on children."

The man nodded and headed for the door. With every step toward the exit, toward freedom, the sting of Gabriel's gaze burning into his back lessened. Anger growing, the Disciple began planning long before his face hit the night air. No one talked to him like that and lived.

No one.

～

What the fuck did I get myself into?

The Apostle sat back down and finished his drink, disgusted at the Disciple, and angry at himself for ever joining forces with an amateur. How could he believe a self-serving idiot like the Disciple would rise to the challenge presented to him?

"You want another, pal?" Bobby asked him. His tone made it clear he didn't consider Gabriel his 'pal.'

"No, one is enough. Overindulgence of any kind is the pathway to hell, my son."

Bobby snorted. "Who the fuck are you? Dear Abby?"

The Apostle threw a twenty-dollar bill on the counter and rose. With a chilling smile that never quite reached his eyes, he winked.

"Dear Abby is a cunt."

Turning his collar to the wind, Gabriel exited the bar, looking left and right, scanning the deserted street with a practiced eye. Absently, he scratched at a scar that lined the side of his face. It was an old wound given to him by a razor-wielding preacher, a self-proclaimed man of the cloth, who'd carved into both sides of Gabriel's face as a teen to 'get the evil out.' That man, Deacon Billy Ray Porter, and his skank of a wife, Jolene, were currently rotting in the ground.

Because no one fucks with the messenger of God.

Still, one good thing came out of that scar—it itched whenever danger was near. A gift for his troubles, a present from the Almighty for his loyalty. He depended on that itch to keep him safe from his enemies. He'd felt it crawling down the sides of his face ever since he'd arrived at Benny's, the tickle telling him he was being watched. Preyed upon.

And that was unacceptable to the man used to being the predator.

The building that housed the bar was one of among a half dozen structures on this block. The area was sketchy, and the roadway—on the outskirts of Sheridan—seldom traveled. In addition, hidden corners and dark alleys created the perfect backdrop for an ambush.

Cautious, Gabriel walked down the east side of the road towards his car. The air was still, and the streetlights cast a dim glow on the empty street. A flicker of movement to his left caused him to pause, listening. He dug into his jacket pocket and wrapped his hand around the grip of a .44 caliber handgun.

An insurance policy in case the Disciple turned out to be just another Judas!

As he walked, shadows spun and twirled in each alley he passed. The ringed moon hung overhead, its glow dimmed by passing clouds and ice crystals that formed a halo effect. A clang down the darkened corridor of an alley to his left caused him to jump, and he squinted his good eye to locate its source. A cat, dark as night and just as spooky, ran from one dumpster to the next, a hunter seeking a food source.

As for predators of the two-legged kind, he saw nothing. Still, he had ample military training and enough life experience to recognize the signs.

He was not alone.

The figure in the black sweats and dark beanie crouched in the recesses of a random alley. He was tired, cold, and berating himself for the hundredth time regarding his mission.

All he wanted to do was recon. All he wanted to do was find out where the hell his co-worker was going.

He expected it was a clandestine meeting, a hook-up with a woman. Or a man.

But it was more mysterious and much shadier than a quick blow job. Hands shaking, eyes tracking the big stranger, he whispered to no one ...

Who the hell is this guy?

CHAPTER NINETEEN

"Are you warm enough?" Jake asked Callie.

Callie's head rested against the passenger window as she took in the distant mountains along Highway 90. She felt drained, weak, and wondered briefly whether there was something seriously wrong with her. The exhaustion had been going on for weeks.

"I'm fine," she said stiffly. Ever since they shared that kiss, things between them were strained. Subconsciously, although she knew it unfair, she blamed him. If he didn't have stunning violet eyes or that amazing body or those 'kiss me 'til I'm breathless,' lips, she would have been just fine.

Conveniently, she ignored the fact that she practically begged him to stay with her—in her bed—following her nightmare.

Jake was uncomfortable as well. He should have reacted differently to her kiss. But good God, did she think he was a monk? He could still smell her tantalizing scent—sunshine and lavender—as it surrounded him, tickling his nose; could still see her gorgeous face and lustrous hair as she leaned over to console him.

Even now, hours later, her scent called to him. It was making him crazy.

Breaking the tomb-like silence in the car, Callie said, "In case I didn't say it before, I wanted to say I'm sorry."

Jake raised his brows. "Sorry for what? Blaze, you know as well as I do, we both wanted that kiss to happen."

"I wasn't talking about that, Jake," Callie clipped. "I was talking about Gus."

"Oh," he said, embarrassed. "Thanks. He was a good boy. I'll miss him."

Callie turned back toward the window. "As for the kiss, I would prefer we chalk that up to an emotional reaction to a sad situation. It was a mistake."

Jake shifted in his seat, annoyed. "Maybe to you, Blaze. Some of us might not see it that way."

Eager to drop the subject, he glanced at the cellphone in her lap, opened to an internet page he didn't recognize. "Whatcha working on?"

She closed out of the site she'd been on. "Uh, nothing much."

Jake frowned. "You understand you're a terrible liar, right? Your voice gets higher, your nose twitches, and your cheeks get red. Hell, I could be a blind man and still see right through you."

Callie's hand flew to her nose. "I do NOT have a nose twitch!"

Jake chuckled. "If you say so. Come on, Blaze. What's going on?"

"Okay, fine, but don't say I didn't warn you. Yesterday, I created an account on LiveFeed. I've been hanging out in the Confessions chatroom for the last hour, trying to bait this guy, hoping he will respond."

"Jesus Christ, what the hell are you thinking?"

"Right now, I'm thinking you'd better adjust that tone, bud."

Jake flipped on the hazard lights and pulled to the shoulder of the road. "Do you even hear yourself? Look, we all know that your sister was reckless. She went headfirst, into the lion's den, without a safety net or an exit strategy. But everything she did, she did to help save someone else."

Irritated, Callie asked, "Meaning?"

"Meaning your recklessness is about something more. It's about revenge."

"Ya' think?" Callie bit back. "My sister is gone, Jake. Dead and buried, while the scumbag who killed her is out there, somewhere, breathing, enjoying life and free as a bird. You bet your ass I want payback! I will never find peace until I find Gabriel. And every day I spend chasing this 'Reaper' guy is one less day spent searching for my sister's murderer. So, yeah. I'll do whatever it takes to end this investigation. If that means luring this killer in and forcing him to make a move, so be it. We need to end this, once and for all."

Jake flexed his hands on the wheel. "Oh, it'll end it, all right. I just hope it isn't with the death of someone else I ..." He clamped his mouth shut, unwilling to finish his words.

If Callie noticed, she didn't let on.

Clearing his throat, Jake said, "We should be at Jed's in about an hour. I want to stop by Ford's place first, though, to check in on him. Something's definitely off."

"Good idea. Shall we phone him first? Let him know we are coming?"

"Nah." Jake flashed a devilish grin. "I say we surprise the bastard."

Jim Ford sat at his kitchen table, a spread of forms and legal papers in front of him. He had been at it all night, searching for his Last Will and Testament. He hadn't thought about that piece of paper for years, but when he stumbled into a murder investigation, he recognized the importance of that document.

Specifically, its importance to one person.

The ring of the doorbell caused him to jump. He seldom received visitors other than food deliveries or the occasional

Jehovah's Witness. When he ignored the bell, the caller pounded on the door.

"Get lost!" he shouted.

"Fuck you!" came the response.

"Jake? That you?"

"How 'bout you open the door and find out, dipshit!"

Cursing, Jim shuffled to the door. "I don't have to," he growled, twisting the knob and opening the door. "I can tell your whiny bitch of a voice anywhere. Hi Callie."

"Hi, Jim," Callie said with a smile. "Is it okay if we come in?"

Ford opened the door wider in invitation, turned, and trudged back to the table before they were inside. He sat down and pointed to the other chairs around the table.

"I suppose you'll be wanting to sit. Just don't think copping a squat means sharing feelings and hugging it out. I'm not one for that Kumbaya shit."

Jake changed the subject. "What is all this, anyway? You getting sued again?"

"No, asshole, I'm not getting sued." He looked pointedly at Callie. "Why do you hang around with this creep, Callie? You can find much better company, I'm sure."

Jake snorted. "Yeah? Like who, you? Forget about it. It's hard to keep company with the guy who ghosted us in the middle of an investigation."

Callie gave Jake a stern look. He wasn't helping.

She turned back to Ford. "Jim, what's going on? It's obvious the Naomi Vaughn crime scene upset you. Did you know her?"

Ford stood and walked to the counter, intent on making his fourth pot of coffee in three hours. "Yeah, I know her. Knew her. We sort of dated."

"You dated her?" Jake said, incredulous. "No offense, old man, but wasn't she decades younger than you? Did she know you are a cop?"

Ford slammed a container of sugar on the table. "It ain't like she's jailbait, Jake. And no, she didn't know I was on the job, didn't even know my first name. Kept myself sort of anonymous by using my middle name."

Jake raised his brows.

"Oh, shut the fuck up. Naomi and I were a one and done thing. We were at a party, hammered and out of our minds. At first, we just hung out, kissed a little. Man, she was a great kisser."

"And then?" Jake asked.

"And then things ... escalated."

"You know this looks bad, right?" Jake asked. "You should've told me or Sawyer the minute you recognized her. Remember Investigation 101? 'A cop who's had an intimate relationship with the deceased should recuse themselves from the case to prevent a blatant conflict of interest.' Or did you miss that class?"

Ford huffed. "Oh, you mean like a certain agent from Quantico who worked the murder of his former lover? But maybe those rules only apply to me?"

Jake shook his head. "Touché. But bottom line? You need to give Sawyer or Dan a statement detailing your relationship with Naomi."

"I told you, I don't have a relationship with her." He gathered three cups from the cabinet and poured them each a cup of coffee.

While he served, Callie took in the room. Jim's kitchen was lackluster and disorganized, but clean. Above the sink was a plaque that read, 'Dream as if you will live forever; live as if you will die today—*James Dean*.'

Ford caught her eyeing the sign. "A reminder that everyone will one day face a day where tomorrow never comes."

She stirred her coffee; the cream creating swirling ribbons of white. "Well, that's cheery," she joked. "Listen, Jim, when was the last time you saw her?" she asked.

"I haven't. Not since, you know, that night we linked up. But she texts me sometimes. Pictures and stuff."

Jake's eyes widened. "Pictures? Like pictures of fluffy little bunnies or pictures that are more, uh, revealing."

Rather than answer, Ford tossed one of the legal documents across the table, followed by a small photo album. Callie picked up the document while Jake went for the photos.

"Do I want to even look at these?" Jake asked.

"Just open it, dude."

Jake cracked open the album and flipped through the pages. His face was unreadable.

"Yours?" he asked after a minute.

"So I'm told."

Curious, Callie leaned over, glimpsing the last picture in the album.

"She's beautiful. Who is she?"

Ford took a swallow of his steaming coffee, his throat burning as the liquid fire found his stomach. "Meet Cassidy Rose Vaughn. My daughter."

"No shit?" Jake asked.

"Nope. In that pile of papers there is DNA proof that I'm the baby daddy. Which, in retrospect, makes me a pretty good suspect in her mother's murder, don't it?" He smoothed a hand across his bald head. "I've been sending Naomi child support payments for the last few months, ever since I found out." He eyed Jake carefully. "Don't go judging me on this, pal. I would make a lousy father. I'm too set in my ways and not about to let a one-night stand turn into a life sentence of formula and diaper rash. But I ain't gonna let that kid want for anything, either."

Callie drummed her fingers on the table. "Does Naomi have family? Someone who can care for Cassidy now that she's gone?"

Ford shrugged. "No clue. Like I said, it was a one-night stand. Still, seeing her like that shocked me, and I panicked. Felt the urge to rush back here and update my will, making Cassidy the sole beneficiary. Not like I have millions of dollars, I know, but at least it will be something for her. I have a call out to my lawyer to ensure any changes will be legal."

Jake carried his cup to the sink. "Look, the team is meeting over at Jed's today. We have a lead on this bastard, a website called LiveFeed. At least two of the victims visited a particular room on the site called 'Confessions'. Detective Callahan over there," he said sarcastically, nodding his head toward Callie, "apparently fancies herself a PI already. She's setting up a sting for this guy, using herself as bait."

Callie rewarded his dig with an icy stare.

"Anyway," Jake continued, "Sawyer should be at Jed's today. If you come along, you can give him your statement there."

Ford shook his head. "I have to finish up this stuff and try to track down Naomi's kin. I need to find a good place for Cassidy before Child Services steps in. I'll call you when I'm done here. If the meeting is still going strong by then, I'll head over."

"Roger that," Jake said. "And Jim? If you can't make it to Jed's, don't forget to reach out to someone in Sheridan County and give a statement. Okay, partner?"

"Yeah, yeah. Now get out of here so I can get this stuff done and head over to Billings."

❧

Fifteen minutes after leaving Ford's house, Callie received notice that she had a message waiting on the LiveFeed site.

"Bingo!" she shouted.

Jake glanced at his passenger. "Bingo what?"

Callie grinned. "You are so lucky to be hanging out with me. I'm a rock star! A certified genius, I tell ya!"

She was so enthused, Jake didn't have the heart to tease her. Much. "Ok, genius—spill it. But give it to me slow, you know, for the poor saps in the car who aren't members of Mensa."

"Funny. I'll have you know that, as we speak, I'm looking at a private message from one 'Nick Fury.' I'd wager that isn't his name."

Jake shook his head. "Not taking that bet, Blaze. Nick Fury, huh? Why does that sound familiar?"

Callie nodded. "I know, right? Does to me as well, but I can't place it."

"Me either," Jake said. "Let's hold off on answering him until we have the team there to chime in."

Callie agreed, and they drove the rest of the way in comfortable silence. When they were ten minutes from Jed's house, Callie spoke.

"Hey, Jake? You know when Jim said that he didn't want to give Naomi Vaughn his real name? That seems so weird to me. I mean, it's not like he's a celebrity or something. What was he trying to hide?"

"No clue," Jake answered, distracted.

"Have you ever done that? Given a girl a phony name?"

Jake turned down the heater and loosened his tie. He was wearing a navy-blue, short-sleeve shirt that accented his biceps and played off his olive skin. His tie was a milder blue, thin, and splashed with cream accents. Although sharp looking, Callie hardly noticed he was even wearing a tie until he started pulling at it.

She was too busy not staring at his muscled arms.

"Uh, I don't recall," Jake said.

Callie gasped and playfully punched his arm. "You dog! You did, didn't you?"

"In my defense, I was very young," he said, trying not to laugh.

"I can't believe it! Who was the girl? And, more importantly," Callie narrowed her eyes, "what name did you give her?"

Stalling, Jake checked and rechecked his mirrors. The morning sun blazed through the driver's side window, highlighting the brilliant sheen of his hair.

"Come on, G-Man, tell me your secrets," Callie teased.

"Bill," Jake blurted. "I told her my name was Bill."

Callie smirked. "Bill? Wow, originality isn't your forte, is it? Let me guess—last name of Brown? Johnson? White?"

Jake wrinkled his nose at her. "Board. I told her it was Board."

Callie howled with laughter. "You didn't! Board? Bill Board? Oh, my God, seriously? Did she die laughing?"

Jake winked. "Not until I told her I had a sister, Peg. And two brothers, Clip and Switch. Oh, and my Grandpa ..."

Callie doubled over, hysterically laughing, tears rolling down her face. "No! No more! I can't breathe! Oh, my sides hurt!"

Jake was cackling like a hyena, trying to stay on the road. "Ma —my Grandpa," he wheezed, "his, his nickname was Boogie."

Callie snorted, which made them laugh even harder. By the time they pulled into Jed's driveway, they had finally stopped laughing long enough to get out of the car.

Then Caleb zoomed by on his skateboard, and they started howling all over again.

～

Jed greeted them at the door, his face flushed.

"Hey, guys. Abby is in the dining room, Curtis is at yet another murder site, and Sawyer and Ford are MIA. Hopefully, they show soon."

"No clue about Sawyer," Jake said, "but we just left Ford. He has some personal stuff to finish up and then he'll be along. What's this about another killing? And why the hell are you so cranked?"

Jed ignored the last. "They found another body, this one over in Shell Canyon. Technically, Shell is Ford's territory to cover, but apparently, he made his absence official and took some personal days. DCI is covering and, since this murder looks related to the Grant and Vaughn homicides, Curtis caught the case. He'll fill us in when he can." Jed spoke directly to his brother. "Right now, though, I need to borrow Callie a minute. Why don't you head in, and we'll join you in a few?"

Keeping his curiosity under wraps, somewhat put out by the secret he was not privy to, Jake walked away. Once he was out of earshot, Callie turned to Jed. "What is it? Is Caleb alright? Faith?"

"No, no, Caleb is fine. Faith is, well, I'm not sure what Faith is. But the reason I pulled you away is that you have a visitor."

Callie frowned. "Really? Who on earth would come here to ..." she paused, then gave out an enthusiastic yelp. "Oh, my gosh! Darbs! And my boy, Blue! I can't believe I forgot they were coming! Where are they?"

Just then, Callie heard Blue's distinctive bark outside. Grinning, she rushed through the front door, placing a hand over her eyes to shield the sun. Unable to see him, she brought her fingers to her lips and whistled. Seconds later, Blue came barreling from around the side of the house, ears flapping in the breeze. She could swear he was smiling.

"My boy!" Callie yelled, as he plowed into her legs, nearly knocking her over. She plopped down on the walkway, pulled him into her lap, and scrubbed his back and belly.

"When it's my turn, I prefer a neck massage," came a voice from behind.

Callie shot up. "Darbs! Oh, man, it's good to see you!"

The women hugged for a long time. "I am over-the-moon, tickled to see you, too!" Darby said. "Geesh, it seems like it's been forever and a day. I've missed your face. Blue has, too."

"And I've missed you both. I have so much to tell you, but I need to get to a PIPPS meeting. I promise I will fill in the details later, but long story short? There's a second serial killer on the loose, one who's leaving rosary beads at his crime scenes. I figure it's a fan boy, a copycat, or Gabriel is involved."

"Huh. I don't remember reading anything about rosary beads being left at Gabriel's homicides. Didn't see it on the nightly news, either."

Callie nodded. "Because it wasn't. As far as I know, the police never released that information to the media. Holding that kind of info back helps separate the legit leads from the crazies. Which means the only way someone would know about it is if they were involved in the investigation or had a friend or relative working the cases."

"Or... they were in contact with Gabriel," Darby said.

"Exactly."

"Dang! I tell ya, Cal, I really hate that guy. Okay, come show me where I'm bunking and get to your meeting. The sooner we find this piece of crap, the sooner you'll come home to Fredericksburg, right?"

Callie didn't answer. Instead, they faced each other, holding hands, and chatted about life back in Virginia.

"Have you spoken to Ryan?" Darby asked. "He's too cute when he talks about birthing babies! He began his clinical rotation in Obstetrics and all he talked about last week at Gram's was placentas and umbilical cords. He's gonna make a great daddy someday."

Callie chuckled. "Yeah, he always was a nurturing soul. I miss all of them. Even Finn," she said, quirking a brow. "How is he? Really?"

"No idea. We haven't seen or heard from him since you left Virginia."

"What do you mean? Where is he?"

"No one knows. He took off, right about the time he heard you were leaving for Montana. He was none too happy. He has some ranch hand looking after things. Truthfully? He's been acting weird."

Callie quirked a brow.

"Well, weirder than the normal Finn weirdness," Darby rushed to say.

"Katie's death hit him hard, too," Callie said. "But I can't help him until I process things myself."

"Of course! Good golly, miss Molly, but you've been through

the wringer." She rubbed her hands together, excited. "Want some good news? I may expand my operation and was thinking of scouting out the area."

"Darbs, what are you talking about?"

Darby's eyes glistened. "Look, Stacy was your best friend, and Kates was mine. But they've both crossed over, Cal. I like to think they are having a blast—dancing on raindrops, fly-fishing in a crystal-clear stream, and stuffing their faces with ice cream and gumdrops." She smiled sadly. "You and I have a bond, a thread that binds us forever—our love for Kate. And I'll be hot-damned if I let that thread get so darned thin it will snap. So, if the person who was closest to my bestie hangs her hat in Montana, then I'm gonna hang my hat next to hers."

Callie was dumbstruck. "You plan to move out here? To Montana?"

"Not exactly. Not full-time, anyway. I figure I'll buy a cute little cabin, find an empty store to rent in a peak location, and make *Time and Time Again* a franchise. Business has been crazy good. Some days, inventory flies off the shelf. And ever since I opened the online store, it's even crazier. People love this stuff, so I figured why not open a second store and capitalize on the trend? Once I get it established, I can find someone to run it while I'm at the Virginia store. And versa, vicey," she said with a grin.

Callie was beaming. "I don't know what to say! This is amazing! Of course, I'll help you! Maybe we can get Jed involved, see if he has a hook with any realtors." She squealed and jumped in place. "I'm so excited! This is epic, girl! We are gonna rule the world!"

Darby laughed and jumped with her. "Yeah. We'll either rule it ... or blow it to bits!"

∼

Ford was just wrapping up his paperwork when the doorbell rang again. Ignoring it, he gathered his legal documents in a folder labeled, 'Last Will and Testicles,' a juvenile joke that still made him smile. His search for Naomi's family brought him nowhere. Since she'd gone missing, Naomi's friend, Suzanne Morrow, had been caring for Cassidy.

Ford found Suzanne's name and number from the police report filed when Naomi went missing and phoned her. A pleasant woman, Suzanne assured him that Cassidy was doing well. She also let him know there was no way she could keep the baby. Her husband had been very upfront when he and Suzanne had gotten married about the possibility of children in their future.

He didn't want them. And she'd promised she was okay with that.

The pounding on the front door startled Jim. He'd forgotten someone was out there. Swearing, he stomped to the door and yanked it open, intending to give the trespasser an earful.

"What the fu—" he yelled, stopping as soon as he recognized his guest.

"Hello, Jim. I come bearing gifts," the visitor grinned, holding up a brown paper bag. "I was just checking on you. You left that Vaughn crime scene in a hurry. Mind if I come in?"

The last thing Ford needed was company. He had to get a move on if he wanted to make the meeting at Jed's. "Okay, but fair warning. I gotta be somewhere, so I only have a few minutes."

The visitor smiled. "That's fine. I have to be somewhere myself. But life's too short to pass up homemade blueberry muffins and French roast coffee."

Stomach growling at the word 'muffin,' Ford opened the door and led his guest to the kitchen.

And never once thought that this may be the day his tomorrows never come.

CHAPTER TWENTY

Callie hooked her arm through Darby's as they walked toward Callie's apartment.

"I'll give you the fifty-cent tour before we lug your bags up there. You may decide after seeing it you want a bit more room to spread out."

"Pu-lease!" Darby said, rolling her eyes. "I've lived in apartments the size of an acorn. Compared to those, this will be the Taj Mahal! So, while I have you alone, what else is going on?"

Callie shrugged. "Same old, same old. Wake up, shower, have a bite to eat, then crawl inside the mind of a lunatic."

"And Jake?" Darby asked with a sideward glance. "What's the skinny? How are things?"

Callie raised a brow. "Taken up mind reading, have you?"

Darby remained silent.

"Okay, alright. Jake and I have gotten to know each other well over the last few months. Too well, I'm afraid. What the hell is the matter with me? Why do I feel this magnetic pull whenever I'm around him?" She looked down, unable to meet Darby's eyes. "I'm embarrassed to say it out loud, but I kissed him."

Darby kept her voice neutral. "Okay. And?"

"And I instantly regretted it. Well, not instantly. It was amazing. Amazing and intoxicating and wrong."

"Wrong how?"

"Jesus, Darbs. Katie was crazy about him. I have no business staking that claim."

Darby stopped and spun Callie to face her. "Don't be a bunny, Cal. There is no claim. Look, at first, I felt the same way as you. Even after I saw how Jake looks at you, I couldn't accept you and Jake as a couple. It felt like, I don't know, treason?"

"And now?"

"And now I realize it's almost half a year since Katie has been gone. She's moved on and is where she's supposed to be. She's found peace, Cal. Don't you think it's time you do the same? Don't you think Kates would want you to live?"

"It's not Kates holding me back from living, Darbs," Callie said, teary-eyed. "It's me."

Jake stood just outside the dining room doors, waiting for Jed to appear. When he did, Jake laid a hand on his chest, stopping him.

"Spill it, brother. What's all the secrecy with Callie?"

"No secrets. It's just Darby and Blue, here for a visit. I figured Callie could use a pleasant surprise about now. She's been served up a ton of shit sandwiches lately, hasn't she?"

Jake frowned. "No lie there. I think I served her one of those sandwiches myself yesterday."

"How so?"

Jake scrubbed his face, irritated. "Because I'm a jackass. Because I was upset about Gus, and I kissed her."

"Gus? Why, what happened?"

Jake sighed. "I lost him, Jed. Sully called last night, said he was fine when he left for work, but when he came home ..."

"Aww, shit, man. I'm sorry. He was a great dog."

Jake nodded. "He was. And even though he had many more

years than I expected, it still stings. Callie was comforting me, trying to help." He ran a hand through his hair. "She kissed me, and instead of pulling away, I dove right in; made myself at home, practically sucked her face right off her skull."

Jed smirked. "But she kissed you first, right? I don't see the issue here. Would have been rude not to reciprocate."

"Give me a break," Jake snapped. "The gentlemanly thing would have been to back off. I should have known it would bring her grief. She feels guilty, I feel guilty. The whole thing blows. And the worse part? Although I feel like shit, I know I'd do it again tomorrow."

He gripped the dining room door, and Jed stopped him. "Wait. One question, though. How was it? The kiss, I mean."

Jake dropped his head back, staring at the beams on the ceiling. "It was ... staggering. Incredible and magical and different from any other. You know, when Kate and I kissed, it was electric, like a shock that tore through my system and ignited a flame in my belly." He straightened his head and found Jed's eyes. "But with Callie, it was all that and more. Aside from the fire shooting through my veins, the kiss seemed, I don't know, deeper somehow. In that moment, I felt possessive and connected and whole again. It was as if she'd climbed into my body, into my soul, and filled a space that'd been empty for months. Maybe even years."

Jed patted his brother on the back. "Sometimes, we are so busy looking at the chaos behind us, we fail to see the beauty in front of us. Sometimes, we lose the world but gain the universe."

Jake crossed his arms. "Lovely. Where did you get that? Pinterest?"

"Nah. Saw it in an advertisement for condoms."

Jake hooted and they both bent over, laughing.

"What's so funny?" Callie asked when she entered the main house.

Jake stood up straighter. "Um, nothing much. Darby get settled?"

"Not yet. We dragged a few suitcases and Blue's bed up the stairs, but could use a hand with her bigger bag." Smirking, she added, "She packs just like me."

"Not a problem. Why don't you stay here and get us a good seat? I'll grab the rest of her stuff and meet you back here."

Jake found Darby leaning into the passenger door of her VW, ass wiggling as she strained to pull a bag out of the cramped space.

"Ho, ho, there," Jake called out, "you're gonna hurt yourself. I've got it."

Darby moved away from the car door. "Appreciate it."

"So, how was the trip?" Jake asked, as he freed the suitcase, a lame attempt at conversation. After what transpired between them in Virginia, he was feeling self-conscious around Darby.

Darby understood his discomfort. She was feeling it herself. "It was good. Long. But Blue is a fantastic co-pilot. Never complained once, even though he's used to traveling in a much larger car. I swear, though, he was giving me the stink-eye with every bump we hit."

Jake grinned. "Yeah, it is tight in there, isn't it?"

She smiled but didn't answer. "So, uh, how are things here? Is Callie okay?"

"Good days and not so good ones. One day at a time, right?"

Darby narrowed her gaze. "Sure, I suppose. And you? Have you figured it out yet?"

He gave her a blank look, and she rolled her eyes. "Men! I swear you need to be hit in the head with a hammer sometimes! Do you remember what we spoke about last time?"

Jake frowned. "Yeah. And I still don't understand what you mean, Darby."

She laughed lightly. "Oh, contraire, mon frere. I think you do."

Jake lifted the bag and headed to the apartment stairs. "If you say so. I'll put these in the living room for you."

"Thanks a bunch. If Callie asks, tell her I took Blue for a walk, will ya? And Jake?"

He turned.

"Don't let the scars of the past define your future."

He gave her a quizzical look, then ascended the steps, muttering, "What the hell is this? Hallmark week?"

∽

Ford took the last bite of his muffin and checked his watch. "Dude, I don't want to be rude," he said to the man across the table, "but I should've been in Billings about forty minutes ago. Appreciate you checking in though."

He stood and stuck out his hand, a clear indicator that he was ready to wrap it up. The entire visit was bizarre. His gut told him this was more than a welfare check. This guy was snooping, prying into his private life.

Ford would have none of it.

"Oh, I didn't mean to keep you," the man said, standing. "Just looking out for you. You know, we gotta watch out for our own. These cases ..." he stopped. "Did you know that there was another murder?"

Ford shook his head.

"Yeah, somewhere over by Shell Canyon. Tragic stuff. Hard to wrap your head around it, right? Have you heard any news about leads on this maniac?"

Ford checked his watch again. "Not much. I think a tech we have working with us may have found a connection between the homicides. Jed and Callie are running down some leads as well. In fact, there is some stupid internet site the fucker is using. LiveFeed, I think it's called. Anyway, Callie is a smart cookie," he smiled warmly. "You know, she actually had the stones to set up an account and try to lure this Reaper prick in. Yeah, she's got more guts than most men I know."

His companion kept his face neutral, hiding the maelstrom

that churned in his gut. "Well, I don't know her well, but she certainly is courageous."

"Uh, yeah," Jim said, distracted. Suddenly, his head felt light, his limbs weak.

The visitor watched, fascinated, as beads of sweat dripped down Jim's temples. The temperature inside was cool at sixty-three degrees, yet Jim's face looked like he was in a sauna.

"Hey, you okay, partner?" the man said. "You're looking a tad peaked."

Jim took a step forward and felt the room spin. On wobbly legs, he grabbed the back of a chair and slumped down. Slurring his words, trying to keep his head up, he said thickly, "Wha' the fuck? Wha' did you give me?"

The man grinned. "Just a sedative. Can't have you fighting me, can we? You would no doubt win such a battle. No matter. In a war of wits, I beat you, hands down." He pulled a syringe from his jacket pocket. When Jim tried to stand, the man gently guided him back to his seat. "Now, now, we'll have none of that."

Ford's limbs were numb, his brain scattered. His vision tunneled into pinpricks of light, and, as the curtain descended, he blacked out.

When Ford came to, his visitor was saying something about a crime scene.

"It was a horrid sight, truth be told. Poor girl was just lying there, needles poking out of her flesh. Did I mention she was naked? She was. Well, except for her shoes and the handkerchief clutched in her palm. I believe it was white, though impossible to tell with all that blood on it. Even the little shamrocks on the edging were stained red."

Ford made an animalistic sound, thrusting his arms outward, trying to push against the table. His arms fell short by a few inches.

"So, anyway," the man continued, indifferent to Jim's efforts, "your end will be a shocking and tragic conclusion to what was once a stellar career. I can see the headlines now ... 'Agent James Ford, a decorated law enforcement officer, hid a nasty secret for years.' Yes, indeed. A serial killer dwelling in our own backyard."

"Why?" Jim said, eyes closed, summoning the strength to battle the overwhelming fatigue.

"I do apologize, James. I picked up the bandana you dropped when you fled Naomi's crime scene. Wasn't very professional of you, was it? No matter. Once it was in my possession, I realized its value."

Ford's eyes flashed with anger as he tried to rise again.

"I placed it in Madison's fist—did I mention her name? No, I'm sure I didn't. She was a spitfire, that one. Madison Gibbs." He sighed. "Oh, well. She's quite dead now. As you will be soon. You know, it's strange how things just fall into place sometimes, isn't it? I only came here today to gather information about the investigation. I had no intention of ending you. But when you told me of the plan that Callahan woman has, wanting to trap me? Well, it's obvious those boneheaded investigators are getting close, and we can't have that, can we? No, it's much better this way. You go down for the killings and I move on, find another place to play."

"You," Jim rasped, his vocal cords dry as dust, "You fucking pile of garbage. Once this shit wears off, I'm coming for you. I'm gonna, gonna rip off your arms and beat you to death with 'em!"

The man clucked his tongue. "Going to be hard to come at me when you're dead, partner. See this syringe here?" He waved it back and forth under Jim's nose. "Once I inject this beauty, it's over. Ever heard of succinylcholine? Difficult to get ahold of, but well worth the effort. It's a marvelous drug, paralyzes every muscle in your body, including your diaphragm and the intercostal muscles of the ribcage. If you paid attention in science class, those are the muscles needed for respiration." He reached into the other pocket of his jacket and pulled out a razor. "And this is the way you will die—a shocking suicide by slicing your own wrists. Gruesome, I know, but necessary."

Jim growled and lunged with all his might. He wrapped his would-be killer around the waist, and they toppled to the floor, the razor skidding along the kitchen tile. Scrambling, scratching for purchase, each man stretched an arm out, reaching for the blade.

Only one man got there.

~

When Jake opened the dining room doors, Callie glanced up just in time to see a shadowy figure fly down the stairs, sail through the foyer, and disappear behind Jake's back.

Jake never noticed it.

Her gut clenched, and her mind whirled. Another ominous figure, another warning. And she still had no answers to what it all meant.

"She's all set," Jake said to no one in particular. He took a seat next to Abby and across from Callie. "So, what'd I miss?"

"I was just telling Jed how much I appreciate him welcoming Darby to his home." Turning to Jed, she said, "I think once you get to know her, you'll understand why she is so special to me."

Jed smiled. "I'm sure I will. She seems lovely."

Jake adjusted his seat. "She's something, all right," he said, with a hint of sarcasm. "Any word on Sawyer or Curt?"

"Curt is just getting to the recent crime scene. He will reach out to us when he has more info. As for Sawyer, still no word. No contact with Jim yet, either." He smiled widely. "But Abby is here, and she has some interesting developments."

Abby smiled shyly and cleared her throat. She'd changed her hair color from brown at their first meeting to a vivid pink. Somehow, it suited her. "Well, yes, I've a few things to share with you," she said, putting on a pair of hot-pink reading glasses. "I guess the most important thing is that the administrators of LiveFeed refused to divulge any information regarding exchanges that took place in the Confessions room. The man I spoke to was apologetic, but emphatic. He said that the room was a 'safe haven' for all its users and to violate that trust would put them out of business."

"Kind of figured they would say something like that," Jake said, annoyed.

"Right," Abby said, "but we aren't sunk yet. We were able to get Arthur Sinclair's laptop from his family, and Evelyn Leonard gave us permission to look through Nora Grant's computer as well."

"And Naomi Vaughn's?" Callie asked.

Abby shook her head. "We have her cellphone but, unfortunately, we can't locate her laptop. There is a good possibility she had it in her car and the killer took it with him."

"Rats!" Callie said.

"I'll come back to what I found on Naomi's phone in a minute. As far as the laptops, I can tell you is that both Nora and Arthur had LiveFeed accounts and had extended conversations in the Confession's room. Arthur believed he was speaking with a thirteen-year-old girl named Jules Winnfield. His tone, his language, was disgusting. It makes you wonder how many other little girls this creep preyed on. God rest, of course."

"If there is a God, the 'creep' will get no rest," Jed bit back.

"True. As for Nora, her contact went by the name of Samuel Jackson."

"Hold on a minute," Jake said. "Samuel Jackson? I remember he played a role in *Pulp Fiction*. Character was Jules Winnfield."

Callie gasped and looked at Jake. "Nick Fury. Wasn't that Samuel Jackson's character in *The Avengers?*"

"Hold on," Jed said. "What's this about Nick Fury?"

Callie pulled out her phone. "After creating an account on LiveFeed to lure this guy out, I went into the Confessions room and spilled my secrets. Today, a man named Nick Fury contacted me, wanting to chat. I haven't responded yet."

Jed scowled, his piercing gaze finding Jake. "And you're okay with this? Callie dangling like a worm on a hook?"

"Of course, I'm not okay with it! What would you have me do? Take away her phone and send her to bed?"

Callie's face flushed from both embarrassment and anger. "Um, hello? I'm sitting right here. Appreciate it if you'd not talk about me as if I were a child!"

"Sorry," Jed said, shamed, "just concerned about you."

Sullen, Jake said nothing.

"I'm a big girl. I keep my eyes open and don't take crazy chances. And I wasn't planning on answering him until I presented it to all of you."

Jake looked at Abby. "What did Nora talk about with this guy?"

Abby's face fell. "She spoke from the heart about feeling guilty for her little brother's death. He died in a fire that she accidentally set."

Jed whistled. "A fire? That's grim."

As soon as he said those words, something clicked into place in Callie's mind. "Holy crap, I get it!"

"Get what?" Jake asked.

"Get the whole thing. This creep goes on LiveFeed looking for a particular kind of person. Someone with warts, someone who feels remorse for what they've done in the past. He kills them and leaves a clue behind. For Nora, it was a block of wood; for Arthur, a can of bean soup and a basket of apples. And Naomi had a crown and gold thread."

"Right, but what does it mean?" Jed asked.

"Don't you see? He is playing out stories from Grimm's Fairytales. *Frau Trude* was a tale about an old woman who turns a girl into a block of wood and tosses her into a fire. In *The Juniper Tree*, a woman decapitates a young boy by slamming the lid of a trunk of apples on his neck. The stepmother then makes bean soup from his body."

"Ew," Abby said. "That's disgusting. These are from fairytales?"

"Yeah, well, the 'Brothers Grimm' are notorious for being fairly gruesome. I would bet the crown and golden thread at Naomi's crime scene signify the story of *Rumpelstiltskin*. You remember? A girl's father, trying to impress the king, brags that his daughter can spin straw into gold. So the king, a greedy fellow, locks up the girl and threatens to behead her if she does not do what was promised. Desperate, she elicits the help of a little man named Rumpelstiltskin, promising him her firstborn child if he helps her."

"Remind me to keep any future kids away from this book," Jake said dryly.

Callie laughed. "No kidding. Now, when the young girl grows older and has a daughter of her own, of course, she cannot part with her. Distraught at the thought of giving her up, Rumpelstiltskin finally makes her a deal. If she could guess his name within three days, he would give up his claim to the child."

Rapt, Abby whispered, "And did she? Guess his name?"

Callie nodded. "She did. She followed him one evening and found him chanting his name over a fire."

The doorbell rang, and Jed rose to answer it. "I guess we know what 'Reaper' on the bodies signify. That's probably Ford or Sawyer at the door. Be right back."

Jake rubbed his chin. He'd forgotten to shave, and the friction against his fingers sounded like sandpaper.

Callie found it sexy as hell.

"I wonder," he began, "if there are any other Grimm-type murders he's committed elsewhere?"

Abby raised her hand. "Funny you should ask. I cross-referenced ..."

She stopped speaking when Sawyer walked into the room. Everyone, except maybe Sawyer, registered Abby's reaction to him. He was brawny and cute, his red curls peeking out from beneath his Colorado Rockies baseball cap.

"I'm so sorry I'm late." Glancing at Abby, he added, "I apologize, Miss. I didn't mean to interrupt."

His smile was dazzling. Abby dropped her head, incapable of speech. Thankfully, Callie noticed and spoke for her.

"No worries. Abby was just telling us about some connections she may have found to the murders."

Jed chimed in. "Glad you could join us, Sawyer."

Sawyer grinned. "Sorry, bud. I was working on my bike and lost track of time. It's outside if you want to check it out later. She's a beauty."

"I will, soon as we're finished here." Turning his back to the others, he said, "We need to discuss that other matter as well."

Sawyer nodded, then took a seat next to Abby.

"Be right back. I forgot to put out some cookies and cakes, courtesy of my personal assistant."

When he left the room, Callie whispered to Jake, "Personal assistant? Uh oh, that's not good. Have you seen her since we've returned?"

"Faith? Nope."

"Jake, you must feel the tension in this house," she continued in a whisper, "it's ten times what it was when we left. I wonder what's going on?"

"No clue. But I hope to hell whatever it is gets resolved soon. The whole thing's giving me a rash."

"Well, don't expect me to scratch it for you."

"Not a problem," Jake said. Winking, he added, "Not exactly the itch I'd like you to scratch, anyway."

Hidden behind the massive doors outside the dining room, Faith tipped her head back and leaned against the wall. She'd heard Jed refer to her as his 'assistant', heard Callie talk about the tension in the house, despite her valiant attempts to keep her voice low. Faith's world was crumbling, her secrets bound to be discovered.

What the hell did you expect, idiot? You joined forces with a bunch of cops and investigators! Fucking moron!

Decision made, she crept from the dining room and made her way to the kitchen. Silently creeping out the back door, she tip-toed toward the guest cottage. She would pack a bag with some things and sneak out in the middle of the night. No regrets, no tears, no clues to her whereabouts.

And no looking back.

CHAPTER TWENTY-ONE

A few minutes later, Jed walked back into the dining room with a tray of sweets.

"Help yourselves. The lemon bars are my favorites."

"You'd best be careful, or you'll ruin your boyish figure," Jake teased. "Faith is spoiling you rotten."

Ignoring the ribbing, Jed took a seat. "It occurred to me as I walked in that I failed to welcome Sawyer Mills to the group. He comes highly recommended by Ford, and any friend of Jim's is a friend of ours."

Sawyer gave a quick nod to the others.

Jake continued. "Abby was just telling us about some recent information she's uncovered."

Abby adjusted her glasses and checked her notes. "Yes, I found something. A few things, actually. First up, the locked cellphone found at Naomi's crime scene is no longer locked, and it definitely belonged to her. I was able to get in easily, to tell the truth. Years of doing cyber security have taught me that many people use important dates in their lives as passwords. Naomi was no exception."

"Her daughter's birthday?" Callie asked.

"Actually, it was the year she graduated high school. I feel like she wished Father Time would turn back the clock. Her texts to friends hinted that maybe motherhood was not for her." Abby licked her lips, nervous. All eyes were on her, and she hated being the center of attention. "Naomi used the same password for almost everything. I was able to log into LiveFeed, which got me into the Confessions room. The conversations there were ... disturbing."

"Disturbing how?" Jake asked.

"Um, like the things she said, admitted to. Like not wanting to be a mom, wishing she would have the courage to give Cassidy up. In one conversation, she spoke about giving birth as a teenager to a little boy and giving him up for adoption. She, um, also admitted to being a cutter."

Callie frowned. "She cut herself?"

"Yes," Abby breathed. "Pretty regularly from the sounds of it."

Jed jotted down some notes. "Did you see the name of the person she was talking to?"

Abby flipped through her papers. "Yes. His name was Elijah Price."

Callie looked at Jake. "Wasn't that a character in the movie *Unbreakable*?"

Jake nodded. "Yeah. Samuel L. Jackson again. What is it with this guy and Jackson?"

Callie shook her head. "Could be the killer's name is Samuel, or that he deeply identifies with something in the actor's life. Or maybe—probably—he just likes the guy and thinks it's clever to use his character names."

"With the added plus of having another way to fuck with the cops," Jake said.

"That, too. This killer is toying with us. He's asserting his dominance and superiority by dropping clues, waiting to see if anyone 'gets' it."

"And banking on being far too smart to get caught," Jed said, taking a lemon bar, then offering one to Callie.

Politely declining the sweet treat, Callie said. "Exactly. He's scouting out victims and passing judgement on their past acts. Arthur Sinclair, Nora Grant, and Naomi Vaughn all had secrets that, I'm guessing, they weren't too proud of. This guy taps into their guilt, their biggest regrets, and then swoops in as punisher."

"And executioner," Jake growled.

"Unfortunately," Callie said. "Reminds me of another killer we know who crowned himself judge, juror, and executioner."

"Yeah," Jake growled, "Gabriel fucking Devine. What are the odds we have two narcissistic killers working the same angle?"

"Astronomical, if I had to guess," Callie answered.

After a moment of silence, Sawyer addressed Abby. "Have you found anything else? IP address, something this guy said? Anything that will pinpoint his location?"

Abby gnawed at a cuticle. "I've checked all the victim's devices I've had access to. In each case, the suspect used a sophisticated IP blocker with a masking feature. Essentially, the program reroutes internet traffic through a Virtual Private Network, or VPN, and encrypts it. This application also comes with a kill switch that instantly disconnects if a breach is suspected."

"Great," Jed said, disappointed. "Anything else?"

"Just one more thing. I entered the details of each homicide into a program I developed last year. It's still in its infancy, but it allows me to discover parallels to other unsolved crimes in the country that haven't yet been entered into a national databank. I collect information from several sources regarding unsolved murders—police reports, television and newspaper accounts, social media statements—and combine them to create a list of similar crimes and a potential profile of the suspect. Think of it like ViCap on steroids."

Callie frowned.

Abby nodded in understanding. "I know, Callie. Keeping all these acronyms straight can be confusing. ViCap stands for the Violent Criminal Apprehension Program. It's a database developed by the FBI and designed to assist law enforcement in identifying and correlating crimes. Police can enter information relating to their unsolved violent crimes to, hopefully, find any link or similarity to other cases across the nation.

"Got it," Callie said. "Thanks for the explanation."

Jed raised a brow at Abby. "Back up a sec, Wonder Woman. Am I to understand that you've created your own database? Do I even want to know if it's legal?"

Abby smiled shyly. "You most definitely don't want to know. For the search, I first entered how the victims died. According to the medical examiner, the killer or killers slashed Arthur's throat, burned Nora alive, and strangled Naomi."

"Unusual to see different methods of killing, isn't it?" Jed asked.

Callie was the first to answer. "It is rare, but not unheard of. How they kill means something to them, although we may not see it yet. Perhaps he believes the punishment must fit the crime or found one method riskier than another and adapted. Essentially, a killer can change his MO or even how he kills, but the fantasy remains the same."

"Right," Abby said. "So, for this program, I also entered the items left behind at each scene. Lo and behold, I got several hits, but only one stood out. The NYPD is investigating a murder that took place a few months ago in Brooklyn. The man's name was Joey Fabrizio, and a quick background check revealed he was not exactly a nice man. He owned a contracting business but rarely did any actual building or repairs. His specialty was fleecing his customers, particularly the elderly."

"Charming," Jake said.

"For real. Anyway, it was a gruesome homicide discovered during a welfare check requested by his family. Local police arrived and found Joey in his basement, naked and hog-tied. The slit in his throat was so deep, first responders initially thought he'd been decapitated, just like Arthur Sinclair. Next to the body, written in blood, was the word 'pig'. Police questioned the next-door neighbors and found out they heard what sounded like pigs squealing earlier in the day. But sadly, no one thought to call the cops."

"Sounds like a nightmare," Jed said. "What makes you think it's related to our killer?"

"It's not so much the cause of death as what the killer left behind. On the cellar floor, as if dotting the 'I' in pig, was a sterling silver bell."

Callie drummed her fingers on the table. "You know, in college, I did a ton of research about the impact on a child's psyche from violence seen on television and in storybook fables. I know a few dark tales and this New York murder sounds like another Grimm's story. In a fairy tale titled, 'How Some Children Played at Slaughter,' two young boys play a game about a farmer's market. One boy, in the role of a butcher, slits the throat of a pig. The boy's little brother played the pig."

"Jesus. You're sure this is a kid's book?" Jed asked.

"Unfortunately. Over the years, though, they've rewritten some stories to take out the... Grimm, so to speak." Callie answered.

Abby sighed. "Thank God for small favors."

"But New York, though?" Sawyer asked, scratching his chin. "It's a little far to travel for our guy, right? Copycat?"

"I don't think so," Abby countered. "The Fabrizio murder occurred months before any of these victims."

Jed directed a question at Callie. "What are you thinking about motive here? TJ Palmer's preliminary report said there was no sexual assault on either Nora or Naomi. Could this guy be gay? Asexual? Impotent?"

Before Callie could answer, Sawyer jumped in. "Rape doesn't always go with murder, Jed. You can take a life without defiling a body first. Isn't that right, Callie?"

She quirked a brow. "If you ask me what he did to these women constitutes defiling a body, but you're right. Sexual gratification doesn't always need to come from intimate contact.

Rather, it may be the act of killing itself that satisfies the killer's sexual urges. That said, I think these murders are rooted in intense anger rather than sexual stimulation. And, although this guy could very well be climaxing during the act of killing, it's not the primary reason he kills. I would be interested to know if the coroner found any semen on the bodies or clothing."

Jed turned to Sawyer. "Can you reach out to the Medical Examiner? See if he has any DNA findings we don't know about yet?"

"No problem. I'll give TJ a call after the meeting."

When Jed's cellphone rang, he excused himself and walked to the hallway. During the break, Jake asked Abby if she'd had time to investigate the email Gabriel sent Callie.

"I did." She directed her next words to Callie. "I'm really sorry but, unfortunately, the sender of the video used a burner email and a TOR browser."

"TOR?" Jake asked. "What is that, exactly?"

"TOR stands for The Onion Router," Abby explained. "It's an internet browser that reroutes and encrypts messages, making your web-based activity virtually impossible to detect. Child pornographers, human traffickers, drug cartels, all reroute their correspondence via an anonymous browser to mask their activity. It's easy to use and quite effective."

Jed returned to the group and held up his phone. "Hey, Curtis, I'm putting you on speaker. Tell them what you just told me."

"Hey, everyone," Curtis began, "wish I had better news. I'm up here in Shell with what appears to be the latest victim from this Reaper guy. Her name is Madison Gibbs, a fifteen-year-old junior in high school."

"Fifteen?" Callie asked, stunned.

"Yes, unfortunately. A month shy of her sixteenth birthday. Killer did a number on her, too. A guy living in the woods in Shell Canyon discovered the body. She was surrounded by prickly pear cacti and buried beneath a pile of brush and twigs."

"How was she killed?" Sawyer asked.

"Not sure yet. Medical Examiner from Big Horn County is on the way now. I can tell you she has dozens of syringes embedded in her body. Bastard even jabbed some into her eyes. I don't know, maybe he injected a poison or something? She has a slit wrist as well, but the cut is superficial. My gut tells me the guy did it only to gather enough blood to spell 'Reaper' on her abdomen."

"Christ," Jake croaked.

"Yeah, it ain't pretty."

Callie tried to maintain a professionalism, which was close to impossible when thinking about such a young victim. "Anything left at the scene?"

"Yeah," Curtis said. "A crown, a silver bell, and a set of rosary beads. Oh, and she had something clenched in her fist. A neckerchief or scarf that I'm betting used to be white before it became saturated in blood—more blood than you'd find from the small gash on her wrist. There's a design around the edges of it, too. Clovers, I think."

Callie swallowed hard. "Shamrocks." She glanced at Jake. "The bandana I gave Ford ..."

Jake stood up so fast his chair went flying. "No! No way! Don't even go there, Blaze! You can't possibly think Ford ..."

"Of course not," Callie said. "I don't know him well, but I know you. If you say it's impossible, I believe you."

"What?" Jed asked them both. "You guys recognize that bandana?"

Callie shook her head. "I don't know if it's the same one. We can't afford to assume."

"Assume what?" Sawyer said, giving the first glimpse of emotion during the entire meeting.

Jake angrily pulled his chair back to the table and sat. "Assume that the bandana the victim held in her hand is the same one Callie gave to Ford."

"What are you talking about, Jake?" Jed asked.

Jake looked at Callie. "While we were at the Naomi Vaughn crime scene, Ford smacked his face into a tree branch and got a bloody nose. Callie gave him her shamrock bandana to staunch the bleeding."

"Holy shit," Abby whispered.

"No! Not holy shit, Abby!" Jake spat. "There is no holy shit! Christ on a cracker, Jed, you know Ford! He's saved my ass more than once. Saved yours too, from what I recall. Remember that pissed off ex-husband from Greybull you were following? The guy built like a brick shithouse?"

Jed dropped his head. "Yeah, I remember."

"Yeah, I do, too. He nearly kicked your ass when he found out you were tailing him. It was Jim who set him straight."

Jed shrugged. "I know all that, bud. But think about it. How does a bloody piece of cloth from the Naomi Vaughn scene end up over an hour away in Shell? Clutched into Madison's hand?"

"Obviously a plant," Callie jumped in. "Which means either the killer was waiting in the woods, saw Jim drop it, and picked it up. Or ..."

"Or our killer is a cop, in on the investigations." Jed hissed.

"At the very least, maybe someone involved in the case." Callie said.

"Well, I don't give a rat's asshole what any of you think," Jake fumed. "I will never, ever believe that the guy I've known half of my life is a serial killer."

"Calm down, Jake, you're gonna stroke out. We'll figure this out," Curtis said.

Callie folded her hands and pushed them to her lips. "Since Ford is a no-show, Jake, you'd best tell them about him and Naomi. If we are going to get to the truth, everyone needs to be on board the same train."

Jake nodded and, resigned, told the group about Jim Ford, Naomi Vaughn, and a little girl named Cassidy.

. . .

Disappointed in himself for spouting Ford's business, yet knowing he had no choice, Jake leaned forward in his chair. "You all need to hear what I'm saying—James Levi Ford is incapable of committing these crimes."

"I agree," Sawyer said. "Although, nothing for nothing, we've all seen what people can do in the heat of the moment."

"Heat of the moment?" Jake snapped. "Was it the heat of the moment four fucking times? Maybe five, if you count the New York guy?"

Jed raised his hands. "Gentlemen, please. We will get nowhere if we argue between ourselves. I say that, until we know otherwise, we act as though Jim Ford is innocent."

"Agreed," Sawyer said.

"Whatever," Jake grunted. "So, I'll get back to my original point—what the hell is going on here? How is it that this motherfucker can operate so far under the radar?" Speaking directly to Jed, he snapped, "It's time we released this shit to the media. We need to warn people."

"If we tip our hand and let him know we are on to the website connection, he's gonna ghost us, Jake," Sawyer said.

"So, we don't give that up," Jed responded. "We can let the public in on the killings, ask them to be careful, go with the 'see something, say something' premise, but keep the internet site out of it."

"How the hell are you going to do that?" Jake asked. "The website *is* the connection. Without mentioning that, we aren't giving the public dick."

Abby raised her hand. "I might have an idea. What if we included a bunch of generic information, but not the internet stuff? We could say several killings have led us to believe we are dealing with a serial killer. Then we say the usual stuff—don't go out alone, be aware of your surroundings, stay indoors at night and keep off internet dating sites or apps. That way, we've planted the seeds of caution in risky situations without pointing out specifically the LiveFeed site."

"That could work," Jed said. "Curt, what do you think?"

"I think it's a good call, although I'd leave the press release to either the FBI or the Sheriff's Office."

"I'll reach out to my boss, get permission to write up a press release," Sawyer said.

"Okay, great. So, what else, ladies and gentlemen?" Jed asked.

Jake rubbed his forehead, a dull throb growing beneath his right brow. "Is it just me, or does anyone else feel like this guy is always two steps ahead of us? He killed Sinclair in Ten Sleep, right? So, while the Sheriff and DCI spent days investigating that, Nora Grant's remains were found over two hours away, in Tongue River. Then, as we're spinning our wheels with that murder, Naomi's body shows up in Little Goose. And now, this Madison kid is found while we're still working the Vaughn murder site. Each homicide occurred quite a distance from the other and involved crossing over the Bighorn Mountains, which, we all know, is a time-consuming trek." He snagged a chocolate chip cookie from the dessert tray. "This douche is escalating, growing a pair with each kill. It's as if he knows, geographically, where we're focusing our investigation each day."

"Like insider trading," Abby said. When they all gave her a questioning look, she said defensively, "Not that I know much about that, but it is similar. Like someone has the inside scoop of where the investigators will be."

"Someone like Ford," Sawyer said quietly.

"Give it a fucking rest, Mills!" Jake yelled.

"Sorry," Sawyer said. "Low blow, you're right."

Frowning, Jake turned to Callie. "The rosary thing is throwing me. You're sure this 'Grimm Reaper' shithead isn't Gabriel?"

"I'm not sure of anything, Jake. All I can tell you is my gut is saying that Gabriel isn't doing the killing. Doesn't mean he isn't privy to it, though."

"Perfect. Can this day get any better?" Jake said.

"Don't worry," Callie soothed. "Eventually, Gabriel's going to trip on his ..." She stopped speaking, suddenly fascinated by the corner of the room.

"What? What's wrong?" Jake asked, concerned. He turned, searching the room for whatever drew her attention.

He saw nothing.

Callie paled and grabbed Jake's hand. She seemed to have forgotten they were not alone. "We have to go. Now."

"Why? What's going on?"

Trembling, she said, "I'll explain on the way. Please, Jake, let's just go, okay?"

Jake nodded and stood. "Uh, guys? Callie and I need to take care of something, but we'll be back ASAP." He pulled Callie to her feet and called out, "Thanks for the update, Curt."

"No problem."

"Okay," Jed said, confused. "It looks like we are about done, anyway." Noticing Callie's complexion, he added, "You okay, Cal?"

She swallowed, not trusting her voice. "Can you let Darby know I'll be back soon? I hate to leave her here alone,"

"She's not alone," Jed said. "Go do what you have to do. I got you."

∿

After the meeting, Jed and Sawyer walked outside to chat in private.

Squatting down near Sawyer's motorcycle, Jed said, "She's a beauty, man. You did a great job with her. Is that ceramic coating on the exhaust?"

Sawyer grinned. "Yep. New pipes and a high-heat ceramic paint. Not only protective, but it provides a great finish."

"I used to ride back in the day," Jed said, nostalgic. "May need to take it up again. Caleb would love it." His eyes flashed over a wide splotch on Sawyer's thigh he hadn't seen earlier.

"Oil?" Jed asked, nodding toward the offending stain.

"Yeah, probably."

"Could be blood," Jed said, standing. "Your hand looks pretty chewed up there."

Sawyer smiled. "Hazards of having big paws when working in a tight space." He stuck his hands in his pockets and lifted his shoulders. "I assume you came out here for another reason besides the bike, huh? Maybe wondering if I got any info on your tenant?"

Jed shifted his stance, uncomfortable. "I reached out to you because Curt said you have contacts in Philly. There may be someone who came across Faith or this Graeme Duncan fellow. From her description, it sounds like this guy was a powder keg, so maybe he had a run-in there with authorities."

Sawyer nodded but said nothing.

"And to be clear, I'm only checking up on her out of concern. Something in her story doesn't add up, and she's not talking. If Faith's in trouble, I want to help."

Sawyer cocked his head. "I'm going to tell you what I know, but understand, Jed, that as a federal agent, I have a job to do. I'm going to need to speak to your border." His foot found a small rock, and he kicked it to the edge of the driveway. "Did you know that Graeme Duncan is dead?"

Jed nodded. "Yes, that much Faith told me. Wouldn't say how, though. Just that he got what he deserved."

"I think his family would disagree with her. According to my sources, his parents thought he'd give both Jesus and Moses a run for their money." Sawyer hesitated. "Someone shot him in the back about eight months ago—three times, point blank, with a .38 Special. At first, police figured it was a pissed off client he'd represented as an attorney. They've since gone in another direction."

"Christ," Jed whispered.

"Oh, it gets better. Duncan had a wife and child, but no one has seen either of them since the killing."

"Faith and Caleb," Jed sighed.

"Negative. Graeme Duncan's wife's name was Emily, formerly Emily Weston, adoptive daughter of Randall Weston."

Jake's brows shot up. "Randall Weston? As in the billionaire oil tycoon who owns Weston Industries?"

"That's the one. Guy has been searching for his daughter and grandson since the murder. Eight months of spending beaucoup bucks with no results. It's like Emily and little Tyler just vanished off the face of the earth."

"Wait, Tyler? So, where do Faith and Caleb fit in here? Do you think Emily and Tyler are really Faith and Caleb? That Faith is using an alias?"

Sawyer dug out a toothpick from his shirt pocket and tucked it into his mouth. "Not sure. The police reports didn't mention a Faith or Caleb McTavish. But there is a person of interest they are looking for."

"And that would be?"

"The Duncan's nanny. Woman named Fiona Clark."

"Holy shit," Jed rasped. "Is that why you want to talk to Faith? Do you think she knows something about this Fiona Clark?"

Sawyer's silence told Jed all he needed to know.

CHAPTER TWENTY-TWO

"You want to tell me what that was all about?"

Jake turned up the heater as they cruised down Route 90 toward Hardin and Jim Ford's home.

"How much farther?" Callie asked.

"Same as when we came in from there to Jed's house. About fifty minutes, give or take. Now, can you tell me what's going on, please?"

Callie fidgeted in her seat and gazed out the window, the scenery a blur. She couldn't look in Jake's eyes, nor could she face the spirit in the seat behind her.

The same one who visited Jed's dining room.

"Callie? Come on, lady. You're scaring me."

He sounded desperate. Wounded. She didn't know what was worse—his hurt expression as she kept him in the dark, or the pain he would experience when learning the truth. "Look, Jake. I know nothing for sure yet. Let's just get to Ford's so we can figure it out."

Jake swiped a hand through his hair. "It's bad, though, right? Did Katie come to you? Give you some inside intel?"

"No," she whispered. "Not Katie. It was Jim."

Jake had a second of confusion, followed by a moment of clarity. "Jesus Christ, he's dead? Is Ford dead?"

In answer, Callie grabbed his hand in hers, her heart aching when she glimpsed the single tear that slid down his face.

Jake's fist pounding on the door caused Callie to jump.

"Ford? Ford, you in there?" he yelled. "Open up, man!"

While Jake continued to beat on the door, Callie framed her eyes with her hands and peeked through a side window. "I don't see anything."

Hopeful, Jake asked, "Maybe he went out? You know, all this spirit stuff is new to you, Blaze. Could it be that you misread the message or something?"

Callie chewed her thumb. "I don't think so. Why don't you look for another way in?"

She continued ringing the bell and knocking on the door until Jake returned. "No good?" she asked.

"Nothing. This place is locked up tighter than a virgin in a ..." he stopped, as if suddenly remembering who he was with. "Uh, it's locked pretty tight."

Callie removed her jacket and wrapped a portion of it around her hand.

"Blaze, what the—oh hell, no. Let me do that."

Smiling sweetly, she threw her fist through the sidelight window, found the deadbolt, and unlocked the door. "You're a cop, Jake," she whispered, stepping over the shards of glass now littering the threshold. "This is breaking and entering. You could lose your job."

He followed her inside. "Nice jab you got there. You get cut?"

"Nope," she whispered again. "I'm fine."

"Why the hell are you whispering?"

She grimaced. "Am I? Sorry, it's my first felony."

Jake opened his jacket and checked the weapon secured in his shoulder holster. "Nah, no criminal intent." He turned to her and winked. "Unless you're planning on jacking something? Otherwise, you could probably plead it down to unlawful entry or trespassing."

"Gee, thanks. I feel so much better now."

They walked to the kitchen, ears straining to hear even the slightest movement inside the house. It felt as though they were trampling over a graveyard.

Or tiptoeing through a landmine.

"There," Callie said, pointing to the kitchen table. "How about you check his laptop while I look around?"

"Uh, no. I have a better idea. Why don't I look around while you check the computer? The cop in me needs to clear the building first."

She narrowed her eyes. "What happened to the 'locked up tighter than a virgin' thing?"

Jake snorted. "Yeah, yeah, so humor me. We just broke into the home of a cop who's not answering our calls or texts. A cop who's arrested a shit ton of bad guys."

"Fair enough. How about we compromise? Since that laptop isn't going anywhere, why don't we both take a look around?"

Jake nodded and gently pushed her behind him. "You stay right behind me, you hear?"

She forced a smile, then saluted him. "Aye, aye, Captain."

"Wiseass," he muttered.

Jim's apartment was small, with a combination kitchen and living room, two bedrooms, and a bath. Aside from the massive entertainment center that occupied an entire wall, the only furniture in the living room was a sofa, easy chair, and a scarred end table.

Not exactly a space crawling with hiding places.

They wandered to the hallway and hit the closest room on the left. Jake went through the door first, Callie on his heels, a firm grip on his jacket. Inside was a twin bed, miniscule closet, and three-drawer oak dresser. A TV tray doubled as a nightstand.

"Guest room," Jake said unnecessarily.

Backing out, they continued down the hall and entered the bathroom, its rose-colored sink and clawfoot tub telegraphing the age of the apartment. In the far corner of the room, a magazine rack and toilet sat opposite a stand-alone shower. Jake crept over to the shower and, after giving Callie a shrug, slowly reached out a hand.

Wrapping his fingers around the edge of the shower curtain, he yanked it back. "Gotcha!"

Callie yelped. "Jesus, Devereaux, you scared me half to death! Who'd you think was in there? Norman Bates?"

Jake smirked, the pit in his stomach dissipating. The house felt peaceful, the atmosphere benign.

"You never know. I bet Janet Leigh checked the shower every day of her life since she made that movie."

Callie blew out a steadying breath. "I bet she did. Come on, let's go."

They returned to the hallway, stopping at the last door on the right. It was closed but not shut entirely, enabling them to see a sliver of the room behind the door: dresser, throw rug, window.

"Hey, Jim?" Jake called out. "You decent?"

No answer.

He tried knocking. "Jimbo? Look, man, I have Callie out here. She doesn't need to see your naked ass. We're coming in."

He palmed the door open, Callie's breasts pushed against his back, her soft breath kissing the nape of his neck. The space was dark; the curtains drawn. His eyes swept over the room, adjusting to the dim lighting, finally landing on the still figure on the bed.

Callie saw it at the same time and gasped, her hand brushing the wall for the light switch.

The first thing she noticed when light bathed the room was Jim Ford standing in the corner, away from the bed, near a potted plant. He looked lost, pained, confused.

And spectral. Unbodied.

"Jesus Christ," Jake croaked, taking in the scene. Blood was everywhere. It covered the bedspread and the sheets, created rivers of red on the floor. It spattered the wall behind the headboard, its crimson shapes and patterns creating a macabre Picasso-like painting.

"Oh, God," Callie gasped.

"Fuck me," Jake ground out, struggling to keep his feet planted. He wanted nothing more than to race to his friend. Instead, he turned to Callie. "This is a crime scene now, Blaze. Only one of us should enter and check that he's ..." He swallowed hard, grasping the futility of anticipating a pulse. "Can you call the cops? Maybe get a look at that laptop before the police get here and confiscate it? Just try not to touch anything."

She nodded. "I'm so sorry, Jake."

As she moved away from the door, she noted the figure still standing in the corner of the room. Jim Ford, it seemed, had no idea he was dead. Jerking her head toward the kitchen, she started down the hall, hoping he would follow.

Instead, he moved next to Jake and stared down at the body on the bed.

His body.

After dialing 911, Callie stood at the table in front of Ford's laptop and read a letter that sat frozen to the screen.

If you're reading this, I'm already dead. I simply could not live with myself, knowing what I've done. I pray this will serve as not only my confession but as my last will and testament.

I killed them all. Sinclair, Grant, and Naomi. Sweet Naomi. But my biggest regret is that I killed a child. Madison Gibbs was so young.

But she was tainted. They all were tainted.

I tried to fight it, truly I did. But I bear the demons of a childhood teeming with abuses so foul, I dare not speak of them here. These fiends in my mind, these bringers of chaos, are my constant companions. They whisper to me, a cacophony of voices echoing off my brain, telling me to do things. Horrible things. Unforgiveable things.

And I cannot listen to their shrill voices any longer.

I have a sister in Oregon who knows nothing about my daughter. I have provided her contact information on a separate sheet of paper and attached it to my legal papers. Please reach out to her about caring for Cassidy. Naomi had no kin, and my sister Patrice is my only hope. Forgive me.

James L. Ford.

"Bullshit!"

Callie grabbed her throat, startled. "Jake. I didn't hear you coming. Are you okay?" She knew it was a stupid question the moment it left her lips. But it was all she had.

"I'm about as far away from 'okay' as I can be. His wrists are slit." Scowling, he said, "No, not slit. Annihilated. Just pieces of meat, slashed in a frenzy, vertically, horizontally. Some cuts look so deep, it boggles the mind how a person could find the strength to keep cutting. The blood loss is massive."

"Psychological pain can give us superhuman willpower and determination," Callie choked, tears filling her eyes. "Although, his choice of weapon is unusual. Jim had access to more lethal methods of harming himself. Bleeding to death takes … time."

"It makes no sense. This whole thing makes no fucking sense," Jake growled. "Did you call the Big Horn Sheriff's department?"

Callie nodded.

"Why didn't he eat his gun, Blaze? Hang himself from the ceiling or ram his truck into an underpass or over a bridge?" He clenched his jaw. "Jim Ford was a tough as nails, old-school type of guy. Some might even call him chauvinistic. Doesn't this suicide seem kind of, I don't know, feminine?"

"We don't know what was going on in his head, Jake. Maybe he'd seen botched attempts using a gun that left the victim alive but disfigured. Or attempted hangings that resulted in living with severe brain damage. I'm sorry, but it feels like you're reaching for a rational explanation where one doesn't exist."

Jake nodded at the screen. "So, what about this, then? This so-called suicide note. I'd bet my left nut he didn't write it."

Callie searched his eyes. "Why?"

"Just look at the language he used. Cacophony? I doubt he'd ever heard of the word. The phrase 'shrill voices' or saying, 'bringers of chaos?' Ford doesn't ... didn't talk that way. You know what he'd say?"

She shook her head.

"He'd say, *'Sayonara, fuckers. I'm out.'* Period, end of story. There's no way in hell Jim Ford wrote this."

"Okay, say I believe you," Callie said. "How did his killer know about Cassidy? Patrice? Did you even know he had a sister?"

"Yes, I did. They had a falling out years ago but before that, they were tight. As for how the bastard who wrote the note knew about Cassidy, it's all right there in his legal papers. We were here when Ford was amending his will. All the killer would have to do is open the folder."

"True. So, what's next? Wait for a crime scene crew?"

"Pretty much."

"And Cassidy? Are you going to call Patrice?"

Jake hung his head. "I guess I am, aren't I?" He moved to the far side of the table and, using a pen, opened a manila folder stuffed with papers. While he searched, Callie moved to the living room. Unsure where Ford was, or even if he could hear her, she spoke.

"Jim? Are you here? Can you hear me?" She looked back at Jake, who'd stopped what he was doing to listen. Voice cracking, she said, "Your journey here is complete, Jim. It's time to find the light."

Tears rolled down Jake's face. He ignored them and nodded in encouragement.

"Don't worry about Cassidy," Callie continued. "We'll take

care of everything. Your only job now is to step into the light, into a new beginning."

A few minutes passed before either of them spoke. "Did it work?" Jake asked.

"No clue. Maybe? I don't see him anymore, anyway." Blowing a curl away from her face, she said, "Gosh, I suck at this. Not being able to communicate is so frustrating! I don't know how Kates did it all those years."

Jake joined her in the living room. The wayward curl she'd tried to breathe away fell back over her eye, and he swept it to the side of her face.

"Kate eventually found a way," he said. "Automatic writing, remember? But she had years of practice with this stuff. You've been dealing with it for what? A few months? How about you cut yourself some slack?"

She sniffed. "I guess. So, what now? Should we stay inside?"

"I think we've contaminated the scene enough, don't you?" he said wryly. "Let's wait outside. I took a picture of Patrice's number." Voice strained, he added, "Maybe you can call Jed while I call her? He needs to know."

"I will," Callie said. "And Jake? I'm so sorry. In the short time I knew him, Jim seemed like a good man."

"He was a good man," he said thickly. "But he was an even better friend."

Outside, Jake paced the sidewalk in front of Jim Ford's home, cellphone to his ear. Callie was on the front step, giving him privacy as he broke the news to Jim's sister, Patrice.

"Hello, Shadow," Katie said, taking a seat next to Callie.

"Now you show up," Callie whined. "You know, I coulda used you back there." Sighing, she stuck out her right leg and stretched her foot.

"Your ankle bothering you?" Katie asked.

"Only when I walk on it too much. Or sneeze. Breathing sometimes ramps up the pain, too," she quipped.

Her heart squeezed as she watched Jake pace the walkway, shoulders slumped, face a mask of pain.

Katie concentrated on her sister's face. "I got him, by the way. Ford, I mean. He's safely crossed over."

Callie bent her leg, actively trying to rub away the ache from her previously shattered ankle. The tear that rolled down the side of her face went unnoticed to her.

Katie noticed.

"I don't think I can do this anymore, Kates," Callie said. "This 'see the dead' stuff just isn't for me. Honestly, how did you not go insane?" She paused, then answered her own question. "Check that; I know why. It's because you're you."

Katie quirked a brow.

"No, I'm serious. You've always handled things better than me. School, parents, friends. And men." She glanced again at Jake. "I've spent my whole life as a spectator, spying on you, seeing how you handled things, then doing my best to imitate you. Like some kind of pathetic poser."

Katie chuckled. "Do you hear yourself, Cal? Who was the one who stood up to the bullies when we were kids? That would be you. Who garnered invites to all the parties, the proms and dances, refusing to go unless someone invited me, too? I lived the life of a nerd while you were the life of the party. It was you that people went to with their secrets or problems or delicious ideas of mischief and mayhem. Do you remember any of this?"

Callie shrugged.

"And your courage in that basement, dealing with a psychopath? Even after Gabriel branded you and fractured your ribs and shattered your ankle, you still stood up to him, Cal. Using nothing but your wits and a rusty nail, you got close enough to blind the bastard. So don't talk to me about not being able to handle things, Shadow. You're the queen of handling things."

Callie nibbled on the side of her thumb.

"And men?" Katie continued. "You had more boyfriends than I could count!"

"Not anymore," Callie said, resigned.

"You sure about that?" Katie said. Standing, she turned her face toward Jake. "You're in love with him, you know."

She said it plainly, without question or feeling. It was simply a statement.

Callie rose and cocked her head. "I think you've been dipping into Jesus's wine supply, Sissy. Jake is your soulmate, not mine."

Energy draining, Katie began to fade. "I used to think so, too. But he's not, Cal. My destiny is already here ... with me. Someday, I'll introduce you two but, until then, follow your heart."

Callie stood stone still, shocked into silence, her sister's words playing on a loop in her mind.

My destiny is already here. Follow your heart.

∽

Jed stood in the front yard, watching Sawyer's back as he walked to the guest house. In front of him, Darby and Caleb were playing a game of 'keep away' with Blue and Lucky.

"Hey, Darby," Jed said, as he walked across the grass, "you settling in alright?"

Darby jumped up and caught the frisbee Caleb tossed, then threw it back to him. "All good, Jed. Thanks again for letting me stay here. And Blue, too, of course."

"No problem. You're welcome to stay as long as you like. I have to say, since you and Jake and Callie have arrived, Caleb is like a different kid. I don't think I've seen him happier."

"He's a good boy. Shame that he can't speak." Smiling, she added, "Something tells me he would have a lot to say."

"I think you're right about that. I believe that one day, he will speak again."

"Oh, I'm sure of it!" Darby said, grunting as she tossed the disc again.

Jed watched the frisbee sail over Caleb's head and directly into Blue's mouth.

"Sorry!" Darby yelled, laughing. "My bad!"

Jed smirked. "Nothing like a gob of dog spit to make frisbee fun! Anyway, I just stopped to say hi before I head over to the guest house."

Darby frowned. "Oh, are you looking for Faith? Because she left about an hour ago. Looked to be in a bit of a hurry, too. Gave Caleb a super-long hug and hightailed it out of here."

Jed rubbed the back of his neck. "Oh, I see. Strange. She usually mentions it when she runs errands." He turned to leave. "Thanks for the info. I guess I'll catch her when she gets back."

Darby looked confused. "Um, alright, but you may be waiting for a spell."

"How so?"

"Because right before she peeled out of the driveway, she loaded her car up with boxes and a few suitcases. It looked like she was going on a trip or something."

"I still don't get why this guy would frame Jim for the murders," Callie said as they waited outside of Ford's apartment for the Big Horn medical examiner. "Why Jim? And how the hell did the killer get that bloody bandana?"

"Ford probably dropped it at Naomi Vaughn's crime scene," Jake said. "You saw how wigged out he was. Which, if that's the case, brings us back to two possibilities—either the suspect was in the woods, watching us, or the killer is part of the investigation."

"Or," Callie said, pained, "Jim really is responsible."

Jake glared at her.

"I know it's not something you want to consider, but hear me out. What if Ford is responsible for Naomi's death but not the others? You said yourself that Ford was a player, that he went after anything in a skirt. And he told us, in no uncertain terms, that he didn't want to be a father to anyone. Maybe he killed Naomi in the heat of the moment and then, panicked, made it look like it was a Grimm Reaper killing."

"And what about the other victims? What about the bandana that Madison Gibbs had clutched in her hand?" Jake said, annoyed. "How do you explain that one, Nancy Drew?"

"I-I can't. Not yet. And I'm not saying I believe Ford killed Naomi. All I'm saying is that we need to come up with an alternative to what investigators will conclude. Jim had motive, means, and opportunity. We need to find another explanation for these killings."

"No," Jake said, "not another explanation. We need to find another suspect."

CHAPTER TWENTY-THREE

The Apostle stretched out on his stomach, watching two figures in front of the immense cabin playing frisbee. He recognized the blonde as Kate's best friend, Darby Harrison.

What the hell is she doing in Montana? And who is the kid?

He flipped up the eyepatch covering his left eye and pressed the binoculars close. Adjusting the right lens, he spanned the property.

Come on, fuckers. Where are you?

Thanks to his new 'friend', he'd seen their picture at one of the crime scenes, knew they were in the area. Common sense and a quick google search of Devereaux's family left him with only two options—Jake's brother, Jed, or his parents. He'd tried Jed's house first and now, since he'd seen Darby, knew he'd found the right place.

His plan was just to scope it out, get the lay of the land, so to speak. Later, after meticulous planning, he'd make his move. His sister and that FBI man ruined everything. He felt a shiver run up his spine as he imagined them on their knees, at his mercy.

What was that saying about revenge being a dish best served cold? Indeed, he'd waited months to settle the score.

His vengeance was damn near glacial.

A sudden breeze touched his neck and, expecting an intruder, he rolled to his feet and spun. Years of military training honed his ability to sense danger, to calculate risks and proceed with caution. Crouching low, he scanned the surrounding grassland, his breathing imperceptible. Waiting a beat, he slowly exhaled, his mind still on high alert.

A black squirrel raced up the ridge behind him.

Tracking the animal's frantic path, Gabriel extended his arm, stuck up his thumb, and pointed his index finger. Miming a gun, he whispered "pow" as he pulled the imaginary trigger.

Yeah, you better run, you dumb fuck.

Resuming his surveillance, he spotted a male approaching Darby as she stood on the lawn. After chatting with her for a minute, Jake Devereaux, hair blowing in the breeze, hunched down to speak to the kid. Something about him was off, though.

Different.

Annoyed, Gabriel adjusted the right eyepiece to further sharpen the image and waited, not-so-patiently, for Jake to stand again.

When he finally did, Gabriel gasped. "It's not him!"

The man in the lens was several inches taller than Jake Devereaux. He walked faster, as if he had places to go, people to see.

And he had a noticeable scar over his eyebrow. Gabriel knew for a fact that Jake Devereaux did not.

Where's your brother, dickhead? When I find him, I find that bitch sister of mine.

His phone vibrated and, pulling it from his pocket, he read the notification telling him he had a message on LiveFeed.

This fucker is working my last nerve ...

He clicked open the app and read the newest communication from his Disciple.

Hello, partner!

I'll be in touch soon to schedule a meeting at our place. Working on something big, something that will make you so hot, you'll blow your wad.

Fondly,
Me

Gabriel's face flushed, anger building.

Vulgar piece of shit. Blow my wad? Who the fuck does he think he's talking to?

He clicked out of the app and backed up in a squat until he could no longer see the house. Then, mind whirling, he headed down a dirt road to his car. This was all wrong. He should have realized the Disciple didn't deserve the honor of the task, that he was more a minion of Lucifer than a servant of God. No, something needed to be done, and Gabriel should be the one to do it.

After all, he was the Apostle. But first, he needed to think, to plan.

He needed to go to church.

~

The Disciple watched, amused, as Gabriel jogged down the back road to his vehicle. He so enjoyed spying on the putz.

That they both ended up in the same place, watching the same home, watching its occupants, was much more than coincidence. Their minds seemed in sync, working as one.

At least, most of the time. At least as attuned as they could be when one part of the duo was the strong, dominant one while the other, submissive and weak.

Mouse-like. Cowardly.

To be fair, he didn't know for sure if Gabriel was a coward. But, at the very least, he'd proved himself to be a blowhard, a voyeur who gained pleasure from witnessing the Disciple's work while doing none of his own.

For whatever reason, the priest had an interest in the Callahan woman and Jake Devereaux. An interest that went far beyond curiosity and straight into disgust, even anger, when seeing the photo of the two of them. Yet, he did nothing about it.

The Disciple knew he could use that information to his advantage.

Humming '*Every Breath you Take*,' by the Police, he made himself comfortable on a low rock and pulled out his phone. Aware that investigators had linked the killings to LiveFeed, he needed to plan his next move carefully. Logging into the website under the alias Nick Fury, he sent a cryptic message to Callie Callahan.

And then he waited.

When the Big Horn medical examiner arrived and the scene was secure, Jake and Callie left Ford's home and headed back to Jed's place.

"I still can't believe he's gone," Callie said sadly. "Should we get Cassidy from the sitters? Ford's notes said Suzanne Morrow could not care for Cassidy much longer."

"No, Patrice is handling it. She and her husband are catching a flight first thing tomorrow morning."

Callie worried her lip. "Is she going to keep her, then? Cassidy?"

"Sounds like." He looked over, noting her frown. "Don't worry, Blaze. Ford was one of my best friends. There is no way in hell I'd stand idly by if they force his kid into foster care."

Callie relaxed. "I was hoping you'd say that." Her phone dinged, showing an incoming message, and she grabbed it from her back pocket.

"Trouble?" Jake asked.

"It's him. Nick Fury. I guess he's impatient because I didn't reply to his first message."

"What's he say?"

"He wants to meet me later today in a restaurant called Stoney's. You know it?"

Jake nodded. "Yeah, I know it. It's about forty miles from Billings and in the middle of freaking nowhere."

A finger tapped her lips. "Hmm."

Jake pulled the car over, instantly knowing her thoughts. "No way, Callahan! There is not a chance in hell I'm going to let you meet this asshole!"

She quirked a brow. "That so, Tarzan?"

"Fine, fine, let me rephrase—there isn't a snowball's chance in hell I'll let you meet this asshole!"

"Dammit, Jake!" she said, raising her voice. "You have no right to tell ..."

"Okay, alright!" he shouted, cutting her off mid-sentence. "How about this? I strongly disagree with any notion or plan you have that puts you, at any time and in any place, directly in contact with this douchebag! That better?"

"Better? Did you get dropped on your head as a child or something?" Face flushed, she shouted, "Has anyone ever told you that you are insufferable? Arrogant? Pushy?"

"No, never!" he yelled back. After a beat, his lip quivered as he fought a smile.

They both lost the battle and howled at the absurdity of his answer. When their laughter died down, Callie spoke again.

"Don't you get it, though?" she asked softly. "He doesn't know we are onto him. You can follow me there, monitor my every move. Hell, I can wear a wire, record everything." She took his hand in hers. "Believe me, it doesn't give me the warm and fuzzies thinking about meeting this guy, either. But Jake, this may be our best opportunity. We need to wrap this up so we can concentrate on finding Gabriel."

He grabbed her chin in his hand and moved his face close to hers, his eyes dazzling pools of violet. Staring at her lips, he whispered, "It's a good thing you're so amazingly beautiful, because you've got to be the most stubborn woman on the planet."

Callie held her breath, searching his face, sure he was about to kiss her. He did not.

"Okay," he sighed, aware he'd lost the argument before it even started. "But we need an angle. Tell him you can't meet today, but you can tomorrow. That will give us time to figure out our next move."

"Sounds like a plan, Stan."

He gripped the wheel tighter but said nothing. He'd been a cop for a long time and relied on his instincts to tell him when something didn't smell right.

And right now, this whole thing reeked.

~

When Jake and Callie pulled up in front of the house, Jed and Darby came out to greet them, Blue and Lucky on their heels.

Pulling Jake into a bear hug, Jed said, "Christ, I'm sorry, Jake. I know you guys were tight." He released him. "I still can't believe it. Suicide? Jim?"

"That's because it wasn't suicide," Jake said. "Someone set this up. I would bet my own life that Jim Ford would never take his."

"Okay," Jed agreed. "I'm with you on that. Let's go inside and try to figure this shit out."

Darby grabbed Callie's hand. "We're right behind you. Give us a minute."

Jake nodded and, with a knowing look at Callie, he and Jed went inside.

"Okay, cookie," Darby said, "spill it. Are you okay? Finding Jim Ford must have been brutal."

"It was," Callie answered, stroking both dogs. "But as hard as it was, seeing the look on Jake's face? That was torture."

Arm in arm, they walked toward the house. "I bet. It's hard watching someone you love in so much pain."

Callie jerked to a stop. "Love? You been talking to Kates? Look, it's true we've been through a lot together, but ew, love him? I don't, I don't love him. Not like that, anyway. I mean, how could I? He's the most arrogant man I've ever known! He's bossy and obnoxious and ...and his feet stink."

Darby laughed. "Really? That's your take? His feet smell?"

"Well, I don't know for sure," Callie grinned, "but I bet they do. Anyway, I care for him as a friend. The same way I'd care about a puppy—a disobedient, furry little puppy that constantly chews my shoes and pees on the rug."

"Keep telling yourself that, girlfriend. Maybe someday, you'll believe it. So, about Kates. You hear anything lately?"

"Yeah, she showed up at Ford's house, helped him cross over."

"Happy to hear that."

They continued their path to the front door. "Hey, Darbs?" Callie asked. "Can I ask you something?"

"Ask away, girlfriend."

"Did Kates ever mention a love interest other than Jake? Or Kyle?"

"Not that I can remember. Why?"

"Um, well, she mentioned something weird the other day, something about Jake not being her soulmate. And today, she told me her destiny was already on the other side. With her. You think she means Kyle?"

"Kyle Walker? Nah. Meaning no disrespect to the dead, I don't see him as her one and only."

"But if Gabriel hadn't killed him? Do you think they would have stayed together?"

"No way, Jose. Kyle and your sister had tons of relationship issues, long before Gabriel entered the picture." Darby thought for a moment. "There is one person your sister was head-over-heels in love with, though. And, although she never said he was her one and only, I remember how crushed she was when it ended. This all was early on, you understand, when we were still fighting the acne and insecurity of our teen years. The guy's name was Michael Trent."

"Michael? I don't recall meeting a Michael."

Darby chuckled. "That's because you didn't meet him, dorko. He was over a century dead, died during the Civil War. Anyway, she had it bad for him, and he for her. But he called it off, told her she had plenty of living to do."

"Wow. Kates never told me about him."

"How could she? You didn't know she could see dead people yet. You didn't find that out until Stacy Egan died."

Callie dropped her head. She missed her best friend, Stacy, tremendously. "You're right, of course. I wonder if this Michael is the destiny she spoke of?"

"You know what I wonder, Cal? I wonder how long you're gonna try to convince yourself you don't have the hots for Jake." Smiling, she pulled Callie into the house by her forearms. "That's what I wonder."

Jake and Jed were standing in the foyer when Callie and Darby entered the house.

Stuffing his hands in his pockets, Jed addressed the group. "Any of you guys hungry? I can rustle up some grub if you are."

"I can't speak for everyone, but there's no way I could eat now. My gut is a mess," Jake said.

"I'm fine, too," Callie answered.

"Well, I have to say, I could eat the tail end of a cow right now," Darby said. "Sorry, but my body works contrary to most people. In times of sadness or stress, I get ravenous. Eat like a Blue Whale." She shrugged an apology. "Did you know those bad boys of the sea eat over a million calories a day? Crazy pants."

Jake smirked. "Everyone deals with stress differently. I bet Faith can fix you something, though. Right, Jed?"

Jed looked uncomfortable. "About that? I'm wondering if I could borrow Callie for a minute. I have a favor to ask."

Jake put his arm around Darby. "Sure, no problem. I'll be in the kitchen, feeding my whale friend over here."

When they were out of sight, Jed said, "Look, this favor I have? It's a big one, especially given what you've been through. So, if you can't do it, no harm, no foul, okay?"

"I'm sure it's fine. What do you need?"

"Like I said, it may be too tough for you now, so don't feel obligated."

Callie smiled. "Jed? As Darby would say, why don't you just spill it?"

He cleared his throat. "Okay. Um, it's about Faith. She's taken off, God knows where, and some questions have come up regarding her past. I can't get into the details yet, since I really know nothing concrete, but there is a criminal element involved."

Callie's eyes widened. "Criminal? How criminal are we talking?"

"Criminal enough to warrant your speaking to Caleb. I need answers about his past and am hoping you can get through to him."

Callie walked the few feet to the dining room and sat down heavily. "I have no problem speaking with Caleb, but I need to know ... what are you hoping to learn?"

Jed sat next to her and folded his hands on the table. "I'm hoping to learn if she is who she says she is. I need to know what secrets she's keeping and what she's really doing here. And most of all, I need to know that she didn't kill Caleb's father."

The Disciple looked down at the reply message from Callie and smiled. So predictable. They were giving themselves a day to weave their web, to trap him. It was almost unfair how easy it would be to turn the tables. He would go to Stoney's place and wait outside. Let them stew for hours, wondering where 'Nick Fury' could be. Once they tired of the game and tried to leave the parking area, he would approach them. Just an old friend, marveling at what a small world it was finding them here.

And then he would strike. Neutralize Devereaux by killing him quickly and proceed with his plans for the girl. He knew exactly what he would do with her, precisely where he'd take her in the mountains.

When he rose to leave, mood elevated, he noticed Callie getting into a car with the boy he'd seen playing frisbee. The child was young, no more than five or six, and the Disciple wondered who he belonged to. No matter. He was a kid and, according to Gabriel, kids were off-limits. Taboo.

Like the forbidden fruit from the Tree of Knowledge.

But the Disciple was not in the Garden of Eden. He could eat whatever fruit he fucking wanted. He would take a stand, demonstrate that he was in charge, not that gutless holy man.

And how better to do that than to go against the Apostle's wishes and ignore his threats.

As he watched the woman and child drive away, a delicious plan formed in his mind. He rushed down the small hill that had been his perch for the last few hours, desperate to get to his car. He needed to catch up with the woman and the boy.

The hell with the meeting tomorrow. He had a much better plan in mind.

~

"You sure you don't mind coming to the store with me?" Callie asked Caleb, as he climbed in the back seat and buckled his seat belt. She wasn't really expecting an answer, but to build trust with the boy, she thought she should ask.

He nodded, and she walked around to the driver's seat and

started the car. "Great," she said, turning toward the back seat. "I'm still new to the area and could use a navigator."

Caleb smiled in response and Callie pulled the Jeep away from the driveway, heading toward the main road. Her plan was to get him alone, engage him in conversation, without fear of saying something to draw the wrath of his mother. Callie had high hopes that, even if he couldn't speak, he could answer yes or no questions.

She just needed to find the right questions.

A pop song came on the radio, and she turned the volume up, acting goofy and miming the song's artist.

Caleb shook his head, trying to hide his smile.

"What?" she said, looking at him through the rearview mirror. "You never saw anyone break it down while driving?" Checking the GPS, she smiled. "Well, it's your lucky day, kid. We have a twenty-minute drive and I've got moves for days. Just wait until I find a hip-hop station!"

Pleased with how it was going so far, she drummed her fingers on the wheel, her mood light. Mind playing over different scenarios, searching for the best yes or no questions to ask, Callie failed to see the car closing in behind, its driver on a mission known only to him.

And, minutes later, she heard the twisting crunch of metal—long before she felt the impact with the trees.

CHAPTER TWENTY-FOUR

"The Boy and The Snake."
A Cherokee Legend

The Apostle had always loved that folktale. It was a legend that spoke about a young boy who took pity on an old, dying snake. The snake asked the boy to carry him up the mountain, to a place that had long been his home, so he could see the sunset before he died. But the child was hesitant and questioned the snake's motives.

"No, Mr. Rattlesnake, for if I pick you up, you will bite me and I will die," the boy said.

"No, I promise," said the rattlesnake. *"Just take me up the mountain."*

The boy agreed, and the two watched a lovely sunset together. When it was over, the snake asked the boy to carry him twice more, and the boy complied. On their last journey, just as the boy was lovingly placing the snake on the ground, the reptile turned, sinking its fangs into the child's chest. The boy cried out, yelled that he'd trusted him, helped him, and now he was going to die.

And the snake replied, *"You knew what I was when you picked me up."*

The accuracy of the tale damned near brought a tear to Gabriel's eye. It served as a reminder to trust no one. And it served as validation that his companion, the Disciple, surely knew who Gabriel was when he spilled his secrets to him.

In his bedroom in the back of the rectory, he packed a small leather bag with surgical gloves, syringes, and two vials of insulin.

He'd made his plans, concocted his web. Now, he need only wait for his prey to land on the silky trap.

It was time to end his Disciple.

Two hours later, the Apostle sat in the vestibule of St. Michael's, chatting with the church's groundskeeper. The man, a fixture in the parish for over thirty years, had told Gabriel about a piece of land owned by the church. This property, an old farmhouse on twenty acres with a barn, was no longer in use and could easily sell at a profit.

"So, I was thinking, Father," old Mr. Dietrich said, "that we could use the money from the sale of the old house for the roof repairs we need. I found another leak last Wednesday, this time in the rec room the kids use for choir practice. Somethin' needs to be done or we're looking at a serious black mold issue."

Gabriel folded his hands, feigning concern. He didn't give two shits about the roof on the church, but he played along. "I see. Yes, Bob, I understand your concerns. Perhaps we should go out there, to the old farmhouse, and look around? What is it? Fifteen miles from here?"

"Thereabouts. Years ago, the original rectory burned to the ground. Thankfully, the church itself took minor damage, but the fire left our parish in a tight spot. We needed to find lodging for our priests, lickety split. Someone found this property, and the church snapped it up. I think the plan was to sell it once we rebuilt the rectory, but you know how it goes—out of sight, out of mind."

"Indeed. Well, I say we check it out. Who knows? Maybe we

can use it as a retreat house for visiting priests or even lease the property. I wouldn't balk at a steady rent paycheck to pay the heating costs in winter." He winked, sealing the deal.

Mr. Dietrich had no way of knowing Gabriel had already seen the outside of the property, taking a drive there when the groundskeeper first brought it up. If the inside was in livable condition, Gabriel planned to move there himself.

Fix the place up, make it a home.

And turn the big red barn into a new classroom for his students. It would afford him space and privacy to conduct his lessons.

It was time to get back to his holy work, time to return to the beginning.

To the genesis of his mission.

"Shadow? Shadow, wake up! Hurry!"

Callie groaned and put a hand to her head. The throbbing in her brain was only second to the shooting pains bursting through her left arm.

"Come on, Shadow. You have to wake up."

Still groggy, Callie turned her head, searching for her sister. "Kates? What happened? Where am I? Where are you?"

"I'm here, Shadow. Right here. There's been an accident and you and Caleb are in danger. You need to move. Now!"

Like a drunk who awoke in the glare of a police car's flashing lights, Callie sobered quickly at the mention of Caleb. Clearing her mind, she looked to the back seat and saw the boy slumped to his side, breathing but not moving. The only thing keeping him upright was his seatbelt.

Wincing, she reached back with her right arm and shook him. "Caleb? Buddy, can you hear me? Wake up, pal."

Caleb groaned but didn't move.

Staring out through the splintered windshield, Callie tried to get a handle on where they were. She'd only been in Montana for a short while and hardly had time to learn the roads. Grudgingly, she acknowledged that even if she'd had the time, it wouldn't have helped.

On a good day, she couldn't find her way out of a paper bag.

But neither of those things deterred her from studying her surroundings. Still, she couldn't grasp a location. She reached into the cupholder, blindly feeling for her phone, her eyes in constant motion. A knock on the driver's side window caused her to yelp.

"Well, hello," the familiar face said. "Trouble?"

Callie breathed a sigh of relief. "Boy, am I glad to see you! Yes, it appears someone has run us off the road and Caleb is hurt."

Perhaps if she hadn't hit her head, she would have found it odd that the man had asked if there was trouble.

The front of her Jeep was demolished, buried into a thick tree. Caleb was semi-conscious, and her left forearm was bent at an odd angle. Asking if there was trouble was like asking a member of the Donner Party if they'd like a sandwich.

"Oh, goodness. Alright, well, my car is right back here. Can you walk?"

Callie tested her limbs as she sat in the car. "Yes. Can you get Caleb?"

The man smiled. "Of course. Let's get you out first, though."

He yanked open the driver's door and helped her to her feet. As they walked to his blue Toyota, something danced in the back of Callie's mind, a fact she knew was vital to remember but escaped her.

Perhaps if she hadn't hit her head, she would have recognized the Toyota as the same one that ran them off the road.

And perhaps she would have been able to fight harder when she noticed the syringe in the man's hand.

Just before it entered her neck.

"Hey, Jed? Where you at?"

Jake stood at the foot of the stairs, the silence of the house unnerving.

Where the hell is everyone?

"Callie? Caleb, you here?" He moved back to the kitchen, where he'd left Darby and a hot bowl of chili.

"How's the grub?" he asked her.

"Delish," Darby gushed. "Thanks for feeding me."

"My pleasure." He took a chair at the breakfast bar. "Wonder where everyone is? It's like a ghost town in this house."

The slam of the front door brought him to his feet. Smiling, he quipped, "They must have been reading my mind."

Jake walked back to the foyer and found Jed near a hall table, going through his mail.

"Where have you been?" Jake asked. "Where's Callie and Caleb?"

Jed continued to flip through his mail, separating the junk from the bills. "They went to the supermarket down the road."

"What? Are you insane? Jesus Christ, Jed, there's a maniac on the loose just itching to get his paws on Callie! Why the hell did you let her and the kid leave without one of us watching them?"

"Calm down, man. The store is only thirty minutes down the road. Callie is helping me try and get answers from Caleb about Faith."

"What kind of answers? Where is she?"

Jed frowned, no longer seeing the mail he was sorting. "Gone. Although where, I haven't a clue. Took all of her stuff, though."

Jake grabbed his arm, and an envelope fell to the ground. "Wait, what? She moved out? Without her kid?"

"Looks like. And I know she loves that boy so there must be a good reason. A shit ton of stuff has happened since we last talked, Jake. Sawyer found out some … some concerning information about Faith's past."

"Concerning how?"

"I'll tell you all about it, but let's include Darby in the conversation. This is a story I'd rather only tell once."

As they made their way to the kitchen, Jed forgot all about the mail and the envelope that had fallen to the floor.

The one addressed to "My dearest Jed."

～

The first thing Callie noticed when she opened her eyes was the smell.

It was a clean scent, with the sweet smell of rain and earth and pine. She was on the ground, her hands tied behind her back, dirt and pine needles pressing into her spine. There was a beat-up truck to her right, and when she tipped her head back, she spotted a cabin about fifty feet behind her. Although the house and truck appeared long abandoned, it gave her hope that, perhaps, someone was nearby in this dense forest and close enough to hear her screams.

So, she screamed. Loud and proud and unapologetically, she bellowed and howled as forcefully as her lungs would allow.

But the only response was the high-pitched whistle of an eagle overhead.

Grunting with effort, she attempted to sit up. Her body was weak and her limbs heavy, as though immersed in mud. Her vision was fuzzy, while every move she made magnified the pounding in her head. It was all eerily similar to how she felt after being drugged by Gabriel—with ketamine, Rohypnol or GHB— months ago.

Before the worst day of her life.

For a second, she contemplated the odds of being roofied and kidnapped not once, but twice, in a lifetime—in a year, even.

It's hell to be popular, she thought, dangerously close to hysterics.

Of course, as always, Callie would not let hysterics or fear or anything else stop her from fighting. She was a survivor, a Callahan.

And the Callahans never raised the white flag. They burned it.

Groaning, she willed herself to roll to her side and came face-to-face with Caleb. His skin was pale, his little body still.

"Caleb?" she whispered. "Caleb? Can you hear me?"

"Well, welcome back to the land of the living," a deep voice said from behind. "For a minute there, I thought you were dead. And then I thought, 'oh no, too soon!' We haven't yet begun to play."

Callie's stomach plunged, and her pupils dilated. Panting, she dropped her head and looked toward her feet. Her brain was currently working on one cylinder, and she didn't trust her memories of the crash. She needed to see her captor's face again.

When their eyes met, he removed his baseball cap and bowed.

Fresh fear scurried down her spine as the memories broke in waves, bathing her mind, threatening to submerge her. She remembered all of it. The man who came to 'help' them, the man who drugged her.

And the scariest part of it all? His name was nowhere near their 'potential killer' list. Jake would never suspect him. None of them would.

Which meant she was on her own.

She studied his scalp, noting the evidence of bleeding and scabbing. A frantic pattern of bald patches circled his crown.

Trichotillomania, she thought. She'd seen it to varying degrees during her clinical rotations. Admittedly, she'd never encountered such a severe case.

"I apologize for my appearance," he said, as if reading her mind. "Thought I had this thing beat, but then, bam! The stress piles on and I start yanking again!" He chuckled. "Do you know I pull to a tune in my head? Can't stop a session until the song is done, either. Yesterday, it was 'Yankee Doodle Dandy.' Today? Who knows?"

Callie wriggled, trying to get her hands up to her lower spine. A sharp, stabbing pain in her left forearm took her breath.

"Easy, there, missy. Looks like you have a nasty break."

Grinding her teeth, swallowing the pain, Callie asked, "I take it you're the Reaper? Clever, given the whole Grimm's fairytale schtick you've got going on. What was it? Mommy issues?"

She understood as a psychologist she shouldn't mock him. For one thing, it was unprofessional. It could set him off further, shutting down any hope of communicating with him. It could also serve as a catalyst, escalating his anger.

At the moment, she didn't care. And she couldn't help herself.

"Oh, wait, I know. Daddy was a meany?"

"Careful, lady. You don't want to fuck with me."

"Oh, shut up. I'm not afraid of you. I have faced, and survived, far worse assholes than you. Frankly, watching paint dry would interest me more than hearing your sociopathic excuses for why you do what you do." Callie fought to steady her voice, surprised she hadn't peed her pants yet.

But she was good at faking courage. She'd done it her entire life.

"So, what's the plan, jackass? What are you going to do with us?"

"I'm going to do a favor for a friend." Bending down, he grabbed Callie by the ankles and pulled, dragging her further into the brush.

Twisting, screaming, her legs pumped to get free of his grip while the fingers of her right hand moved over the ligature at her wrists. She felt for the knot that secured her bonds, but her hands were damp, slick with the sweat that comes with fear, and merely slid off the rope.

As he pulled, her head bounced across the forest floor, pain exploding behind her eyes. When he finally stopped, they were in the center of a small clearing.

"End of the road, I'm afraid," he said menacingly. "But, before we part, I just have to say how much I love that LiveFeed site. Man, that Confessions room has worked like a charm for me." Chuckling, he added, "Nick Fury. Classic!"

Callie rolled her eyes. "Yeah. You're a freakin' genius, *Nick*."

Frowning, he wiped his mouth with the back of his hand. "You know, you never should have let it slip that you were afraid of enclosed spaces, bitch. This might be a little rough for you."

He picked her up under her arms, pitched her backward, and she fell into nothingness. Plummeting, her shrieks echoing off the walls of the abyss and her body curled tight, she braced herself for impact. It took only a few seconds.

It felt like forever.

Her left shoulder and knee took the brunt of the fall, agony pulling the breath from her body. The collision with the ground loosened the rope binding her wrists, and she wriggled free. Gasping for air, she struggled to sit up.

A noise from above alerted her. She looked up, horrified to see her captor standing at the well's opening, Caleb in his arms.

"You've got company!" the man yelled. "Hope you've tidied up the place!"

Callie screamed as he leaned Caleb over the edge. "No! He's just a child! Don't do this!"

But it was too late. Arms flapping at his side, Caleb's small body hurdled through the dark at incredible speed. Callie pushed off the ground, wobbled to a stand, and stuck her arms out to catch him.

She missed.

~

Jake paced in front of the house, Darby and Blue at his heels while Lucky tried to keep up.

"Jake, I swear, you're gonna give yourself a coronary if you don't calm down," Darby said, maneuvering Blue between her knees and stroking his head. "She hasn't been gone that long, right? And didn't your brother just leave to track them down? Heck, if I know Callie, right now they are sitting inside an ice-cream parlor, slurping on milkshakes and eating French fries."

Jake shook his head. "No, I don't think so. I can't explain it, but I have a bad feeling."

Darby's hand stilled. "Did you have a vision or something?"

"Uh, no. I don't have 'visions', Darby. I have my gut, my instincts, which I believe are just as accurate. Maybe more so. It's hard to put into words, but the more time I spend with Callie, the more I can *feel* her, even when she's not there. Feel her, I don't know, essence? It's disturbing and fascinating all at once."

Darby narrowed her eyes. "So, what is it you're feeling? Where is she?"

The subtle shake of his head and slump of his shoulders changed Darby's mind in an instant. Callie and Caleb weren't off having fun, sharing a laugh and an ice-cream.

They were in trouble. Serious trouble.

Caleb missed Callie's outstretched arms, instead landing squarely on her chest. They tumbled backward to the ground, Callie cradling his head and absorbing the force of the fall.

Caleb was uninjured.

"Are you alright, bud?" Callie grunted. She didn't know what hurt worse—her arm, her knee, or her head.

In answer, he began to cry.

"Don't cry, pal. It's going to be okay, promise. But I need your help to figure a way out of here. You think you're up to the challenge?"

Sniffing, he nodded and stood up.

Callie bit her lip and tried to stand as well. Splinters of pain shot down her leg from her knee to her toes and she yelped.

"Caleb," she said, swallowing a wave of nausea, "I think I'm going to need some help standing. Can you do that?"

The boy nodded and walked around to her right side, bent his knees, and placed her arm over his shoulder. Callie folded her right leg close to her body, leaned into Caleb and, with Herculean effort, slowly stood.

Once standing, she clutched the boy to her side and, trembling from the cool air, scanned her prison. The walls were crude, rough, constructed of various kinds of rock. A damp chill permeated the air and droplets of water ran down the stone sides. But the well was essentially dry.

Dry and deep and small. A confining space that could fill with water at any moment, drowning them in an instant. How strong were the walls? What if they collapsed? What if they ran out of air?

Suddenly, clumps of dirt fell from above. Callie looked up to see their only source of light waning as a wooden lid scraped against stone, sealing them in their tomb.

She felt the unwelcome but familiar sensations taking control. Her hands trembled and her heart pounded. She felt dizzy, disconnected from reality.

Collapsing to the floor, she bent her legs and put her head on her knees. Her throat tightened and her lungs burned.

She knew they were going to die, knew they were running out of oxygen.

And she knew she was in the throes of a panic attack, but was helpless to stop it.

CHAPTER TWENTY-FIVE

"... and if he died first, she would go down to the grave with him." —*The Brothers Grimm, "The Three Snake-Leaves."*

"I ... can't ... breathe."

Callie hunched forward, feeling her heart kick up yet another notch. She cradled her injured left arm and rocked back and forth, hyperventilating, waiting to die. The well had become a tomb, a coffin, snatching air and life and hope.

Agitated, lost in her own fears, she forgot she was not alone until a tiny hand touched her shoulder. She turned her tear-stained face to the side and gazed into Caleb's worried eyes.

Please, God! Help me help him!

Closing her eyes, she took several calming breaths, calling up the image of her loved ones. Of Kates.

Of Jake.

She grabbed Caleb's hand, still resting on her shoulder, and squeezed. "I'm sorry, Caleb. It's just that, sometimes, small, dark spaces terrify me. My mind plays tricks, telling me stuff that isn't true."

The boy squeezed her hand back.

Forcing a smile, she asked, "How about you help me stand again? We need to look around, see how we can get ourselves out of here." She sighed, both to steady her breathing and in resignation. "I wish we had some light. He took my phone, so no help there."

Caleb stepped back and stomped his feet, lighting up the sides of his *Spiderman* sneakers.

Callie clapped her thigh with her right hand. "Wow! Caleb, you may have just saved our bacon!"

He smiled, put her arm over his shoulder, and helped her stand.

When Callie was steady, Caleb pulled off a sneaker and handed it to her. She limped to the closest wall and smacked the shoe against it. A flash of light illuminated a small area immediately under the sneaker.

The beam of the shoe only spanned about a foot. At this rate, it would take her hours to explore the well.

"You know, bud," Callie said, holding up the shoe, "it may be faster if you do this. My knee has me moving like a one-legged server at IHOP."

Caleb just stared.

"IHOP," she grinned. "Get it?"

He rolled his eyes but smiled shyly. Walking closer to the well wall, he inched along, hitting his shoe against the stones every few feet. Halfway around, he felt, rather than saw, an old two-by-four, about eight feet long, that sat propped against the wall. He pulled it over to where Callie stood.

Essentially blinded by the darkness, she couldn't recognize what he was dragging until he reached her. "Great work, Caleb! Let's see if this is long enough to reach the top of this hole."

Gingerly, she hobbled to where she assumed the center of the well would be, trying to ignore the voice screaming inside her head, warning that they would soon be out of oxygen; that the walls were seconds away from collapsing.

Giving herself a mental slap, she refocused and raised the wood scrap as high as possible.

And felt only air.

"Well, so much for that. It's too short. Or I am," she cracked. "Keep looking. Maybe there is another piece in here."

Caleb sniffed but didn't move.

"Caleb? You okay, buddy?" He sniffed again and her heart squeezed.

Oh, no! He's crying again!

"Come here a second, bud," she said.

Caleb walked over and grabbed her around the waist.

She dried his tears with her shirt. Stroking his head, she said, "You know, it's okay to be scared. I'm scared, too. But we're going to be fine. I bet everyone is looking for us. And Faith? Gosh, I bet your mom is scared silly. She will never stop looking for you!"

She felt Caleb's head tilt to look at her. "She's not my mom," he croaked.

Callie froze, stunned. *Oh, my God, he spoke!*

~

Bored, Gabriel was polishing the communion chalice when he received the latest message from the Disciple:

Meet me at Benny's! I have a surprise for you!

Gabriel's first thought was to reply, 'fuck you, douchebag.' His patience was growing thin. Still, he was curious and held his tongue.

For now.

~

The Disciple walked into Benny's Bar and Grill carrying a book and wearing a smile. He easily found a seat at the bar and looked around.

Once again, he'd picked the perfect meeting place. Even the name of the town the bar was in was magical—Story, Wyoming. He patted the book on the stool next to him.

Everything was falling into place. The stars had aligned, leaving the universe in sync with his plans.

He looked around once again. It was late afternoon and business was light. In an hour, bored housewives, desperate to escape their children, and married men, looking for a different kind of escape, would swarm the joint.

A masculine-looking woman at a corner table tried to catch his eye. She had a face full of piercings and dozens of tattoos covering her neck and arms. When he chanced a glance, she raised her glass in acknowledgement.

He studied her as a scientist might study a lab rat: closely cropped hair, muscled arms that peeked out from beneath a ragged T-shirt, acne scars dotting her cheeks.

Is she joking? He thought, disgusted. *Why on earth would such a creature think I'd be interested?*

Bobby, the burly bartender who was swiftly becoming his nemesis, stepped in front of him. "Are you ordering here, pal, or just takin' in the scenery? This ain't no park and ride. Order or leave."

"Yes, yes, of course I will order," the Disciple said nervously. "Why come into a bar if not to order a drink, right?"

Bobby folded his beefy arms and said nothing.

"Um, how about a recommendation? What do you have that's potent and carries a wicked name?

Bobby grunted. "I got whiskey. *Bulleit* whiskey sounds badass. But, if you're lookin' for a girly drink, there's always a Red Devil."

The Disciple forced a chuckle. "I see. Well, not looking to get in touch with my feminine side today."

Bobby frowned.

"Yes, let's have a bite of the *Bulleit,* por favor."

While Bobby poured, the Disciple drummed his fingers on the bar top, tapping in beat to a country tune blaring from an old jukebox. It was a song performed by Trace Adkins called *'Honky Tonk Badonkadonk.'* He liked the tempo but thought the lyrics silly.

An entire song about a woman's backside? Ridiculous.

A burst of air from the right blew his cocktail napkin to the floor, and he turned. He watched as the Apostle scanned the bar, locked eyes, and strode towards him.

"Good to see you, my friend," the Disciple said, lifting his book from the stool beside him. "Have a seat."

Gabriel grunted in response, focusing on the other customers in the bar. He narrowed his gaze when he spied the beast-woman in the corner ogling him.

She licked her lips seductively, and his face flushed. "What's with her?" he asked, nodding his head toward the woman.

"Who?" the Disciple asked innocently, suppressing a grin.

"Her," Gabriel said gruffly. "Mrs. Buzzcut over there."

The Disciple snickered. "Oh, her. She's harmless. Ignore her." He hesitated. "Unless, of course, you're interested? Not my cup of tea, but I don't judge."

He was provoking Gabriel, gaging his reaction. Gabriel refused to take the bait.

"I'm a priest," he said coldly. "I don't do women."

"Yeah, well, it's a stupid rule. Me? I got 'em lined up, especially when they find out what I do for a living. But your Holy Orders with their oath of celibacy? Unnatural, if you ask me."

"Yeah, well, no one asked you," Gabriel said, taking his seat and ordering a drink from Bobby. "So, what's all this about a surprise? I hate surprises."

"Oh, you'll love this one," the Disciple said, patting Gabriel's shoulder. He held up the thick, gold-bound book that had been keeping Gabriel's seat. "You have your bible, Padre," he said, shrinking back at his companion's hard stare, "and I have mine."

"A book of Fairytales?" Gabriel questioned. "This is your go-to? Your strength?"

The Disciple chuckled. "I suppose that's one way to put it. This book was a double-edged sword for me growing up. But, if I've learned anything as I've aged, it's that a sword with two sharpened edges cuts twice as deep."

"I've no clue what the fuck you're talking about. Make your point."

The Disciple opened the front cover of the book and pulled out two Polaroid pictures. After making sure Bobby was at the far end of the bar, he tossed one photo on the counter. "Merry Christmas," he said proudly.

Gabriel picked up the first picture and stared. His stomach churned as his brain tried to absorb what he was seeing. A woman, bound, lying on the ground, surrounded by trees. Her eyes were closed, her face bruised. From the angle, it seemed the photographer was standing some distance away.

No matter. He knew immediately who the woman was.

"I see you're speechless," the Disciple quipped. Throwing down the second picture, he asked, "How 'bout now? Cat still got your tongue?"

The Apostle picked up the photo, drew in a quick breath, and dropped the image as though it were flames licking at his fingers. He stared down at the picture on top of the bar, momentarily speechless. The boy in the photo, on his back at the bottom of a pit, looked to be about five or six years old.

Gabriel's hands shook, and he sat on them, fighting to keep them at his sides, rather than where they wanted to be.

Around the Disciple's neck, squeezing until the man's eyes bulged and tongue swelled.

Finding his voice, Gabriel whispered, "What did I tell you about kids?"

"Are you serious?" the Disciple asked. Anger growing, he spat out, "Hey, I did you a favor, Gabe. And yeah, yeah, I know you don't want me to call you out by name. Too fuckin' bad. I did you a solid, man. Try to show a little gratitude."

Gabriel's jaw tensed. He imagined himself jumping to his

feet, pulling the pretentious prick's head back, and slitting his throat. Instead, he played along.

"You're right, of course. I believed I needed to deal with Callie myself to move on. Now, I see you were right all along. As long as she's dead, I'm happy."

"Not quite dead yet," the Disciple corrected, "but being buried in that well, in the middle of nowhere? It's only a matter of time."

Gabriel winked. "Dead is dead, right? Whether it takes a minute or a day, soon she'll be dancing in hellfire as Lucifer's bitch."

The Disciple narrowed his gaze, skeptical. "And the boy?"

Gabriel shook his head. "Tragic, I'm sure. But collateral damage is always a possibility in our line of work, isn't it? I am curious, though. How did you find such a remote setting?"

"Oh, that was easy. I was scouting out possibilities and just came across it."

"Came across?"

"Sibley Lake. It's an active campground, but there are also a shit-ton of empty cabins up there with no one around. One of them had a rusted out pickup and a dry well. Except for worrying that the woman would regain consciousness during the two-hour drive from Billings, it was perfect."

Gabriel tucked that information away and took a sip of his vodka tonic. "This calls for a celebration! Next round's on me!"

The Disciple raised his glass. "To our brilliance! You know, as busy as I've been, I've even managed to set up a sad-sack FBI agent."

Gabriel winced. *If you say Jake Devereaux, I'll fucking gut you right here!*

Forcing a smile, he clinked glasses to meet the Disciple's toast. "Do tell."

"Nothing to it, really. I just planted some DNA evidence at one of the murder sites," he smirked, proud of himself. "Dumb shit was fucking up our investigation, anyway. Not that I wasn't planning on throwing in some red herrings, but the guy was making us all look bad. Once his FBI pals discover Jim Ford's suicide and letter of confession, the case against an 'unknown killer' will take a sudden turn."

Gabriel handed the photos back and waved Bobby over. "Two more, my good sir. And keep 'em coming! We've much to celebrate, much to plan!"

Including my plan ... get this fucker shit-faced and end him. Tonight.

～

"What did you say?" Callie whispered to Caleb. They huddled close, her hand on Caleb's head.

"I said she's not my mom. She's someone else, just pretending to be her."

Callie exhaled the breath she'd been holding. "I don't know about you, bud, but I need to sit down." She pulled him with her to the ground and settled him between her bent knees. He leaned back against her, and she stroked his hair, trying to ignore the pounding in her head and the throbbing of her arm.

"There's a lot to unpack there, Caleb," she said. "Must have been hard to carry that secret for months. By the way, you have a very nice voice. I'm glad you trusted me enough to use it."

He said nothing.

"Maybe we should start from the beginning," she offered. "If Faith isn't your mother, who is she?"

Caleb used a finger to draw circles in the dirt at his feet. "Fiona," he answered after a moment. "She was my nanny when we lived in Pilladelpia."

"Philadelphia you mean?"

Caleb nodded.

"Okay, so how did you guys end up here? Where are your parents, Caleb?"

He looked up at her. "Tyler," he whispered. "My name is Tyler. Fiona made me change it when we left. She changed hers, too."

Callie tried to digest the information. "I see. Why did she do that, Caleb? Or would you prefer I call you Tyler?"

"In here, you can call me Tyler. But if we get out ..." He didn't complete his thought.

"Okay, then. Tyler it is. So, why did she do that, Tyler? Why did she change your names?"

Tears filled his eyes. "I saw my daddy in the kitchen. He was on the floor, bleeding. But I can't remember what happened. Only that it was awful."

Callie sensed that whatever Caleb, or Tyler, saw that day was responsible for his catatonia all these months. It was only the dire circumstances they faced now that released him from his verbal prison.

She squeezed him closer. "I'm so sorry, little man. But once we get out of this hole, I'll talk to Faith. I'm sure there is a logical explanation."

The boy shook his head. "No! You can't tell her I told you! She said we had to keep our names a secret." He buried his face in his hands. "She said we had to hide."

Callie pulled his hands away from his face. "Hide from what, Tyler?"

His shoulders sagged, and he whispered, "From the Bogeyman."

~

"Well, shit," the Disciple slurred, "I'm a little tipshy. Not tha' I'm a lightweight, you unnerstand. Jus' not used ta drinkin' like this."

Gabriel did his best to keep his expression neutral. Although they had the same number of empty glasses in front of them, Gabriel was sober as a judge.

Or a priest, he thought, impressed with his wit.

All it took was a little ingenuity and a splash of luck. It turned out the Disciple had a bladder the size of a walnut. Every twenty minutes, he would leave his seat and head to the bathroom.

Allowing Gabriel to empty his drink into the Disciple's glass.

"Don't give it another thought," Gabriel said. "I know you aren't used to imbibing like this. But maybe you should slow down. There's no shame in a man admitting he can't handle his liquor."

Gabriel was baiting him, testing his machismo by luring him into a pissing contest. Predictably, the Disciple fell for it.

"Fuck that!" he barked. "Bobby! Line 'em up!"

Five or six drinks later, the Disciple was having difficulty staying upright. The bartender cut him off three drinks ago, but continued to serve Gabriel.

And Gabriel continued to fill the Disciples empty glass with his.

Bobby either didn't notice or didn't care. When the Disciple staggered to the bathroom once again, Gabriel reached into his jacket pocket for the syringe full of insulin hidden there. Keeping his hand out of sight, he uncapped the needle and waited.

He'd done his homework. Insulin was an invaluable medication, capable of prolonging life for countless patients who were insulin deficient. For the non-diabetic, though, a fast-acting dose of insulin could be an effective way to kill.

An overdose would most likely turn up during the inevitable autopsy, but he didn't give a shit. He'd been careful to stay under the radar.

He was always careful.

The Disciple returned to the bar and plopped on his stool. "I better get moving," he said thickly. Eyeing the man behind the bar, he added, "Bitch won't serve me, anyway."

Gabriel nodded. "Understood. But, before you go, I have something special for you."

"Can't wait," the Disciple said, sucking the last drops of whiskey from his glass.

Gabriel reached into his pocket and withdrew the needle. *"You knew what I was when you picked me up,"* he whispered, emptying the contents of the syringe into the Disciple's thigh.

"Ouch! What the ...!"

"Problem?" Gabriel asked.

"Not sure," the Disciple said, absently rubbing his leg. "Bee sting, maybe."

A few minutes later, Gabriel watched, fascinated, as beads of sweat materialized along his companion's forehead. "You okay, partner? You look like shit."

The Disciple touched his forehead. His hands were shaking, his vision blurred. He reached out to the bar to quell the dizziness. "I ... I don't feel so good."

"You know," Gabriel sneered, "the good book tells us we reap what we sow. Push me and I push back. You disregarded my orders and took another kid after I expressly forbade it. You took Callista even after I told you she is mine to deal with, mine to punish. You think you're a tough guy? Meet your worst nightmare, asshole."

The Disciple's eyes widened when Gabriel's words cut through the fog of his brain. He stood and swayed for a moment, finally crashing to the ground in the throes of a full-blown seizure. Foam bubbled from his mouth as he continued to convulse, a spasming leg kicking his barstool to the ground.

A woman screamed and several men shouted to call 911, their pounding feet echoing off the wooden floor as they rushed to render aid. The crowd surrounded the man with the rolled-back eyes and blue lips, barking out contradicting advice on how best to treat a grand mal seizure.

Gabriel picked up the Grimm's Fairytales book and stood, tucking the photographs securely inside the pages of the book. Bending forward, he laid the book next to the dying man and walked away from the figure contorting on the floor, away from his Disciple.

Away from Sheridan County medical examiner, TJ Palmer.

CHAPTER TWENTY-SIX

G abriel left Benny's Bar and Grill feeling pretty damned proud of himself. He'd not only eliminated his Disciple, but he did it undetected, in front of dozens of witnesses who assumed TJ Palmer had a seizure disorder.

If that didn't speak to his omnipotence, his mission, he didn't know what would.

Whistling softly, he made his way back to his car, the peal of an ambulance siren growing closer.

Good thing Palmer has connections in the M.E.'s office. Fucker needs a hearse, not an ambulance.

A shuffling noise startled him, and he stopped, breath caught in his throat. A hooded figure, crouched and moving quickly, darted behind a parked car a few feet to his right.

Feigning a calm he didn't feel, he tracked the shadow in his periphery. The faceless stalker was an amateur, unfamiliar with the rules of the hunt. Gabriel continued to walk, head down, planning his attack.

Opportunity knocked a few feet later—in front of a broken streetlamp, under the awning of a specialty store.

Gabriel ducked into the covered entryway of the closed shop, waited for the figure to pass, and pounced. Hooking one arm around the intruder's neck and placing the other against the back of the man's head, he squeezed.

"You better be following me 'cause you're looking for redemption, son," the Apostle growled. "Otherwise, you're a dead man."

The mystery man gasped and clawed at Gabriel's arm. "Wait, wait," he wheezed, "I mean you no harm!"

Gabriel let up slightly on the pressure he was delivering to the man's throat.

"What the fuck are you doing then?"

The man took a deep breath, filling his lungs with precious oxygen. "I-I was just following the man you were meeting."

"Why?" Gabriel asked, applying pressure again, sending a signal that he expected an honest answer.

"TJ has been acting odd, is all. We're working on a big case, and I need to compare notes with him. But he's ignoring me, not answering my calls. I figured I would follow him to find out what's so important that he ignores me."

The Apostle put his lips near the man's ear. "But why are you following *me*, asshole?"

The stranger gulped. "Well, I saw you leave without TJ, and I was curious about who you were."

The Apostle digested that explanation.

It's so fucking lame it's probably true. Still, he could be a threat. How much did he see?

Gabriel debated snapping the man's neck against letting him live.

Decision made, he adjusted his hold on the stranger's neck. "Give me your driver's license and cell phone," he commanded. Then, handing him a pen, he added, "And write your cell number on my palm."

Shaking, the man did as he was told.

With one arm still around the stranger's neck, Gabriel stuck the man's license between his teeth and took a photo of the two of them using the man's cellphone.

Releasing his captive, Gabriel tucked the driver's license into a pocket and handed him back his phone. "I know who you are now," he threatened, tapping his pocket. "And I know where you live. If you decide to grow a brain or contact the police, I want you to look at the picture I just took. Think of it as a reminder that you work for me now. When I contact you, you best come running." Annoyed, he jerked his head. "Now, get the fuck out of here before I change my mind and crush your windpipe."

The man took off at a trot, occasionally stumbling on the uneven sidewalk. He reached his car, not knowing where the Apostle had gone.

Because, terrified of what he might see, he never looked back.

Thirty minutes later, the Apostle stepped out of a downtown department store with a burner cellphone, a diet soda, and a pack of salted peanuts. Once he got back to his car, he called directory assistance and jotted down the number of the business he was trying to reach.

Scanning the radio channels, he found a local Christian station, tipped his head back, and closed his eyes. By the time Lauren Daigle's *Light of the World* was over, her angelic voice left him in tears. Wiping his eyes, confident in his decision, he picked up the phone.

Vengeance belonged to him, not to his Disciple. He made the call.

~

When Jed pulled up the drive, Jake and Darby flew out the front door to greet him. He'd barely parked the car before they yanked open his door and fired their questions.

"Tell me you found them," Jake said.

"Are they at the market? In a park? Oh, maybe they went for

ice cream. You know Callie loves ice cream." Darby was babbling, her go-to move during a crisis.

Jed climbed out of the car, frowning. "No, I didn't find them. I found the car, though, buried into a tree about fifteen miles down the road."

"Jesus Christ," Jake said hoarsely.

Jed put a hand up. "Don't jump to conclusions. Although the airbag deployed, I saw no evidence of serious injury. The steering wheel isn't bent, and, although the windshield sustained damage, it doesn't appear anyone went through it."

"Comforting," Jake said sharply.

"I've called the Billings PD. They have no reports of an accident on that stretch of road but are en route to the scene."

"Why the fuck didn't you call me immediately?" Jake snapped. "I need to get a look at that car!"

"Yeah, I figured as much. But I also figured you'd be in no shape to drive after hearing how I found it." Looking at Darby, he added, "Either of you. So, I called the cops and headed straight back here to pick you both up. We'll head over to the scene together. On the way, we can call some of the local hospitals and towing companies. Maybe Callie called a garage or something."

Jake clenched his jaw. "This is bad, Jed. She's with a little kid in an unfamiliar area. She wouldn't have any idea who to call out here. Except me. I would've been her first call."

Darby nodded. "Yes, she would have called Jake. I don't like this."

"You think I do?" Jed ground out. "I'm the one who sent them both down that road."

"Okay, bub, don't even go there," Darby said. "For all we know, they're yakking in the passenger seat of a warm tow truck, laughing about their adventures."

Jed raised his brow. "Laughing about totaling her car? I doubt that. And if a tow came, why is her Jeep still there?"

Jake headed inside to get his keys. "I don't know about you

two, but I'm starting a search." To Jed, he said, "I got Darby. You stay here and make some calls—urgent care facilities, hospitals, local garages. And update the Sheriff's Office that they didn't make it home."

"Hold on a second," Jed said. "You're a wreck, brother. You've no business driving in your mental state."

Jake simply glared.

"Okay, fine. But be careful. You're no help to Callie or Caleb if you get yourself killed."

Darby and Jed stood in silence while Jake went to get his car keys. Darby's sniffles caught Jed's attention.

"Oh, hey now," he said, hooking an arm around her shoulders, "don't do that. Don't cry, Darby. We'll find them. There's no other option."

She nodded. "I know. But I can't help thinking about the last time Callie went missing. She ended up kidnapped, chained, beaten. And Kates ended up ..." She couldn't say the words.

"Not gonna happen!" Jake said from behind. "No way in hell I'll let another person I care for die in the hands of Gabriel or another psycho fuck. We're going to find her. We're going to find them both."

He got into his SUV, Darby right behind him. As they took off down the road, Jake held a white-knuckle grip on the wheel while Darby replayed the words he'd just spoken.

No way in hell I'll let another person I care for die in the hands of a psycho fuck.

Jake had finally accepted what Darby knew all along; he was falling in love with Callie.

She only hoped his realization didn't come too late.

At a loss about what to do next, Jed headed to Faith's cottage. She'd been gone when Sawyer Mills tried to interview her earlier and, after doing a cursory check of the home, Sawyer returned to his office to do a bit more digging.

Jed, on the other hand, was certain there was a logical explanation to Faith's actions. He simply couldn't wrap his head around Faith being a con artist or kidnapper.

Or worse.

When he entered the cabin, the first thing he noticed was the silence. The space felt insignificant, hollow. Faith's presence, even when she wasn't home, had always been strong.

Or maybe that was just an illusion.

As Jed walked through the rooms, he couldn't help but feel like he was trespassing. He was invading her privacy, poking through her personal things.

But she'd left him no choice.

Finding nothing of interest in the main living areas, he walked to her bedroom. Everything looked in order. Her bed was made, and the curtains drawn. A necklace with a blue-green gem lay across an otherwise empty jewelry box on the dresser. The pendant was a gift from him, a thank-you for all she'd done to make his life easier. He'd agonized about what type of stone to get her, finally settling on the beauty of turquoise.

Apparently, the gift meant more to him than it did to her.

He checked the dresser drawers and found them empty. Walking to the nightstand near the bed, he picked up a mystery she'd been reading and flipped through the pages. After opening the single drawer and finding only hairpins and dust, he swept his hand beneath the edge of the mattress.

And found her diary.

~

"I'm thirsty."

Tyler sat in front of Callie, cross-legged, playing with the Velcro tabs on his sneakers. They were taking a break from banging the shoes on the walls and shouting for help.

"I am too, pal." Callie patted her jacket pockets, looking for the tin of mints she sometimes kept there. All she found was an ancient pack of gum.

"How do you feel about gum that's probably older than you?" she asked. Holding out the pack, Tyler wriggled out a piece.

"You know not to swallow that, right?" she asked, only half-joking. She had no children and didn't know if gum was age appropriate for him.

Talk about a ridiculous worry, Callahan. Chances are excellent that we'll both die in this well.

"Yeah," he said, somewhat insulted, "I know that. I'm not a baby."

"'Course not. How about we try looking around again? We only got halfway around the first time."

She grabbed Tyler's shoulder with one hand and wobbled to her feet, careful not to put pressure on her left leg. "Can you hand me that board? I can use it to help keep my balance."

Using the two-by-four and the wall, she stabilized herself. "Maybe you should walk the rest of the well with your super-duper sneaker lights, and I'll start hollering again."

Hugging the wall, inching around a well as black as night, Tyler pushed on. Twenty minutes later, he called out. "I found something, Callie! I think it's a wooden bucket!"

"Great work, bud! Now, follow my voice ... that's it, you're getting closer. I can smell your minty-fresh breath."

Tyler, one arm waving in front of him to navigate the unlit cavern, bumped into her and handed her the vessel.

Using her fingers, Callie felt the pail for cracks or breaks in the wood, then thumped on the bottom. "Seems reasonably solid. It makes sense there's a container down here. That's how they would pull the water from the well."

She placed it on the ground and sat. "I'm sitting on it now," she explained in the darkness. "If it holds my weight, I might be able to stand on top of it to increase my height. Then, I can try to use the plank to lift the lid."

She bounced in place for a minute, bracing to hear a

thunderous crack, expecting her ass to crash through the pail and slam to the ground. But the bucket held.

"Yay, I'm skinny!"

"Huh?"

Callie used the plank to help her stand. "Nothing. It's a girl thing. How about we try to find the center of this place?"

They plodded along, Callie hopping on one foot while Tyler carried the bucket until they reached what they thought was the center of the well.

"Okay, here's what we do," she said. "I'm going to need your help to stand on this pail. Once I'm up, you hand me the board, and I'll see if we can reach the top. Deal?"

Tyler bent down once again to allow Callie to use his shoulder. She placed her right foot on the bucket and pushed off Tyler's back. The vessel ricocheted off her heel and sent her crashing to the ground.

"Dammit!"

Tyler's voice shook. "Callie?"

"I'm okay, just need to center my foot better. We can try again, but first, we need to find that stupid bucket."

This is impossible! She thought, despondent. *I can't see anything!*

The flashing rainbow of colors from Tyler's heels provided little relief from the gloom. Callie felt herself slipping, free-falling back into the arms of panic.

Kates! she pleaded silently. *I don't know what else to do! Help me!*

Tyler stood close to Callie's leg, his body shaking. He grabbed her hand, a comforting expression of solidarity from one so young.

His tiny fingers were ice cold.

The touch of his freezing hand de-escalated Callie's panic. "You're freezing, Ty! Here." Callie shrugged out of her jacket, careful to avoid pulling on her injured left forearm. "Here," she said again, handing him her coat, "my sizzling personality will keep me warm."

Saying nothing, still trembling, Tyler donned her jacket.

Come on, Kates! This kid is going to freeze to death!

Hope slipping away, Callie sighed against the plank and tried again. "Help us! Can anyone hear me? We need help!"

For several moments, the only response was the eerie echo of her own words. But then, a welcome and familiar voice reached her ears.

"I'm here, Shadow," Katie said. "Help is coming."

Callie nearly collapsed in relief. "Boy, am I glad to see ... wait. Where are you?"

A few seconds later, Katie's shimmering form appeared and, with it, a glimpse of light. Still, Katie's essence seemed dimmer here, and most of the well remained in shadow.

"Kates, we're in real trouble," Callie said, speaking openly. "No one knows we're here. We are in the middle of nowhere and about ten feet underground."

Before Katie could respond, Tyler, in childlike wonder, whispered, "Are you an angel?"

Despite dealing with the bizarre reality that was now her life, Callie was stunned. "Tyler? Buddy, can you see her?"

In awe, he said, "She's beautiful. Do you think she's seen my mom and dad?"

Callie's heart squeezed. It was a question no five-year-old should ever have to ask a spirit. "Ty, this is my sister, Katie. She's going to help us get the heck outta dodge." Hesitating, she asked, "Aren't you, Kates?"

"You know I can't interfere directly, Shadow." Then, grinning, she added, "Although there's nothing forbidden about shedding a little light." In a blink, dozens of brilliant orbs, radiating with the glow of a thousand lightbulbs, pierced the gloom of the well. "And no one told me I couldn't bring a few friends along."

Callie watched the light show in fascination, her eyes filling with tears. "Holy moly, you always knew how to make an entrance, Kates!" Spotting the bucket, she pointed it out to Tyler. "Let's try this again, huh? Only this time, we can actually see what we are doing!"

"Hurry, Cal," Katie urged. "You know we can only sustain this light for a short time."

Callie huffed. "Hurry? Oh, you're a riot, girl. I have a busted kneecap, a broken arm, and probably a concussion. And you want me to hustle?"

Katie ignored the jab. "If you stand on the bucket, maybe you can reach high enough to lift the lid."

"My thoughts exactly. Okay, kiddo, let's give this a go."

A dozen attempts later, Callie faced the truth—she wasn't tall enough to move the lid of the well. It appeared to be a heavy piece of wood, and she could barely tap it with the plank. She was amazed she hadn't lost her footing and broken her neck yet, balancing on the pail like a circus sea lion.

"Callie, it's getting dark again!" Tyler yelled.

Callie had noticed minutes earlier that most of the orbs had dimmed. "This isn't working, Kates!"

"You're right. Stay where you are and just try tapping the top. Hopefully, the banging noise will transfer above ground."

Katie's form faded.

"Wait! You're going? Are you insane? Help us, Kates! Please!"

She disappeared completely, but not before Callie and Tyler heard her parting words. "Don't give up, Shadow! I'll be back as soon as possible. And, with any luck, I'll bring help."

With Katie's fading light, the well became a tomb once again. Callie stepped off the pail, leaned the plank against her body, and shook the cramps from her right bicep. Pins and needles had developed in the hand of her fractured arm and her left knee throbbed.

But worse, she feared for Tyler. A child's body had a remarkable way of compensating for trauma. It was entirely possible that Ty had suffered hidden injuries from either the accident or the fall. At the very least, his age put him at greater risk of severe hypothermia.

They were out of options and damned near out of time. Callie was cold, exhausted, drained physically and emotionally. She wanted nothing more than to curl into a ball on the floor and go to sleep.

Instead, she climbed back on the wooden bucket, lifted the two-by-four once again, and started tapping.

CHAPTER TWENTY-SEVEN

Jed returned to the house, Faith's diary in his jacket pocket. Concerned about Callie and Caleb, he felt the urgent need to contact Jake before examining the entries.

Blue barreled in from the kitchen and greeted him in the foyer.

"Hey, big guy," Jed said, scrubbing the dog's neck. "Miss me?"

Blue's tail wagged wildly, stirring the air in the hallway. The envelope that had fallen off the entry table earlier landed at Jed's feet. Staring down at the neat print, he didn't need to open it to know immediately the envelope was from Faith.

Just as he picked it up, his cellphone rang.

"Jed? Curtis here. I have some news you won't believe. I just got off the phone with Dan Cummings. Right now, he's out in Story, Wyoming, investigating a medical incident at a joint called Benny's Bar and Grill. It seems one of the bar's patrons fell deathly ill earlier today. The victim is currently in a coma at Sheridan Memorial."

Absently, Jed flipped over the envelope in his hand and looked at the back. "I'm guessing, since Dan's involved, foul play is suspected?"

"It is. According to witnesses, the guy had a major seizure, dropping like a rock to the floor, unconscious and barely breathing. Since Story is pretty far out there, Dan arrived before the paramedics and found a Grimm's book of fairy tales at the victim's side. Inside the book were a few photographs of a crime scene that Dan described as 'deeply disturbing.' He isn't sure what happened to the victim yet, but believes that whatever put him in the hospital was done intentionally."

"Grimm's? You think this guy is another Reaper casualty?"

"Not exactly," Curtis said. "I think the guy may actually be the Reaper."

"Holy shit! Who?"

"Someone close enough to the investigation to manipulate data and leave us chasing our tails." Curtis blew out a breath. "It was TJ, Jed. Medical Examiner TJ Palmer."

The lights of a police car on the side of the road acted as a beacon, guiding Jake and Darby to Callie's wrecked car. They pulled to the shoulder and walked toward the patrol car.

Two Billings police officers stood next to Callie's vehicle. The younger cop was furiously scribbling on a clipboard while the other eyed Jake and Darby as they approached.

Jake nodded in greeting. "Gentlemen," he said, flashing his badge. "I'm Agent Jake Devereaux, and this is Darby Harrison. The woman who was driving this car is a friend of ours. She was traveling with a young boy. Any signs of them?"

The older cop, whose nametag read 'Ptl. J. Bryant,' shook his head. "Afraid not, Agent. And, unfortunately, I have a tow on the way. I need to get this car off the road."

Jake scanned the area. Tire marks ten feet behind him indicated Callie had, at some point, hit the brakes. "Okay with you if I have a look around?"

The cop swept out his hand. "Be my guest. I'll be in the squad car with the rookie, going over his report."

Jake stepped over to Callie's car and opened the driver's side door. Fast food wrappers, empty water bottles, and napkins littered the floorboard. He eyed a smear of blood in the center of the steering wheel.

"Shit, she must have hit hard," he said to Darby. "See there? That's blood. And it looks like the contents inside the car went flying."

Darby wrinkled her nose. "Uh, actually, her car usually has a lived-in feel to it."

"You mean it's a mess, right?"

She shrugged. "Yep. I can't remember the last time she cleaned her car."

Grunting, he looked to the backseat. "Nothing here. No blood. I'm going to check around for her phone. She rarely carries a purse, right?"

Darby nodded.

Jake checked the seats, floorboards, and glove box. "I don't see her phone, so at least that's something. When was the last time you tried calling her?"

"Two minutes ago, when you asked me to. And two minutes before that, again when you asked me to."

"Yeah, well, I'm asking again. I want to make sure her phone isn't buried in here somewhere."

Darby tried, and after four rings, got Callie's voicemail. "Just her away message, Jake. Wherever her phone is, it's not here."

After giving Officer Bryant his card and asking him to call if he got any word, Jake and Darby headed down the road toward the supermarket.

"I'm freaking a little," Darby said. "What if this Reaper guy is invincible? Like Gabriel?"

"He's a man, Darby. They both are. Have you ever heard the phrase, 'If it bleeds, we can kill it?' I think it's from a Schwarzenegger movie."

"I'm more a Romcom gal. But seriously, what if we can't find them?"

"Oh, we'll find them," Jake answered. "I don't care if I have to flip this mountain on its head. We'll find them."

~

Jed held his phone, waiting impatiently for Curtis Valdez to send him a copy of the Polaroids found on TJ Palmer. Dan Cummings had sent the images to Curt who, after scrutinizing the photos, recognized Callie and Caleb. It appeared they were trapped in a hole or underground room, somewhere in the Bighorn Mountains.

Before contacting Jake, Jed wanted to get a look at the images himself. He hoped he could recognize the area and give them a good place to start a search.

As he waited for the pictures to load, the business phone rang in the office. Jogging through the living room, he got to his desk and picked up on the sixth ring.

"You've reached PIPPS, Private Investigative and Personal Protection Services. How can I help you?"

"You can't," the caller snarled. "But I can help you. It's about the kid who lives with you. And my bitch sister."

Jake began recording the call, a less-than-legal upgrade provided by Abby. It was the first time he had used it.

"I take it this is Gabriel?"

"Wow, you're a regular Sam Spade, ain't ya? Well, listen up, Sammie. I happen to have some intel I'm willing to share on Callista's whereabouts. And the kid too, of course."

"In exchange for?"

"Would you believe I'm doing it out of the goodness of my heart?"

"It's my understanding that you don't have a heart. Come on, Gabriel. I know your type. You aren't doing this for nothing."

"Let's just say I owe Callie a visit. We have some personal business to attend to, and I can't very well settle things if she's dead, can I?"

Jed grabbed a pen and paper. "So, you're saying you don't want Callie to die? Sorry, but that's not how I heard it."

"Of course I want her dead, asshole. But at my hand, not that dickhead who took her. Speaking of, have you discovered his identity yet? The guy you're searching for is named Palmer. You're welcome."

"I found that out from a cop friend thirty minutes ago. Try to keep up."

"Did your pig friend also tell you he died like a dog?"

Jed froze. *This fucker doesn't know Palmer is still alive! Let's keep it that way.*

Ignoring Gabriel's last remark, Jed asked, "Okay, so where are they? Where are Callie and Caleb?"

Gabriel cleared his throat. "I'm afraid I don't have a precise location, Sammie. You'll find some photographs in a fairytale book near Palmer's body. He told me he took them to an area in the Bighorn Mountains called Sibley Lake. There's an active campground up there, as well as a bunch of cabins. My sister and the boy are there, somewhere, trapped in a dry well. He also mentioned an old pickup truck and an abandoned cabin nearby. I believe I've given you and that bastard brother of yours enough information to find her." Chuckling, he added, "Let's hope you do. It would be a shame if the whore died before I had the chance to kill her."

"Sibley Lake is a sizeable area, Gabriel. Did Palmer say anything else? Any other landmarks? Or, maybe, how far this well is from the lake?"

"Oh," Gabriel snapped, "you mean like coordinates? Well, a'course, surely he did. He gave me the latitude and longitude; told me it was behind the Rings of Jupiter and to the right of a big ol' buffalo's asshole. What do you think, dipshit?"

"I just meant ..."

"Goodbye, Sammie."

When the phone clicked off, Jed dug his cellphone out of his pocket and checked the photos Curtis sent. Unfortunately, aside from a view inside of the well, the pictures held no identifiable markers. Walking back to the hallway, he steeled himself and dialed Jake's number.

~

Callie's foot slid off the water bucket for the third time in fifteen minutes, sending the pail flying and throwing her to the ground. Her right thigh burned, protesting the effort of holding her weight alone. She tried to do a 'controlled' roll each time she fell, protecting her left side.

She learned quickly she sucked at a controlled roll.

The damp air was siphoning heat from her body, turning her muscles to jelly. Her lips were raw as, deep in thought, she mindlessly gnawed at them. She needed a plan, but the freezing temperature in the well had turned her brain to peanut butter.

Tyler, too, was barely hanging on. He sat cross-legged on the floor, his back against the wall, Callie's jacket pulled up to his chin.

"Tyler? You okay, bud?" Callie asked, tucking her hands into her sleeves for warmth. "I think you should move around, heat your muscles. It will keep you warmer."

Tyler mumbled.

"Come on, Ty," she pleaded, struggling to her feet. "You need to get up. How about you come over and help me with this stupid bucket?"

"I'm tired, Callie. Please?"

His speech was thick, as if forming a coherent sentence was a struggle. Callie could hear his teeth chattering between words. If help didn't come soon, Tyler would die of hypothermia.

They both would.

"Oh, please, Kate!" she whispered. "Hurry! We can't last much longer!"

If nothing else, Callie Callahan was known for her tenacious attitude and her stubbornness. It was a trait that she'd always considered a liability.

Now, aware of the stakes, she thought of it as an asset.

Giving it some more thought, she decided that waiting for a ghost to save them was foolish. As a mass without a body, Katie could only do so much. No one, and nothing, would get them out of this hole faster than wits and perseverance. Determined, she pushed her shoulders back, swiped the hair off her tear-stained face, and tapped the ground with a hand until she felt the overturned pail. Setting it upright, she leaned against the two-by-four and climbed on the bucket once again.

Her strength seemingly on life support, she struggled to make as much noise as possible. But the faint tap-tap-tap of the plank against the lid of the well was like an omen, a foreshadowing to an end she wasn't ready to face.

Fuck that, she thought. Fate would not win.

She tapped harder.

$\sim$

"Jake, where are you two?"

Jed was in the driveway, loading his truck with supplies.

"At the market. There's no sign of either Callie or Caleb. Darby went into the store and spoke to some employees while I canvassed the parking lot. No one has seen them. We're leaving here now to swing by the Billings Police station."

"That won't help, Jake. I don't think they made it beyond where the jeep crashed," Jed said. "I know where they are. Sort of. It's not an exact location, but I know the general area."

"You're stalling. What's going on?" Jake asked. "Tell me where the hell she is!"

"Just listen, okay? Curtis called and told me about a man found unconscious in a bar in Story. He had a Grimm's Fairytales book and some pictures."

"Grimm's? You found the Reaper? Or is it another of his victims?" Jake asked.

Darby tapped Jake on the shoulder. "Hello? Can you share please?"

He pulled to the side of the road and switched the call to speaker. "So, who is the guy? What's in the pictures?"

"They are photos of Callie and Caleb in an underground container. An insider told me the location is somewhere up in Sibley Lake. As for the pictures? Let's just say it's clear that they've been kidnapped."

"God dammit!" Jake swore.

"Oh my God!" Darby cried out. "Who did this?"

Jed pinched the bridge of his nose. "Medical examiner TJ Palmer. It looks like he is the Grimm Reaper. The problem is, he's comatose at the moment, so we can't even squeeze him for information."

"Back up a damned minute," Jake said. "Who is this insider?"

"Gabriel."

"Gabriel? Gabriel Divine is the one who told you they are somewhere in Sibley Lake?" Jake asked, stunned. "How does that bastard even know? You actually talked to the fucker?"

Jed threw the last of his gear, a backpack of food and water, into the truck. "Yes, he called. I know, I know, it's a lot to unpack. I'll tell you all about it when I see you. Right now, I'm going to reach out to Curtis and Dan, see if we can get a search party together. Maybe they even have a helicopter available. I'll meet you at the entrance to the Sibley Lake campground, and we'll figure this out."

Darby spoke first. "Jed, grab one of Callie's shirts and bring Blue. He's a search and rescue dog, after all. I know how to handle him. If he can catch her scent, maybe he can help us find her."

Jake nodded, impressed. He should have thought of that, would have thought of it if he wasn't scared out of his mind.

"Yes, good idea. We are about an hour and change out from Sibley Lake. How far are you?"

"At least two hours. Listen, don't do anything until I get there. Hello? Jake, did you hear me? Stay put until I get there!"

The soft click on the line told him Jake had already hung up.

"We really should wait for Jed."

Darby looked around the entrance of the campground, a shiver racing up her spine. "There is, like, no one here. Freddy Krueger or Hannibal Lecter could be right around the corner, and no one would hear us scream."

Jake ignored Darby's rambling and grabbed another jacket from the back of his car. "Look, I get that it's scary. Hell, I'm a little worried myself. But I'll be damned if I wait another forty-five minutes for my brother to get here."

"I get it. But, you promised."

"Uh, no, actually, I didn't. Jed said he would meet us here. I never agreed to it."

"Oh, come on, Jake!" Darby said. "We can't go off half-cocked, so to speak. What if we get lost?"

Jake grinned. "*We* aren't going to get lost because *we* aren't going. I need you to stay here and wait for Jed and Blue. I have my cell. Call me when he gets here, and we will link up with the dog."

Darby folded her arms. "Well, sure," she said dryly, "that's a brilliant idea. And here I was, thinking the first rule of Boy Scouts is don't split up!"

Shrugging into his overcoat, he winked. "I flunked out of Boy Scouts. Too many rules." He checked his holstered weapon and zipped his coat. "I'm out, Darby. Stay in the car, lock the doors, and text me when Jed gets here."

He entered the gates of Sibley campground and turned his collar up. It was late afternoon, and the temperature was dropping. If he didn't find Callie and Caleb soon, he feared they would succumb to the cold.

And if they did, he didn't think he could bear it.

Twenty minutes later, Jake came to a clearing in the deep woods. He stopped and checked the signal on his cell phone and, as expected, he had no service. Opening his messages, he studied the photos of Callie and Caleb in their underground prison.

Dammit! Nothing here looks like this fucking picture!

Desperate, he continued forward, heading toward higher ground. "Blaze! Caleb!" he called out. "Can you hear me?"

He stayed on course, repeating the pattern of calling out and quietly listening. The only response he got was the chittering and chirps of various woodland residents. He checked his phone when he reached the top of a rocky slope and, although the phone display no longer warned 'no service,' he had barely one bar showing on the screen.

Perched on the rise, he looked around, intimidated by the immense forest. For the first time, Jake let his mind wander to that forbidden place, the place where fear clogged his throat and hope no longer existed. His legs swayed, and, unable to support his weight, he fell to his knees.

And prayed.

He prayed to the Gods and the angels and even Satan himself.

And then he prayed to Kate.

"Red, I don't know if you can hear me," he croaked, his voice shaking, "but I have to try. I need help here. Serious help. Your sister and a little kid are missing." He felt the sting of tears and struggled on. "Life threw you and me a curveball, sweetheart, and I hate that. Honest to God, I do. We could have had a shot at forever. But the fact is, we didn't. Fate and God and your fucking brother made sure of it." He sniffed. "I am truly sorry for you, Red, I am. But I can't feel bad about my feelings for Callie. I won't feel bad."

He sat back on his heels, feeling incredibly small and insignificant amid the grandeur of the mountain. "Callie is ... incredible, Kate. But I'm sure I don't have to tell you that. She's been my constant companion for five months now and I still learn something new about her every day." He smiled sadly. "Did you know she hates sushi? And peas and wet jeans and half-assed rain showers instead of full-blown storms. And she cries. Oh, Red, she cries a lot. She cries when she's happy or sad, frustrated or angry. Hell, I've seen her cry when she's hungry."

He stood and paced in a circle. "She makes my stomach flutter and my legs quake whenever she walks into a room. It's like she's crawled under my skin and made herself at home there. When we are apart, I count the moments until I can drown in her eyes and bathe in her scent again." He tipped his head back, his tears blurring his view of the sky. "Jesus, Red, I can't function, can't breathe, without her by my side. I need to find her."

He put his hands on his hips and tried to gather himself. His thoughts were more an enemy than the vast mountains or the waning daylight. The possibility of a horrific outcome played endlessly in his mind. He wiped his eyes once again and spun, trying to decide which way to go.

Before he could choose a direction, an unexplainable peace washed over him, blanketing him with comfort and calming the maelstrom in his mind. A chill swept down the nape of his neck, raising the hair on his skin.

There was a fluttering of fingers, a gentle touch on his shoulder. He sensed a presence behind him, but remained rooted in place. And then a voice, soft and sweet, broke the spell.

"She'll be fine, FBI guy," Katie soothed. "Just listen."

Incredulous, Jake frowned.

You're losing it, Devereaux.

Still, unable to help himself, he looked left and right but saw nothing. He felt alone once again, the harsh panting of his breath the only sound he heard.

He strained, listening, willing the wildlife to shut up, praying he'd recognize anything out of place in these woods.

Come on, dammit!

Finally, a faint noise, floating on the breeze, reached his ears.

He stood taller, listening.

Nothing.

After a moment, he started to move again, convinced he'd imagined it. And then, stronger, unmistakable ...

Tap. Tap. Tap.

Legs pumping, Jake tore up the slope, clumps of dirt kicking up behind him.

"Callie!" he shouted. "Blaze, can you hear me? Caleb?"

He reached the top of the incline and stopped, concentrating on the surrounding sounds. The tapping noise appeared louder here, telling him he was close.

"Hang on, sweetheart! I'm coming!"

He dug his phone from his pocket and studied the photos Jed sent him. Comparing the landscape, he spotted a rusted red truck in front of a dilapidated shack identical to the image in the picture. Stomach in knots, he sprinted toward the cabin, willing his feet to go faster.

We found them, Red. Sweet Jesus, we found them!

~

Callie wobbled on top of the bucket, her right bicep burning as she struggled to hold up the wooden plank. She had no clue how long she'd been banging against the lid of their tomb, but it felt like forever.

With daylight waning, the temperature in the well had gone from freezing to downright arctic. She weighed her concerns about starving to death against the odds of dying by hypothermia. There was no contest.

At least, it won't be painful.

Barely able to stay awake, trying to hold it together, she focused on her primary concern ... Tyler. Despite her repeated attempts to engage him in conversation, he had stopped responding to her twenty minutes ago.

"Ty? Bud, you still with me?"

Callie listened, hoping for at least a groan or two. But there was nothing. Incapable of admitting defeat, summoning every ounce of strength and determination she possessed, she refocused on the task before her.

Because losing gracefully was never an option.

And, as long as there was breath in her body, she would keep fighting.

Two minutes after that thought crossed her mind, Callie collapsed.

CHAPTER TWENTY-EIGHT

Jed, Darby, and Blue crested the opposite side of the hill and met Jake just as he reached the cabin.

"This has to be it!" Darby cried. "It looks just like the pictures! But, where?"

"Shh," Jake said quietly, "there was tapping earlier."

After a minute, Jed said, "I don't hear anything."

"She's here. I know it," Jake said, still whispering. "Look around for an indentation, bare spot, maybe a well cap. Careful where you step, though. I've already twisted my ankles a dozen times in animal burrows."

Less than a minute later, Darby called out. "Here! Over here by the truck, guys! Blue's found something!"

Sprinting to the pickup, the men followed Darby's gaze to the plywood at her feet. Blue sat to her left, whining softly.

"There's a good boy," Darby said, squatting down to give Blue a hug.

"Jed," Jake said, panting. "Here, grab a corner."

Using a strength borne only from fear, the men tossed the heavy sheet of wood as if it weighed nothing.

Peering into the hole, Jake called out. "Blaze? Honey, can you hear me?"

"Take this," Jed said, handing him a flashlight.

Jake bathed the black abyss with a cone of light. The vision he saw, one of two forms curled together, lifeless, caused his stomach to freefall.

"It's them," Jake croaked, heart in his throat. "We're too late."

~

Sheridan Memorial Hospital
Fourth floor

The man in Room 404 lay motionless under the crisp white sheets.

Next to the bed, behind a curtain, the steady beep of the monitor displayed stable vital signs. A nurse, wearing cheery scrubs printed with koala bears and hearts, checked her patient's catheter for patency, and hung another IV bag of medication.

Wrapping her stethoscope around her neck, she took a seat in a bedside chair and scribbled notes on a clipboard. The sound of padded footsteps entering the room drew her away from her task.

"Any change, Tatiana?" asked Maggie, the shift supervisor.

"No, nothing. His vitals are holding, but he remains in a minimally conscious state. Neurology was in earlier to see him, but it's anyone's guess when, or even if, he will wake up."

"And what level of functioning he'll have if he does," Maggie said.

"Sadly, yes."

"How about family? Has anyone come forward to claim him?"

Tatiana sighed. "No, poor lamb. Looks like he had no one." She glanced at the clock on the wall. "Shift change already? Boy, my day flew by. Just let me finish up here, and I'll be out to give you report. Is Sid still standing guard?"

"He just left. Replaced by a very young, very yummy, man

335

who looks a lot like Captain America." Maggie winked. "And I don't see a ring on it."

Tatiana laughed lightly. "You're incorrigible, you know that? I wonder how long the police will continue to watch him." Whispering, she added, "I mean, it's not like he's a flight risk. He doesn't seem to be responding to treatment. I don't think our guy here is coming back to us."

Whispering herself, Maggie said, "They have no choice. He's been placed in police custody, suspected of committing horrendous crimes. Sid tells me that 'our guy' is a very bad man. If it was me in charge of the investigation? I wouldn't take my eyes off him."

When her supervisor left, Tatiana emptied her patient's urinary bag and adjusted his blankets. Bending down, she said, "There you go, Thomas. Have a good night."

Cocooned within his coma, TJ Palmer heard nothing.

~

Sheridan Memorial Hospital
Second floor

"Hey, Cal? Do you have any plans to wake up? Be nice to chat with you while I'm still dead."

Callie's eyes fluttered, and she squinted against the bright light at the foot of the bed. "Kates? Is that you?"

"Of course, it's me, Shadow. I'm the only ghost I know who will put up with your nonsense."

"Testy. Maybe switch to decaf, Kates."

"Hilarious. But while you're over there cutting the jokes, I'm still shaking, thinking how close you came to joining me over here. I swear, if I weren't already dead, your antics would kill me."

Callie groaned. "Where am I?"

Katie moved closer. "You're in the hospital. We nearly lost

you. Again. But thankfully, you'll live. It's going to take some time to recover, but you'll undoubtedly do that in your usual way —blowing off the doc's advice and rushing the healing process."

"Everything is so fuzzy. My head hurts."

"You had a car accident, Cal. It gave you a pretty good concussion, on top of some other nasty injuries."

Callie's mind continued to stretch for memories just out of reach.

"You know I can't stay, toots," Katie said, her light dimming. "I'm still recharging my batteries after the last visit, but I needed to check on you." She paused. "And I wanted to introduce you to someone."

Another glowing figure came forward, as bright and warm as Katie's had ever been. The man wore a Civil War uniform, black combat-type boots, and a winning smile.

Katie grinned. "Do you remember when I told you that Jake wasn't my future, Shadow?"

Mesmerized by the man in uniform—a spirit who'd been dead for centuries—Callie merely blinked.

"It's because, as luck would have it, my soulmate was already on the other side, waiting for me." She held her hand out to the handsome man beside her, and he grabbed it. "Callie, meet Michael Trent. My destiny."

~

"You know she's safe, right, Jake?" Jed put a hand on his brother's shoulder. "You, on the other hand, look like shit. When was the last time you ate anything?"

Grinding his teeth, Jake shrugged away from Jed and paced the hospital corridor near the waiting area. "I'm not hungry. What I am, though, is pissed off! I want answers, Jed."

"Yeah, well, me, too. But falling over from low blood sugar won't help anyone."

"I'm not leaving this hospital!"

"Hold on, boys," Darby jumped in, "you're both preachin' to the same choir. How's this for an idea? Jed and I will go down to the cafeteria and grab an assortment of sandwiches and bring them up for you. That way, you don't have to leave, and we won't have to scrape your ass off the floor."

"Fine, whatever. I'm going back to her room. If she wakes up, I don't want her to be alone."

Jake pushed open the door to room 216 and found Callie awake, attempting to sit up. He rushed to her side.

"Easy, sweetheart. Go slow."

Callie frowned, the top of her skull pounding. "Jake? I must have dozed off again. What happened? Where's Kates?"

He took her hand. "What happened is you scared the shit out of me. As for Kate, I'm not sure." Smirking, he added, "I haven't seen her."

"Everyone's a comedian," she mumbled. Grabbing the side rails, she tried to pull herself up and was immediately hit with a wave of nausea.

"Whoa, slow down, champ. You have a concussion and some torn ligaments in your knee. Did a number on your left arm, too. Never let it be said that Callie Callahan isn't an overachiever."

"Swell," Callie said. "Got any good news?"

"Well, somehow, your right ankle is fine. Even after your fall, all the pins and screws in your ankle are still in place. I guess your left side hit the bottom of the well, taking the brunt of the impact."

The mention of the well and the fall was like a key unlocking a door. "Oh, God! I have to go!"

She tossed the covers aside and tried to roll to her right side. Immediately, Jake was there.

"Are you insane, woman? Did you hear what I just said?"

"Tyler! Where is Tyler?"

As soon as the words left her mouth, Jed and Darby stepped

into the room. "He's safe, Callie," Jed said. "Thanks to you, Tyler is going to be fine. Aside from hypothermia and a few bumps and bruises, he's okay. They have him in a room upstairs in the Pediatric wing."

Jake raised a brow. "What's that? Who is Tyler?"

"Caleb's real name is Tyler Duncan. Long story," Jed said. "I'll tell you about it in a minute. I have a ton of info to share with all of you."

Callie massaged her forehead, a ridiculous attempt to push the hammering in her brain through the bone of her skull. "I still don't know how I got here. How did we get out of that hole?"

Jake poured her a glass of water from the bedstand. "What's the last thing you remember, Blaze?"

"I-I'm not sure. My memories are scattered. Kates was here earlier and mentioned a car accident. I don't remember that."

"Kates was here?" Darby asked excitedly, taking a chair by the bed.

Callie nodded. "Yes. At least, I think she was. Who knows, maybe I dreamed it." She gave Darby a knowing look. "But I don't think I did. She brought a friend."

Darby grinned. "Michael Trent?"

"Michael who?" Jake and Jed asked in unison.

Callie sighed. "Not important right now. Anyway, I don't recall the accident, but I remember being tied up and thrown in that well by ... someone. And then, that same man hurled Tyler over the side, too. Son of a bitch never blinked an eye."

She took a sip of her water and continued. "Somehow, I was able to catch Tyler as he fell. Well, sort of. Probably more like I broke his fall than caught him."

"You probably saved that kid's life, Callie," Jed said. "That was a helluva fall."

Callie's eyes widened. "Oh, I remember now! I can see his face, see the evil in his eyes as he pushed me into that well." She reached out for Jake. "The Reaper is TJ Palmer!"

Jake took her hand, then sat on the side of her bed. "Yes, we know. Palmer was in a perfect position to get away with it all, too. As the county M.E., he could manipulate data and lead us down blind alleys, all while keeping tabs on our progress. We're still learning about his activity, but it appears the bastard has been on a killing spree for some time." Jake's voice dropped. "Palmer framed my best friend, made it look like he was the Reaper—right before he killed him."

Callie squeezed his hand. "I'm so sorry about Ford, Jake. He was one of the good ones."

"You're not wrong. What else do you remember, sweetheart?"

"I was cold, colder than I ever thought possible. I remember trying to lift the lid of that freaking coffin we were in. I used a length of wood we found to hit the cover, maybe knock it to the side and get some light in, but I was too short."

Darby patted Callie's knee. "We aren't short, Cal. We're fun-sized!"

Callie grinned. "I like that. Anyway, I could feel it coming; the anxiety, the panic. I was having trouble breathing, focusing. It felt like the walls were caving in on me. But Ty? Man, that kid was amazing. He kept me grounded, talked me off the ledge, made me try harder. His light-up sneakers helped us find a bucket for me to stand on. I'm so relieved that he's okay." Her eyes met Jake's. "He is okay, right? You aren't just telling me that to protect me?"

Darby spoke first. "He's fine, Cal. Jed and I are going to head up to the Pediatric Unit to check on him in a minute. Poor kid. What a mess."

Callie's face dropped. "I can't imagine how he feels. I wish I could have done something sooner, recognized the danger. I should have seen it." She picked at the corner of her blanket. "He spoke, you know. Tyler. We were both exhausted and, I expect, preparing to die. And then he spoke."

Darby clapped her hands. "Did he? For real and for certain? Wow, that's great news!"

Callie smiled. "It is. His voice is so melodic and sweet, I

could listen to it forever." Her vision blurred with unshed tears. "That child has been through so much in his short life, but he never complained in that hole, not once. Lord knows, he certainly had reason to. I wish I could have done more to help him."

Jake quirked a brow. "Done more? Do you not understand how amazing you are? Callie, you saved that little boy. You saved yourself. That stubborn Irish temper wouldn't let you roll over and die, wouldn't let you get sucked into that dark chasm of anxiety. Instead, you continued tapping with that damned plank of wood, and I heard you."

With a little help from a friend, he thought.

Later, he would tell Callie how her sister helped him find that well. For now, though, he kissed the back of her hand and whispered, "I'm so damned proud of you, Blaze."

Callie, doubtful that she'd done anything right the last few months, ignored the compliment. "I'm still confused about how you knew where to look for us. I mean, I get you heard me making noise, but how, in a mountain range so vast, did you know where to look?"

"Gabriel," Jake said plainly. "He called PIPPS, gave Jed a description of the area, even sent some pictures TJ took we could use as a reference. Then, because Gabey-boy is such an upstanding guy, he double-crossed his protégé, tried to kill him with an overdose of insulin. Pity that asshole Palmer didn't have the good sense to die, though. As we speak, he's comatose in a bed on the fourth floor."

Jed gave Callie a lopsided grin. "Yep. And the best part? Gabriel doesn't know Palmer is still alive. I bet we can use that to our advantage."

"Interesting," Jake said.

"He must be slipping; it's not like Gabriel to miss his mark," Callie said. "Still, I wonder why the man who wants me dead would save me."

"For reals!" Darby huffed. "Although I'd be lying if I didn't admit to feeling a twinge of gratitude. After all, whatever his motivation, he saved your life."

Jake growled. "Gratitude? Sorry, Darbs, but the only thing I feel toward that fucker is rage."

"Me, too," Callie said. "So again, I ask. Why help me?"

Jed pulled a seat over to the bed. "I suppose even the Devil himself has a line he will not cross. For Gabriel, that line is crimes against children."

"Not to mention, he wants the pleasure of killing me himself," Callie said.

Jake nodded. "That, too. Somewhere along the line, Gabriel and TJ linked up. We know the why of it—crazy begets crazy, right? We just don't know how or even when that happened."

Callie pinned her gaze on Jed. "So, is Caleb part of what you need to talk to us about? I assume since you know his real name is Tyler, you also know Faith isn't his mother?"

"Yeah, I know," Jed said, his voice gruff. "A week or so ago, after realizing Faith's story had more holes than a block of Swiss, I asked Sawyer to look into her background. He has a ton of police friends on the east coast and, since Faith spoke about living in Philadelphia, I figured that was a good place to start."

"Okay," Callie said. "Did he find anything?"

Jed walked back to the corner of the room and picked up a folder that sat on an unoccupied chair. "He did. We still don't know the complete story, but we've pieced together some of it. This," he pulled out a 5x7 photo from the manila folder in his lap, "is Graeme Duncan, Tyler's father."

Darby peered over the bed. "He's handsome."

"Yeah, not anymore. He was shot to death about eight months ago."

Darby's eyes widened. "Geez Louise! You mean Faith's husband was murdered?"

"Not her husband, Darby," Jed answered. "Graeme was married to Emily Weston, the adopted daughter of billionaire

Randall Weston. My sources tell me he's been searching for Emily since Graeme's killing."

"Searching?" Jake asked. "Is she missing?"

"She is. No one has seen her for about eight months. Investigators had her pegged as the prime suspect in Graeme's murder until they learned about the nanny."

Darby rolled her eyes. "Seriously? This is starting to sound like a Lifetime Movie."

Callie groaned. "My scrambled brains are having trouble keeping up, Jed. If Faith isn't Graeme's wife, if she isn't Tyler's mom, then who is she?"

Jed shrugged. "Not a hundred percent on this, but I'm guessing she's the nanny. Her real name is Fiona Clark. Sawyer and I are working on unraveling this mystery, but we think Fiona took Tyler on the run with her. She changed their names and traveled to Montana, pretending to be his mother."

Callie rubbed a hand over her eyes, trying to follow the conversation. Her skin was pale, accentuating the bruising on her body. "But why? Why the charade?"

Jake tossed a warning look at his brother. "Maybe this isn't a good time to hit her with this stuff."

"No, I want to hear it," Callie objected. "Do you think Faith or Fiona or whatever killed Tyler's parents?"

"Maybe. I don't know," Jed answered. "I found Faith's diary right after she took off. Judging from the little I've read, it's certainly possible she's involved. In her last entry, she admitted that her Scottish accent is fake, a hoax to further cloak her identity. Not something I'd expect from an innocent woman."

"Cheese and rice," Darby whispered. "Where is she now?"

"Gone."

Jake stood and stretched. "Gone? Do we know if her absence was voluntary?"

"It was," Jed responded bitterly. "She split as soon as she realized Sawyer and I were on to her."

Callie shook her head, then instantly regretted it. "I can't believe she would leave without Tyler. If I know nothing else about her, I know she loved that little boy."

Jed took another photo out of his folder and tossed it on the bed. "So did she. Meet Emily Duncan, Tyler's biological mother. Faith left this photo in my foyer, along with a request to pass the picture to Tyler. I don't expect he has any family photos."

Callie studied Emily's image. "She's beautiful. Any idea where she is?"

Jed shrugged. "No one knows. Her sister reported she and Tyler missing after authorities found Graeme's body. The original theory was that Emily killed her husband in a rage, then ran off with Tyler. But Emily's family never bought that scenario and filed a missing person's report. Now, after all this time, I think the cops fear Emily Duncan is dead."

Jake took the picture out of Callie's hand and stared. "Man, she looks familiar to me," he mumbled to no one in particular.

"I thought so, too," Jed said. "Must have one of those faces."

Jake shook his head. "Nah, that's not it. It'll come to me."

Jed's gaze shifted to Callie and the dark circles beneath her eyes. "You look wiped, Cal. Get some rest. Darby and I are going to head up to see Tyler."

Jake walked them to the door. "Jed, you realize you pretty much just handed us all a leaky bag of shit, right? You're already stretched thin working your regular cases. Now, on top of finding Gabriel, we have to search for Faith as well."

"And Emily Duncan."

Closing the door after Jed and Darby, Jake whispered, "And our sister, Lacy Jane."

CHAPTER TWENTY-NINE

I t took several hours before the man in the alley by Benny's Bar gathered enough courage to go home. After all, the crazy person who jumped him knew his name and address. What if he'd decided to pay a visit? What if he changed his mind, instead deciding to kill the man who'd seen everything?

After he got home, panting and beyond terrified, the man tore through his apartment, checking all the doors and windows. Once confident he was secure, he walked to the bathroom and peeled off his clothes. His wet pants clung to his thighs, making removing them difficult.

He had no recollection of peeing his pants, but apparently, he had. He'd never thought of himself as a coward. Time and time again, he'd proven his courage to the world. But there was something about this encounter that created a fear in him he'd never known existed.

Stepping into the shower, he stood under the steaming water and closed his eyes. Hyperventilating, near panic, his mind raced. He'd seen the killer's face; knew what he'd done.

And now, TJ's murderer knew all about him as well. Short of disappearing entirely, there was nowhere to hide.

Drying off, the man dressed, went to the den, and fixed

himself a gin and tonic. Sitting on the sofa, hands trembling, he tried to convince himself the entire experience had been a dream. A nightmare.

After all, this wasn't some third-rate movie. This was his life.

He dug into his pocket for his phone and clicked on the photo icon. Instantly, the image of a wide-eyed man with an arm around his throat and urine-drenched pants stared back at him.

Embarrassed by his cowardice, he gulped down his drink and snapped the phone shut, shattering any illusion that the encounter in the alley was a dream.

The sudden blare of his ringtone startled him, and he yelped. Stomach flipping, butt-clenching, he stared at the unknown number on the screen. His gut reaction was to say, 'fuck it,' and let the call go to voicemail.

But the psycho knew where he lived; the last thing he needed was the bastard showing up on his doorstep.

Taking a steadying breath, he answered the call. "Hel-hello?"

"Well, hello yourself. Remember me? Allow me to properly introduce myself. I am known as the Apostle, but you can call me Sir."

The familiar voice shot fresh fear through the man's body. "I-I remember."

"Excellent. I'd hate to think I failed to leave an impression. Now, we have much to do and little time to do it in. But first, I must give you a name, one that describes your role as my assistant more accurately."

The man nibbled on a hangnail but said nothing.

"I wonder ..." the Apostle said, his voice trailing off.

After a minute of silence, the man dared to hope the Apostle had hung up.

He did not.

A quick intake of air, the snap of two fingers, and then, "Have you ever heard of Simon of Cyrene?"

Confused by the question, petrified that any answer would be wrong, the man stayed silent.

"Hello? Are you listening to me, asshole?"

"Sorry, yes. Yes, I'm listening." the man croaked. "But I-I don't know Simon of Syria."

"Cyrene, you idiot. Simon of Cyrene. He was a man who helped Christ bear the weight of his cross while he traveled the road to crucifixion. I believe you can help me carry my many crosses, as Simon did for Jesus. It's quite the honor, truth be told. I'm entering a new chapter in my life, a chapter written exclusively for me and authored by God himself."

"I-I see," the man said, although clearly he did not. "And what is it you'll have me do?"

The Apostle closed his eyes, basking in his new role, ignoring the man's question. "We shall call you 'Simon' for now. Clever, don't you think? Soon, the world will know you as the first follower of the man who would be king."

"K-King?" the man asked.

"Focus, Simon! I'm the Chosen One. I am on a path to divinity."

There was a disturbing sound, the unmistakable vibration of a zipper gliding past its teeth. The Apostle let out a moan, his rapid breathing and grunts telegraphing precisely what he was doing.

Cringing at the obscene sounds on the other end of the line, his assistant waited.

Just before the line went dead, a whispered voice cut through the man's core, threatening to let loose his bladder all over again.

"I am the Messiah."

The man dropped the phone to the floor, as though letting go of it would free him of his torment.

And then, Simon of Cyrene, unwilling assistant to a sociopath, wept.

～

Six days later.

"Are you sure you'll be okay to travel, Cal?" Darby asked. "You just got out of the hospital. Maybe you should hang out here and let me spoil you rotten before you get on that plane to Virginia."

They were in Jed's dining room, Darby standing near the table while Callie sat in her wheelchair. "Honestly, I'll be fine, Darbs. Don't forget I'm not traveling alone. I have June Cleaver to take care of me. I'll be surprised if he lets me powder my bottom alone."

Darby chuckled. "Don't be so hard on him, sis. He went through hell when Palmer took you and Tyler. Can't blame the guy for not wanting to let you out of his sight."

"I know, I know. And I appreciate it. But sometimes, that gorgeous man can—" she stopped speaking when Jake entered the room.

"Gorgeous, huh? Oh, Blaze, you're making me blush."

"Don't flatter yourself, Barney. I wasn't talking about you. You sure have an inflated ego, don't you?"

Jake winked. "And you sure are a terrible liar. Anyway, I'm finished loading the car. Do you have everything? I see you've got your chair, but what else? Meds, crutches, sling?"

"Yes, mother, I'm good," Callie said dryly. She grabbed Darby's hand. "Now, are you sure you don't mind handling things for a few weeks? With Tyler staying here, it's a big load we are putting on your 'fun-sized' shoulders."

"Ha! Don't worry about my shoulders, Cal. I've learned over the last few months they can handle a ton."

Darby was staying in Montana with Jed to help care for Tyler. They all agreed it was too early to know if sending Tyler to live with his grandfather was safe. Little was known about Randall Weston, Emily Duncan's disappearance, or the killing of Emily's husband, Graeme.

Until they were sure of Randall Weston's innocence in either crime, they decided to keep Tyler close.

Sawyer and Curt agreed that, for now, they would keep Family Services in the dark about the boy. The plan was for the team to dig deeper in the next few weeks, even traveling to Philadelphia, if necessary, to uncover the truth about what happened to the Duncans.

When they were satisfied with the answers, they would hand Tyler over to his family.

"I am more than good, Cal," Darby said. "We have some big plans! I still need to find a building for my store, so Jed's agreed to help me look at property around here. In return, I'll pitch in and help with the day-to-day stuff for PIPPS. I'm excited about it!" She tilted her head. "And what plans do you have for your recovery? You'll need to make some doctor appointments in Virginia, like neurology, orthopedics, physical therapy. Oh, and don't forget you can't put weight on your knee yet, and your arm is going to be in a cast awhile, so your butt needs that wheelchair. Maybe stay on the ground floor at the cabin." She put a finger on her chin. "What did I forget?"

Callie laughed. "You're adorable, you know that? Don't worry, Darbs. Remember, I have a hook in the medical field with Ryan. Finn is going to be up my ass, and Jake is staying at the cabin with me. We'll be back before you know it." She rolled her chair back and forth. "I need to go home, girlfriend. Reboot, recharge, spend some time with Grams. And handle, you know, some unfinished business."

"Like Amara?" Darby asked.

During her week of hospitalization, Callie confided in Darby and Jed about her newly discovered sister.

"Yes, like her. But I need to be careful. If there is the slightest possibility that Gabriel doesn't know he has another sister, I'd like to keep it that way."

Darby nodded. "Good thinking, Cal."

Jake released the lock on Callie's wheelchair. "And I need to tie things up at Quantico. The bureau okayed the transfer I put in for, so I'll start in the Billings office next month. And I, too, need to take care of some unfinished business."

"Selling the townhouse?" Jed asked from the doorway.

"Nah," Jake said sadly. "This is much bigger than real estate. I need to lay a dear friend to rest."

~

In the backyard of the Callahan cabin in Falls Church, Virginia, Callie sat in her wheelchair, taking in the scenery. The Rappahannock River was especially quiet on this lovely spring day, making it easy to hear the surrounding wildlife. She turned when she heard the crunch of grass behind her.

"You're out of ginger ale, so I got you an orange juice," Jake said, handing her a glass. "I'll go out later and get some supplies." He sat next to her on a flat rock, enjoying the view. "Sure is beautiful here, I'll give you that. You feeling okay?"

Callie smiled softly. "I should be asking you that, Jake. After all, you are saying goodbye to a loyal friend today. That can't be easy."

Jake stood and walked to an urn that sat next to another grave. "It's not, but Gus deserves a special place to rest. I can't think of a better site than right here, with his buddy, Chance." He picked up the urn and played with the top of it. "If I didn't say it before, thank you for letting me do this."

Callie's eyes filled. "Oh, Jake, you never even had to ask. Gus is family." Wiping a tear, she asked, "Do you want to sprinkle his ashes on top or bury him next to Chance?"

"I think I'll dust him over the grave. Gus always loved the wind in his face." Choking, voice raw, he said, "He hated to be confined. He loved fresh air and sunshine and ... freedom."

After saying a prayer, Jake shook out the contents of the urn, watching it float and spiral in the wind. "Well, that's that, isn't it? Funny how years of life and love can come down to a container of ash."

Callie gestured for him to come nearer. "That's just it, though, Jake. It's not. Life is about loving and learning and leaving an imprint on the hearts of the people you touch. What remains after death means nothing; it's how you lived, what you did with that life, that matters."

Jake sat back down next to her, taking her hand in his. "I believe you, Callie. And I think if I've learned anything, it's that we can't take life for granted." His eyes found her lips, and he leaned in, eager to taste their sweetness.

Startled, Callie moved back. "I'm sorry. I want to, I do. It's just ..."

Jake squeezed her hand. "I get it. Hard to get close with a person between us, right? Even if that person is a ghost."

"No, Kate made it clear she was with her true love. I know that now. But in the back of my mind, I sometimes wonder if you do."

Jake looked shocked. "Callie, you can't possibly think ..." He leaned closer. "You know what? It doesn't matter what you think. I will wait for as long as you need. I'm not going anywhere."

His words touched her, and she began to cry.

"Hey now," Jake said, "none of that. You're going to get your cast all wet."

She sniffed, smiling.

Jake's demeanor changed from jovial to somber. "I know you believe I compare you to Kate, Blaze, and I get why. You've been compared to her your whole life." He picked up a small rock and skipped it across the river. "But I know exactly who you are. You are a stubborn and reckless woman who's loyal to a fault."

He moved to the front of her wheelchair and got on his knees. "You have a weird-looking pinkie toe on your left foot and a heart-shaped mole on your neck. You sometimes snort when you laugh and have the most amazing dimple on your right cheek. You're funny and maddening and literally take my breath away whenever you smile at me."

"Jake, stop ..."

He put a hand up. "You're compassionate and giving and beautiful beyond compare. And you believe in people, Blaze. You believe in me." He kissed her forehead. "I will wait until the end of time for you if I have to, because, God help me, I adore you. In this life or the next, I choose you. I will always choose you."

Callie sniffed. "Oh, Jake ..."

He pushed on. "No, I need to finish. Callista Grace Callahan, I know exactly who you are. You are the woman I love with a passion and fierceness I never knew existed." He dropped his head in her lap. "I would die for you. God as my witness, Callie, I would. And that scares the hell out of me. Because I have never felt that kind of love before. Ever,"

She lifted his head off her lap and held his face in her hands. "I do *not* have a weird pinkie toe. But I love you, too, Jacob Devereaux, with all that I am. And I expect I always will. Now, shut up and kiss me."

He smiled and moved closer, whispering into her lips. "Yes, ma'am."

$\sim$

Two glowing figures stood near the woods, hand in hand, watching Callie and Jake by the river.

"Your sister seems so happy, love," Michael said. "Are you sure we should tell them? Prepare them for the evil to come?"

Katie shook her head. "No, Michael, you were right. Callie has finally found peace. Let's give her today, at least. The darkness will still be there once she's healed." She rested her head on his shoulder, afraid to voice the fear in her mind.

And that darkness will follow us, consume us, drag us to the depths of Hell.

Unless we destroy it first.

ACKNOWLEDGMENTS

Bask in your success, but never forget how you've achieved it.

This book would not have been possible without the love and unconditional support of so many people in my life.

Family is everything, and I have the best. A million thanks to my husband Mark, (my strength and the love of my life) and our children Jennifer, Brian, Jared, John, and Jordan. You've always been my biggest supporters and loudest cheerleaders, no matter what path my life has taken. I love you all with everything I am.

An extra special shout out to Jordan, my beautiful daughter, and the 'runt' of my litter. Jo, you have been my sounding board and confidant and have come up with some pretty crazy plot twists! I could not have completed this book without you.

Love you more than you know what.

I never thought I could adore any child as I adore my own. And then, I met my grandkids. To Declan, Ava, Raylan, David, Connor, Mila, Dean and Piper.... Being your Nana has been—and always will be—the greatest honor in my life. Love you all crazy mad.

To my mom, Mary Quinn... the president of my fan club, long before I had a fan club. Thank you for policing my spelling and correcting me when I crush, kill, and destroy innocent punctuation.

Love you, momma.

Special thanks to my 'third' daughter, Lara Noll. No matter how down I am, no matter how much I doubt myself, you are always there to pick me up. You're such a bright light in this family, Lil, and I couldn't love you more.

To Lori Martin and James Quinn, the best damned siblings anyone could ask for—love you both, you filthy animals.

And, as always, thanks to all my cherished friends, especially my 'bookends', Cynthia Rich-Boyd and Mary Hoffman. You stand beside me when I'm overwhelmed and kick my butt when I waver. I love you both beyond words.

There are always a few angels on my shoulder, whispering and encouraging me to push on. The loudest voice belongs to my best friend, Lisa, while the most persistent comes from my cousin, Kevin.

But the title of 'powerhouse' goes to my much missed and loved mother-in-law, Janet Noll.

'Grammie', you were a beautiful and strong force packed into a tiny five-foot body. I love you dearly and am so fortunate to have called you mom.

~

In other news... some unsolicited advice I received when I began this writing journey was to 'write what you know,' and 'stay in the lane you're comfortable with.' Of course, as an unapologetic lane changer, I did the opposite. I dove in, headfirst, and placed a serial killer in a geographical area I knew little about.

Because I'm a rebel like that. And I love a good challenge.

But it's how one reacts to such a challenge that defines a person. A victory means little without someone to share it with. Having the backing of the best group of people, the best tribe, is non-negotiable.

Oh, and a phone—you definitely need a phone.

The first person I 'cold-called,' was Patrol Captain David Hartley of the US Forestry Service/ Tongue Ranger District, Wyoming. Captain Hartley was knowledgeable, kind, and provided invaluable information about Tongue River and the surrounding areas. Thank you tremendously for your patience.

My next call was to the Medicine Wheel Ranger District, where I spoke to a nameless female ranger (nameless because I suck and failed to record her name) who gave me ideas on the foliage, terrain, and the best places to hide a body on Bighorn Mountain. She stayed on the line, politely answering the most bizarre questions, and did not hang up.

Thank you for listening to the rantings of a crazy woman. If I were you, I'd have hung up.

To Assistant Chief Patrick Smith, US Park Police (ret) and SAC Scott Hinson of the Investigative Services Branch, National Park Service (ret), I appreciate you both sharing your vast experience with me and explaining the inside workings of a homicide investigation.

And to the man, the myth, the legend, Michael Burke, NYPD (ret). Thanks for all the support from both you and the fine men and women of the amazing non-profit group, Brothers Before Others.

But you owe me, bud😊

A big thank you to Don DeJarnett, treasured friend, successful author, and a virtual fountain of information regarding the Montana/Wyoming area. I thank you for relating the stories and legends, your insights into the accessibility of 'kill sites,' and the many hand-drawn maps you made for me. I am forever in your debt.

Thank you, Chelsea Ryan, for introducing me to 'Grandad' Don and for being my 'fourth' daughter. Love you lots.

To KT Lyon, my Scottish friend and fellow author. Thank you for ensuring I didn't butcher your country's beautiful style of speaking.

Too much, anyway 😊

Writing the manuscript is only part of the process. To my editor, Sian Phillips...thank you for your support, your wisdom, and your ability to polish my words while still letting my voice shine through.

To my cousin and 'twin', Brian Quinn, you rocked yet another cover, brother. Your brilliance is, at times, blinding.

Finally, to Law Enforcement Officers everywhere...

We see you; we salute you.

We recognize your strength, courage, and the sacrifices you make each day. Stand tall, shoulders back, and kneel to no one but God.

Because you are all warriors. And you've earned the right to be proud of the colors you wear.

Peace out, my friends.

DISCUSSION QUESTIONS

1. One daunting task that faces an author is the challenge of writing authentic characters. Which character did you like the best? Could you see yourself or one of your personality traits in any of the characters?

2. The setting of this book is in Montana and Wyoming. Did any descriptions of the area or mountains make you more likely to want to visit?

3. Poor choices in life can be dangerous. Is there any character in the book who you would like to lecture about the perils of the decisions they made?

4. Did you guess the ending of the book? Which twist shocked you the most?

5. This book has many scary moments, including scenes of supernatural phenomenon and horrible deaths. Which scene did you find the scariest? Are there any scenes that stayed with you long after you finished the book?

6. How long did it take you to read the book? Was it a slow burn or more of a race to the finish?

7. Have you read "The Apostle's Fury", the first book in

the series? If so, how did the pacing and overall plot compare to "The Disciple's Fury?" Do you plan on reading "Final Fury," the last book in the trilogy?

8. There have been many studies on the connection between siblings, particularly twins. In The Disciple's Fury, Callie struggles with the sudden absence of her sister, as well as her own feelings of survivor's guilt. Do you believe that Katie would have as much difficulty as Callie in coming to terms with her sister's death?

9. How did you feel about the relationship between Callie and Jake? Did you find it difficult to reconcile Callie's romantic feelings for her sister's ex?

10. What did you think about the style of writing? Are there any scenes or sentences that stayed with you for a while?

11. Do you believe in the paranormal? Have you had any experiences similar to those described in the book?

12. Do you have any extraordinary animals in your life?

13. Would you recommend this series and/or this author to friends and family?

14. Did you find the book believable? Did you understand the explanations for the forensic and investigational procedures done by law enforcement?

15. Finally, what do you imagine will happen next? Any thoughts as to the direction Book 3 will take? Where do you think the characters will be at the conclusion of the series? Should this series be a spin-off featuring PIPPS investigations with Callie, Jake, and Jed?

SHADOW SISTERS BOOK THREE: FINAL FURY

I hope you enjoyed reading *"Shadow Sisters Book Two: The Disciple's Fury."* Continuing the journey of the Callahan family and friends has been such a joy. It will sadden me to see this trilogy end with the third and final installment, *"Shadow Sisters Book Three: Final Fury."*

(Unless Callie, Jake, and the gang continue their adventures in a new series? Time will tell!)

But, if and until then, read on to see what's in store for the conclusion of the 'Fury' books!

Rebecca Sue Caraway kneeled on the dusty floor of the barn, arms shackled in irons above her, and watched as droplets of blood splashed to the ground below.

Seven cuts over seven minutes in the seventh hour of the day. Her punishment for committing one of the most grievous offenses, one of the most cardinal of sins.

At least, that's what her captor had told her.

She tipped her head back and examined the slashes marching in formation on her forearms. As a nurse, she understood she was in no danger of bleeding to death. The cuts were superficial and, although painful, too shallow to hit an artery. No, her immediate concern was dehydration, shock, or hypothermia.

And, of course, her captor. The man who held her prisoner was her biggest threat.

Becky Sue had no idea how long she'd been trapped in the old barn. The hours and days seemed to fuse, melting into a succession of horrors her mind could not process. She closed her eyes and took a calming breath, willing her racing heart to slow down. It was a relaxation technique she'd demonstrated for many of her patients before they faced a painful procedure.

She was learning first-hand that the method was useless. Fear was fear and pain was pain. No amount of measured breathing could ease the agony of skin debridement in a burn victim, or the anxiety a patient felt before undergoing cardiac bypass.

And no cleansing breaths could erase the spine-chilling terror that comes with knowing a psychopath wanted to end you.

She tugged once again at the chains that bound her and winced. Every move sent blinding pain through her body. The delicate skin under the iron cuffs was raw. Her knees throbbed from kneeling, while the intense heat spreading across her shoulder blades threatened to become an inferno.

Besides the shackles biting into the flesh of her wrists, the slant of her body was also contributing to her misery. Strapped by the waist to a column behind her, the chains that secured her arms hung at least a foot in front of her, leaving her upper torso suspended. The angle forced her shoulders to take the brunt of her weight.

Admittedly, it was a considerable amount of weight.

Becky Sue wondered if being fat—obese, truth be told—would be a deciding factor in her survivability. Could she have escaped if she were thinner? Model thin, like Kate Moss or Angelina Jolie? A petite girl with slender, graceful hands that could easily slip out of the restraints? She studied the cold steel around her wrists and shook off the idea that skinny would equate to survival.

The only thing one could consider 'slim' on Becky were her wrists. Even Kate Moss would be screwed.

Rebecca's inability to slim down was not for lack of trying. She'd lost track of how many diets she'd tried, how many gym memberships and pills and 'quick-loss' programs she'd paid for in her quest to drop the pounds.

Nothing worked.

In the end, the only thing lighter was her wallet. Like a needy friend or an unrelenting virus, her weight was always there, lurking in the background, a thing that wouldn't leave. Her doctor attributed it to hormones, while her friends blamed the high-stress career she had chosen. Phil, her personal trainer, accused her of binge-eating and 'not wanting it badly enough.'

Soon after Phil had given her his 'professional' opinion, she fired him and went out for fries and a milkshake.

Because Becky Sue understood it was a combination of problems—issues that would take years of therapy, calorie counting, and strenuous workouts to resolve. At this point in her life, it all seemed too overwhelming. So, for now, she accepted her weight, even learned to live with it. After all, she still believed herself to be an attractive woman.

What was it they said? There was just more of her to love.

'They' obviously never considered a madman seeking to punish people who, in his eyes, committed one of the seven deadly sins.

Apparently, Rebecca Sue Caraway's sin was 'gluttony.'

$\sim$

The Apostle stood naked in his bedroom, slick with sweat, and gazed at his reflection in the mirror. He'd just completed a ten-mile run—hobble, truth be told—and his upper leg was on fire. He rubbed the area where FBI Agent Jake Devereaux's bullet had pierced his thigh and groaned, hurting but proud of himself for completing the run.

The agent's bullet had nearly taken away his ability to walk. Now, here he was, not only walking, but running.

Glory be to the Father!

He smiled into the mirror, liking what he saw. Chiseled jaw, ripped abs, arms the size of tanks. During his time at St. Michael's, the

Archangel Church, he worked diligently to increase his size, stamina, and strength.

The road before him would not be easy. His task? To prepare his place on earth, become qualified to wear the crown offered to him. And the only way to do that was to prove himself by unmasking the evil ones, the beasts who've committed the deadliest of sins, and eliminating them, one-by-one.

He would begin with the swine in the barn.

For, not everyone was chosen; not everyone was given the key to eternal life.

Not everyone was worthy of becoming the Messiah.

A TALK WITH THE AUTHOR

What was your inspiration behind the *Shadow Sisters* series?

Ghosts.

That's it, in a nutshell. I wish I could give you deeper insight, come up with a more compelling explanation.

But, in the end, it simply started with ghosts.

Ever since I was a child, I've been fascinated with the paranormal. The Hooker Man, Bloody Mary, Ouija boards. You name it; I did it. My friends and I would scare ourselves silly, run screaming out of the room like, well, like we just saw a ghost.

And they would vow to never mess with anything supernatural again ...just as I was planning the next seance or future drive-by of a haunted house.

I know, right? Weirdo.

The bald truth is I have witnessed some pretty strange stuff over the years and continue to do so. Some experiences I've written about can be found on my blog (Quinnnoll.com) but they represent only a fraction of my experiences with the paranormal. Most of these incidents I hold close to the vest, locked away in a vault in my mind, protecting both my privacy and the personal nature of the visits.

So, since the paranormal has become almost routine to me, it only made sense to create a character that had similar experiences.

Fast forward to the actual idea for the *Fury* books. One day, as I was burning sage because, well, that's what you do when a nasty spirit enters your world, a thought popped into my head.

"Maybe if Ted Bundy's mom had done this, the evil would have left him."

Or he would have caught fire. Either way, it would be a win/win.

So I'm burning and thinking about the cancerous individuals who live among us, the soulless ones who reek of moral decay, and am thinking, 'Gee, wouldn't it be cool if a serial killer goes after someone who has a pipeline to the dead?'

It started that quickly. Because you might not know this, but guess what my other fascination is? Yeah, you aren't wrong.

Serial killers.

But not because of some off-the-wall, 'I want to be pen pals' kind of thing. It's because I've always struggled to understand how an individual could become so ugly, so cruel.

So void of decency and good and remorse.

And I've found there is no answer. Because you cannot solve a puzzle that's missing pieces. And we will never uncover all the shredded parts that make up the essence of a killer.

Describe your writing process for this book. How long did it take you? How many hours a day did you work on the content?

As my second book in the series, I found the writing went much smoother and faster. I'd learned what not to do—edit the hell out of it as I write. I did that in the first book and eventually realized all it did was halt the creative juices. Now, I try to avoid too much 'on the spot' editing until I complete the scene or the chapter.

As far as how many hours a day, I would sit down about 9am, after my morning walk, and work until about noon. Then I would have brunch (I usually skip breakfast) and write afterward until about 4 or 5, depending on where I was in the story. If I found myself on a roll, I'd keep going until I rolled down that hill.

There is a strong religious slant to this series. Are you a religious or spiritual person?

I was raised Catholic, and as a child, attended Mass every weekend, every holiday, every holy day. As I got older, I questioned some beliefs found not only in Catholicism, but in organized religion in general. As a result, I classify myself more as a spiritual person than a religious one.

In these *Fury* books, I tried to show how one can pervert and twist God's word to rationalize their particular brand of crazy. We've all seen it before...people slaughtering the innocent under the twisted idealism that they committed their crimes 'in the name of God.'

Bullshit.

There is no God who would either condone or urge His followers to kill that which He created. Period.

Do you get emotionally invested in the characters as you write difficult scenes?

Holy cow, yes! There were a few scenes in *The Apostle's Fury* where I literally broke down in tears and had to walk away from my laptop. In *The Disciple's Fury*, some graphic scenes of violence or terror caused me to pause and remind myself that this was fiction, not real life.

I believe that a writer needs to be invested in his or her

characters to write authentic fiction. After all, if I don't believe in them, how do I expect my readers to? The series literally came alive to me from the first sentence of the first book, and I fear it will devastate me when the trilogy comes to an end.

Do you have a playlist you listen to when writing or do you prefer complete silence?

I actually do have a few writing playlists I listen to with noise-cancelling headphones on (because I can listen to tunes but everyday household activity I find distracting.) The playlist depends on my task at the time. I listen to 70's music when I'm editing and classical music when I'm writing. Go figure.

Do you have any aspirations to switch it up after this series and change genres?

I've thought about doing some cozy mysteries. These are books that can be part romance, part suspense, but without the graphic details you see in many romance novels or thrillers. My favorites in this genre are the Rose Gardner mysteries by Denise Grover Swank. Sure, you got your murder, your crazy people, your romantic lead. But much is left to the imagination, rather than spelling it out. It's like Alfred Hitchcock movies.

You don't necessarily have to see the gore to get the pants scared off of you!

Finally, what is it you want your fans to know most about you?

Gosh, that's a tough one. I guess I would say I'd like them to know how much I cherish their support. It's easy to jump on the Stephen King or Nora Roberts train, because those authors (deservedly) are successful and well-known. For the rest of us, we depend on readers taking a chance on a new writer and spreading the word. My readers have done just that and have left me beyond grateful.

Above all, I just want folks to enjoy my stories. Escape for a little while and treat yourselves to a safe fantasy world.

Life is terminal at best. Be good to each other, believe in something other than yourself, and never forget that there is no such thing as coincidence...only design.

Peace out, my friends.

—Q

ABOUT THE AUTHOR

Want More Quinn?

For updates, bonus content, and special giveaways, be sure to visit me at Quinnnoll.com and sign up for my newsletter! *Shadow Sisters: The Beginning*, a short story detailing the Callahan sister's early years, is available to download free when you sign up for my newsletter!

Happy reading!

Quinn Noll

Quinn Noll
Writer. Poet. Dreamer.
www.Quinnnoll.com